Also by Rachel Khong

Goodbye, Vitamin

Real Americans

REAL
AMERICANS

A Novel

Rachel Khong

Alfred A. Knopf   *New York*   2024

THIS IS A BORZOI BOOK
PUBLISHED BY ALFRED A. KNOPF

www.aaknopf.com

Library of Congress Cataloging-in-Publication Data
Name: Khong, Rachel, [date] author.
Title: Real Americans : a novel / Rachel Khong.
Description: First edition. | New York : Alfred A. Knopf, 2024.
Identifiers: LCCN 2023009880 (print) | LCCN 2023009881 (ebook) |
    ISBN 9780593537251 (hardcover) | ISBN 9780593537268 (ebook) |
    ISBN 9780593802373 (open market)
Subjects: LCSH: National characteristics, American—Fiction. |
    LCGFT: Domestic fiction. | Novels.
Classification: LCC PS3611.H66 R43 2024 (print) | LCC PS3611.H66 (ebook) |
    DDC 813/.6—dc23eng/20230310
LC record available at https://lccn.loc.gov/2023009880
LC ebook record available at https://lccn.loc.gov/2023009881

Front-of-jacket images (top to bottom, details): *Chinese Ornament*,
Metropolitan Museum of Art, N.Y.; *Lotus* by Ohara Koson, photograph
© Minneapolis Institute of Art / Bridgeman images; *Skyline*, CSA Printstock /
Getty Images; *Chinatown, San Francisco*, photograph © Look and Learn /
Bridgeman Images
Jacket design by Linda Huang

Manufactured in the United States of America
First Edition

For my family

Like you, I was raised in the institution of dreaming.

—CAMERON AWKWARD-RICH

Real Americans

BEIJING, 1966

SHE ISN'T AFRAID, but he is. They stand, in the darkness, before a glass case of old things. A Ming dynasty inkstone. A chrysanthemum carved from horn. A Song painting stamped with ruby-red collector's seals. And on a silk pillow, so slight it could be missed: an ancient lotus seed with a legend behind it.

The story goes like this: One night, long ago, a dragon emerged from the sky and dropped this seed into the emperor's open hand. His advisors huddled near to examine it. *What fortune!* they remarked. This seed would grant the emperor his greatest wish. Unfortunately, he died that night, while contemplating his options. He might have asked for immortality.

She takes a hammer from her knapsack. With all her strength, she strikes the glass. It makes a beautifully clear sound as it shatters. Quickly, the two get to work, securing the relics. It is an attempt to spare them from the Red Guards' destruction—an act of protest, small, against a movement she's no match for.

The seed is unspectacular, so old it resembles a stone. Yet she's aware it contains an entire future: roots, stems, leaves, blooms, to seeds once more—encoded, like she is. Her heart pumps blood, her lungs take in air, she sleeps, wakes, eats, excretes. Will her life be long or short? What has she chosen, she wonders, and what has chosen her? She likes the fragrance of gardenias, but not the scent of lipstick. She doesn't mind the rain. She is in love, which feels, to her, at once easy and hard, elemental and ungraspable—like vanishing and eternity at the same time. She wants to ask of every person she meets: Is it this way for you?

"Hurry," her companion says.

A door slams, loudly. Someone is here. The footsteps draw closer. They flee.

Outside, she opens her fist. On her bleeding palm rests a stolen seed. The story is fiction. And yet: Why shouldn't the wish be hers?

PART ONE

Lily

CHAPTER 1

1999

MY ALARM RANG AT seven and I pressed snooze as usual. The second time I awoke, it was still seven. This happened occasionally, these blips in my existence. I got blank stares whenever I tried explaining them, so I didn't anymore. The feeling I had was that time wouldn't move. A second would refuse to pass as it usually did, and I would find myself trapped in a moment—unable to progress beyond a minute or two.

My bathroom mirror, flecked white with toothpaste, reflected me to myself. Lines from the pillow were pressed into my cheek. I ran my fingers over the indentations. The toothpaste flecks gave the effect of being in a shaken snow globe.

In the kitchen, the same drain flies circled the sink, unless they were new ones—the former ones' progeny. Debbie never washed her dishes, and her lipstick-rimmed mug sat balanced on the edge of the sink, like a dare to raise the issue. Warily, I ate a piece of toast with blueberry jam. The toast crunched as it always had. Some jam got on my cheek, and in swiping it from my face I removed some blush. Now there was a void in my coloring. I would have to redo the makeup, but it relieved me to see that the regular laws of physics continued to apply.

Outside, I regarded my surroundings with suspicion, as though they were a dream I might wake up from. Like everyone, I had recently watched *The Matrix*. Would it be so bad to discover that life until now, or some portion of it, had been illusory—an advanced society's highly realistic simulation? It might actually be a relief.

Downstairs, Mrs. Chin restocked the key chains of her souvenir shop. She was arguing with Mr. Peng, who owned the salon next door. Seeing me, they paused their quarrel.

"Lei hou, Lily," Mrs. Chin said with a wave, pronouncing it *lee lee*. She'd taught me exactly three words of Cantonese: *Lei hou ma?* How are you?

"Lei hou ma!" I called back. "I'm okay," I added, in English.

Mrs. Chin's hair, newly permed, shimmered with auburn highlights—Mr. Peng's handiwork. From a plastic bag with a happy face on it, she pulled out a bun. The yeast smelled sweet. Did I want one? I shook my head. Not today.

The bell on the café door gave its meek ring. I ordered my regular latte—the latte I shouldn't have been buying, because I didn't make any money. I sat to drink it. A dark-haired man held a bagel to a child's small mouth, waiting for the child to accept a bite. I followed his gaze to the New York City street, where nothing appeared out of the ordinary: people, pigeons, bags of trash. Holding the bagel steady, the father's mind traveled elsewhere. It was a look I remembered my mother wearing when I was a child—one I resented. How dare she think of anything but me?

The father and child began to speak in another language I couldn't make out. Then the man turned, suddenly, catching me in my stare. I dropped my gaze, feeling my ears redden.

There were the regular café sounds: the low rumble of milk being steamed, the crinkling of paper bags when pastries were slid in. A man in his fifties, a Wall Street type, ate a cookie noisily and peered at his pager.

I returned to the register to order the coffee I brought to my boss every day. It was a dark roast stirred with two pink packets of Sweet'N Low, made paler with half-and-half, until it was "the color of Halle Berry," he'd instructed proudly on my first day, as if that wasn't a terrible thing to say.

On the four blocks to the office I dodged tourists wearing backpacks and bucket hats, holding red bags from the discount designer store. They moved slowly, their faces stupid with awe. I walked fast, with purpose, gripping the cup of coffee, which burned through its cardboard sleeve, proud to be inured to a cityscape that instilled marvel in everyone else. When I entered the immense glass building, I did so with a sense of importance and authority: I *worked* here. I was an unpaid intern, but still.

Our building was new, a futuristic marvel of glass and steel that curved slightly upward. The elevator was a point of pride. It took me to the twentieth floor within minutes, where I handed Jerry his coffee, which he accepted in his sausagey pink fingers without a word. The flesh on his ring finger bulged around his wedding ring, the way trees grew around old signs or objects. I remembered a photo from the magazine, from somewhere in the Pacific Northwest—a tree growing bark over a boy's bicycle, as though swallowing it. The boy who'd owned the bicycle was an old man by now. Jerry nodded, to indicate the coffee was to his liking.

I spent the next four hours brightening images. When Jerry left early, as he did every evening, I opened Usenet. I had never posted before, so I created a username: *TimelessinNY*. I typed out my question: *Does anyone ever feel like time gets stuck? I have these moments when time won't move. A minute lasts forever.* Awaiting responses, I searched for "jobs for art history major." Curator, docent, teacher. It was difficult to picture myself as any of those things. I would be graduating in the spring, and what I wished for was some clear way forward—some passion, like my parents had, that would give my life meaning. I had not inherited their gift for science or, sometimes it seemed, for anything at all.

Before I left for the day, I checked the message board for replies. There were none.

⌁

At the company's holiday party, the tree was false and towering. The Santa was Latino, his red velvet suit emblazoned with the company's logo. A boy band's Christmas album played too loudly. Our larger parent company had rented out a floor of a hotel in Chelsea, lined with windows, giving us a 360-degree view of Manhattan. With money they weren't paying me, I thought. Before leaving for the party, I'd noticed a run in my only pair of black stockings. I drew a line on my calf in Sharpie, a trick my freshman-year dorm-mate had taught me, to make the stocking appear intact.

I picked up a triangle of toast, black beads of caviar clumped on it. The city offered wealth to us in glimpses: Even a college student could eat caviar, or drink wine from crystal. We'd be reminded that we weren't—rich, that is—the moment we returned to our minuscule apartments, where we slept in loft beds and shared closet-sized bathrooms. Even the put-together people—the people who dressed exquisitely, expensively—I had come to learn, didn't necessarily inhabit livable places. Often they dug their elegant clothing from piles on chairs that were their only furniture.

I'd have to be vigilant if I wanted more caviar. Media employees mobbed the stressed young server holding the silver tray. I wondered what this party was doing for their morale. It was obvious who worked in fashion, food, celebrity gossip. My own coworkers wore skin-baring dresses—we'd seen little skin all winter—and ladled punch out of a fountain that frothed uncontrollably.

My fellow interns lingered as a pack by the hors d'oeuvres, finding strength in numbers. Seeing me, they waved, beckoning me over. Most, like me, went to NYU; a few went to Columbia or SUNY. All of them were drinking the alcoholic punch, though many were underage. This went uncommented on, because it was implicit: This was our salary. The other interns were uniformly blond, round breasted, affable. It was plain to see that Jerry, who had done the hiring, had a type. I was the anomaly.

I picked up a shrimp and swiped it through cocktail sauce. It was cold and tasted only faintly of the sea. Shrimp cocktail involved a disorienting amount of chewing, and there was always a moment, eating it, when I thought, *Too much flesh.* But I had this amnesia about the shrimp-cocktail-eating experience: I forgot how I felt until I was in the act of eating my next one.

I scanned the room for a trash can, not noticing Jerry approach. I'd have preferred to avoid him tonight, but now it was too late. Beside him stood a man, tall and golden haired, who looked to be in his twenties.

"Lily, this is my nephew," Jerry announced, with some pride.

Jerry had cocktail sauce at the edge of his mouth, crusted like blood.

"And this is Lily," he said to the nephew.

He slapped the nephew on his back. I held up the shrimp tail and shrugged at the nephew, like, *Sorry, wish I could, but I can't shake your hand at the moment.*

"She's Korean," my boss added.

I wondered why he said that—with such confidence, and as though it would be of interest. I felt instantly weary.

"Chinese," I clarified to the nephew, once my boss was gone.

Jerry migrated to the flock of blond interns, where one by one they brightened at him, as though he were a god. He had the power to transform any of us from unpaid to paid interns, so, in a way, he was. In the past he'd also introduced me as Thai. We worked in travel, but he couldn't manage to keep it straight.

"Sorry," the nephew said. "That was weird."

He was distractingly hot—athletic but not vacant, a muscular nerd. Unlike the other men at the party, media types wearing T-shirts that were loose around their collars, he looked at home in his suit, which was fitted. He didn't appear as though he'd borrowed it for this occasion. He was definitely not my type. Muscles intimidated me. I deliberated how much more to drink. I inched toward the punch fountain and he followed.

"I'm Matthew," he introduced himself, scratching the back of his neck, which I couldn't help but admire. "What do you do here?"

"I'm an intern," I said, filling a glass with punch. "In the art department. Mostly I search for stock photographs. Or collect invoices from photographers."

I pressed my hand to my punch glass. Cold. I moved it to my neck. Hot. It was likely I was not dreaming; it was likely this was reality. I'd been wary in the wake of the morning.

A gaggle of gossip magazine staffers glanced over at us, interested in the handsome nephew's movements.

"What'd you work on today?"

Matthew appeared genuinely curious, as though he wanted to continue the conversation, which surprised me. I was used to people looking around for someone more interesting once I told them what my position was.

I'd processed invoices. I'd verified hotel features—comparing photos to their stated amenities. I'd also researched potential photographers for an article about millennium projects—architecture and celebrations meant to commemorate the year 2000. The Millennium Wheel, for example: a Ferris wheel being built in London, designed by a husband-and-wife team.

"It's big, right?" Matthew asked.

"The world's tallest," I confirmed.

The music stopped abruptly. We quieted with the crowd.

"Good evening, everyone," came a voice over the speakers.

We turned our attention to the stage. The raffle was beginning, announced the energetic hired emcee. We had each been given tickets at the beginning of the party, and I dug mine out of my purse.

"Three, eight, five, six . . . ," read the emcee. I heard sighs of disappointment.

Of course I won nothing. I wasn't a lucky person. I'd never defied odds. Even my being born a Chinese woman had been likeliest, of all possible humans. My cubicle-mate, Amy, screamed with glee. She ran to the stage to collect her prize: a shrink-wrapped Discman in a box. Again I thought of the cost of the Discman, the salary I was not receiving.

The emcee read out another number: "Three, eight, seven, seven." More groans of disappointment. Again, not me. Matthew was staring at his ticket.

"I think that's me," he said.

He made his way up to the stage and collected a forty-inch plasma TV. He returned to my side and stood it up next to us, and shrugged, as though this sort of thing happened regularly. The emcee continued to read off winning numbers, and Matthew leaned toward me.

"Do you want it?"

"Are you kidding?"

"I've got a TV. I don't actually know what I'd do with this."

"Wow," I said, disbelieving. "I mean . . ."

"Why don't you take it and see how you like it? And if you don't, you could sell it. It's a nice TV. You could get a few grand for it, at least."

"This is crazy," I said, "but okay."

"Do you need help getting it home?"

I looked at him.

"I'm not coming on to you," he added quickly. "It's just . . . no offense, but this party isn't that amazing."

This was a true thing: This party was not that amazing.

"Well, sure," I said. "Why not. Hang on."

I ran to the snack table, wrapped some cookies in a napkin for the road, and put them in my coat pocket. Matthew picked the TV up easily, and outside, I held my arm out to hail a cab. One pulled up. The driver was grinning both in his ID card and in real life. In the cab we held the TV awkwardly across our laps, unable to move, not speaking.

In front of my apartment he unbuttoned his dress shirt and handed it, along with his coat and tie, shiny and blue, to me. Holding the TV, wearing only his white undershirt, his muscles bulged, modestly, as he carried it up my three flights of stairs. Debbie was in Nebraska for the holidays.

While I moved books off the table that would serve as the console, he found the cable jack and electrical outlet. He lifted the TV onto the table, with an elegance that surprised me, and pressed the on button. The weatherman appeared. I gasped.

"God, thanks," I said, handing his shirt back to him. "This is incredible. Never has a stranger given me a television."

"It's not like I'm nothing to you. You make it sound like I came in from off the street."

"You're not nothing," I agreed. "We had a conversation. It was . . . five minutes?"

"Maybe even ten."

"Maybe even ten!"

"It's perfect there," he said, buttoning his shirt.

I tried to make out his tone—sarcastic? The screen was laughably enormous in my tiny apartment.

"Wait," I said, and fished the cookies out of my coat. They were Danish butter cookies, the kind that came in a blue tin, nestled into cupcake papers. "A reward." The cookies were crumbles now. He poured them into his mouth all at once, which I liked.

He didn't say anything for a moment, dissolving the cookies with his saliva. I admired his eyes, which were an intense blue, more like ice than water, so light they were nearly transparent. My own eyes struck me as common, in comparison. They were brown, and moderately cool, as all eyes were. But a certain type of eyes made you think: *Those can't possibly be real. A human body made those?* Matthew's were in that category. He was beautiful, I'd observed all night, but suddenly it hit me with force, like wind, and I regretted that he would soon be gone.

"Do you want my number?" I blurted, surprising myself.

He said nothing for a second, and it was the longest second of my life. I'd said the wrong thing, I realized, mortified. He'd said he wasn't coming on to me, and now I was coming on to him. He turned away from me and located what he needed: He tore off a corner of an empty cereal box from my recycling bin. He handed it to me, and I wrote my number down.

CHAPTER 2

I WOKE UP AT seven, out of habit, still wearing my dress from the party. I fell back asleep. When I woke up again it was late: nine. I ran to the bathroom, splashed my face, and pulled a skirt and stockings on, before realizing it was Saturday and relaxing. I noticed the Sharpie on my leg and tried to rub it off, succeeding only in smearing ink across my calf. I regarded the giant television that now swallowed my living room. My answering machine blinked with a message.

"Hey. I was wondering if you wanted to have dinner tonight? It's the stranger who gave you a TV, by the way."

Matthew proposed a restaurant I'd never been to, because I didn't make enough money to eat there. It was where celebrities went, I'd always imagined. Or CEOs. I knew about it, though, because everybody knew about it.

I called the number he left. He picked up immediately. I repeated the name of the restaurant he'd proposed.

"Seriously?" I asked. "You're paying?"

Under ordinary circumstances I would not have been so forward. I would have suffered quietly through dinner—enjoying yet not enjoying it—and waited to see what happened when the bill arrived.

But these were not ordinary circumstances. I proceeded as though I were in a dream. I was certain I wasn't his type, either. He must have dated astonishingly beautiful women.

"Of course," he said.

His father had canceled on him, he explained, so he had a dinner reservation—made months ago—that would otherwise go to waste. I put my hand over the receiver.

"What the hell," I said aloud. What the hell, as in *What is happening,* and what the hell, as in *Who cares, let's see.*

"You didn't finish telling me about millennium architecture," he said.

There was a black cloud-shaped stain on the couch cushion—my mascara. Officially, it was my roommate's couch. I flipped the cushion over.

"It's certainly worth a very expensive meal, this knowledge."

"Pick you up at seven."

It was ten. *Don't you dare spend the next nine hours thinking about this,* I warned myself. I made myself a series of promises: I would spend a maximum of one hour getting ready. I would not obsess, or overthink, or try on multiple dresses. I would not apply, remove, and reapply my makeup. I would enjoy this improbable free meal and not expect or hope for anything more.

I turned on the TV. Politicians were saying uncharitable things to each other, business as usual. On another channel, a Princeton scientist was describing his successful experiment: His team had been able to modify mice to make them smarter, by manipulating a single gene—by halting its expression. The scientist was Chinese, I was proud to see. It would be a topic of conversation—something I could discuss with my mother.

At six I threw on my favorite black dress and a set of earrings I already knew went well with it. I applied makeup and spritzed on ancient perfume and regarded myself in the mirror. I ran a wet paper towel across it to remove the toothpaste flecks.

"Pretty good," I said to the mirror. "Pretty good to good."

Exactly at seven, a black town car materialized at the curb. I hurried out.

Beside the car stood an older man who said, "Lily," and opened the door for me. I got in the car—confused, then relieved, to see that Matthew wasn't there.

"I'm Lily," I said, trying to fill the silence, before remembering he'd already greeted me by my name.

"I'm Mitchell," he said.

From the driver's seat, he looked like he could have been Matthew's father. He had light blue eyes that I caught glimpses of in the rearview mirror. Or maybe I was just bad at telling white people apart. In movies, actors were always playing one another's parents and children, believably.

When we arrived at the restaurant, I promptly opened the car door for myself. But Mitchell moved fast: He was there to take my hand and help me down. A gust of wind blew then, a chill against my stockinged legs. I hugged my coat more tightly. Up to this point I'd been so blithe, and the cold snapped me out of it. Suddenly I was nervous.

"Have a nice meal," Mitchell said. "See you in a bit."

Inside the restaurant I gave Matthew's name—I didn't know his last name, but she knew who I meant—and the hostess led me across the vast restaurant to the table where he was already seated, sipping a glass of water. When he saw me, he stood and smiled in this amused way, as though we already shared a secret.

"You made it," he said, taking my coat from my shoulders, handing it to the hostess.

"How could I pass up a free dinner?"

"No one ever should."

The server brought us menus: a lengthy wine list, unfamiliar words in microscopic font.

"What do you think?" he asked.

"Please don't make me choose."

"Should I pick based on what I know about you?"

"What do you know about me?"

"I know that you like TV, and dinner."

"That's pretty much all there is to know."

While he examined the list, I surveyed the room. A group of men in suits raised glasses. A well-dressed family with two young children sat stiffly, disturbingly quiet.

To our left, a man in his sixties held hands, across the table, with a much younger Asian woman. I could hear that her English was broken and felt embarrassed on their behalf. I wondered if I could be mistaken for an escort. I wondered if the people around us were leaning closer to listen for my foreign accent. They probably didn't care— everyone had their own private universe of concerns; they weren't as nosy as I was—but it was hard to shake the feeling. I glanced again at their table: The Asian woman, as though she could hear my thoughts, returned my gaze challengingly.

"Does my uncle always do that?" Matthew asked.

"Do what?"

"Introduce you by what kind of Asian you are."

"Let's see. . . . Third time he's done it now?" I said. "It's fine. Anyway, I'm used to it."

"I'll say something. It's not cool."

"Don't worry about it. I don't want to embarrass him."

"But it's embarrassing."

"I can't even speak Chinese," I said.

I don't know why I said this, as though I were proud of it. I wasn't proud, but I wanted to wield it as proof: I was as American as they came.

"No?"

"My parents never taught me. Hey," I said, ready to change the subject. "You know that I like TV and dinner. I don't know anything about you. What do you do?"

The sommelier returned with two thin-stemmed crystal glasses and a green glass bottle. Carefully, he poured the wine and we watched, in silence, paying tribute to his care: He wiped the condensation from the bottle with the napkin from his arm. The color of the wine in my glass was pale yellow, tinged green. It tasted like grass, in a good way.

"I'm in finance," he said.

"Like . . . you're a banker?"

"Private equity. I promise it's not interesting."

The meal arrived in small courses. Raw clams, one for each of us, glistening with sauce, shallots suspended like jewels. Red and pink leaves in an architectural arrangement. A plate stacked with pieces of a chubby miniature chicken—squab, the menu said; *pigeon*, Matthew translated.

"What are you going to do? After college?"

I was certain I was drinking wine but the liquid in my glass never seemed to lessen, by magic, or by miracle. Once I caught her after the act: our server, hurrying away, her ponytail swinging.

"Maybe you can help me figure it out."

"What did you want to be? Like, when you were a kid?"

"An architect." I laughed, a little sadly.

I was never going to be a scientist, like my parents—interested in life at the molecular level, in things even smaller than molecules. Architecture had seemed to me so glamorous: imaginary structures, made real. But quickly it became clear that I lacked the drive. I didn't live and breathe architecture the way my classmates did. So I switched my major to art history. In the end, I wasn't the sort of person who yearned to shape a landscape. I wanted only to observe it.

"I'm hoping a job opens up at the magazine."

"I could talk to Jerry, if you want?"

"No," I said quickly. "Thank you. That's kind of you."

He was twenty-seven, five years older than I was. He'd gone to Columbia. He played racquetball, went to Knicks games and the movies, enjoyed mysteries and biographies. He was really good at giving manicures.

"I don't believe that."

"That doesn't make it untrue."

I swore to myself that I'd remember each dish, but would forget what we'd eaten the moment the plate was taken away.

"So you grew up in Florida," he said.

"For the most part. I was born in New York, actually. On Long Island."

"Where? I was, too."

"Nassau County."

"Me too. We were in Middleport. By the harbor."

"No way!" I said. "I was born there and we left when I was four. I don't remember much about it."

"We were there until I was nine." Matthew paused. "That means we were there together."

"Did you notice me? Did you think to yourself, *Wow, what an attractive baby*?"

"Now that you mention it, I remember you! The attractive baby."

My only memories were flashes: A playground by the water. Dogwood trees that bloomed in May, a profusion of flowers—the first flower I ever learned the name of, and it puzzled me.

"Do you remember the guy who was always feeding the ducks?" Matthew asked. "He would give these blue rocks to kids."

I touched his forearm in excitement. I had one of those blue rocks but had never known why. The rocks were Earth, Matthew said. Meant to remind us of our own smallness.

I couldn't imagine a child comprehending that—that we were so insignificant, that we didn't matter. Even now, it was something I understood in the abstract—not in any real way.

"Is that depressing?" I asked. "Or liberating?"

"Depends on the glass, I guess." He lifted my glass of water. "Half full."

"Okay, so, we both like TV and dinner. And we were born on Long Island. Not a lot going for us, I have to be honest."

"And travel," Matthew said. "We like traveling."

"Yeah, I get to do a lot of that as a penniless intern."

"Did you study abroad?"

"France, last year. Paris."

"I went there, too. We could have run into each other at a café."

"Except you were born five years too early."

"Or you were too late."

"I *love* Paris," I said, overemphatically, and felt my cheeks redden the moment the words left my mouth. I often wondered what percentage of things I said were truly original, and how much of what I said I'd heard said before and was only repeating.

"An unconventional view. Another thing we have going for us."

He teased me lightly, and let me tease him in return. Ravenously, I cleared every plate.

"I'm loving how much you love this."

"I'm going to forgive you, this once, for commenting on how much a woman eats."

"I didn't mean that. I just meant you seem like you love it."

I'd been committed to taking this night with a grain of salt. I wanted to be as casual with relationships as the other twenty-two-year-olds I knew, but had never been able to manage it. I was surprised by how easy it was, talking to him.

"I do," I said. I did. "Aren't you going to eat that?"

He'd taken a small bite of his portion of venison. The butter, opaque on top, was clear as it ran down the sides. He pushed his plate toward me.

"I'm sorry your dad stood you up."

He flinched a little at the mention of his father—so lightly I might have missed it, had I not been carefully watching his face.

"Trust me, you're much better company."

"Lucky for me."

"I'm the lucky one."

"I'm not debating luck with you. You won a TV."

We were halfway through our second bottle of wine, a Napa cabernet, and I washed the venison down with it. The wine felt drying on my tongue, perfect to chase the butter and meat, making me want more of both. By this point I'd stopped noticing our surroundings. It was only the two of us, and our conversation turned manic.

"I'm not good at haggling," Matthew was saying. He meant in the world: At his job he regularly negotiated, but he had trouble when faced with a street vendor. Even as he was saying it, I couldn't remember why we had started on that topic of conversation.

Between us, the candle was on its last legs: a flame in a liquid pool of wax.

"There's so much power being wielded over nothing," I found myself saying, impassioned and not knowing why. "School is bullshit. It's all bureaucracy. I can't wait for it to be over."

"It's not just school." Matthew shook his head. "It's everything. Say your flight's delayed, and the person at the airline counter says they *can't* get you a ticket for the plane that's leaving conveniently soon, but *can* get you a ticket for another plane. And the more you argue with this airline employee, the less he or she will be willing to give you that thing you want badly—the plane ticket from New York to Paris, or the seat next to your boyfriend, or whatever it is you want."

He looked at the watch on his wrist. It was gold and ticked softly. It was sobering to consider how expensive it might be. A year of my rent—more. And last night I'd given him cookie crumbs.

"Hey," he said. "What are you doing tomorrow?"

I planned to get brunch with a friend, and had a haircut scheduled, but I said, "Nothing."

"Should we go to Paris?" I thought I heard him say.

"What?"

"Let's go to Paris," he repeated. "Let's go now," he said, making eye contact with our server, nodding for the check.

On the plane, we chattered, frenetic, covering ground urgently and exhaustively, like everything we needed to say had to be said *now*. Still wine-drunk from dinner, we got drunker on the champagne the stewardess served. Midflight, she popped open bottles with a practiced ease, as though it were something they taught French children in grade school. I imagined the cork punching a hole in the side of the plane and sending us spiraling out of the sky. What a way to go, I thought, on the way to Paris with a stranger. Had I told my parents that I loved them? Not recently enough, I feared.

He'd grown up in New York, then Connecticut, the second youngest of six children, four of them sisters. I'd been alone. As children, we'd both longed for the happy medium.

Had he ever done this before? I wondered aloud. Taken a stranger to dinner, and then Paris?

"Never," he swore, holding his palm up solemnly.

"A different city?"

"First time taking a stranger anywhere."

When we started to descend, it was with so much turbulence that Matthew ceased talking, leaned back, and sharply inhaled. He'd closed his eyes and appeared frightened. I raised the armrest that divided us and reached for his hand to hold it. Until now, we hadn't touched, and the contact gave me a jolt.

It had seemed probable that things were headed in a romantic direction—here we were, on a plane to Paris, after all—but nothing physical had actually transpired, and I wondered, lightly, if I had been reading this entire situation incorrectly. I pictured myself in the future, telling a girlfriend about the weekend, laughing. *We went to a fancy dinner. Then he took me to Paris, platonically.*

Matthew gave my hand a small squeeze in acknowledgment but kept his eyes tightly shut. His hand still in mine, I spoke assurances: Turbulence meant we probably *weren't* going to die. Someone had told me this once and I accepted it as the gospel truth. We were only experiencing a disturbance in airflow. I tried to keep my voice steady, despite my own fear. While I spoke, he nodded to indicate that he was listening, eyes closed.

"Do you want me to stop talking?"

It occurred to me that it might be unpleasant—to hear about turbulence while experiencing it.

He shook his head.

"Don't stop," he said softly.

He was truly frightened, this grown man beside me. Most likely we were flying through clouds, I continued. Clouds held differences in atmospheric pressure; clouds were not uniformly dense. Clouds were suspended, liquid droplets, and when they got heavy enough, that was rain. Wasn't that amazing?

Statistically, the descent and landing were the most dangerous parts of a flight. I didn't mention this. The plane landed forcefully. Beside me, Matthew kept his eyes shut. The possibility remained that the plane could burst into flames. This was what I worried about, after landing. Even though we'd evaded one terrible ending, another could be in store.

The cabin lights came on, and the stewardess's voice crackled over the intercom, welcoming us to France. I clutched our customs forms and passports. In his passport photo, he was young and serious—newly of age and wanting to prove it. He looked unlike he had at dinner, but like he did now—a boy.

Matthew turned to me and gave a small, sheepish smile. His hand gripped mine, and he twisted our fingers together. Before I could register what was happening, he reached his other hand around the back of my head, brought my face to his, and kissed me.

Matthew spoke shyly to the taxi driver, embarrassed about his French, which sounded fluent to me. We'd lost the morning, so it was afternoon here: The winter sun streamed in through the windows, and the old stone buildings looked slick, almost wet, with light.

I followed him into the lobby of the hotel, then to our room—more spacious than I was prepared for, with fresh flowers on both bedside tables, a king-sized canopy bed. From the balcony I could make out Notre Dame and the Seine, birds diving, majestically, like kites.

He placed my purse on an upholstered armchair and lay on top of the bedspread, not bothering to take off his shoes. I lay down, too, beside him. On our sides, we faced each other. I touched his jaw, gently, disbelieving. Was this real? The moment felt protracted, endless. I had been one person, going to dinner last night, and now I was someone else entirely.

We kissed again, chastely, like a husband and wife, and fell asleep. When we woke up it was to church bells ringing. The room was dark, the sun having set. Matthew pulled me close. I was certain my makeup was smudged or gone, and my breath was awful. I wanted sex but worried about how I must look and how I must taste, and I couldn't stop my mind from churning with the worry. I'd never had a good first time with anyone.

He didn't ask what I wanted and I was relieved. I wished I were a woman who could list what she wanted, confidently, as though ordering from a menu. But I wasn't that.

His hair smelled of synthetic roses, exactly like the Herbal Essences I used. It charmed me, that he didn't feel the need to use a men's shampoo, with its supposed masculine fragrance.

His thumb had a callus on it. He ran it, lightly, over my thigh. I kept my hands over his, clutched to his knuckles as they held my hips down. With his mouth he worked me until I came, too loudly. He kissed my neck and unwrapped a condom. He got on top of me, and into my ear, thumb on my collarbone, he asked, "Is this okay?" It seemed a great effort to nod, to manage a yes.

Afterward, we lay silent. My hair, wet with sweat, clung to my forehead and his chest.

"Okay," I said, into the silence, and we both laughed.

It was evening when we left the hotel. The night was crisp, the city lit and enchanted. Vendors turned chestnuts over fires, diffusing a sweet, toasted scent. Matthew remembered a bistro he liked, in Montmartre, and led us to it from memory.

His French was better than mine, but the waiter shifted to English after a few French exchanges. We shared lamb, lentils, a salad. The salad was entirely leaves—some jagged and green, others frilled and purple—dressed with whole grains of mustard that popped in my mouth. The lentils came with a soft egg and the yolk, punctured, was better than any sauce. I had never had a meal like this before—simple, yet perfect, unlike the previous night's dinner, which insisted on its own complexity. Yesterday's multicourse menu had been born of striving and time, but this one came from something different: care, what felt like love. Matthew studied my expression as I ate, hoping I'd be pleased.

We weren't strangers anymore, I mused aloud.

"Do you agree," he said, "that I'm not nothing to you?"

"You're not nothing to me," I said, feeling that this was the beginning of something. That, after this, because of this, my life would not be the same.

CHAPTER 3

MATTHEW APOLOGIZED: HE HAD a busy week at work leading up to the holiday. But he called me the day after Paris, and the day after that. He called me every day that week, as though I needed reminding that he existed. He was an asset manager at an investment bank. I searched for the average salary online and was stunned. Surely someone paid like that was busy. But the calls kept coming, never with an agenda, only to say hello, the way I'd done with friends as a teenager but hadn't since.

"It's for you," my mother said, her hand cupped over the telephone receiver.

I was in Tampa to spend Christmas with my parents. He asked what they were like. They'd immigrated to the U.S. from China, by way of Hong Kong. My father was as he appeared: cheerful, uncomplicated. Gifts for him were generic, copied from television: wide ties, leather belts. He was genuinely thrilled, receiving gifts like these.

And my mother? She was impossible to describe.

"They're scientists?" Matthew asked.

Both were geneticists. But to my father, science was a job. He had friends and other interests. Whereas my mother was a scientist like someone might be a painter—wholly, and obsessively. It was her entire life.

Our yard was a blanket of green—not grass, but clover. As a child, I didn't understand why people thought four-leaf clovers were luckier than those with three leaves. If you looked closely at our lawn you would see it was full of four-leaf clovers. My mother had located the mutation that gave clover its fourth leaf—previously thought impossible, because clovers are deceptively complex, with double the chromosomes of humans. What she wanted was to make her own luck.

I heard Matthew's secretary's voice in the background, informing him that he was needed. She sounded young and impatient. It was her job to be concerned with the demands on his time, and who was I, this intrusion on his tightly packed schedule? I identified with her. I wasn't accustomed to speaking this way with anyone—without purpose, as though time weren't finite but unlimited.

I wished we could stay on the phone forever. The moment I hung up my mother would ask, *Who was that?*

What she actually wanted to know: *Who are you? Who do you plan on becoming?* And the truth, which I couldn't admit outright, was that I didn't have any idea—not yet.

The next week: We saw each other over dinner, over drinks. On cold nights, we kissed against brick walls, my arms around him, inside his warm coat. In bed, we had long conversations, my head pressed to his chest, so close I could smell the bar soap on his skin.

He lived in the West Village, in a condo that seemed always, by some magical force, to be the right temperature. A functioning thermostat, I supposed, which *was* magic, if you were used to living the way I did, with a radiator that ran too hot or not at all.

Entering, what I noticed—what surprised me—was a pot of bright orchids in the foyer. Immediately at the door they greeted you, eight of them in an elegant chain. Fuchsia and speckled, like miniature lion's faces. Their leaves were a deep, shiny green, and the flowers appeared well cared for.

They were his only plants. Though it was the largest New York City apartment I had ever been in, spanning two floors, it was uniformly sparse, without much personality.

Next to the orchids a brass vase sat on a stack of art books, beside a glass mister that looked vintage—out of place among the very new things. I wondered if it was something an ex-girlfriend had proposed— orchids in the foyer, knickknacks arranged just so. I imagined this ex-girlfriend selecting the flowers, teaching him how to mist them. These must be the books she most loved, which he'd kept because they were remnants of her. He seemed able to read my thoughts, because he said, "I copied it from a catalog."

"What?"

"The whole thing. This . . ." He searched for the word. *"Tableau."* He gestured with a flourish, which made me laugh.

"You did this yourself?"

"Is that surprising?" he asked. "I really did copy it. It's embarrassing."

He picked up a booklet from the coffee table and flipped it open to a dog-eared page.

"Here."

He pointed to a photograph: a rectangular planter exactly like his, with the same fuchsia orchids in it, the same books, and the same brass vase and glass mister, not vintage at all, but on sale for two hundred dollars.

The TV he'd given me went unwatched because if one of us spent the night, it was me. His TV was even bigger—I could see why he didn't need another. He paid for cable and had hundreds more channels.

His bathtub was kept sparkling clean and free of dust by his housekeeper, Jenny. The first time we met, I was in the bathtub. She said something to me in what I recognized as Mandarin, but when I looked stunned and didn't respond, we both blushed, embarrassed. She lived in Flushing, I learned from Matthew. She was my age, with a baby.

Confessions accrued: He told me that his mother had killed herself when he was eight years old. His younger brother had taken his own life, at nineteen. Was sadness inherited? he worried. I turned toward him, pulled him close, insisted *no*.

The night we'd met, when I'd told him about the Millennium Wheel, in London, he hadn't mentioned he'd seen it already, in person. On a business trip last month, he'd walked along the river and encountered the wheel hovering at an angle—like it was playing a game of limbo. They were raising it in two phases, two degrees per hour. It wasn't that he'd planned to keep this from me. He'd liked hearing me talk, with so much unearned authority, about it. And I had never even been to London.

I was reading a novel set there—a New Year's book, a London

book—about a friendship between a man from Bangladesh and a man from England. In bed I passed it to Matthew. When he opened it, my mother's clovers rained down, onto his chest—two-dimensional four-leaved confetti. I'd been pressing them, I'd forgotten. I picked each specimen off of him, placing each clover on the bedside table. I looked up to find him staring.

"What is it?"

"Nothing."

He was smiling.

"Tell me," I insisted.

"There's no one like you," he finally said.

⁓

I wore my favorite black dress, and Matthew, a suit. Mitchell deposited us at a stone building on the Upper East Side, and an elevator that smelled of gardenias delivered us to the top floor.

It wasn't any New Year's Eve. At least, that was how it felt. Afterward we would realize that Y2K had been a lot of worry over nothing. We would laugh at the fact we'd ever thought otherwise. We were entering a new millennium, the year 2000, and more than a few of us believed that the world might end—that some unknown catastrophe would happen if our computers thought the year was 1900. Matthew predicted everything would be fine: The media was making a fuss, as it liked to. But I knew that even he was worried, because all week he'd stayed late at the office, burning his data to CDs.

"Matthew!" a man, I assumed the party's host, bellowed at the elevator doors.

He was tall and blond like Matthew, wearing a specious grin. He held a glass that tinkled with ice and something amber, and leaned down to kiss me, routinely, on the cheek.

"I'm Jared," he introduced himself. "How's this guy treating you?" He didn't actually expect an answer.

The men talked in low voices about something unintelligible to me, and I followed. I worried we were the first to arrive, until we passed from the kitchen into an outdoor space where people were gathered, thrumming, around a rectangular pool, and Jared turned to me and said, pleasantly, "You should meet my wife." It sounded like a line from a movie. Had everyone learned how to speak and act from movies? Did Jared genuinely believe that women at parties were meant to speak with other women at parties?

Jared's wife was wearing a sequined, backless dress—it seemed that all the women were—so you could see the indent, the line, that went all the way down her back. Despite the heat lamps, it was chilly, and the fine hairs on her arms stood up, translucent toothbrush bristles.

"I'm Lily," I introduced myself.

Her rings tapped loudly against her glass when she switched her wine from one hand to the other.

"I'm Lily, too. Did your mother like the flower?"

"I've never asked her."

We smiled mildly at each other. Her eyes lingered on my dress.

It was the same dress I'd worn to dinner with Matthew—a thinning rayon. I was noticing now that it was thinner in places than I'd remembered.

"You have a beautiful place," I said quickly.

"Thank you," she said, brightening even though she was already bright.

Jared appeared with our drinks, scotch for Matthew and champagne for me. I felt relief when he and the other Lily were greeted by another couple, swept into conversation.

"We'll have fun," Matthew said to me, not sounding convinced himself.

Around us, fairy lights glowed like brilliant stationary fireflies. In the surrounding high-rises, in windows here and there, men and women bent over their desks—working, for some reason, on New Year's Eve. What work did they do that could be so important? From a distance, they looked like dolls. Whatever they were doing was easy to dismiss as inconsequential. It was something I did, back then—disregard what I didn't understand.

Servers in white circulated with miniature foods and plucked empty, abandoned glasses from concrete planters.

Everyone seemed to know Matthew and was exaggeratedly polite to me. They regarded me noncommittally, their eyes resting but not engaged, like I was a TV commercial that would flash past, given a moment. With certain people Matthew spoke with sharpness, impatience—in tones he never used with me. It made me wonder about what he did for a living—how it was he earned his money. *It's not interesting,* he'd said over our first dinner.

I was one of a handful of Asian women, and silently I wished for more of us, or none at all. One of them hung off the arm of the only Black man, who wore a large signet ring on the hand that stroked his companion's bare back. It disturbed me, the kneading of her naked back, as though she were entirely dough. In fact, many men were doing this to many women—stroking backs, openly. I sipped more champagne.

I was separated from Matthew, and a man cornered me into a conversation about how he'd just come back from a trip to Shanghai— how the city was changing, you wouldn't believe the traffic. I said I wasn't from Shanghai, or even China, that I had been born here—in New York, actually—but none of it mattered to this not-Chinese man. I excused myself: I needed to use the restroom.

In the bathroom, I laughed aloud. It was obvious when every-thing in a bathroom had been picked based on cost. My landlord had skimped on everything—vinyl flooring, the flimsiest taps, the cheap-est toilet and fixtures—and here it was as though everything had been selected for its expense. The floor and counters were marble, and the fixtures looked polished and Scandinavian. An expensive candle released its luxurious fragrance—money, literally burning. A mirror hung across from the toilet; I watched myself as I peed out the costly champagne I'd been drinking all night. My lip liner was asymmetri-cal, I realized, embarrassed. My mouth's shape was wrong. And I was wearing way too much blush. I tried my best to wipe it off with my palms but only made it worse.

"Brenda!" people called to an older woman, pressing their faces against hers. Brenda seemed to be in her fifties and had arrived with a much younger man. She had once been beautiful, I was sure, but now it wasn't clear. She had lipstick on her teeth and I could see the foundation in the lines of her face, like mortar between bricks. Yet she carried herself like a million dollars, speaking loudly, as though she knew everyone, as though this were *her* party. Jared and Lily were deferential to her; she held some power over them.

Out of the corner of my eye, I noticed Matthew, a few yards away, standing with a thin woman, almost as tall as he was. Her hair was straight and shiny and brown—like hair that was swished in shampoo commercials, the vibrant "after." Unlike the other women, she wore a dress that was plain and loose. *Even without trying*, the dress seemed to say, *I can be more beautiful than you.* They stood close, with familiarity. They were perfect together.

As if they could sense me watching, they both turned to look at me, at the same time someone shouted, "Countdown!" and began: "Ten!"

Matthew made his way through the mass of people. It was nine, eight, seven, six, and five when he got to me.

"Happy New Year!" people cried, and blew noisemakers that had been passed out to everyone else.

Matthew kissed me, optimistically. He kept his hands on my face afterward—a compensatory act, I couldn't help but think, making up for what I had noticed.

Around us, the city sparkled blithely. And layered over the feeling of being in love was a coating of something more insidious—a conviction that this couldn't last. I didn't belong here. Of course I didn't belong.

"I'm going to miss you. I'm sorry I have to go."

In ten hours, he would be flying to see his father and stepmother in Berlin.

"Are these your real friends?" I asked Matthew.

"It's complicated," he said.

He didn't speak to the brunette again, but periodically I felt her glance our way. Knowing she was monitoring me, I laughed harder and smiled more widely with whomever we were talking with. I wasn't out of place, my laughing and smiling indicated.

I wasn't not drunk. The world around me was fuzzy and golden. It was a new year. That always made me a little bit sad. As though something were wrong with the old one.

At the bar, the young man who'd arrived with Brenda waited for the bartender's attention. Close up, the man looked older—at least thirty. Beside Brenda—who was across the room now—he'd looked like a little boy.

"What are you drinking?" he asked.

"Just champagne."

"Two champagnes," he said to the bartender.

He handed me my flute and, as he did, noticed a smudge. He gave me the other glass and rubbed the smudge off with his tie, which had colorful little crayons printed on it. It made me like him immediately.

"I'm Stan."

"Lily," I said, clinking my glass to his.

"I take it you're not from this world."

"Is it that obvious?" I shook my head. "Is it my dress? Be honest."

"No, no, nothing like that." He drank half his champagne in one swallow. "You seem like you're paying attention."

"Very low bar." The champagne hurt my throat going down. I hardly tasted it anymore. "And you? Are you?"

"Am I what?"

"Part of this world?"

"It's complicated," he said, echoing Matthew. "I'm an artist."

"You use crayons?" I motioned to his tie.

"As a matter of fact, on occasion I do," he said, and smiled. "But I pale in comparison to most five-year-olds. I'm more of a painter."

"What do you paint?"

"That's not a question to ask a painter."

"Sorry." I blushed. For all the art I'd studied, I didn't personally know any artists.

"I'm teasing. They're mostly abstractions. I use oil. I have to talk about it—especially in places like this—but I hate it. It's all bullshit."

"The painting?"

"The talking about painting."

"And you're with her?" I gestured to Brenda.

Stan drank the rest of his champagne, then waited for me to finish mine.

"It's complicated," he repeated.

He asked for two more champagnes, and I admired his profile. Stan was good-looking. Not conventionally, but specifically. His nose was crooked, like it had once been broken. A small patch of one eyebrow was missing. I followed his gaze, which rested on Brenda.

"Time—it's the one thing they can't buy. I've wondered if that's why owning art appeals," Stan mused. "They buy my paintings because they want to own time itself. A painting is the next best thing."

"The time you spent making it."

"The actual spent time, yes—my time, accumulated. In a way, it's compensation for my time."

"So these are your customers."

"I hate that I need to sell it. I would paint for nothing, you know? But I have to live. In art as a product there is no longer patience, or presence—only commodity."

"That sounds like it could be on one of those placards," I teased. "At the museum."

"Am I being pretentious?" He laughed. "I'll save it for my artist's statement."

Matthew materialized, then. He touched my arm; the gesture was meant more for Stan than for me. Stan's demeanor changed as he registered that we were together.

"Matthew," Stan said, aloof now. They shook hands. "How's business?"

"The same. Endless. And painting?"

"The usual. Endless despair."

To see them side by side reminded me how strange it was that Matthew was the one I was with. He laced his fingers with mine, confirming it.

⌒

He returned from Berlin bearing gifts. Standing in my doorway, he looked too tall for it, and was. He bent down to kiss me. He was wearing a scarf that grazed my neck when he leaned down. I couldn't touch him: There were garlic peels stuck to my fingers and I held my hands in claws. I worried I smelled like grease. My apron was a thrift store purchase that said "Hot stuff coming through."

I'd spent a few days cleaning but the place looked the same: like a crumbling Chinatown apartment, darkened grout on the kitchen counter like shrimp veins. Debbie had conveniently stayed in her room all day, avoiding my cleaning spree, then disappeared before Matthew arrived, no doubt filing this occasion away, in her head, as something that would need repayment. There would be a night down the line when she would need me to disappear, and I would have no choice but to do it.

"Hi," Matthew said. Through the wall, my neighbor made violent noises, trying to get his throat clear. "Smells good in here."

My small Formica table flickered with candles I'd stood up in drinking glasses; they leaned slightly. Music played—a mix CD I had labored over.

"Wine?" I asked. He nodded.

I opened the bottle of wine I'd paid twenty dollars for, more than I usually spent, and as he drank it I worried: Was it good enough? It tasted fine to me—like wine. A chicken roasted in the oven.

He placed gifts on the table: one small, one large. He folded the paper bag and leaned it against a table leg.

"This isn't fair," I said. "All I made you was this mix CD."

"It's a really good mix," he said.

In the smaller box was a lavender bottle of perfume, made of glass so thick it seemed it wouldn't break if I threw it. He admitted that his sister Jenna had helped him choose it. I spritzed it on one wrist: It smelled like pepper and herbs and trees; I didn't have the words to describe it, except that I loved it. It made me think of my mother, who kept cloying department store perfumes spritzed on pieces of paper. She had never allowed herself a full bottle.

The larger box contained a dress: black silk, filmy. It fit perfectly, as though he had taken my measurements in my sleep. In the mirror I looked grown-up, like one of the women I admired on the street.

He'd been embarrassed by the dress I'd worn to the New Year's party, I thought. He must have wished I were wearing something else, and this was why he'd bought me this dress.

"It's okay if you hate it." A worried expression came over his face as he noticed the complicated emotion in mine.

"How could I hate it? It's beautiful."

It wasn't a lie. It was perfect, the sort of dress I wished I knew how to buy for myself, let alone had the money for. It wasn't the dress. It was what the dress represented—what he must have thought about me. When I caught my reflection in the silver of the toaster, I resembled someone else.

"Is something wrong?"

"I love it," I insisted, trying to erase the unease from my voice.

The chicken was done. The recipe said I had to let it rest, so I left it on the countertop.

"How was the trip?" I asked.

"It was fine." His parents were the same. They had a new dog, a Boston terrier. The dog's name was Hans. By the third night the family had run out of topics of conversation.

"They asked if I was seeing anyone."

"What did you say?"

Matthew put a hand to his neck and rubbed it.

"I didn't say anything," he admitted guiltily.

I poured myself more wine.

"Don't worry. I get having weird parents."

"They would have asked too many follow-up questions."

"I get it," I said, trying not to sound mad. It was completely unfair: I would have never told my parents about a relationship after only two weeks. I *hadn't* told them. And yet my life felt changed. I wondered if his did, too.

The timer chimed, and the chicken was ready to be cut into, and we ate it—it was dry—and I asked what Hans was like, and he said "cute and exuberant," and all the while I wondered what I was to him. I'd had casual relationships in the past—attempted them, at least. I wondered if that was what this was—a casual thing I'd misunderstood as something more serious. Maybe I'd been too lovestruck to pick up on the clues.

I tried to make a salad like what we'd eaten in France, but it was mustardy and sour—nothing like the salad we'd had. A leaf fell onto my dress, and the oil bloomed on it. I would have to soak it with dish soap. There was a duck on the dish soap's label. The brand was proud that it had helped clean oil-soaked waterfowl—including two endangered species—after the most recent oil spill in Oregon. If it was supposed to fill me with optimism—this dish soap can clean birds!—it had the opposite effect: It depressed me, that we lived in a world where oil was spilling regularly into the ocean, killing numerous birds, marine mammals, and shellfish, or if not killing them, covering them in oil.

Matthew did the dishes quietly in my too-small sink, and stacked them neatly and carefully. When he was done, he joined me on the couch.

The mix CD ended. The TV's volume was off. On the news was a car chase, police weaving silently through traffic after a speeding van. Matthew placed a hand on my arm, and I tensed.

He was too tall for Debbie's couch, and the couch was dirty. I thought of my apartment as charming—cozy—but with him here it was no longer acceptable, and I saw the charms for the deficiencies they were: my mismatched silver, my foraged flowers, the chips in the glasses. He was wrong here, in my life. At the New Year's party, I had been wrong in his.

"Look, Matthew, I'm happy to see you."

He was silent. I didn't know what I was saying. He watched my face and I wished he wouldn't. *Stop looking at me*, I wanted to shout.

"But?"

He kissed my neck, smelling the perfume, the scent he'd chosen. My heart raced, not in the good way. I felt suffocated, as though he had used all the air in the room, and there was none left for me.

"But . . . ," I continued. "Would it be okay if I spent tonight alone?"

At that moment, Debbie's keys jangled outside and the door opened. She held a bulging bag of takeout. I wondered how we appeared to her. This particular man beside me. My eyes red around the edges, holding back tears.

"Hi," we all said, politely.

Debbie hurried to her room.

"I'm sorry," he said.

He stood, wound his scarf back around his neck, put on his jacket, kissed me again, and was gone. It was a relief, and it was devastating. I put away the clean, dry dishes and pulled the CD from the player. He hadn't taken it with him, hadn't even recalled it was there. I'd spent hours playing song after song, making sure the sequence was correct. Dramatically, I threw the CD in the trash, then emptied the drain catch's contents into it, so the bits of wet food would ruin it.

CHAPTER 4

MY MOTHER AND FATHER sat unspeaking at my kitchen table. My father's hands trembled, and none of us mentioned it. His Parkinson's was getting worse. I poured hot water over yellow-brown bits of chamomile flowers that danced up when the water hit them. My mother watched with suspicion as I filled a glass of water for myself from the tap.

"It's safe to drink. New York water is famous."

"How can water be famous?" my mother asked.

"It makes the pizza good. And the bagels."

"That's a nice TV," my father said.

"You bought that?" my mother asked.

She was always doing this—asking questions about choices that had already been made.

"You'll find a new roommate?" my mother asked.

I nodded. The apartment was crowded with boxes: Debbie's things lined the hallway. After graduation, she was moving back to Omaha.

I'd posted an ad on Craigslist, describing the roommate I wanted: a "quiet professional, 20s or 30s," as though that was what I was.

"A stranger?" my mother asked.

"Everyone starts out strangers. You've never had roommates?"

"I've had roommates," she said, matter-of-factly.

When it came to her past, she never elaborated. She gripped her mug and I noticed new spots on the backs of her hands, light brown circles. My immediate thought was a selfish one, that I should wear sunscreen there.

Earlier, that afternoon, the sky had been an ominous silver, threatening to burst into rain. To my left and right were Chinese students I didn't know: other Chens and Chans and Changs and Chengs. The mortarboard didn't rest comfortably on my head. I'd pinned it into place but my hair was too slippery. The gown was a bright purple, a coarse material that itched against my chest and calves.

Somewhere in Yankee Stadium, my parents sat among the legions of family in the too-grand arena, waiting to hear my name.

The immense space reminded me that I was one of many—common, unspecial. I wasn't graduating with any distinctions. It embarrassed me, that my parents had come all this way for this impersonal ritual.

Our commencement speaker was a television news anchor: famous, though not in a meaningful way. I wondered what my parents were thinking as he declared that we could do anything we set our minds to—a bland television sentiment. But the more trite his statements became, the more they elicited cheers and claps and hollers. We were exceptional, he said to the thousands of us. I noticed the students beside me, international students from Asian countries, not cheering along with everyone else.

I heard my name: only a first and last name, no middle—nothing to mispronounce. As I walked to the stage to collect my diploma, my hat slid farther down, looking silly, like I was poking fun at the ritual.

When other students claimed their diplomas, their entourages whistled and shouted out. But when my name was called I heard only the softest polite claps.

After the ceremony, after dinner, we returned to Chinatown, passing produce vendors and wizened Chinese women wearing softly rippled polyester pants, moving their practiced hands, discerning the better fruit from the rest.

My mother plucked out a cluster of brown fruit, stems bundled together with a rubber band. The vendor regarded us kindly, a Chinese mother and her Chinese daughter. When my mother returned her Cantonese with English, the vendor appeared surprised, then disappointed. She took the folded bill silently and handed us the fruit in a pink plastic bag.

"Longans," my mother said. "I loved these as a girl."

She demonstrated peeling the skin off, biting carefully to avoid the shiny deep brown pit.

"You were so brilliant," my mother remembered with fondness. She spoke as though to herself. "All the tests you took. You always did better than the other children."

I held the fruit, not responding.

I remembered those tests: the smell of pencil, the sequences of squares and circles—choosing what shape did not go with the others. My mother's praise when I scored highly. She'd decided, back then, that I was remarkable, and I could not persuade her otherwise. I was nothing special, I wanted to protest. I wouldn't ever be. But I couldn't say that now, not while she was so happy, eyes closed, savoring the fruit.

I'd made my bed with fresh sheets for them. Before they'd arrived, I'd lugged my only set of bedding to the laundromat.

"You'll stay in New York?" my mother asked, and I nodded. "You have enough money?"

"Yes," I lied.

"The website will hire her, May," my father said to my mother. "No need to interrogate her."

The dot-com bubble had recently burst. Employees were let go, but I remained. No reason not to keep me, an unpaid intern. My student debt was laughable, not that I could laugh at it. I'd maxed out the $3,000 limit on my credit card.

Every so often I went through past statements as a sort of torturous exercise—to reprimand myself for the things I had spent money on in the past, with the hope that I'd learn from my mistakes and never spend money again. Everything I'd ever purchased seemed to me now objectively foolish: cheap earrings that had infected my ears, the mediocre takeout when I could have just as easily eaten Cup Noodles for one-sixth of the price. And all those lattes—what was I thinking?

On a January statement were the groceries for the dinner I'd cooked for Matthew, wanting to impress him. I'd overspent on the chicken, the arugula. The expensive jars of herbs and spices, the pricey mustard I'd bought because I wanted to follow the recipe exactly. The wine I shouldn't have splurged on. All of it gone now, less than nothing.

The morning after dinner in my apartment, Matthew had called. He'd left a message on my answering machine. In the days that followed he left another, then another. "Hey, Lily," each message began. "Could we talk?" He sent Instant Messages. He sent emails that I deleted without reading.

It was terrible of me not to respond—cowardly and childish, I'll admit—but it was easier that way. We weren't right together; anyone could see that. What was the point of pursuing what didn't make sense?

I ignored his communications until, eventually, they stopped. •

We said our good nights. My parents were in my bedroom and I lay on the couch. A firecracker rang out like a gunshot. A car alarm went off, repetitive and urgent. Voices floated in, women loudly laughing about the size of a man's dick. I needed to protect my parents from the reality of how I lived, but was helpless to. When my father passed me on the way to the bathroom, feeling for Debbie's boxes in the dark, I pretended I was asleep. The volume and brightness of the city—they weren't used to it in Tampa. My curtains weren't opaque enough to block out the orange of the streetlights.

It would be easier to take a cab, I said in the morning, but they insisted on taking the subway.

"We're proud of you," my father said.

"We love you," my mother said.

She may have meant it, but it was hard to believe it was true. My mother had not grown up saying *love* to her parents. As a child, she had never heard it said to her. With me, my parents made it a point to speak it frequently. My father was the more convincing. Even with her perfect American accent, my mother said it unnaturally, as though *love* were a foreign word. For her it was, doubly.

On the street, we said our goodbyes. I watched them wheel their suitcases away until I could no longer make them out, among the other Chinese men and women.

An envelope was on my nightstand. Inside, there were twelve hundred-dollar bills. A note from my father said: *Don't tell your mother.*

What I insisted to myself was that I didn't hope to see him, but the truth was when I walked through the West Village, which I did from time to time, I did so slowly. If I saw a man on the street—tall, blond, with the right width of shoulders—I would forget to exhale. But it was never him.

Not far from Matthew's was an exercise studio. An introductory deal was painted on its windows: your first class for fifteen dollars.

Inside, the pert woman seated at the front desk informed me that a Pilates class was starting: Would I like to join? She pronounced it *puh-LA-tees*. Fifteen dollars, she assured me, was a steal. A week of lattes, I thought. More affordable than health insurance.

I knew I shouldn't be here. Every job application I'd submitted had gone unanswered. I was living off my father's hundreds. It was dangerous to even leave the apartment because somehow I inevitably returned with twenty to forty fewer dollars than I had started out with, without understanding how. In this city, every encounter was a transaction, requiring money.

The mirrored studio was packed with women, all of them thin, with clean, light hair tied into ponytails and clothing like a uniform: tight pants cut off at the calf, spaghetti-strap tank tops that showed off the definition in their arms. I'd always exercised in downgraded clothes, and here I was in gym shorts and an old T shirt. Each woman seemed to have her own rubber mat and square blue bottle of Fiji water.

In the sea of blondes, to the side were two Asian women. They stood close together, chatting. They wore the same spaghetti-strap tops that everyone else wore, and the same tight pants. Noticing me, my bewilderment, one of them waved me over.

"I think they have mats you can borrow," the one who waved said.

"I'll go see," her friend added, and disappeared.

She returned promptly with a mat, then helped me unfurl it onto the floor beside hers.

"Thank you," I said. "I've never done this before."

"You're going to love it. Pablo is the best."

One of the women rooted around in her purse and pulled out a hair tie for me. I pulled my hair into a ponytail.

When Pablo entered, the room quieted. He was short, tanned, compactly muscled. He wore a headset, like a pop star. The lights then dimmed, and music began to play. It was a song by Britney Spears, about being lucky. Everyone around me dropped down to lie on their back, and I did the same.

My shorts billowed around my thighs and my T-shirt kept riding up. I needed tighter pants for exercising, I thought. A tank top that fit me more snugly. I was thirsty, too, and I wished I had one of those blue plastic bottles of water.

Then the music stopped, harsh lighting flicked on.

"We're getting some food nearby," the Asian woman who'd gotten me the mat said. "Want to come? My name's Hong, by the way."

"And I'm Theresa," her friend said.

At the restaurant, Hong ordered in rapid Vietnamese, impressing me. She'd grown up in Northern Virginia, near DC, in a large Vietnamese community. Her parents hadn't ever had to learn English. When our bowls of pho arrived, I followed their leads, squeezing hoisin and sriracha into a small plastic dish decorated with blue flowers.

Hong and Theresa dug into their tangles of noodles with green plastic chopsticks, messily and unself-consciously, their foreheads growing shiny with steam and sweat.

"Don't worry, it gets easier," Hong said.

"I was sore for a week," Theresa said.

Theresa had grown up in California, in a suburb of Los Angeles with an Asian majority. Her parents called her by her Korean name. I didn't have a Chinese one.

They marveled at my childhood: shoes in the house, dinners of meat loaf and mac-'n'-cheese. I didn't try Chinese food until I moved to New York.

My mother and father had spoken English in the house, never Chinese. Every Christmas Eve, a plate of chocolate chip cookies materialized on our mantel, with a glass of milk that neither of my parents could drink, because they were lactose intolerant. They must have poured Santa's milk down the drain. It was as though they followed a guidebook on how to be American. To the children I went to school with, these efforts didn't matter. Even if I ate the same bologna-and-white-bread sandwiches the other kids did and spoke perfect English, I had a face that marked me as different.

"And your parents immigrated as adults?" Hong asked, incredulous.

I shrugged. They'd wanted to be American.

Hong and Theresa talked as though they were childhood friends, even though they'd met only a year ago, in class. I felt envious and impatient—a longing to belong with them.

After we parted, I returned to the studio, where the woman at the desk seemed surprised to see me again so soon. It was money I shouldn't have been spending, but I bought a multiclass pass with one of my father's crisp hundreds.

CHAPTER 5

AT WORK, THE WEB became my primary research tool. Guidebooks and libraries were outdated, in comparison. I typed "Athens, Greece" into Yahoo! and found accounts of people who detailed their journeys by the hour—minutiae that might have been edited out of a book. Online I found countless photographs—not the overly composed photos in print magazines but exuberant, intimate snapshots of amateurs, vibrant and immediate, as though I could reach out to touch the clear, rippled ocean. I could open a new window to travel to Beijing, or the Great Wall of China. It was mysterious, this phenomenon: Online, the hours passed like seconds. Months disappeared this way. Yet I would be hard-pressed to tell you what happened in my real life.

December came. Our annual holiday party was on a stricter budget. No extravagant raffle, no hired Santa. Instead, a finite amount of beer and wine sat atop a desk, draped in a plastic tablecloth creased with fold marks.

I nursed the small hope Matthew might be in attendance. But the moment I arrived I knew that he wasn't. I would have noticed him immediately. I tried not to be disappointed.

I picked up a gingerbread cookie and had begun to wash it down with room-temperature beer when a young woman approached me.

"Lily, right?"

She was dressed too fashionably to be in news, but not quite fashionably enough to be in fashion. Most likely she was from the gossip magazine. She refilled her plastic cup with chardonnay, to the edge. The older gossip staffers looked wizened with hatred and pettiness, so she must have been new. She was young—my age. She extended her hand.

"I'm Sandra," she introduced herself. "You're friends with Matt, right? Matt Allen?"

Who was she? Matthew had told me he didn't like to be called Matt, but what if things had changed, or what if she knew him more intimately?

"Yeah," I said. It had been almost a year since we'd last spoken.

"Is he cool?"

I didn't answer right away, wondering if she would elaborate.

"A good friend of mine recently started dating him," she said. She searched my face for a reaction, and I tried my best not to have one. "I was wondering if I needed to warn her."

"I don't think so."

"There's always something wrong with people that attractive."

I laughed, liking her.

"He's a good guy," I said, and meant it, even as the inside of my chest twisted. So he was dating someone. "Stamp of approval. Who's your friend?" I asked as casually as I could manage.

"My college roommate," Sandra said. "Angelica Veers. Veers as in, like, the cosmetics company."

In my purse, my mascara and lipstick were both Veers.

"They sound perfect for each other."

"She said he might be too, like, socially awkward for her." Sandra laughed.

Just then, Jerry approached. Sandra slipped away.

"You clean up well," he said. "Why don't you wear nicer clothes more often?"

"Well, I would. But you kind of need money for clothes."

"Very funny. You're very funny sometimes."

"Thanks." I drained my cup and glanced at my watch. Ten. It was past time to go.

"I've been thinking," he said. "You might make a good assistant photo editor."

"You've been thinking it?"

"Top of mind. I'll let you know my decision." Jerry winked then.

Luke, our new contributing editor, appeared when Jerry left. He was a column of black: His daily uniform was black jeans with a black shirt, black leather boots. A silver hoop in one ear. He had overheard our conversation. In the office, he didn't conceal the fact he disliked Jerry.

"Wait, you don't get paid?" he asked, dismayed. His green eyes met mine. "That's messed up."

Each month, I scraped out a living piecemeal: a few hundred from research assignments from Luke—work he didn't actually need outsourced but I gratefully accepted—and the rest from gigs gotten through Craigslist. I walked a Chihuahua with limbs like chicken wings, who tired easily. I assisted a photographer by holding up panels that, incomprehensibly to me, affected the light. I stood in line at a bakery for a rich woman who wanted to buy highly sought-after cupcakes as gifts, but whose schedule could not accommodate the wait. What did a gift mean, I wondered, if you weren't the one to spend the time obtaining it? More than once, I considered selling Matthew's TV. But I couldn't bring myself to.

Past Mrs. Chin's souvenir shop and Mr. Peng's salon was a small, crowded store wallpapered in scratch tickets. It sold SIM cards and bus tickets along with the scratchers. It became a ritual: I bought a single scratch ticket whenever I was paid for a gig.

"Set for life" seemed the most appealing to me, as a concept. To be set for life would mean never having to strive again. After my first scratch card, I understood how people got hooked: I liked the feeling of the metal coming off under my penny. Even when I had scratched off enough to see that I hadn't won, I continued to scratch. I liked to scratch off all it was possible to scratch. But, as suspected, I wasn't a lucky person. I never won.

The Park Slope brownstone where I was dog-sitting had slanted floors that rumbled when the F train passed. I wondered if I was imagining it at first until I saw that the water in the aquarium was slanted, too. It was the last week of the month, and rent was due in days. Even after this gig, I would still be short three hundred dollars.

My job was to care for an English bulldog and several exotic fish. The dog was Reginald and the fish were unnamed. As instructed, I halved a pill, crushed it into powder, and stirred it into the dog's food. Because they were bred for companionship, bulldogs suffered especially from separation anxiety.

The brownstone was paradise with two couches, multiple armchairs. I no longer had a couch because Debbie had taken it. I made mental notes about the décor: what I could copy when, sometime in the future, I could afford furniture. You could tell how rich people were by how large their plants and rugs were. They had enormous ceramic pots of birds-of-paradise that might peck your eyes out, monsteras like the open palms of giants. A living room rug the size of my apartment. Reginald had his own bed, lined with angora.

The sofas and armchairs were a spotless white, not a single stain anywhere. Finding the wine collection, I saw why: All the wine was white. They didn't drink red.

A half-full bottle of chilled chenin blanc was in the fridge. The homeowners had insisted I should help myself to anything, so I poured myself a glass. I reasoned it couldn't be too fancy because the label looked amateurish: a clip-art illustration of grapes.

Poor Reginald breathed in a belabored way. I wiped food from the folds in his face with wet wipes. I brushed the short hair on his back and stomach; he enjoyed this. On their computer I looked up the wine. It was eighty dollars.

The wineglass was hefty in my hand: real crystal. If they asked me to return, I would ask for more money.

On the desk sat an orchid plant that reminded me of Matthew's, the same fuchsia speckles. I remembered the older man with the Asian woman at the restaurant. I thought of Brenda at the New Year's Eve party—of Stan, and what it cost him to live, to make his art. I poured myself more of the wine. I opened my browser to Craigslist, to the personals.

I could invent a fake name. I could create a whole persona. A normal name, difficult to verify as real. Michelle . . . Kwan? She was a figure skater. Michelle Chang, then. I created an email address and drafted a listing for Craigslist. "Sugar daddy wanted," I typed. Did "sugar daddy" connote incredible wealth? I wasn't looking for luxury. All I needed was rent money. It could be a one-time thing. My fingers trembled as I typed: "Spoil me. Let me be your Asian mistress. I'm twenty-three, with brown eyes and long black hair, seeking a gentleman to help me out financially. Help me, so I can help you." I finished the wine. I stared at the web page, finger on the mouse—hesitating. My chest tightened with nerves. Reginald looked at me, panting neutrally. Was this wrong? I'd gone on dates with men and let them pay. This wasn't so different, was it? I clicked submit.

Responses appeared in my inbox right away: most vulgar and brief, not serious contenders. But one caught my eye. It was written in full sentences, grammatically correct, courteous. "Hi Michelle," the message said. "I'm interested." He had caveats, which I found encouraging: Discretion was important to him. He wanted to make sure I didn't have any venereal diseases. He was married and couldn't pass anything on to his wife. I wrote back: I was discreet and didn't have any diseases. When could we meet?

"What about Wednesday morning?" he responded. He named a café in midtown.

He would be wearing a blue tie, he said. He would be holding a newspaper in his hand. I didn't describe myself. I didn't tell him what I would be wearing. All he knew was my age and that I was Asian.

My wine was gone and I looked around, as though someone were here, judging me. Reginald was asleep, head on his paws.

Wednesday came. At the crowded café, numerous Asian women stood in line for coffee. I spotted him immediately: He sat at a small table, looking tense, newspaper in his hand, eyes darting from one woman to the next.

He'd said he was in his fifties but hadn't said early or late. Now I saw that it was late. His hair was sparse, and white at the temples. His tie was too short, resting on his rounded belly. His suit looked shiny and synthetic, and was too large—the shoulders didn't fall where they should have. He didn't appear particularly wealthy. I wondered about his wife—how their life together was arranged. I tried to picture him naked. Hair poked out at the top of his shirt, as though reaching for sunlight.

What am I doing? I thought suddenly, my own shame arresting me.

People on their way to work walked briskly past me in their suits, without the slightest idea of what I had done.

So far I'd gone unnoticed. He continued to glance from Asian woman to Asian woman, wondering who might join him at his table. One wore a skintight dress that accentuated her breasts and constricted her movement to small steps. Her pointy acrylic nails tapped impatiently against a café table. He watched her, with eagerness, then disappointment, when she embraced a young, beaming man with gelled, parted hair—a banker, maybe.

How could I have considered this a good idea? I felt sick, my stomach whisked with regret. I pitied him, his hopefulness. He would find his Asian mistress, but who was I kidding? This was a job—an opportunity—for someone else. His eyes met mine. Did he know it was me? I reached for the door and left.

When I called home, my mother answered. I almost hung up at the sound of her voice. She expected better of me.

"I'm sorry," I said. "But I need money."

CHAPTER 6

MY MOTHER'S REFRAIN WAS that once I figured out what to do, professionally, the rest of my life would click into place. It wouldn't be like that for me, I tried to explain, but she didn't believe me. "That's what you think now because you haven't found it," she insisted, and wearily I agreed, so the conversation could end. But I knew she was wrong: There was no *it*. In my art history classes we'd studied artists whose impulses to create were so overwhelming, they came at a terrible expense to their actual lives. Van Gogh's severed ear, Pollock's alcoholism, Caravaggio's violence. I wasn't one of those people. If I was, I would know it already.

Hong's mother could not have been more different from mine. In silence, she had waited in the lobby through our Pilates class, our showers, and now she sat in the boutique, smiling and nodding when we held dresses up, or conferring with Hong in Vietnamese. She didn't speak any English.

"She says you're so pretty," Hong translated, and I blushed.

"You're so much prettier."

"I'm not going to translate that."

I was sent into the dressing room with a bright blue silk dress. It was thin and I wasn't wearing the proper bra for it. I emerged, swaying for their approval, like a tropical fish on display.

"That looks *amazing* on you," Theresa said.

"You *have* to get it. You just have to," Hong said.

Her mother said something to her in Vietnamese.

"My mom loves it, too!"

I shook my head. "I can't." I didn't even have to look at the price tag. In a shop like this I already knew it would be too much.

"You *have* to," Theresa said. As if it mattered at all to her. Why couldn't I just say that I didn't have the money? "You'll wear it everywhere. It'll be worth it."

I considered my reflection. It *was* a beautiful dress.

There was a rapping sound on the window.

"Uh," Hong said. "There's a hot guy outside?"

Luke was outside, waving goofily. He let in a breeze when he entered.

"What are you doing here?" I crossed my arms over my chest.

"My place is just around the corner," he said. He was incongruous among the frilled things, in his black clothes. "It looks good on you."

"Doesn't she *need* it?" Hong asked.

"It's nice."

"Don't encourage them," I said, shaking my head.

"Well, my vote is yes," he said. "See you at work, Lily. Nice to meet you all."

"Who was *he*?" Theresa asked.

"A coworker." My face was overheating and I willed it to cool down. Hong's mother spoke to her.

"My mom thinks he's very handsome!"

I tried to put the dress back on the rack.

"Is it the money?" Hong asked. "What if we buy it for you?"

"Don't! Fine, fine, I'll buy it."

I took out my credit card. I hoped the charge would go through. My balance was hovering right below the limit. I could return the dress, I reasoned, if I needed to. The shopkeeper folded it in tissue, then placed it in a paper bag, stamped with the store's logo.

At home, I noticed the label: It was the same designer as the dress Matthew had given me. I laid the dresses on the bed side by side and saw that they were identical, but different colors. As though everyone had decided that this was the dress I should wear. I hadn't soaked Matthew's dress in dish soap and the oil stain, ancient now, was still there.

⌁

"What the fuck?" said Rose, Jerry's assistant.

I had never once heard Rose curse. She was Canadian, exceedingly polite. I looked up from the computer, where I had been correcting photos from a Tokyo nightclub, removing dancers' red eyes. Rose stood at the window, a hand over her mouth.

Luke went to her side. They made a jarring pair: him, black clad, and her, in a candy-pink dress. His regular smirk evaporated.

"Fuck," Luke muttered.

My coworkers followed: the sound of chairs against floor, the whooshes of email sending. At the window, I blinked. I couldn't be seeing what I was seeing.

To the south, gray smoke plumed from the World Trade towers, like a volcano. Jerry turned on the television in his office. We'd never known why his job required a television. In horror, we watched the second tower fall.

A plane had been hijacked, the news anchor was saying. *Planes.* Rose began to weep, and Luke stood with his hands balled against the windows, as though he were ready to smash them.

"Let's go home," Luke said, not looking at Jerry. "Fuck this."

He went to his desk, slid his laptop into his messenger bag. I stayed frozen, motionless and disbelieving, by the window. Jerry put his arm around Rose to console her.

"Let's all go home," Jerry announced, as though he hadn't heard Luke.

"You're in Chinatown, right?" Luke said to me. "I'm in the East Village. I'll walk with you."

We walked close and quickly, not speaking. People wore surgical masks and handkerchiefs over their mouths and noses. My eyes stung. What were we inhaling? Building materials, office furniture, bodies? I tried to take as few breaths as I could and grew lightheaded. Car alarms caroled, a dissonant concert. If the world ended now I wouldn't have been surprised. I remembered the Y2K party on the roof, everyone in such elegant clothes, and how we'd worn the feeling that the world might end so lightly. And now it felt as though it really might.

"This is me," I said.

Mrs. Chin's souvenir shop had its metal door rolled down. A handwritten sign had been taped up: "Closed until further notice," with Chinese characters beneath it. Luke and I stood for a moment in the entryway, littered with grocery mailers.

Luke embraced me when I began to cry. I wiped my nose on his shirt, leaving streaks on the black. He removed a small notebook from his back pocket and wrote something down. He ripped the page out and handed it to me: his phone number.

"If you need anything, call me. Okay?"

I nodded. I couldn't look at him or I'd start crying again.

"Don't be too tough, Lily," he said.

My new roommate had left a note: She was at her boyfriend's. Alone in the apartment, I turned the TV on. Every channel showed the same footage of the buildings, collapsing like sand castles. Worried messages had collected on my machine: my parents, Hong and Theresa, childhood friends, and acquaintances I hadn't heard from in forever but who'd seen the news. I couldn't return their calls because the phones had stopped working.

Two classmates of mine, people I didn't know well, interned there. I hoped they hadn't gone to work that day. I was lucky I was an intern in a different tower. I had been so preoccupied with my own life—the trivial question of what to do with it. Yet here I was, alive.

In the morning, I found Mrs. Chin downstairs, trying to communicate with a policeman. He wore a gas mask, so it was hard to make out his expression. His arms were crossed tightly across his chest, refusing her access to her own store.

"What's going on?" I asked.

"She needs to move along unless she can show me her ID."

"But this is her shop."

"She needs to prove it."

Mrs. Chin faced me pleadingly. I realized she might not have papers.

"Can I show you my ID? I've lived here for two years. I know her— this is Mrs. Chin." I held out my driver's license. "*Please*," I pleaded. After a long moment, he nodded and let her pass.

In the streets, men and women approached, speaking Cantonese, and I had to shake my head, unable to understand. All I knew was *lei hou ma*. I hated that I was so useless.

Because the phone lines were down, a phone company had set up portable call centers.

"Lily," my mother answered, her voice unlike I'd ever heard it, slack and shaking with panic. "You're all right," she said, relieved.

"I'm all right."

"We were so worried," she said. "It's Lily. She's okay," she called to my father. I repeated to him that I was fine.

I hesitated, and then I dialed Luke.

"Can I come over?" I asked.

Luke opened the door and hugged me immediately. His T-shirt smelled like Tide. Despite his frequent traveling, his small space was welcoming, appealing, towers of ragged books in every corner, spines lined and cracked with use, and walls covered in drawings and newspaper clippings. In a corner sat the smallest television and VCR, like an afterthought. He brewed mint tea. The mug looked homemade, thick with violet glaze. He passed a blanket to me—a rainbow afghan his grandmother had crocheted—and I drew it over myself.

I cried as I told him how useless I felt. The blood banks were full. I didn't know how to help my Chinese neighbors, unable to speak the language.

"We'll help," he said. "We'll find a way."

In the morning, at the Javits Center, we were put to work making sandwiches for rescuers, engineers, nurses. Luke had an ease with strangers, and it was the reason he was such a good reporter. He flirted with older nurses, who leaned toward him and grasped his forearm. When I spoke to the same women, they gave me expressions of encouragement. But I never could elicit the same warmth Luke did, with his green eyes and unruly hair and charm.

"Are you two . . . ?" asked one of the women, in her seventies.

"Oh no," I responded immediately.

I turned my attention back to the sandwich I was wrapping. Luke must have made a face for her entertainment, because she laughed.

When people took their sandwiches from me I nodded and smiled—stiffly, wordlessly—but Luke could strike up a conversation with anyone, on any topic. He could lighten anyone's mood. So often,

I wanted to be a different kind of person. Watching Luke, accumulating light dust on his black clothes, I wished I were more like him: someone for whom the effort of connection was simple, even natural.

I did my best to mimic him, hoping my gestures and actions—hardly anything in the face of this immense misery—weren't totally meaningless.

Signs everywhere said: "Avoid Lower Manhattan" and "United We Stand" and "God Bless America." Homemade posters covered walls, held by clear plastic packing tape. The signs written by Chinatown residents bore the same curled, upright scrawl I recognized from Chinese restaurant menus, as though they'd learned to write from the same person. Chinese children waved American flags. No one was interested in buying other souvenirs, so shopkeepers sold flags in every size. Bouquets of flowers, white and yellow and red, tied with huge ribbons like alien leaves, erupted everywhere—makeshift memorials, generic yet necessary.

I stood numbly at a vigil. All of us, young and old, mostly Chinese, cupped small flickering flames. I didn't notice when the candle I held burned down to nothing and the wax melted, a second skin, onto my fingers.

CHAPTER 7

THE DOOR TO THERESA'S apartment was open. I held, by its neck, a bottle of wine—the second-least expensive option at the bodega. A sticky residue remained where the price tag had been.

"You came!" Theresa said. We embraced; she smelled like frying oil. "Come in. Let me find Adam. He's heard so much about you."

I added my wine to the crowded kitchen island, where it immediately didn't matter which it was. I'd fretted so long over which to buy.

Guests held paper plates, translucent and flimsy with oil. Theresa forgot about locating Adam and returned to her post at the stove, flipping latkes. Hong, wedged between two men on the sofa, noticed me and waved me over.

"Lily, this is everyone," Hong said, and made a sweeping gesture.

December brought parties, everyone insisting on joy after September's tragedy. The group greeted me with generic enthusiasm before returning to their argument—impassioned and exasperated—about Enron. As a person who didn't own any stocks, I didn't know how to be part of the conversation. Luke would have known how to participate. I'd considered asking him to come. In the end I didn't; I thought he'd feel left out among my friends. But now I worried that it had been a mistake, coming alone.

"You know they give out this prize," one of the men said. "The Enron Prize for Distinguished Public Service."

"Shut up," Hong said. "Public service?"

"You get a crystal trophy and, like, fifteen K. Alan Greenspan won this year."

"What do you do?" a woman asked kindly, noticing me. Around her, people quieted, waiting for my answer.

"I'm a photo editor at an online travel magazine," I said. It elicited the kind of satisfaction that saying *fireman* might have: People knew what it meant.

"That sounds fun!" she replied, and I nodded as though it were.

Assistant photo editor, officially, but *editor* was in the name. Except for the salary, the job wasn't any different from my internship. It offered health insurance, but the premium was so high that I didn't sign up for it.

"That's all right! You're so young!" Jerry had said.

In late September I received the news I'd been hired in an email. The office was closed, and we were working remotely. In the wake of the tragedy, everyone kinder with one another, Jerry must have felt guilty.

I should have been happy. I'd wanted the job for so long. But it all felt silly, especially now. My mother had always encouraged me to find meaningful work. Choosing pictures for an online travel magazine could hardly count as mattering. While Luke argued with Jerry about the importance of taking political stances—we had a duty to actively address Islamophobia, Luke insisted—I chose between similar images of hotel lobbies or temples in Thailand. Anything Asian, Jerry assigned to me. My days disintegrated as I sat before the computer.

Of course I was relieved to have a job. The concern that had once been most pressing—money, and whether I could make my rent—vanished. I reminded myself to be grateful—mere months ago, the thing I had wanted most was to be employed!—but reprimanding myself was only so effective. My mother's voice echoed in my head: What was I doing with my life? I needed meaning, as she'd said, but how would I find it? Meaning was a slippery fish I was trying to catch with one hand.

Could a life be meaningful if its foundation was something besides work? Hong and Theresa's lives didn't revolve around their jobs. They loved weekends and complained about Mondays. Yet their lives seemed fuller than mine, rich with friends and family and activity.

The woman who asked what I did didn't have follow-up questions. I was about to return her inquiry—why was that always the first thing asked, *What do you do?*—when the group returned to their conversation. I ate a cold latke. It was bland and tasted of vegetable oil, without enough salt.

I glanced at the door whenever it opened, as though I might know the person arriving, though of course I didn't. Theresa and Hong's friends came in mostly heterosexual pairs. Many of the women wore sparkling engagement rings. Each couple appeared to know the others. I regretted not inviting Luke, at the same time I was glad I hadn't. All the Asian women, Hong and Theresa included, hung off the arms of white men. I was relieved I wasn't one of them, even though I had been, in the not-so-distant past.

I inspected the framed photographs in the hallway: Theresa and Adam in front of the Parthenon; Theresa and Adam holding a friend's cartoonish baby; Theresa and Adam on the beach, windswept and sunburned, the camera reflected in their mirrored sunglasses.

"Hey," a man said. "I don't think we've met." I recognized him as Adam, Theresa's Adam, from the photos.

"I'm Lily."

"Lily!" he said, embracing me.

His face was close to mine and I saw that his eyes were glassy; he was drunk. He kept a hand on my waist. I tried to step back but he moved with me. I could feel my neck growing hot. What if someone saw us and got the wrong idea?

"I love your place," I said, moving another step backward. "Theresa's incredible. Congratulations, by the way." I hoped mentioning his fiancée's name might encourage him to remove his hand from my waist. After a too-long moment, he did.

In the kitchen, Hong and Theresa stood side by side at the sink, hands wet with soap, like sisters. Hong said something into Theresa's ear and she laughed. I felt envy expanding, like cotton candy being spun in my chest. It would have been easy to say good night, but I didn't want to interrupt them—didn't want them to have to accommodate me. I slipped out without saying goodbye.

The smell of oil followed me home. It was in my hair and clothes. Even after I showered, it lingered.

The following weekend, another party. Flowers decorated the long tables, candles gave off their orange glow, a pizza oven radiated heat. Platters of meatballs, in pyramids, sat on the tables. On giant wooden boards rested wedges of sulfurous cheese, salami folded into roses, and fake-looking bunches of grapes. Ice buckets held Italian beer in green bottles, beaded with condensation. Jerry, thinking no one was watching, slid an entire salami rose into his mouth.

My dress was tighter than I'd realized, with a neckline that plunged toward my small chest and accentuated my bad posture. I'd arrived wearing a faux mink coat I'd found at the thrift store but shed it quickly because two people, one after the other, commented on it. I didn't want to have to talk about the coat all night, which had no good story. I surrendered it at the coat check—our poor intern took it—and now I was not only cold but exposed, and slouching. At twenty-four I still didn't know how to choose the right clothing for myself.

By the refreshments, Luke held his beer in an odd way, as though it pained him. When I approached, he showed me why. With a magician's flourish, he opened his palm, revealing trash in his hand, a crumpled napkin and toothpicks—the detritus of at least ten meatballs.

"That's your dinner?"

"Not entirely. I haven't had dessert."

"Fancy editor like you. Why don't you leave the scavenging to me?"

"Hey," Luke said, as though remembering something. "You look pretty."

I'd never seen him in anything but his all-black uniform. Tonight he wore a blue jacket. His dark, wild hair hadn't been tamed, but I liked it that way. I was softer with him now, feeling a kinship, feeling grateful for the nights he'd let me stay with him, lonely in September. Nothing had happened, then. If he tried to kiss me tonight, I realized, I would let him.

I scanned the room for Sandra. A voice over the intercom announced the raffle. My raffle ticket was in the pocket of my coat, which I'd checked. I didn't bother to get it. I knew, already, that I wouldn't win.

"Our first prize is . . . an iPod!"

People murmured with excitement and peered at their tickets. I crossed my arms, trying to keep warm.

"Are you cold?" asked a voice beside me.

It wasn't Luke, whose attention was on the stage. I turned to my left: It was Matthew. I must have made a noise, because Luke glanced over.

"Take this," Matthew whispered.

Matthew took his coat off and draped it over me. I put my arms through the sleeves. I could feel Luke's eyes on us, curious.

Then he pressed his raffle ticket into my hand.

"What's an iPod?" I asked.

"It's like a Walkman," he said.

The emcee read out the numbers, then repeated them.

"That's you," Matthew said. "Go on."

Walking to the stage to collect my prize, I remembered the enormous TV. This came in a small white box I could hold in one hand.

"I can't," I said to Matthew, extending the box to him. "It's yours."

"What if we shared it?"

"You mean, like, joint custody?"

"No." He shook his head. "That's not what I mean."

I'd imagined this encounter happening years in the future, when I was grown, when I understood myself: I'd know exactly what to say, and how to describe, with perfect confidence, the ways in which I was wrong for him—we were wrong for each other. But there were also the inarticulable things, which came to mind in scents, in colors, impressions I didn't have language for—the rightness I felt with him. Not in his contexts, but with him specifically. I'd missed him. I could decide—here, now—to stop overthinking things.

"Want to get out of here?" I said. "This party is not that amazing."

He smiled.

"See you at work," I turned to say to Luke.

CHAPTER 8

HE WANTED TO PROVE his skill as a manicurist, which he'd mentioned at our first dinner and I continued to express skepticism over. We were in his bed. It tickled when he placed the cotton balls between my toes. He held my calf in his hand—the most intimate pedicure. Now each toenail was the color of a sand dollar. Next he would paint the fingers, a gray blue, like a sky threatening rain. His sister Jenna had left nail polish in the guest-room bathroom.

"How'd you get so good at this?"

"Don't move," he said.

He blew on one painted hand. He shook the container of topcoat and, intently, applied it neatly to my nails. I liked how serious his face became.

"Were you amazing at coloring in the lines?"

"It was having so many sisters. I was their indentured manicurist."

"No!" I laughed. "How old were you?"

"Honestly? Age five through . . . maybe high school?"

"What!"

"I wasn't very cool, in case that isn't obvious."

"I find that hard to believe."

"They bribed me. Baseball cards as a kid, beer as a teenager." He set my hands down on two hardcover books he'd strategically placed. "There."

"I'll buy you beer."

"Mani-pedi for a six-pack."

"A steal, honestly."

"Hey," he said. "I have two surprises."

"You mean, two *more* surprises? That you're a manicurist is pretty surprising."

He presented our iPod, which he'd loaded with songs. Engraving was free, and he'd gotten it engraved—formalizing the fact that it was now ours: "Matthew and Lily." He showed me how to move the cursor with my finger to locate playlists here, albums and artists there. One of the playlists was labeled "L+M." I picked it up using only my palm and touched it only using the pads of my fingers. He put the earbuds in my ears because the polish wasn't dry enough for me to do it myself.

When I pressed play, I was surprised to hear Elliott Smith's sad voice. The squeak of the guitar strings made my skin feel tight. It was the mix I'd given him—the CD I'd thrown away that night I'd felt, so strongly, that we should stop seeing each other.

"I memorized it," he said.

"Creepy," I said, but I was flattered.

I hadn't known he was paying attention. The song transported me back to that night, how bereft I'd felt, how certain with the disappointment that we weren't meant to be. I pressed stop.

It was easy, picking up where we left off. At his place, everything was the same: the orchids, still alive, with new blooms, in the foyer. When we tried to catch up there was oddly little to say. He could summarize the past two years, and I could do the same, in a matter of sentences. It should have required more—recounting the time—and yet I could have said more about my day than I could two years. I was certain I was a different person, a changed person, and yet I couldn't say how. It wasn't as though I had grown straightforwardly, the way a tree grows. My mother might have said that certain cells had been replaced by newer cells—skin cells, intestinal cells, red blood cells— where others, like my neurons and bones, had deteriorated.

"Surprise number two," Matthew said. "Close your eyes. Give me your hand."

I offered one hand and he turned it over, careful to avoid the wet nails. He placed something cold and metal in my palm. I opened my eyes and saw it was two keys on a ring.

"Oh."

"So you have them," he said.

My manicured hand resembled someone else's—unfamiliar, with the gray blue. Though I admired the colors, I saw, now, that they weren't right with my skin tone.

"I want to do this," he said. "I don't want to lose you again."

Matthew wore an imploring expression. He'd missed a day of shaving and the light hair was coming in around his jaw.

We had been spending nearly every night together, though I made sure, every few days, to return to my apartment. It was an effort to remind myself: This was where I would be, if the relationship failed.

I imagined certain women, women raised differently, constituted of different stuff, running blindly into love, not afraid of what might happen afterward—how things might end. Could I be a woman like that?

Each morning, he woke at five, made himself coffee and a smoothie, and left for the gym. He smelled like the woods, like tobacco. He was embarrassed when I found the bottle of cologne. He seemed able to do more in a day than I could, as though he had access to more time.

Each night, we talked until one of us fell asleep—usually him first. You can fall in love with a person, watching them sleep—and I did. I loved him, already. I hadn't been careful, like I'd intended to be. It had happened in spite of me—without my permission. But I didn't tell him. I withheld it. I could feel the words, like physical weight in my mouth, wanting to spill out. But if I said it I wouldn't be able to undo it, and then where would that leave me?

Matthew blew on my hands. With the lightest touch, he ran the pad of his thumb over one of my nails to check that it was dry. He gathered my hands in his. I'd been holding my breath, and I let it go.

"Me too," I said. "I want to do this, too."

～

All over Matthew's condo there were mirrors, so it was as though we shared the space with our doubles. When he held me I looked, instinctively, to our reflection. It was like pressing a bruise, wanting to see if the pain lingered. I wanted to see how contradictory we were, as a pair, the difference of our physical bodies: him blond, built, tall; me with my plain black hair and average height and face that didn't look good, I believed, unless I wore makeup. It was a face that made people ask: *Where are you from?*

In our reflection, I saw an all-American man with a foreign woman, even though I was also all-American.

"You're beautiful," Matthew said, catching me, somehow reading my mind.

"Stop," I said.

"You are," he said. "You know what I thought, the first time we met?"

"What?"

"*I need to ask her to dinner—that beguiling young woman clutching a shrimp tail.*"

Matthew thought I was more special than I believed I was. Who was right, and who was wrong?

Love irrigated everything with new meaning. Loving him fully and well—this was a task I felt up to. I was used to an atmosphere of unease that traveled constantly with me; when I was with Matthew, it lifted. Both of us had been lonely; we weren't anymore. If our bodies disappeared—if they vanished—and what remained was only our souls, I was certain they would share a resemblance. Both of us had been formed like stones in a river, washed over by our parents' expectations—the forceful currents of them. No wonder we were drawn to each other.

My issues at work didn't vanish now that I was salaried. Jerry's superiors weren't happy with the website's engagement numbers, so his moods swung back and forth. Frequently I was a target of those moods.

"You should quit, Lily," Matthew said. "You hate this job, anyway."

"What about money?" I asked.

"What about it? What do you need? I can give it to you."

I shook my head. He didn't understand.

"It's fine," he said. "I promise, it's really, really fine. I make a stupid amount of money. I couldn't spend it all myself, even if I tried."

All I could think of was my mother—her disappointment. Whenever we spoke, I tried to talk to her about Matthew, and she would steer the conversation to my professional life.

She took me to her lab when I was nine, I told Matthew. I realized I'd never shared this story with anyone. I was still ashamed. It had happened so long ago and should have been absorbed into the comprehensible past—a tellable anecdote, like any other story from my childhood—as distant as myth. And yet, perhaps because I hadn't aired it, it felt recent, and painful.

She'd hoped that I'd fall in love with the work of becoming a research scientist, the way she once had. She'd hoped I might be seduced, as she had. But to me, the fact that everything was invisible rendered it nonexistent. It was terribly simple of me. All I saw were hands in blue gloves, pipetting clear liquids into petri dishes— I couldn't make sense of it.

I must have seemed bored. I must not have asked the questions she wished I would ask. Afterward, when I begged to get ice cream, she said no, that we were going home. She was like a child who had been refused, and was lashing out. And like that, we were both upset.

I knew, then, that I had disappointed her irrevocably. I adopted her belief in me: that I was small-minded—and would be for my entire life. Now I thought it was naïve of her, too, to believe that particular moment—me so young, displaying a child's typical response— represented anything.

I remembered so clearly the disappointment on her face, the fear that I would never amount to anything—anything significant, anyway. And to date, she was right: I hadn't. I was beginning to think it might be fine with me—being ordinary but happy. But this would never be acceptable to her.

She had always longed for more. She had always wanted more than one life could contain.

Matthew said he would have his assistant get my checking account information. She would set up an automatic payment.

"Just to tide you over," he said, and I didn't refuse. "So you can decide what you want to do next, you know? Instead of being forced to take whatever."

He refilled my jam jar of wine. We were in my apartment, and his eyes fell to the empty space in the living room where a couch should have been, then looked to me, suddenly, like he had an idea.

"Move in with me," he said.

"I don't know, Matthew. How much is the rent?"

He shook his head. "There's no rent. It's all paid for."

I didn't reply. What was I so afraid of? I worried that I was doing things in the wrong order: entering a relationship without yet knowing the trajectory of my life—who I was supposed to be. I was afraid to form a self around a person who might disappear from my life as easily as he'd entered it. But Matthew punctured my thoughts.

"I love you," he said, articulating what I'd been too afraid to.

CHAPTER 9

WE LEFT OUR RAFFLE TV on the sidewalk for a lucky New Yorker. I was used to moving being stressful. But the day was painless—hopeful, even.

He wore his white undershirt, carrying my things, reminding me of the night we met. Mrs. Chin embraced me and waved shyly at Matthew. Mr. Peng gave me a plastic comb—a parting gift.

Jerry fired me, as I'd known he would. Matthew came to console me, incongruous in his suit and tie. He helped me pack my desk. Jerry's jaw dropped to see us together. He hadn't known we were dating. That night, he called, full of remorse: "We might actually have a place for you, going forward. Not in your current role, but something else?" It was satisfying, to tell him no—petty and pleasurable, to hang up without saying goodbye.

Every Friday, Matthew had money wired to my bank account. Like magic, the digits of my balance grew higher. One thousand dollars a week, more than I had ever earned at a job before. I spent it on groceries for dinners I had waiting for Matthew when he arrived home from the office, but even then, I couldn't use it all. Week after week, my balance grew.

Life merged with his was undoubtedly easier: Money made it so. The pristine white kitchen, its marble counter that glistened. Matching silverware and glassware. No unintentional duplicates, no warped plastic spatulas or branded beer openers. I spritzed the orchids, replaced the soaps, as though I were living someone else's life. For weeks, I hesitated to call it "home." I kept my few belongings in a corner of the bedroom, in case I'd have to leave at a moment's notice.

Matthew discerned this. "Why don't you redecorate?" he prompted. More money appeared in my bank account—a budget for furniture, the balance so high I was reminded of the scratch cards I used to buy. Was this what it felt like to win the lottery?

I selected furniture from catalogs, replacing Matthew's impersonal choices with cozier ones. An overstuffed armchair that invited lounging in, a dining room table of warm maple—its grain hard-won, acquired through age. Never before had I purchased furniture that wasn't secondhand. The armchair came wound in plastic and hissed when unwrapped. I remembered the Park Slope brownstone— Reginald the English bulldog, bred until he could no longer breathe easily, the patterned rugs and potted plants. I bought Persian rugs and immense plants in hand-thrown ceramic pots; they brought a warmth that had been lacking. Money made decorating almost too easy. Everything could be new. But furnishing with only new things made a space feel artificial. At the flea market, I found an antique lamp and carved credenza—objects with histories, the perfect finishing touches.

"Incredible," Matthew said.

I had a talent for this: for considering a space, creating a home, anticipating needs. Larger questions overwhelmed me, but this was a question on a human scale: What did a person—two people—need? This, at least, I comprehended.

Hong and Theresa insisted on meeting Matthew. At the bar, I almost didn't recognize them: They arrived wearing more makeup than they usually did. Matthew loomed over Adam and Tim, who were both broad and short, only a few inches taller than I was. Adam greeted me, a kiss on each cheek, not appearing to remember he'd acted improperly.

While Adam and Tim excused themselves to fetch our drinks, Theresa and Hong asked questions, their eyes fixed on Matthew: How had we met? Who had introduced us? How long had he lived in the West Village? It was obvious they found him beautiful.

It was an interrogation: How and why were we together? What was the reason he was with me at all? Hong and Theresa both flushed from the alcohol. Their cheeks were red and their eyes were glassy. I didn't share this genetic trait.

Why were we all in relationships with white men? I wanted to ask. I didn't know the answer. Had Hong and Theresa's white partners dated Asian women previously? Were we interchangeable? Had Adam cornered me at his party because of how I looked? Matthew didn't have any Asian ex-girlfriends. That made him different, I concluded. But was I right to believe this, or was I just lying to myself?

Of all available people, we had chosen white men. The word *chosen* didn't strike me as correct. Falling in love didn't seem to me a choice. It was disorientation. And was it my choice, I wondered, if the person I desired was desired so unsurprisingly by these women, too?

Hong and Theresa were different with their partners from when it was just the three of us. They spoke more softly. They put hands on their partners' arms, possessively. They laughed at unfunny things, out of politeness. They looked constantly to their partners, while their partners looked to Matthew—everyone seeking approval. I wondered if I was acting different, too—if they could register the changes in me. I wondered if they, like me, didn't like what they saw.

The phone was ringing when we got back home. I hurried to pick it up.

"Hi, Lily?" a woman greeted me.

"Yes?"

"This is Lily. The other Lily. From the New Year's party? A few years ago now."

"I remember," I said. "I'll get Matthew."

"Actually, I'm calling to talk to you. I thought we could get to know each other."

"Oh?"

"Could we get brunch sometime?"

I was surprised. At her party, she'd seemed uninterested in speaking with me—relieved to be drawn away. The fact that I was with Matthew—it changed things, apparently. This was getting tiresome.

"Sure," I agreed, nevertheless. It wasn't as though I could say no.

When the other Lily said *brunch* I had pictured a crowded, shared table, elbow to elbow with hungover New Yorkers wearing sunglasses, prattling in an attempt to keep night-before regrets at bay. This wasn't that. We met at a hotel—her suggestion. She was in the lounge area when I arrived. She stood and gave me a bony, floral hug.

A server guided us to upholstered chairs at a small table, amid couples with crossword puzzles, families with glasses of orange juice.

Lily held the menu, showing off the rings on her fingers—real gold that shone. Underneath the table, I removed the brass ring I was wearing and slipped it into my purse. I'd bought it while shopping with Hong and Theresa. It was play jewelry compared with hers, and I hoped she hadn't noticed it.

Lily asked for coffee, which our server poured from a silver pot. Croissants arrived, swaddled in a pressed white napkin. I took one and Lily did the same. I finished mine quickly. She tore hers up into small pieces. The server returned to brush the crumbs off the table with a long, thin tool.

Our entrées appeared—asymmetric: Lily's small cup of yogurt with granola and fruit, my enormous platter of smoked salmon benedict, hollandaise sloping generously down its sides, and home fries in a separate dish. I'd thought the point of brunch was to eat two meals at once—it was in the name—and now realized that not everyone believed this. Lily didn't remark on the discrepancy.

Instead she asked me questions relentlessly, as if interviewing me. She asked what I'd studied in college, what I did for a living. She waved a hand when I tried to ask about her, as though her answers were less interesting. My food grew cold.

After the requisite inquiries about myself, she began to ask about Matthew. Like Hong and Theresa, she wanted to know why we were together. None of them concealed it well.

"I'm so happy you reconnected," Lily said. She took a small bite of her parfait and chewed it. "Matthew had a hard year. We all did."

Of course all of New York—the entire country—had mourned. The grief was total, obliterating. But I wondered what it was like where she was, on the Upper East Side, so much farther from the towers.

"That's so interesting that you're from Florida," she said. "Has he taken you there? To Miami? He has a beautiful place, an investment property, right on the beach."

I shook my head.

"Or the Hamptons? He must have taken you to the Hamptons."

I shook my head again. He hadn't mentioned the Hamptons. I could see her revise her perspective: I wasn't as important as she'd believed me to be.

"He will," she insisted. "We went last week—to Florida. That's why my hair's this blond right now." She laughed—with relief, I thought, satisfied to have uncovered proof I was temporary. "Have him take you!"

Lily could tell me who the brunette at her party was, it occurred to me. I could feel the question forming but was too afraid to actually speak it. I already detected in Lily's questions her disbelief that I was living with Matthew. I didn't want her to know that I couldn't quite believe it, either.

I had no way of knowing when brunch would conclude. Her parfait remained uneaten, despite the fact that I'd done all the talking. Finally, she nodded at our server for the check and insisted on paying for the meal, even though she had eaten a tenth of what I had, in calories.

"Let's do this again!" she said, and wordlessly I nodded.

I brought it up casually, lightly, as though I didn't care. We were standing before a painting: an abstraction of ocean blue with a burst of color, like confetti, in the center. It reminded me of the photos I'd seen of trash accumulated in the ocean. Stan circulated; it was opening night of his show. I clutched warm grapes and a plastic cup of room-temperature sauvignon blanc.

I wanted to pick out a painting for one of our blank walls. But the colors of this one weren't right.

"Lily said your Florida place was nice," I said to Matthew. "I had brunch with her."

Lily had pulled to the surface a worry I'd kept submerged. Why hadn't he mentioned Florida? Why hadn't he mentioned the Hamptons? What did I actually mean to him?

"Do you want to go?" He seemed surprised.

I wanted to test him: *How important am I to you?* But he didn't even register it as a test. He reacted as though I were only asking about dinner.

"Hey, you two," said Stan, interrupting.

"We're talking about Miami," Matthew said to Stan. "The condo."

"You haven't been to Miami?" Stan teased.

"And *you* have?" I said, feigning offense.

"We want to buy something," Matthew said. "But Lily says the colors aren't right."

Stan put his hands over his heart, mimicking hurt.

"That's not what I mean!"

"Show me what you mean, then," Stan said. "I'll do a special one just for you."

"I do want to go," I said to Matthew as Stan was pulled away by his gallerist. "You went there as a kid, right? I want to know what it was like for you."

"We can go," Matthew said with some resignation.

Whenever I brought up his family, he grew rigid, hard shelled. *How important am I to you?* was my more pressing question, though I didn't ask it.

Stan reappeared. "Take the jet!" he said, with mischief.

"The what?"

It was his family's jet, Matthew explained, shared among the siblings. He hated to use it and preferred to fly commercial. So his family was that kind of rich. Naïvely, I hadn't been aware.

"I'm not with you for your money, if that's what you're worried about," I teased.

Wearily, he smiled, and brought a nervous hand to the back of his neck.

"That's a joke, by the way," I added.

"That's not what I worry about with you," he said.

CHAPTER 10

WE DRESSED IN DARKNESS. The moon hung, faded, in the morning sky.

Mitchell drove directly onto the tarmac, where an airplane in miniature waited. At the bottom of the staircase, two women greeted us, beaming—our stewardesses. They looked cold, with their thin-stockinged legs. I'd always thought *gams* was an odd word to mean "legs," but *their* legs—long like arms—looked exactly like gams.

Inside, the pilots greeted us in British accents—two amiable older white men. The interior looked the way it did in the movies, beige leather armchairs with tables between them, where a CEO might sit discussing important affairs.

"You good?" Matthew asked.

I nodded. He kneeled before me and gestured to the base of the seat, a brass lever.

"By the way," he said, "these swivel."

He pushed the lever down and spun me, and I laughed. Then he moved to the couch seat, at the rear of the plane. Within moments, he was fast asleep—unconscious through the plane's ascent. I remembered our flight to Paris, how afraid he'd been. But this, he was accustomed to.

"Coffee?" one of the flight attendants asked.

She had the coffee pitcher already in one hand. Her necklace dangled when she bent to pour it, like it wanted to hypnotize me: a cursive gold J.

Did I want an omelet? Anything else? Juice? The coffee tasted like it was from a café, not a plane, and the mug was heavy in my hand—real ceramic.

"Okay, an omelet," I said. "And, sure—I'll take juice."

The orange juice came in a real glass, and tasted freshly squeezed. The omelet was served on a real plate, and I ate it with a real fork. The eggs were real, and oozed cheese.

I used a toilet with a plush seat, with a lid that folded down to look like it wasn't a toilet at all. I washed my hands with a brand of hand soap I recognized from the bathrooms of the restaurants that Matthew had taken me to. It smelled like a garden—no false notes in it. While Matthew slept, the plane warmed and filled with golden sunlight.

We were there in no time at all. In Miami, a bald man in a black suit greeted us, beside a polished black town car. All of it shone in the sunlight: the car, his head, the wedding ring on the hand he stretched out to greet us. I'd gotten used to this, as effortlessly as I'd gotten used to so many once-remarkable things, and thought nothing, now, of getting into cars to be driven by strangers.

The sky was gray but the wind hot like breath, as though it were being blown by giant lungs. My long skirt whipped around my legs.

In the chilled, air-conditioned car, we didn't speak. My nerves felt alive inside me. Matthew seemed to know: He squeezed the hand that was in my lap, and as he did, my eyes met the driver's, in the rearview mirror. Immediately, I looked away. I wondered what he thought of us—if he thought we were terrible people, people who couldn't drive themselves.

In the week leading up to the trip I'd been seized with worry. My swimsuit was too old. I went shopping in a panic. At Bloomingdale's, I put four bikinis on my credit card—Matthew's money. I could feel the cashier, with her gold name tag that said "Monica," searching my face, trying to get a handle on me, but I never met her gaze. Did other women feel this way when they went shopping, buying multiple options in a panic? I signed the receipt and fled.

At home I tried on each bikini and peeled each off, one by one. Terrible, terrible, terrible. Each reminded me of a different way in which I fell short: my too-small breasts, the layer of fat around my stomach, the stretch marks on my butt that none of the swimsuits completely covered. I couldn't return them on the same day and face the same cashier. In the end I kept one suit, only because I had to: a green string bikini consisting of triangles that reminded me of a jack-o'-lantern—its eyes and smile.

Around us, palms bent with the wind, and I pictured their tops flying off like toupees, while we sped along inside of our protected shell, unaffected. From Miami to Key Biscayne we drove over what Matthew told me was the Rickenbacker Causeway—a bridge so long I couldn't hold my breath over the length of it. And then the island itself: imposing white buildings with windows like mirrors, beaches of pale sand with scattered plants, which Matthew said were sea grape, leaves that were round and shiny and green.

The car slowed, approaching a gated group of three tall buildings.

"This is it," he said.

In the lobby, a smiling, tanned, dark-haired doorman greeted Matthew.

"Santino," Matthew said. "This is Lily."

Shaking his hand was like handling cold leather. It was clear they had known each other for ages—since Matthew was a child.

Santino appraised me openly, with unabashed bemusement. His gaze told me that he'd met Matthew's previous girlfriends, and I was merely one in a long line of them. I wondered how I compared.

The elevator doors opened right into the apartment, which somehow was already the perfect temperature, with a vase of flowers and fresh fruit in a bowl on the counter—fake-looking green apples. *Somehow*, though of course all this had been finely calibrated by people doing invisible work. The steel refrigerator was without smudges, the beds tautly made. The fridge was bare but for glass bottles of sparkling water, inert as bowling pins.

Matthew dropped our bags, opened the windows and sliding doors to let the breeze blast in. We were so high up the ocean looked peaceful. Matthew picked a green apple from the bowl and crunched into it—not fake.

"Is this what you expected?" he asked, and I had to laugh.

How could I have known to imagine this?

———

The restaurant he chose for us was Peruvian, within walking distance. There weren't many options on the island, he explained, and this was one of the better ones. He ordered three different ceviches, circled by plantain chips.

I was a freshman in college when I'd tried my first ceviche, celebrating with friends at a restaurant near Union Square. I'd noticed the word on the menu and contemplated its pronunciation when Evan, who was the birthday boy, ordered the snapper ceviche. When it came, it looked like plastic food—the false food in display cases at some Japanese restaurants.

"It's good," Evan had said, and I'd raised my eyebrows.

"Is it cooked?"

"Sort of," he said. "The acid cooks it. The lime juice."

Evan held up a piece of fish—half translucent, half opaque—and put it in his mouth. Later I'd understand that the only white boys who knew about ceviche at age eighteen had grown up rich. In college, everyone had acted poor, and I didn't know to suspect otherwise. I hadn't known what signs to pick up on.

Matthew had wanted to protect me from a certain kind of wealth his family had. He drew the lines in the sand that I was only now beginning to understand: It was okay to fly to Paris on a whim, on his own dime, but he wasn't eager to show off his family's property. He employed Mitchell and Jenny, but it was with money he made, not money he'd been given.

His Florida was so different from the one I had known. Gleaming and polished, not mossy and mildewing. The condo was too high for the mosquitoes to reach us.

I hadn't told my parents I was dating anyone, let alone that I had moved in with Matthew, or that I had lost my job. I hadn't told them that I hadn't yet found a new one, or about the money that was transferred, each week, to my bank account. I couldn't.

It was a habit, with my parents: omitting information, not wanting to worry them unnecessarily. Though they'd raised me so American, I could never manage the sorts of American relationships my friends had with their parents, where they talked to them like friends.

We ate the fruit out of the sangria pitcher—wine-soaked plum and apple half-moons, with skins that felt chalky against my teeth. My questions grew bolder.

Except for the first night we'd met, Matthew rarely got drunk. Now he was; we both were. His lips and tongue were purple from the wine and I was sure mine were, too.

"At Stan's show you said, 'That's not what I worry about with you.' What is it? That you worry about with me?"

"It's my father," he said. "My whole family."

"What about them?"

"They'll hire a private investigator. To look into you."

"They did that to your last girlfriend?"

"See, that's a perfect example."

Our dessert arrived, a plate of alfajores. He grabbed one.

"My ex's father belongs to my father's country club. I've known her since I was *eleven*. And yes."

"Yes?"

"Yes, they investigated her. Even though we'd known each other forever. These are really good, by the way," he said, powdered sugar on his lips.

The investigator found out she had auditioned to be on a season of the reality television series *The Real World*. It wasn't that anyone forced him to break up with her, but their relationship was not long for the real world, after that.

Everything blurred. I didn't notice the bill come, I didn't notice Matthew pay it. All of a sudden, we were too drunk and laughing over nothing, and racing each other home. The asphalt gave way to sand, and we were on the beach, surrounded by palms that leaned and swayed, intoxicated as we were.

"Let's go swimming," he said.

"What?" I asked. "Now? We're so drunk."

But I followed. We kicked off our shoes. He ran and I chased him, onto the beach, where the chairs had been gathered and umbrellas closed, everyone evacuated: the people, the iguanas. We stripped down to our underwear and waded in. I wrapped my arms around his neck, my legs around his torso. I could almost forget my misgivings here, in the water, in the darkness—the worry that this couldn't last. Matthew was a strong swimmer, and I trusted that he would have been able to save me. The moon was full and round over us and its reflection shimmered in the water like a pearl we could swim for, even touch. Afterward, we couldn't find our shoes. We walked barefoot all the way back.

In the lobby, Santino was off. It was the night security guard, who didn't, as far as I could tell, think anything of me, of us—two dripping people taking the elevator up, without shoes. He'd seen stranger. We got into the shower, rinsed the ocean's salt water off our bodies, climbed into bed still damp, pressed into each other.

The sunshine woke us. We hadn't had the foresight to pull the shades down. One of my arms, in a trapezoid of light, had burned to pink. He blew on my arm to cool it, and in that moment, what love was seemed so clear to me: the need to guard against loss. If I lost him, I thought then, feeling his cool breath against my hot arm, I would never recover.

There was a lizard in the kitchen—a small, slow one. How this lizard had gotten to the fifteenth floor, we didn't know. We supposed it could have come up in an elevator, and it must have. We laughed, imagining it.

It was brown and large eyed—innocent seeming. We debated its age: Was it young? Ancient? We tried to usher it into a plastic bag, and of course it refused to walk willingly into the bag. The ground beneath its feet, cold marble, was likely not what lizards were used to experiencing. It was so far from home. This lizard was probably accustomed to hot rocks, to the sand on the beach, or to the rough bark of trees.

"We could ignore it," Matthew said.

"We're not ignoring it," I said, aghast. "You could pick it up?"

He made an expression that told me that wasn't going to happen. "Or you could."

We positioned the plastic bag on the ground and again the lizard darted elsewhere.

"I have an idea," he said. He opened the kitchen drawer, removed a metal spatula. He gestured to me with it. "Get the bag ready," he said.

I held it open. I braced myself for the worst-case scenario: the lizard running past the bag, up my leg, and into my mouth.

With one quick motion Matthew slid the spatula beneath the lizard and flipped it into the bag like a pancake. I tied the bag shut. Solemnly, we rode the elevator down, the lizard almost weightless, my hand on Matthew's arm. It was Matthew who gingerly opened the bag, who released the lizard onto the sandy beach. It scurried away, each leg moving in tandem with an arm.

"So long, comrade," he said, saluting it, and I loved him.

CHAPTER 11

MATTHEW'S CAR WAS A red convertible, purchased in his early twenties with his first paychecks. I whistled when I got in. "Embarrassing," he said. I liked watching him drive—his serious profile, his arm shifting—because usually Mitchell chauffeured us.

His entire family convened in the Hamptons for the Fourth of July—Matthew's father and stepmother included. He would have declined if not for me, but I pressed: I wanted to meet them, and he acquiesced.

Matthew hesitated before a large iron gate.

"It's not too late. We can turn back now."

"We're doing this," I replied.

He rolled down the window, pressed a sequence on the PIN pad. The gate opened.

Perfectly green juniper trees lined the long driveway. A fat orange cat lay curled near a fountain, where birds were bathing—yellow and brown blurs, fluttering—but the cat, world-weary, couldn't be bothered. It had been hot when we had gotten into the car, almost too cold on the road with the roof down, but here, the temperature was perfect, warm with a breeze. The ocean was so close I could feel it on my skin and in my hair.

Beyond the fountain, the main house was as white as an egg, with green-shuttered windows. On the wraparound porch was a uniformly smiling welcome committee. I heard the jingle of a dog's collar before I saw the dog itself, wiry hair drooping from its face.

"That's Hans," Matthew said.

Hans stuck his slobbery goatee into one of my hands, and I petted him with the other. I liked meeting dogs and children, with their low expectations.

"Ready?" he asked.

I wiped Hans's saliva on my dress. Matthew took my hand.

"You must be Lily," said a woman with Matthew's eyes but dark brown hair. "I'm Lee." I reached my hand out for a handshake, but she embraced me instead, pressing me against soft linen.

"Jane," said a younger blond woman.

Then Denise, with wrists that dripped in platinum. Their husbands were Bobby, Stew, Ben—each in shorts and a polo shirt. The children, ages four through eleven, were pointed out while they chased one another in a game of tag. And Jenna, wearing a white button-down shirt and culottes, older than Matthew by a year but younger than her sisters. Where the others wore wedding bands, she wore only a sapphire ring and no other jewelry. When she and Matthew hugged, her long hair curtained over his shoulders, and she whispered into his ear.

"Okay, okay." Matthew threw up his hands. "We've already fully terrified her."

Except for the children, everyone towered over me. Matthew's father and stepmother emerged last. They stood on the porch, making it clear we were to approach them, not the other way around.

Matthew kissed them stiffly. I could sense his discomfort.

"Hello, Lily," Matthew's father said. They were the same height and had the same face. He felt familiar because he looked so much like Matthew. "It's wonderful to meet you."

"Mr. Allen," I said. Matthew's father looked to him before responding.

"It's Maier, actually," he said warmly, with some amusement. "It's only Matthew who's opted for a different last name. But please, call me Otto. This is Delia." Delia took my hand in hers and kissed my cheeks. Her teeth were perfect rectangles, white as subway tile, so faultless at her age that they had to be veneers. I thought of my own mother's teeth: uniform from afar, but up close you could see they were a mix, false and real, white and yellow.

"Go on and get settled in," Otto added. "I hope you'll make yourself at home. We'll see you at dinner."

I followed Matthew to our room.

"What did he mean, about your last name?" I asked as soon as the door was closed.

"I'm sorry." He moved a nervous hand to his neck. "I should have told you."

"That you changed your last name?"

I hung my dresses in the closet, arranged my two pairs of shoes, keeping my back to him.

"Allen is my middle name. I didn't want . . . My last name is distracting."

Maier, I thought. *Could it be* that *Maier? The pharmaceutical company?* I had taken their drugs for fevers and cramps. I was on their brand of birth control.

"Why didn't you tell me?"

"I didn't want to scare you off."

"So instead of being scared," I said, "I'm incredibly irritated. You made me look stupid."

"I'm sorry. I wanted to tell you, I just . . . I was scared."

"You were scared," I repeated. "*You* were."

"It's a lot. I keep telling you: It's a lot. I'm sorry."

He looked into his lap. I put my hand on his shoulder.

"It doesn't matter to me who your family is. Okay? I don't care about—" Here I gestured all around: the room, the ocean. "I couldn't care less about any of this. I care about you—knowing you. Anyway, it's fine. They seem nice."

"They can be very charming when they want to be," Matthew said.

"I won't be charmed if you don't want me to be."

At dinner that night, conversation was trained on me. We ate outdoors, at a long table on the deck. It smelled like clams and citronella. I hardly touched the linguine because their questions were so relentless. The wine made the siblings chatty and inquisitive.

Where had I grown up? Florida, central. What did my parents do? They were scientists, in genetics. What was "my background," Lee asked, and I took that to mean, where was I from, where was I *originally* from, and I said my parents had come from China, from

Beijing, but that I had never been there. The dog stole a clam from my plate at that moment, and the tension broke. Everyone laughed. The conversation's focus turned to Jenna, and her dating life, and she groaned. Matthew's father and stepmother perched on the end of the table, opposite us. If they had questions for me, they politely didn't add to the barrage of them.

I envied their ease, this enormous family so unlike mine, who joked with one another. They must never be lonely, I thought.

All week, I mimicked them. Their habits were a well-worn rhythm. When Matthew's siblings lounged by the pool, I did the same. When pitchers of grapefruit and mint cocktails materialized, I obediently drank them. We played bocce ball—I had to be taught. We went out sailing, with a cooler to keep the champagne chilled. On the boat's side was written, in dark navy cursive, "The Beacon."

In the evenings, their chef laid out platters of grilled food: fish, steaks, summer vegetables. Always bubbly water passed around, so carbonated it burned my throat going down. All day, while we lounged and sailed and drank—they were always drinking—the chef prepared our meals. Whenever I passed the kitchen she was engaged in violent activity: cracking lobster shells that splattered against her glasses, or hard-cooked eggs against the counter. The meals would appear— creamy pastas, composed salads—on neat white platters decorated with chive blossoms or tarragon flowers, at once complex yet effortless, divorced from the time and labor it had taken to make them. *They want to own time,* I remembered Stan saying.

"Fluke crudo," the chef said to me one afternoon. She'd caught me watching. She must have been my age—a few years older, at most.

"Can I make a confession?" I said. "I don't know those words."

"It's fish," she said gently. "Raw fish. That's all." And then she'd given me a taste: bright citrus, salty ocean—delicious.

Dinner was served al fresco. The siblings invited the chef to eat with us, which she did, politely and swiftly, before standing up to clean.

The kids sat at a separate table with their Filipina nannies, while the adults conversed. I tried to make out the invisible strings connecting them—taut with tension, or loose, estranged. Lee and Jane were close—like sisters, I thought—where Denise was the oddball. Jenna and Matthew made another pair. Within a day I could tell who had a strained relationship with whom, who believed they lived their life better than the others, who felt judgmental, who judged others for judging. They poked fun at Jerry and how he must have been to work with. Matthew had gone to the holiday party out of pity. Jerry had so hopefully invited the whole family. This surprised me, the willingness to tease him. No single member of the family was representative of the others. Whereas mine was so comprehensible. It was clear who the most important people in our lives were meant to be: one another.

Matthew never really relaxed the way he did when he was with only me. When it was just Jenna I could see his shoulders loosen, but otherwise, around the other family members—especially around his father and stepmother—he didn't engage in conversation for longer than he had to.

I tried and failed to read the book I'd brought. It was a novel in which not much happened, each page a dense thicket of descriptive language and characters in overwrought contemplation, and I regretted the choice. In the pool, Denise's five-year-old son sat on Matthew's shoulders, giggling gleefully, and together they made an imposing aquatic creature.

He emerged. He kissed me on the head and told me he'd be right back. I tensed; he'd promised he wouldn't leave my side. He walked to the kitchen, towel around his waist. He had just taken a glass bottle of pink lemonade from the fridge when his father intercepted him, roped him into a conversation.

"Mind if I join?" Jenna asked.

She wore a sun hat with an enormous brim. Her hair, which had seemed to me brown, looked blonder in the light. She settled quietly into the chair beside me, a heavy *Vogue* in her hand.

She didn't pepper me with questions, the way everyone else did. She was a lawyer—in art law. She dealt mostly with collectors, many of whom were eccentric. And she worked with artists, who were also eccentric. I could see why Jenna was Matthew's favorite.

Wanting her to like me, I confessed more than I meant to: about the magazine, about how I'd been fired, and how Jerry had tried to hire me back when he learned that Matthew and I were dating. I was interviewing for jobs now, I admitted, but wasn't having any luck.

"You know, my friend Roland is looking for help. He's a decorator. He does private homes, hotels here and there."

"Oh." I'd been applying for jobs at museums and galleries.

"Matthew said you transformed his place."

"I don't know about that."

"Would that sort of thing interest you? I'd be happy to put in a good word."

"If it's not too much trouble," I found myself saying.

"It would be the easiest thing in the world. I'll call him."

"Who are you calling?" Matthew reappeared, lemonade in his hand. Though he tried to hide it, I could tell something had happened in the kitchen with his father—some disturbance. In the pool, playing with the children, he'd been carefree. Now he was tense.

"You okay?" I asked, touching his back.

"Yeah," he said. "It's nothing."

Once we were alone, Matthew recounted their conversation: His father was pressuring him to take over his position at the family's foundation. Otto put it in language he knew Matthew would respond to, insisting he could do more good there than he could in his current job. What they funded was diverse: antimalarial drugs, sanitation, agricultural research, family planning. That didn't sound so bad, I said. It sounded, in fact, very noble. But Matthew had never wanted to use his family's name, let alone work with them.

Lee was vice chair, but Otto was old-fashioned—idealized the idea of having the entire family involved, and a son at the helm. Matthew's brother, Thomas, should have been the one to take over. He'd planned to study medicine. But he was gone—forever nineteen, younger than Matthew was now. Matthew's eyes grew wet.

There was a knock on the door. It was dinnertime.

I followed him, as I always did, to the far end of the table, away from his parents. Each place was set with a bowl of smooth red-orange soup. I kept my distance from Otto and Delia because Matthew seemed to want me to.

———

In the morning, in the kitchen, I poured myself coffee. Matthew sat in the living room armchair, facing the ocean. Gulls argued so loudly we could hear them.

"My electric toothbrush bit the dust," I announced.

"Did it?" came a voice that wasn't Matthew's.

At that moment I saw that Matthew was actually on the porch, with Jenna. They faced the ocean, backs to us.

"I'm sorry," I said, flustered. "I thought you were—"

"We do look alike," Otto said warmly. "But he's better looking."

We had never been alone together, and I hoped my unease wasn't apparent. He was sipping orange juice, so I decided to pour myself a glass. It was something to do.

I opened the refrigerator to look for it. Inside were three cartons of what looked to be the same brand of orange juice, labeled with a terrifying, grinning cartoon of an anthropomorphic orange. I shouldn't have been surprised to see multiples. The other day I'd opened a door to what I thought was a bathroom and stumbled across a storeroom of pantry items: cleaning supplies and paper goods, enough to last years. And now I was here, paralyzed before the juice.

"It's too much juice," Otto said, reading my mind. "There was a breakdown in grocery list communication."

He folded his newspaper and approached me. He was wearing a checkered flannel robe, silver glasses, fleece slippers. Was this how Matthew would look when he was older?

Otto reached for a carton and each of us unscrewed a cap. They were both unopened, leaving the last one. I unscrewed that cap and it turned out to be the open carton.

"Thank you. Do you want a refill?"

"Sure," he said, extending his glass.

I poured more juice for him, then a glass for myself, wondering if I should retreat to our room, or join Matthew and Jenna on the deck, or remain here so Otto wouldn't think I was fleeing him, even though that would have been correct—I did want to flee. He had a gentle perceptiveness about him and I worried about what he might perceive.

He clinked his juice glass against mine, in a cheers.

"Do you remember your dreams, Lily?"

The question surprised me.

"Sometimes."

"Do you think dreaming means you had a more restful night, or less?"

"I don't know if it has to do with the quality," I said slowly. "Doesn't it mean you woke up in the middle of it?"

"I dream more when I'm worried about something."

"Are you worried?"

"I'm frequently worried."

"What did you dream last night?" I felt emboldened. He was just a friendly man in a flannel robe. Easier to talk to than Matthew had led me to believe.

"I dreamed that I was a duck." He laughed.

"How did you know you were you?"

"Somehow, I could just tell. And all my children were there too—ducklings."

We were laughing when Matthew came in, crossing the kitchen to the fridge.

"What's so funny?" he asked.

We laughed again, picturing him as a duckling.

Matthew reached into the fridge and pulled out an orange juice carton, not seeming to notice that there were three. Otto and I gave each other a look. Blithely, he poured it into a glass. He'd found the open one on his first try.

On the Fourth, the family's fisherman friend stopped by with a cooler of seafood and a box of live lobsters, who scratched at the cardboard from inside with rubber-banded claws. It wasn't that they didn't want to die. They didn't want to be in a box. They had no idea that death was even on the table.

Inside the cooler were mesh bags of mussels and oysters and shrimp with their alien, antennaed heads attached. The chef got to work—simmering the shrimp with lemon and bay leaves, steaming mussels with wine, stirring garlic into melted butter. Deftly, she shucked oysters, and I asked if she would teach me. She showed me how to plunge the tool in the creature's hinge and, assertively, twist. We nestled them into a platter of crushed ice.

Jane's kids gave me a bouquet of lavender and hydrangea they'd picked. I put it in the pocket of my dress. Matthew appeared beside us.

He picked up an oyster, spooned mignonette over it. He tilted his head back, his Adam's apple moving with the swallow. It overwhelmed me, then: the rush of gratitude, of affection. Of wonder: I loved this man, and he'd chosen me. How could this be my life?

That night, beneath the bursting fireworks, we feasted. Otto tapped his glass to mine. We sat beside each other. I asked about the foundation's work, and he expounded. It inspired me, how much good they were doing in the world. I felt a tinge of shame. I hardly ever volunteered—only at holidays when I remembered it.

The American flag, high on its pole, clinked loudly in the wind. Matthew's knee against mine, hands passing the plates across the table, wiping hands on ruined napkins. I didn't think I could be happier.

CHAPTER 12

MATTHEW PROPOSED TWO WEEKS after the Hamptons. He kneeled on the wood floor of the restaurant where we'd had our first dinner. The restaurant remembered our preferences and sent out dishes accordingly. There was the assumption that we were the same people, with the same likes and dislikes. Yet when I tried to recall the person I'd been, who'd sat across from him then, I couldn't remember her. I couldn't put myself back into her place.

My face grew hot. I wished he would stand up. I hoped no one was paying attention to us, but I knew that everyone was. The space was sparse and everyone—guests, servers, the sommelier—watched with curiosity.

"What are you doing?" I murmured, even as I knew.

He pulled a small box out of his pocket and opened it. Inside was the biggest diamond I'd ever seen close up—not that I had seen many. My mother didn't wear any jewelry, let alone an engagement ring. The stone shone in the box he held, and I didn't dare let my gaze linger, as though it might blind me if I looked too long.

My limbs and skin went numb. My vision blurred, like I was looking at the world through water. It was one of my errors, I knew right away. Time had stopped, and I was outside of it. If I could turn every worry over, I might come to the correct decision.

Among the concerns I had, I worried most of all that nothing was as simple as he said. What was uncomplicated for him would not be the same for me. Even this gesture: It was easy for him to act out this grand, timeworn ritual. Could I say yes? When it seemed so impossible. Yet we could be married, the two of us. It could be that easy.

The plain facts were that we loved each other. We understood each other. Was that enough? That I felt, in the crook of his arm, a rightness—a belonging? Wasn't that everything?

"Okay," I finally said. *Finally*—in reality it was seconds. The world returned to its regular speed. It wasn't even long enough for him to begin to feel nervous about what I might say. He knew I would say yes: How could I have said no?

On my finger, the diamond sparkled in its otherworldly way. We were both carbon, my mother might have said. Yet this shining stone was, somehow, over a billion years old. Being worn by me—even if I wore it my whole life—would only be, for this diamond, an instant in time.

Our server rushed out glasses of champagne. The bubbles leapt, eager, into my face.

I called my parents the next day, while picking dried flowers off Matthew's orchid. He was making pancakes, and the kitchen smelled of browning butter. With my engagement-ring hand, I clutched the dead heads of flowers. With the other I pressed the phone against my ear.

Matthew's family had been quick and effusive with congratulations, as one family member after the other phoned to express their delight.

"You have no idea how relieved I am," Jenna said over the phone. "That it's you, I mean. Welcome to the family."

"He left a burner on, heating up an empty frying pan for who knows how many hours," my mother said.

"What's he doing now?"

"He fell asleep in front of the TV."

Matthew slid the coffee mug before me. He recognized the shift in my face and knew who it was I must be talking to. My mother's voice seemed to come through the phone more hotly than other people's did. During conversations my ear grew pained and sweaty.

"What do the rich people want this week?" she asked.

I'd begun working for Jenna's friend Roland. After I told my mother, she'd repeated, incredulously, "A decorator's assistant." As though the things that I got up to were so unbelievable to her she'd never even known to imagine them.

We were decorating a midtown hotel. An accent wall would be covered entirely in plants. I stared at my ring as I spoke.

"Sounds like a waste of water," she said.

"But think of the clean air."

"That does sound nice." A pause. "Your dad's awake."

"Could you get him on the phone? Could you put it on speakerphone?"

There was a shuffle, and then, my father's voice: "We're here."

"Matthew's here, too," I said. He took the dead orchids from me and held them in his fist. With his free hand, he clasped my forearm.

"Hi, Mr. and Mrs. Chen," Matthew said into the phone.

"We're engaged," I said.

"Congratulations," my father said. "How exciting!"

"Yes," my mother echoed faintly. "Congratulations."

After we hung up, Matthew threw away the dead flowers he'd relieved me of.

"She didn't sound happy."

"She said congratulations," Matthew said. "How can you tell?"

"I just know," I said.

I picked the phone up again and held it to my ear.

"Lily?" My mother was surprised to hear from me again.

"Why are you like this?" I willed myself not to cry but couldn't keep my voice from wavering. "I thought you would be happy for me."

"I am," my mother said. "I am happy." She didn't sound convincing. "You're very young. I'm surprised, that's all."

"You were young, too."

My parents had been married in Hong Kong. My mother said she had barely understood the ceremony, in Cantonese. She hadn't told me much else.

"I was young, too. You're right," she agreed.

She said nothing for a long moment.

"I'm happy for you," she said, finally.

I couldn't help but think it had the ring of "I love you," that foreign phrase she'd adopted—that would never be native, or natural, to her.

CHAPTER 13

WHEN THE RAIN BEGAN, it was lightly at first. The wedding planner put up tents and assured me that dinner could still happen outside. But the wind grew too strong, the rain soaked the tablecloths, and she changed her mind: We would move the rehearsal dinner indoors. The staff pushed folding tables together and draped fresh cloth coverings over them.

My parents would be meeting Matthew and the Maiers for the first time. The living and dining rooms that had seemed so large when I had been here in July suddenly struck me as inadequate. Inside, I watched the storm gather power. The ocean, agitated, reflected the silver sky and sparked with lightning. Indoors it was just as stormy: The caterers clanked the dishes and silverware, the chef shouted orders.

"It will clear by tomorrow," the planner swore to me.

I didn't notice myself tapping my ring against my glass until Matthew took my hand, to steady it. I resented him a little, for not sharing my worry.

Thankfully, Jenna arrived first. The siblings followed with their children and their wet dogs, horrifying the planner with their dripping coats, and the house grew loud with chatter. My nerves wouldn't settle until my parents were here. I wondered if they had gotten lost, somehow. Their hotel was only five minutes away.

I couldn't follow conversations, listening, instead, for the doorbell.

The other Lily helped to choose much of what was happening this weekend, from the flower arrangements to the dress I would wear to the menu for the dinner: something innocuous and "not too exotic," she'd said, thinking, maybe, I wanted a Chinese feast. "Trust me, I learned all this the hard way," she'd added, and laughed. Dinner would be uncomplicated, "New American." I couldn't ask advice from Hong and Theresa. They had planned their own weddings, but they hadn't planned weddings like this—with a budget like this one.

"It's just . . . unexpected," Matthew said, when I admitted to accepting Lily's help.

She tasted cake with us, met with the wedding planner, sourced the linens. She'd picked a dress for my mother to wear: cap-sleeved, in a yellow that would photograph well, she assured me. She'd had it tailored to her measurements. It hung, now, sleeved in plastic, on the coatrack, a reminder that she wasn't here.

They were an hour late, when they arrived at last. The crab cakes and cheese cubes—orange, white, swirled orange and white—had been consumed, and the caterers glanced nervously at one another, unsure of when to serve the salad.

At the door, my parents stood, wet from the rain, black hair like stark slashes against their foreheads.

In exaggerated motions, they wiped their shoes on the welcome mat. Matthew introduced himself. My mother kept a smile—rigid, polite—fixed on it. What a magnificent home, my father said. Such an elegant fountain! One by one, the siblings approached, and my parents greeted them, complimenting them on their children—Matthew's nieces and nephews—so well behaved.

Delia introduced herself as Matthew's mother, and Matthew stiffened at the word. Behind her, Otto held out his hand to shake my father's hand, then my mother's.

"Drinks!" Delia exclaimed, her white teeth flashing. "What would you like?"

"Champagne would be most appropriate, wouldn't it?" my father said jovially.

My mother's face still had its tight smile fixed on it.

Lily removed the dress she'd chosen from its rack and encouraged my mother to try it on. Obediently, she changed in the bathroom. When she emerged in the yellow dress, it was immediately clear that the color, of a pale Easter chick, was wrong against her skin. Lily tried to hide her disappointment. It was apparent from her expression that she was fretting: It would be difficult to get a new dress in time for the wedding.

"It fits perfectly," she said to my mother.

We took our seats at the dinner table, Matthew to my right and Otto to my left. My mother sat across from me, wearing the unflattering dress, behind an overly exuberant floral arrangement—a lilac angled in front of her face. Servers presented us with plates of salad, leaves like a saw's teeth.

Around us, conversation swirled: how the flight was, the hotel. I'd had a couple glasses of champagne and felt light from them. My mother stared at her plate, as though trying to look inside the food, not making any movement toward it. I was embarrassed by her stiffness— worried that her lack of interest reflected on me. The Maiers were probably wondering what a difficult family they were fusing themselves with.

"How did you meet?" my mother asked at last.

This was a question for Matthew and me, yet she looked to Otto as she spoke, voice clear—almost a challenge in it. He must have been a curiosity to her: the richest person she'd ever met—*I'd* ever met—but it surprised me, how boldly she stared.

"At the company party," I said, and she turned toward me, as though remembering it was our question to answer.

"Jerry introduced us," Matthew added.

"Jerry—my boss at the website." I didn't know if she remembered. "Matthew's uncle. You'll meet him at the wedding tomorrow."

"And why were you there, Matthew?" She turned to Matthew now.

"He invited us all. He was so proud of the party," he said. "I thought I'd support him."

Otto raised his champagne flute.

"What good luck," Otto said, "that the two of you met."

We lifted our glasses. Mechanically, my mother raised hers, but she didn't drink from it.

She leaned over to my father, said something into his ear. My father cleared his throat.

"My wife isn't feeling well," he declared.

"But the rehearsal," I protested.

My father stood, apologizing. He clasped my mother's hand. They laid their unused napkins, loosely folded, on their plates. I kept trying to catch my mother's eye but she refused to meet it.

The planner was right: The sun did emerge. The rain had a cleansing effect, and the day seemed more beautiful, rinsed. Before the ceremony, we wandered through the property, to an orchard of gnarled apple trees, older than we were by hundreds of years. In the trees, the apples were golden. There were apples on the ground, too, brown and rotting. Flies swarmed everywhere around the putrid pulp. But what we noticed were the apples that hung, radiant, on branches like arms, extended to us. They were wet from the rain. Matthew plucked two and we ate them, me in my wedding dress, him in his suit, our heads craned at an angle, trying not to drip. It was bad luck for him to see me in my dress, but we didn't care. He was so handsome, and I was the woman he'd chosen. Goldfinches swayed on the branches. We tossed the cores over our shoulders. Not sure where to wipe our hands, we settled on Matthew's pocket square. We tried to refold it, without success. We would need help when we got back to the house. A groomsman would be irritated.

I longed for one of my time errors. I wished I could summon it. I wanted so badly to freeze us here, together, in this uncomplicated moment. How little I cared about linens, or cakes, or seating arrangements—the fuss of it all. A wedding involved witnesses, but who could really see what existed, precious, between us? The entirety of this moment was the taste of apple, cool and sweet, like honey, and how much I loved him, how much I felt I was loved. But time moved forward, as it had to, as it always did.

My father held his arm tightly in mine. Everything felt heavy: the gown, my made-up face, the false lashes that weighed on my eyelids and made a strip of dull black at the top of my vision. I looked past the dark valance, searching for my mother. Her seat was empty.

"She'll come," my father said.

He had no way of knowing this, and we each knew that as well as the other. His hands shook at his sides, his tremor much worse recently.

The day was perfect—temperate for the finely dressed people, as if Lily had personally programmed the intensity of the sun's rays. Otto and Delia sat in their designated seats, on the groom's side. Among the guests were the Maiers' powerful friends: two former presidents from different parties, a few senators, entrepreneurs.

She was sick, she'd said. I had trouble believing the excuse. My mother was displeased with me—disappointed. As usual she had made it about her—even my wedding day. I remembered, as a child, then a teenager, the times she was frustrated or impatient with me. Let her calm down, my father would say. Let her have a moment. *Have a moment*, as though time weren't all of ours, as though a moment could belong to one person. Even now, this belonged to her.

The song ended, the signal for me to begin down the aisle. I closed my eyes. Would our relationship have been different if I had been more like her? If I had uncovered my purpose, followed some ambition? Would she have loved me more?

When I opened my eyes, she was there, wearing the dress Lily had chosen, but a radiant blue—as though transformed by a fairy godmother. My mother turned in her seat, and her eyes caught mine. She nodded, and I began to make my way.

The days at home, after the wedding and before the honeymoon, we luxuriated—sleeping in, ordering takeout, playing board games, eating wedding cake for breakfast, arguing, lightly, about whether to get a pet. I noticed when Matthew would begin to reach for his Black-Berry, before stopping himself and refocusing his attention on me.

We'd taken the wedding peonies home. We owned only one vase—my contribution, when we had merged our things—so we stood the flowers up in drinking glasses, in which they leaned drowsily, perched in the bathroom, on our kitchen counter, on both our nightstands. Each day they grew fuller, giving the impression that they would never die.

On a night we ate pad thai in bed, I tucked a peony behind Matthew's ear. He looked childish, with his long legs folded beneath him: white shirt, boxer shorts, bright pink peony. He forgot about the flower and did the dishes with it. Later in the night, the peony still behind his ear, we sat cross-legged on the floor, and he held his cards fanned before him, eyes narrowed. We were playing Texas Hold'em, using dimes for chips.

"Did you know dimes have nickel in them?" I asked.

"Yes."

"Fuck you." I laughed. "No, you didn't."

"I really did."

At that moment I felt the familiar numbness in my extremities and blurring of vision—one of my time glitches. Our interaction paused. His chest stopped its rising and falling, and I could feel time laid out before me, like a dress on a bed. I could see, arrested on his face, the flinch, when he decided to increase his wager but didn't have the cards to support it.

And like that, he returned to regular speed.

Ten dimes, he counted out, blustery.

"All in," I said, not breaking my gaze.

He folded. I knew he would. But I'd had nothing at all, even less than he'd had, and I showed him my hand. He could have won. Of the two of us, we had already established, he was the luckier one.

The moment we stepped through the door, home after the honeymoon, I realized we'd forgotten to throw the flowers away before leaving. There was a spoiled smell, wilted brown petals like scales on the floor.

"I'll call Jenny," Matthew said.

"I can handle it."

"It's too much work. I don't want you to."

"But I want to."

I was annoyed. He registered it in my voice.

"Whatever you want."

He said it neutrally, deferring, polite, and that irritated me further. Like my mother, he could act as though he knew best, as though I didn't know what I wanted for myself. He retreated to the bedroom.

I swept the petals from the floor and into the dustbin. They flew up and scattered. The stems in their vase had grown slime, and the water smelled like rotting fish. Our food had gone bad in the refrigerator so it was hard to tell which bad smell was which.

A tower of boxes sat in the lobby. I'd forgotten about the wedding registry—all the items we had chosen. They were gifts, but the sight of them overwhelmed me. Greece already seemed years in the past: the sunsets soundtracked by buskers repeating the same popular love songs, the retsina on ice. The dishware and appliances came packaged in abundant Styrofoam that didn't fit into our trash can.

At the reception, after the ceremony, we'd gone from circular table to table, greeting the unfamiliar faces: innumerable relatives whose names I wouldn't retain, the minor celebrities I politely asked the names of. To the former presidents I said it was an honor, even though I'd approved of one's tenure more than the other's. Jerry sat meekly. Our guests stared at me, attentive to my every movement— telling me how beautiful I was.

Hong and Theresa sat at the same table with their white spouses, like an advertisement for Asian woman–white man pairings. How incredible this wedding was, how gorgeous we both were, they gushed. Still, I wondered if they were comparing our wedding with their own. Why was it that friendship invited comparison? Were they judging me for my choices? Maybe they thought this was all too extravagant—too much money. They had no high ground to stand on. They had spent everything they could on their weddings, too.

"You're stunning," Jenna said to me. The woman beside her nodded but said nothing. She was Cora, Jenna told me, the woman I'd seen on the eve of the new millennium, the one I'd worried was Matthew's perfect match. They were childhood friends; they'd gone to their high school prom together. The way Cora moved around the wedding, it was as though it were hers: talking to Matthew's parents, sitting at a table with his siblings, entirely at ease. It was *my* wedding day, and everyone was here to see us. But I could just as easily imagine it was her wedding, she and Matthew had just gotten married, and this was all a cruel joke everyone had played on me.

But no, I insisted to myself. I was his wife. Everyone was looking at me, not her.

On occasion I glanced over at my parents. My mother appeared relaxed, held conversations. I wasn't needed.

"Wow, your parents' English is so good," Hong had said afterward, impressed.

Matthew reemerged. The broken-down cardboard boxes, three into two dimensions, were a stack by my feet. He lifted them up.

"I'm sorry," he said.

"I'm just tired."

"I know," he said, and kissed me. "I know you."

This was the thing he said that I craved the most. More than *I love you*, I wanted him to say that he knew me. Who else did?

CHAPTER 14

OUR MARRIAGE WOULD BE different, we swore to each other. It wouldn't resemble our parents'. In long conversations—in bed, making pronouncements in the direction of the ceiling—we enumerated the ways. We wouldn't ever be too busy. We wouldn't nurse resentments. We wouldn't abandon each other, as my mother was doing, now, to my father.

She'd moved him into an assisted living facility. His Parkinson's had worsened. Though luxurious by Tampa standards—the sort of place where the soft-serve machine dispensed different flavors every day, residents ate from china, and there was an extensive DVD library—I was disappointed. It wasn't my place to say what she should do, and yet I couldn't help but feel that she was exacting revenge on him for some reason unknown to me.

We were so happy together, we wanted to enlarge that happiness with a baby. It was a sort of greed—not for money or recognition, but for love. Before I'd met Matthew I never envisioned this happiness. And now it was like a dare: Could I possibly be happier? Even as I was grateful for what we already had, I wanted more.

I wondered if a child would give me the meaning a career hadn't. I didn't admit this to anyone, especially not my mother, who would have been disappointed to hear me say this. An American woman like me, in the new millennium? Couldn't I use my imagination, my capabilities, to pursue some less conventional life? I knew I was lucky to have a mother who had never expected of me the old-fashioned things: marriage, a family. And yet this was what I wanted, as puzzling as it was to her.

I got pregnant. We told our families. Then I had a miscarriage. The pregnancy was only eleven weeks along, and miscarriages were common this early, the doctor assured me. When I got pregnant again, we waited to share the news. I miscarried again. When it happened a third time, I thought, *This can't be normal. What could be wrong? This must be my fault.* The doctor ran tests.

"It's genetic," I told my mother. She'd called to ask how the appointment had gone. "Something to do with chromosomal abnormalities."

"The doctor said that?" Concern tightened her voice.

"They said we could try in vitro fertilization. We could maybe avoid the problem that way."

Through IVF, Lee had conceived her youngest at age thirty-eight. It was expensive, but nothing we couldn't afford.

Our embryos were screened for gene disorders and chromosomal imbalances, the unhealthy ones set aside. We were given the option of choosing the sex of our child, but I didn't want to choose. It didn't seem right.

It was only a collection of cells, deciding whether or not to implant into my uterine wall, and remain there, and yet I spoke to it, I tried to make a deal with it. Like telepathy with my own body, and this new entity in it. *We'll have a great life,* I tried to communicate to the embryo. *Please,* I told it, without words. *Just stay.*

After an agonizing two weeks, the doctor called. The pregnancy had taken, but I couldn't be relieved—not yet. I could miscarry again. Time passed excruciatingly: a month, then another, then another. Time slowed to a crawl—now I understood the expression. I pictured time as an old man, with long silver hair like a wizard's, on his hands and knees.

On the ultrasound I saw the baby's outline. Was love so flimsy? Was I so easily suggestible? I hadn't met this person—only knew his shape and felt his movements—but already he was everything to me.

CHAPTER 15

IN BEIJING, THE HOTEL bathroom fixtures glistened, unscuffed chrome that mirrored my distorted figure. I was seven months pregnant, and the bathrobe hardly closed around my now enormous midsection. A square pot of orchids rested beside the television, like the ones we had at home: a catalog's idea of elegance. The surrounding view was of other high-rises and ongoing construction—a different Beijing from the one my parents had known. Before leaving, I'd asked my mother what I should see and do, and she said she couldn't say. It had been so long, I was better off reading a guidebook.

"Sorry," Matthew said, putting his jacket on. He had to be in meetings all day.

"I told you it's fine."

"Friday," he promised. "I'll be all yours. We'll get some famous Peking duck."

I straightened his tie. He gave me an envelope of bills: yuan in different denominations.

At first, we were afraid to talk about the baby—as though it might vanish the moment we spoke of it. But he kept growing in size, compared to larger and larger fruits: a lemon, an avocado, a melon. Tentatively, again, we resumed our conversations. We would raise our son differently from how we had been raised. What we wanted, most of all, was for him to grow up feeling loved—wholly, completely, without condition.

I wondered if, unlike my mother, I would be a motherly mother. How would I know which kind I was—the motherly or unmotherly type? Was motherliness something that could be cultivated? I had the memory of standing outside my mother's office door. When I was younger, wanting her attention, I'd had to slip notes under the door. *Can I go outside? I'm hungry. I miss you.* I worried I was being needy, but I *did* need. She'd open the door with a face that tried to hide her exasperation but didn't quite. I could always detect it, the detachment. I would be different with my son. I wouldn't expect him to be a replica of me. I would always let him have ice cream.

Matthew made promises himself, too. We would give our son my last name, Matthew insisted. It was better not to be a Maier.

Reluctantly, he had taken the job with his family's foundation. His new position took him around the world. I'd tagged along on trips to Germany, Italy, Mexico. I was thirty-two weeks along when Matthew said he was needed in Beijing—a weeklong trip. The doctor said travel was fine until thirty-six weeks, so I jumped at the chance to go to China.

"There's nothing interesting to see there," my mother had said, trying to dissuade me.

She'd never expressed a desire to return. This made me curious: Where was this place she'd come from? How could she leave and never want to visit—not even once? I wanted to be able to tell my son something about where we'd originated—more than my parents had ever told me.

The hotel was a mishmash of architectural styles, an attempt to look Western—Roman columns, dramatic archways. In the hotel restaurant, if I wanted, I could order eggs and bacon for breakfast.

A stream ran through the lobby, orange-and-white koi swimming past the glinting, thrown-in coins, like dolls' eyes. Except for the Chinese faces, and Chinese art, it was indistinguishable from any other luxury hotel—built a year ago, the teenage concierge told me, in practiced English he confessed he'd learned from *Friends*. His name tag said "Joey."

"Girl or boy?" Joey asked.

"Boy," I said, and he nodded, approving, before telling me about the sights.

———

On the street, I blended in—no one paid me any attention. Women carried the knockoff version of my real handbag. In some alleyways I could peer into people's cramped living quarters: Children and men watched television on tiled floors, while women squatted over wooden boards, mincing meat with heavy cleavers. It didn't feel right to wear my jewelry there, so I slipped my rings into my purse. And then there were other parts of the city where that jewelry was hardly the most ostentatious.

I searched for some proof of my parents, wondering what streets they'd walked, what they'd eaten, where.

At a hectic wet market—stalls of women exhibiting colorful heaps of produce—a mother halved a grape and handed it to her toddler daughter. A memory surfaced, then: How my mother bought big globe grapes that came in plastic bags with holes, as if they were animals that needed air. Gently, she would peel the skin off each grape, pull the orb apart, and swipe the seeds out with her thumbs. She presented these skinned and seeded halves to me. They tasted a little bit salty, like her hands. It was the one un-American thing she did.

I entered the air-conditioned cool of a museum to use its restroom. Behind velvet ropes and glass: a wall of painted bricks from the Jin dynasty, from the Gansu Province. Agricultural and culinary scenes of men tilling the soil and riding horses, royalty feasting—scenes of life. But in parentheses it said "Replicas." Many other displays bore the same parenthetical. The originals had been destroyed during the Cultural Revolution. A carved silver vessel from central China, an iron lamp from Henan Province. I imagined the copyist, casting silver and iron, trying to make the objects look aged to exactly 1,785 years old. As interesting as the scenes were, they told me nothing about my parents' lives.

Nothing indicated that I was American until I opened my mouth, and then there was invariably disappointment—even scorn—that I couldn't say what I wanted to say with my Chinese face. In America people saw me as Chinese, and here they saw me, unpleasantly, as an American. I knew *ni hao* because it was what the catcalling men in

New York shouted the most, after *konichiwa*. After a day in Beijing, I knew the word *ai*, love. Every song was about it on the radio, toneless.

Here, as in New York, groups of friends, dressed alike, gathered over bowls of dessert, or over lunch. In the park, older women danced to warbled music. Would I have been happier here? As an American child, I had been told I was exceptional. And here, maybe, I might have simply existed, part of the fabric of something larger, and been content.

In Tiananmen Square, placards described the square's history, omitting the massacre. In the wind, red flags fluttered, untiring birds' wings. A beggar reached out his hands to me, entreating. His beard was patchy and uneven, his skin oily. Matthew always gave money to men and women on the street and I so rarely did, making the justification to myself that, as a woman, I was afraid for my safety. But the truth was something else—a reluctance to acknowledge a reality that made me uncomfortable. In the act of giving I conceded that I had more than I needed, and someone had far less than they did. It was for no real reason, it wasn't fair. It shattered the illusion of my own free will—that I had made choices, and those choices had resulted in my life. To look away was easier.

He began to speak, in a mumble, and I shook my head: I couldn't understand. The few teeth he had were yellowed, precarious. I wanted to apologize. I didn't want him to think I wasn't speaking to him because of the way he looked—it was only that I couldn't.

I reached into the envelope Matthew had given me and put two twenty-yuan notes into the plate he made with his spidery hands. I felt a touch on my shoulder. An elderly woman, no more than four feet tall, had noticed. I dispensed her the same amount, and soon I was surrounded. I handed out the crisp bills until a policeman whistled at the crowd to disperse.

Here I was, distributing yuan from my husband, gold and diamonds in my purse. My young mother had come here for university, acquiring her ambition in spite of the political turmoil. How had we turned out so different?

I returned to the hotel and approached Joey at his concierge stand.

"Back already?"

"Where is Peking University?" I asked. I wanted to see where my parents had met.

The train car smelled like a familiar perfume, Calvin Klein, or something from the Gap. Around me, everyone was Chinese: Chinese faces with dark hair, or hair that had whitened or silvered with age, or hair that was highlighted to camel or brown.

I exited at the East Gate station. Cars and bicycles gleamed brightly in the sun.

Immediately I realized my mistake: I had no plan. I couldn't read any of the signs or street names.

The students headed in one direction, a school of fish, so I followed behind. A beautiful lake came into view, willows surrounding it, their leaves like uncut hair. Young couples sat on benches.

"Do you speak English?" I stopped a girl holding a textbook. I recognized the oblong shape of mitochondria.

"Little bit," she said.

I asked her where the science building was, and when she asked which kind of science, I said biology.

"I'm going there. I can take you."

She wasn't pretty, exactly, but the skirt she wore flattered her long legs. Young people were more knowledgeable than I had been at their age. She led me into a large brick building.

"I have class now," she said. "You know where to go?"

"Yes," I lied, and thanked her.

The floors were clean, unscuffed linoleum—brand-new. Inside the labs, students wore matching lab coats and goggles. A boy, wrists as thin as mine, moved narrow pipettes. When my mother had brought me to her lab as a child, it was all serious-faced older men and women. This lab had the same bleached smell, strange, like a vitamin.

I heard students laughing with one another. I wondered how different it was in the sixties. My father had been a teaching assistant— older than my mother, who had been a student. My father might have stood before the chalkboard, hands dusty. Was it immediate? Or maybe it was an attraction that grew. I didn't actually know the story. They'd met in class—that was what they'd told me. I'd never seen photos of them young. If they existed, they'd been destroyed, like so many photos during that era.

Without a plan, I wandered the hallways, peering in. Students emerged from their classrooms, looking wonderingly at my pregnant form. I had hoped to feel some kind of connection to my parents here but struggled to, amid the renovations: walls and floors the same, perhaps, but painted over and redone. When I grew tired, I sat.

A man in an apron, holding a pink box, appeared as lost as I was. Noticing me, he nodded and thrust the box into my hands, along with a plastic knife. I shook my head—he had the wrong person! It didn't matter to him; he only wanted to be rid of it. I opened the box: a cake, with Chinese words and sliced fruit, alternating kiwi and mango. What was I supposed to do with it? I sat back down, pink box on the bench beside me.

Now I was a pregnant woman with a cake—an even more puzzling sight. After several minutes, a different man emerged from one of the closed office doors and waved to me. He was thin, bespectacled, with wavy hair—a hint of whiteness beginning at the roots. He was slightly stooped in the manner of certain tall people. He said something to me in Chinese and I extended the box to him. He opened it, and nodded, and took it from me. He knew what to do with this cake.

"Excuse me. I'm wondering if you could help me. I'm looking for anyone who has been here since the sixties? A professor, maybe? My parents, they went to school here . . . ," I began to say. He regarded me with a blank expression. "May Ling and Charles. In the sixties. I'm sorry, I don't speak Chinese," I added, embarrassed.

He said nothing. He probably didn't understand. After a long pause, he said, in gently accented English, "I can help you."

Then he added, "You look exactly like your mother."

As it turned out, the cake was for a colleague who was, like me, expecting her first child. Hence the baker's confusion. The department planned to celebrate her with a small evening gathering before her maternity leave.

His name was Xue Ping. On his desk rested a bamboo plant in a glazed brown cup, tied with ribbon. A gift from a student. Behind him, a photo of his family. His wife smiled genuinely, with apparent pride. Between them, one child, a boy, stood even taller than his tall parents and held a diploma. He had curly hair like his father, visible beneath the mortarboard, identical to the one I'd worn to my own graduation.

"Is he a scientist, too?" I asked.

"A filmmaker, actually. He lives in London."

"What kind of films?"

"You're not here to talk about my son's films, are you?" Ping said, amused.

"No," I admitted.

"How many weeks along?"

"Thirty-two." I drew a hand instinctively to my midsection, to the baby.

"What brings you here?"

"My husband is on a business trip."

"What I mean is, what brings you to my office?"

Ping pressed a button on his electric kettle. He overturned one of the cups from the clay tea set on his desk and placed it before me. With tweezers, he lifted leaves from a paper bag and put them in the teapot. His hands were steady, unlike my father's.

"I was curious to see the university. My parents never talk about China."

"Mei Ling." He nodded.

"May and Charles."

"Charles," he repeated, and chuckled to himself.

"What were they like? Back then?"

He didn't speak right away, as though deciding what he wanted to share. He slid his glasses off, to wipe the lenses with a small cloth. He poured the water over the tea, and the steam rose between us like a curtain.

"We studied lotus plants," he said gently. "In the lake. Your mother and I."

His eyes rested on me, studying my face, not bothering to hide his curiosity.

"It's strange," he said, "not to know you at all. You seem very familiar to me. Will you give me a moment?"

"Of course."

We drank the tea in silence. My mother had never mentioned him before, but I didn't say this to him.

"Your husband—is he American?"

He meant white American. It was what people meant here. I nodded.

He wondered about me, and I wondered about my mother: How had she become herself? How did anyone become themselves?

He asked what my mother studied now. My parents had worked in genetically modified crops, I explained. Fruits and vegetables. My father was retired, and my mother had taken reduced hours. I couldn't explain their work in detail, and I felt a flicker of shame.

"I didn't imagine she would be working on something like that," he said.

"What do you mean?"

"When I knew her," he said slowly, "she had many dreams."

I said nothing, so he went on.

"I can tell you a story about your mother. If you'd like."

"Please." I nodded.

"I mentioned we studied the lotus plant. The lotus is an important plant, in Chinese medicine. Every part of it is used. The roots, seeds, leaves—used for blood disorders, for increased vitality. And the lotus is ancient—existing at the same time as dinosaurs. We knew that the lotus's incredible, ancient genome could repair its own genetic defects, even if we didn't yet have the technology to understand it. In class, we studied its chemical composition."

While speaking, Ping held his eyes closed, as though remembering was a difficult effort.

"Your mother loved the library, more than anything. Because of Stalin, who believed they were essential to educating the masses, the building of libraries had been prioritized throughout China. In Beijing we had one of the best. Your mother spent many of her waking hours there, among the books.

"In our library, there was a glass display case—the type you find at a museum. Inside the case were precious objects, dating back to dynasties past. Little dishes and bowls; a stone chest for holding jewelry. We were from peasant families, you understand. Nothing we owned was meant to last for generations. So your mother was fascinated by this case, which held objects that were a marvel—older than our grand-parents, our great-great-grandparents. But the thing that fascinated her most was not any of the man-made objects. Beside the artifacts, on a pillow, rested a shriveled old lotus seed. The seed was allegedly from the Qin dynasty—over two thousand years old—and purported to be magic. We joked about planting it. Lotuses are known to sprout after many, many years of dormancy.

"During Mao's revolution, libraries became suspect. All over China Red Guards set fire to whole collections, destroying precious artifacts. Anything old, they smashed or set aflame, without reserva-tion. Your mother worried that the same would happen to our library. She wanted to take the precious items before the Red Guards—who didn't understand their value—did. I thought it was a terrible idea, but I went along with it, not wanting her to do such a risky thing alone.

"One night we hid in the library and stayed after it closed. Your mother brought a hammer. She smashed the glass case with it. She was always more fearless than I was. She had no guilt about it. She was right. Chinese museums have so few old things anymore. So much was destroyed.

"We hid the artifacts, for safekeeping. Then we heard a sound: someone entering the library. We ran.

"Outside, she looked to me, mischief on her face. She'd taken the seed. We were scientists, we didn't believe in *magic*. I was aghast that she had stolen it, but I was excited, too. We could study it. It was easy to comprehend that a tree had outlived you, several lifetimes over, but a seed? For a moment I pretended we were gods, holding a tiny planet. Then your mother closed her fist, brought it to her mouth, and swallowed."

Here Ping paused, drank his tea. "That was your mother."

We looked at each other, a long silent moment. I didn't know what to say.

"Does she like America?" he asked.

"I don't know," I said, honestly.

I'd never thought to ask her that.

"Throughout the years I searched for her name on papers. But I never saw it, and I wondered why."

Classical music played softly, I noticed. Violins. Why hadn't I heard it until now? I'd expected everything to be worse in China. I readily believed what I'd been told, that my American life was better than the lives my parents had left behind. But now I looked again at Ping's family photo. The violin, plaintive, high, reached upward. What did I imagine? That he wouldn't like music, that he wouldn't enjoy tea? Which of us was living the richer life?

"What was the magic?" I asked.

"What?"

"The seed. You said it was magic. What did you mean?"

Ping seemed amused at my question.

"The seed granted a wish. I assume your mother made one, but she never told me what it was."

Ping tore a sheet of paper from his notebook.

"You can't read Chinese?" he confirmed.

I shook my head. I couldn't read or speak it.

He began to write. He held his pen elegantly, high up, like it was a brush. He crossed out a few of the characters, rewrote them. From his desk drawer, he removed a photograph—facedown.

"This is for your mother," he said. "Will you give it to her?"

He sealed the letter. I nodded and put it into my purse. He tore another page from his notebook and wrote another few characters— this one for me. His favorite restaurant for Peking duck.

"You're very American," he said, awe in his voice, as though I were a grove of old trees—improbable. "A real American."

⌒

The contractions began while I was in our hotel room, watching, instead of the television, another pregnant woman in the window of a nearby building. Matthew was at yet another meeting—his last of the trip. The woman was younger than me, wearing lime-green plastic sandals and an apron, and holding a young child on her hip. Clothes hung from a clothesline on her small balcony, crowded with plastic children's toys.

I was relieved to find Joey at the concierge desk. He called for a taxi and spoke rapidly to the driver. In his urgency, he didn't translate. I tried my best not to reveal how much agony I was in, though I wanted to scream. The cabdriver looked constantly in the rearview mirror as he drove, anxious about what might happen in his back seat.

Alone in the hospital room, I couldn't understand the nurses, who spoke impatiently, voices muffled behind their turquoise face masks. They looked to me expectantly for my responses even as I shook my head, uncomprehending; they spoke louder, as though that would help. The pain came in horrible, tightening waves, obliterating any thought. I could only anticipate—and fear—the next harrowing surge, which was a stab and an ache and a folding in on itself, all at once. The tears I'd held back in the taxi poured out. At last, Matthew arrived, apologetic. His presence made clear the need for a translator: An English-speaking nurse was summoned to our side. He grasped my hand, promised I was doing well, swore it would all be over soon. I remembered how I'd assured him during our turbulent flight to Paris. Neither of us had any idea what we were talking about.

When it was over, the nurse placed him against my chest, deep pink, covered in muck: a too-tiny boy, complete and whole, yet lighter than a brick. We'd been considering the name Nicholas, and Matthew had proposed Nico—his mother's father's name. They let him rest against me for a moment before they whisked him away.

I must have fallen asleep. When I awoke, Matthew was there, with containers of food: Peking duck—from a different restaurant from the one Ping had recommended. I was ravenous, and it was good—the dark, sweet sauce over the hot rice, the duck with its crispy skin—but eating in the hospital felt unpleasant, like eating in a bathroom. The nurse brought the baby back; he needed to be fed. Cleaned, the baby was still pink, with light hair on his head. His eyes were blue.

"Is this the right baby?"

"This is Nico," Matthew said softly. "He's too small right now. We'll need to extend the trip so he can grow a little."

"Why are his eyes like that?"

Babies' eyes could start out blue or gray. The irises didn't yet produce melanin; that would come in later, Matthew said. He'd read this in a book. But I shook my head.

The nurses regarded me with quizzical expressions, as though they weren't sure what was wrong with me—what the panic on my face meant. To them, ours was the only white baby in the hospital of Chinese babies.

But this baby wasn't mine. They had made a mistake and they needed to correct it. They tried taking him from me and returning him. But they couldn't fool me: I could tell he was the same wrong baby. The baby who wasn't my baby was brought to my breast, and I let him eat. After a few minutes he peered up at me with his eyes, as blue as the Atlantic, as blue, it struck me, as Matthew's eyes.

In New York, pairs of shoes neatly arranged, like parked cars, awaited us at the front door: women's shoes, the smallest children's shoes. Jenny and her family had been housesitting for us while we were away the extra weeks, Nico in the NICU, but we expected her to be gone when we returned.

Jenny apologized, her face red. Her husband had disappeared, she explained. He'd gone out to drink and gamble with his friends—nothing out of the ordinary for him—but where most nights he usually came back at two or three in the morning, it had been two days, and he hadn't returned. Jenny began to cry, which was a shock, how uncontrollable it was, when I had only ever seen her composed.

"It's okay," I said, embracing her. My body ached and cramped. My irritation was another sensation layered over my physical discomforts. "It'll be okay."

I said this without context. I knew nothing about him, except what she'd told me—that he worked long hours as a cook at a Cantonese restaurant, that he was addicted to gambling. Her newest baby, four months old, was on the shag rug, like a bag of flour thrown on the ground, unsuccessfully trying to lift his head. Her toddler had crawled to an electrical outlet where a floor lamp was plugged in; she hurried to pull him away.

Somehow, despite the chaos of the children, the house itself sparkled: every surface scrubbed clean, shining like new. We had set up the crib before the trip and now we put Nico in it.

The two babies wailed. Their cries were distinct. I knew the sound of my own baby, and the sound of Jenny's.

Matthew called the police chief in Flushing, who was a friend of a friend. He consoled Jenny. It was so like him, to assure her that all would be well: They would find her husband and return him.

That evening we sat in the living room, with our babies. They looked so different. Jenny's baby was almost thin and had dark features, deep brown eyes. He peered at me, trying to comprehend my face. My baby had light hair and light eyes.

Ping's envelope was in my purse. The letter was in Chinese, I knew, but I remembered he'd included a photograph. I hesitated, then opened the envelope carefully, so I could reseal it. The photo had creases in it, as though it had been folded and refolded. On the back was written, in pencil, *1966.*

There, arrested in time, was my mother. I'd never seen her at this age. We had the same face shape, the same long fingers, the same thick brows that I had taken forever to pluck to thinness, when thin eyebrows were the fashion. Her hair was styled into two braids, each tied with a ribbon. I recognized the lake because, only months ago, I had been there, beside the same tree. A willow's branches behind her, a green curtain. Lotus leaves carpeted the surface of the water, made it look as though you could walk across it. And there, beside her, arm around her shoulders, wasn't my father, but Ping.

My mother gazed directly into the camera. It gave the impression that she was looking, across time, to me now. She wore the same slight smile she consistently performed for pictures, mouth closed, practically a grimace—while Ping regarded her admiringly. My father had been the interloper. It was jarring, his omission. Ping and my mother looked correct together: content, as though they needed nothing else.

"Will you translate this for me?"

Jenny gave the letter a cursory look, then pushed it back toward me.

"It doesn't look like it's for you."

"It's for my mother." I paused. "I'll give it to her. I just need to know what it says first."

"My English is not so good." She tried to return the folded note to me.

"It's better than my Chinese."

Reluctantly, she unfolded the letter.

"Mei Ling," she began. "I was surprised to meet your daughter, so

American. You never asked my forgiveness, but here it is. I have a wife and son. I have my work, and I am happy. Forgive me for my curiosity." Here Jenny hesitated. "I wonder where your desires have taken you. I wonder what lengths you went to to achieve what you wanted. I wonder who else you have harmed along the way."

In the little sleep I was able to get, between feedings, I had anxious dreams: I dreamed I was Jenny. I was Jenny but I was somehow me, taking the subway home, changing trains twice before taking the bus, clearing the newspapers off a crowded kitchen table, serving my family rice. Jenny going to bed, without an expensive skin-care routine. Jenny's skin was beautiful. It came naturally to her, without my hundred-dollar face creams.

Jenny's husband appeared in the morning, face unshaven, dark shadows beneath his eyes. I sat at the kitchen table, spreading butter onto toast, sharing tea with Jenny, a baby on each of our chests. He spoke to her firmly in Chinese and she stood, hurrying to put her dishes away and to gather their things. He didn't address me at all, as though he found me, my life, reprehensible. Roughly, he took the bags and their toddler, while Jenny held the baby. The door closed, leaving me alone with Nico, who began to cry.

CHAPTER 16

MY MOTHER STOOD HOLDING a small-wheeled silver suitcase that matched the silvering hair on her head. She had left my father behind in his assisted living facility, not wanting him to travel—not wanting, I knew, to travel with him.

"How was your flight?"

"Let's see him," my mother said impatiently.

"He's asleep."

Jenny greeted my mother and carried her suitcase to the guest room. My mother followed me to the nursery, where the baby was asleep, curled on his side, like a larva.

"He looks like Matthew," she said, astonished.

She reached a hand out to touch the baby's soft cheek.

She had many ideas about what a new mother needed. She didn't want me to take showers, or eat raw vegetables, or drink cold water. The vegetables had to be cooked, the water warm. My mother made food I'd never seen before: chicken with black skin, simmered with rice wine she fermented herself, and heady teas as dark as Coca-Cola. She was never sure how to translate the contents.

I fed the baby and watched TV while my mother fussed in the kitchen. I couldn't fathom the change. My whole life she'd cooked Western foods, following recipes she'd clipped from magazines for meat loaves and tuna casseroles. Now she brewed potions from desiccated things that she and Jenny bought in Chinatown. When I had lived there, I'd wandered into those shops, lined with glass jars labeled with Chinese characters and, in some cases, outrageous prices. The proprietor would begin to speak in Cantonese and I would shake my head and hurry out.

I drank or ate whatever was put before me: Some of the potions tasted woody and dark, like forests. Some were sweet soups that gelatinous things bobbed in.

My mother took on many of Jenny's chores: She cooked and cleaned. She handled Nico with ease, as though she'd tended to a baby recently. I wasn't useful, except as a food source. Neither she nor Jenny said anything about his eyes, which stayed blue, or the fact that, with each day, he looked more like Matthew and didn't resemble me at all.

They spoke to each other in Mandarin. It was a shock: I'd never heard my mother speak anything but English. When the two of them doted on Nico, it was in Mandarin. Jenny was more relaxed when speaking in Chinese. My mother was, too. I liked that Nico was hearing the language but longed to know what they said. Whenever I asked them to translate, they did so half-heartedly: Their translated English lacked the initial energy of whatever they had said to each other.

One morning I found my mother in the kitchen, speaking rapidly to Jenny, and Jenny shaking her head.

"What did you say to her?" I asked.

"I said she should bring her baby," my mother said.

Jenny's own children stayed with a neighbor while she came to work. She was still breastfeeding. She kept her milk hidden in an insulated lunch bag in the fridge.

"Don't you think? He's so young. Not much difference between one and two babies."

Jenny looked to me, needing my permission.

"Of course," I said, nodding. It made sense. Nico didn't need the attention of three women. And yet I felt a pang of selfishness—of, even, jealousy. What if my mother loved Jenny's baby more?

Afternoons, we sat together on the couch, close but not touching, the babies sleeping, watching Chinese soap operas in which the women wore elaborate headdresses and the men had luxurious, shiny hair. Jenny and my mother would translate after the drama had already taken place, tears in their eyes. She loved him, Jenny would say, as if that summed up a monologue. Or they would try to explain why a character had to drink poison, or walk into the river with stones in her pockets. Usually, it was for honor. We took turns picking up a baby if he cried.

Despite my envy of the ease my mother had with Jenny, and Jenny with her, I loved these days we had together. I felt a part of something. I liked hearing them speak, even if I couldn't understand it. The feeling was that everything was as it should be. Here and there I picked up Chinese words: *guāi*, if Nico slept and didn't scream, meant "good, well behaved."

When it was only us, we ate soups and porridges, rice with braised meats. The moment Matthew returned home they spoke English. Our dinners together were Western. Their manner changed, too, when Matthew was around. With each other they spoke loudly: Their voices periodically rose to excited shouts, and they laughed raucously. In English they were milder mannered, polite. My mother had always spoken English to me. Now I wondered if, in doing so, she had not fully been herself.

I didn't give her Ping's letter. The more time that passed, the less possible it was. What had he meant? I could have asked her directly, but I knew she wouldn't tell me. There was a pleasure in withholding this from her, knowing she would have withheld something from me.

I was sobbing when the doorbell rang. My mother and Jenny had tears in their eyes, too. In the drama we were watching, the heroine's mother was traveling miles on her bound feet to deliver a message that might clear up a miscommunication. If she didn't arrive in time, the heroine would have no choice but to poison herself with the vial of cyanide she wore around her neck. It grew increasingly likely the message would not make it to its destination. The music swelled: reedy, warbling instruments growing urgent with emotion.

"Can you get it?" I said to my mother.

I hurried to the bathroom to rinse my face. Quickly, I applied foundation, then blush. A swipe of eyeliner. I hadn't worn makeup since becoming a mother, but I couldn't risk their finding me plain.

When the Maiers had announced they wanted to come see the

baby, my mother was unable to hide her displeasure. They would stay in a nearby hotel, while my mother remained in our guest bedroom. It disappointed her, knowing our days together were numbered.

Otto and Delia stood at the door, unruffled from their flight, shopping bags draped across their arms. I embraced them. They said I looked healthy—a lie. In the bathroom, I'd seen my puffy eyes, how the skin beneath them had darkened and creased from lack of sleep. We spoke softly because the babies were sleeping.

"I hope we're not interrupting," Otto said.

My mother's eyes were red, as mine were. Jenny had moved to the kitchen, to tidy.

It wasn't fair that they were the same age as my parents. They appeared to have more life and energy to them, as though the years they had lived had fortified them, by draining my parents. It reminded me that my father was living a life that was different from ours. I'd sent him photos of Nico and promised to visit, but the fact was that my mother was here, while he was in the company of other seniors, watching animated movies.

The bags contained gifts for us all. We arranged them under the tree we had decorated—my mother, Jenny, and me. It was a Douglas fir we hung with golden tinsel and hand-blown glass ornaments, and needed a stepstool to reach the top of.

Already, I began to mourn the days together with my mother, and with Jenny. But I was pleased to see the Maiers. I liked Otto. I felt at ease with him now, as if ease were acquired, applied in coats of paint, layered over a certain number of gatherings.

"What smells amazing?" Delia asked.

I pulled cookies from the oven—chocolate chip cookies. We offered them milk and tea, and they chose milk, like Santa. It reminded me of the milk my parents dutifully offered to Santa yet couldn't drink themselves. For us, my mother brewed tea.

At the sound of Nico's whimpers through the monitor, my mother and I both stood.

"Let me," I said, though I knew she would have preferred to be the one to leave the room.

I could feel their eyes on me as I went. In the nursery, he calmed almost immediately when I held him. His eyes fluttered closed again, and I could have put him down, then, but I didn't. I pressed my ear against the door, trying to listen for conversation: to see if they were speaking to one another, in my absence. They were talking, though I couldn't make out the words. Like a child, I always wanted to know what people were saying when I wasn't in the room.

With Nico in my arms, I returned to the living room. Their conversation halted; their faces brightened immediately. They were enchanted by the sight of him. I handed Nico to Otto, and Delia stroked his cheek with the back of her hand. Otto had had five more children than my mother, it occurred to me, and knew exactly how to hold him.

Nico was so small in Otto's arms. They looked right together; they looked like family.

Otto and Delia said nothing about Nico's appearance—how light his skin and hair and eyes were, how completely unlike me, and how wholly like Matthew. Did they feel it would be rude?

"And how are you feeling?" Otto asked softly. By now Nico had fallen asleep in Otto's arms, a peaceful expression on his face.

My eyes filled with tears, surprising me. We'd spent the past two weeks together and my mother hadn't once asked me this question. She had hurried into action instead, with her herbal tonics, her directives.

Now she busied herself in the kitchen, cleaning bottles, holding them up against the light to check for scum. Her mind was elsewhere; no doubt she was wishing the Maiers would vanish, returning our time to us.

Then Jenny's baby began to cry. Confused, Otto and Delia looked to me. Nico was placid in Otto's arms. Jenny apologized, her head tilted down, ashamed. She rushed to fetch her baby from the bedroom and bounced him in her arms to quiet him. I could feel Otto and Delia exchange a glance, before they looked to us politely, wondering to themselves who this other baby was and what it was doing here.

⌒

My mother bristled whenever Otto spoke to me. I could tell she was irritated that I liked him. She never asked the types of questions he did; they exasperated her. How could you summarize motherhood? You couldn't. The answerable questions were the only ones worth asking. Was I cold? Was I hungry? What was the state of my milk?

Each day, Otto and Delia claimed the living room, while my mother occupied the kitchen.

In the evenings, on nights Matthew was home, we sat down to meals together, falsely harmonious. Jenny stayed no longer than she needed to and stopped bringing her baby. Every day, she stood silently beside my mother, preparing food, as stiff as a nutcracker. They stopped speaking Mandarin, and in English, their conversation was stilted and formal.

I was nursing Nico when I heard, faintly, an argument begin between the parents. I pressed my ear against the door. Was it about the thirty days of no cold water, about the food my mother prepared? I could only make out every few words. It was superstitious, Otto said, unscientific. How could she insist on it, as a scientist herself? But my mother stood her ground. This was how the Chinese believed a mother should recover after giving birth.

In the morning, sitting with Nico in the living room, I heard their voices come through the baby monitor. For some reason, my mother and Otto were in the nursery together. Otto's voice was soft, low, but clear. They must have forgotten the monitor was there.

"We should hire a night nurse."

"She has Jenny."

"Jenny is a housekeeper."

"Lily doesn't need someone to take care of her own baby."

"Your daughter is exhausted."

"You've already done enough, don't you think?" my mother said. "He's her baby, not yours. Even if—"

"Stop it. We can't talk about this now."

What were they saying? They spoke as though they had a familiarity with each other. They fought like a couple fought, not near strangers.

Both our families had lived in Middleport. Could they have known each other there? The foundation funded scientific research—in many fields, but genetics in particular. It was possible they had crossed paths.

If so, why hadn't they mentioned it? How lucky that we had met, I remembered Otto saying, the night of our rehearsal dinner.

"It is what it is, May," Otto said finally. Her name sounded so familiar in his mouth.

On the jet, Jenny sat stiffly, Nico in her lap. Offered an omelet or coffee or orange juice, she shook her head. I was annoyed that she wasn't more grateful. We were on our way to Tampa. I was taking Nico to visit his grandfather, aware that my mother wouldn't care to come. I needed to speak with my father.

My father's retirement home was a salmon-colored stucco building, taller than the fast-food restaurants and chain stores that surrounded it. Only a fraction of the many parking spots were filled. It saddened me—the anticipation of visitors, and the lack of them.

In the lobby was a Christmas tree, generically decorated, without character. Around me, children and grandchildren squirmed on the floral chintz couches, smashing their hands into the cushions, bored. Or they stood near their elderly loved ones, who glided at a snail's pace with their walkers, tennis balls cut to fit the feet. My father didn't belong here, I'd argued with my mother, but the truth was I hadn't seen him in so long, I didn't know if he did.

The receptionist called to me. My father was awake. She printed out visitor's badges for me and Jenny—even Nico. At the sight of us she grew interested: me, and Jenny, and our blond baby. On Nico, the badge was the size of a breastplate, labeling him "Charles Chen."

In his room, my father waited in his armchair, hair thinned but stubbornly raven colored. I resembled his daughter, even if we didn't share many physical features. I could play his child in a movie, unlike Nico, who would never be cast as mine.

His room was small, but tidy and uncluttered. His shelves lacked books. Instead there were framed photographs, including one of Matthew and me on our wedding day. Here was my father, with whom I'd always had the easier relationship.

Jenny, standing, cheerfully greeted him in Mandarin.

"We're in America," my father said coldly. "Speak English."

Jenny apologized, embarrassed. I was surprised at his rudeness; it wasn't like him. I would apologize to her later.

I passed him the baby.

"He looks like Matthew," my father said, astonished.

Nico began to fuss. My father passed him back to me, distressed by the sound. He appeared agitated by Jenny's presence.

"I'm sorry," I said to Jenny, handing Nico to her. "Could you wait outside?"

Once Jenny was gone, Nico with her, I turned to him.

"You and Mom—did you know Otto Maier? In the past?"

He didn't respond right away. I followed his gaze—to the framed photo on his shelf, of Matthew and me at our wedding.

"Otto is the same," my father said. "They're both the same."

"What do you mean, Dad?" I pressed. Was he lucid? "You knew Otto? On Long Island?"

"I'm tired," my father announced. "Where's Deirdre? Deirdre!"

Deirdre, his aide, appeared. She helped him make his way to the bed.

Suddenly he looked to me, disoriented, surprised I was there. As though we hadn't just been speaking to each other.

"You can go now," he said flatly.

The house was neater than I had ever seen it. My mother had tidied before leaving for New York. The fridge and counters were bare, the carpet recently vacuumed—still showing the Z patterns of its route.

In the backyard, the green was unruly and unmowed. I let myself out the sliding glass doors and bent down to pluck a handful of clovers. All of them had four leaves.

The interior doors had been left wide open—the master bedroom, my bedroom, the guest room—except one: my mother's office door. I twisted the knob, which was locked, as I knew it would be.

I slid a credit card into the door, the way I'd seen done in movies. It stayed closed. I tried a paper clip in the lock.

"What are you doing?" Jenny asked, startling me. She stood behind me, holding Nico.

"I forgot the key."

It was clear Jenny didn't believe me. It would be easy for her to telephone my mother, report on me.

"Nico needs his dinner," I said to her, challenging. The milk I'd pumped was in the fridge. She'd been brought along to tend to the baby, not to question me. Chastened, she left to heat the milk.

In the phone book, I found the number for a locksmith.

"I need help getting into a room," I said sweetly to him. "I locked my key in there. I'm such an idiot."

"It happens more than you'd think," the locksmith replied pleasantly. "With bathrooms, especially."

Within the hour, he was there: a young man with red hair and a battered black toolbox. He asked no questions about how the room had come to be locked or why I needed to get in. I was a harmless woman and he regarded me without any suspicion at all. The door came open easily, with a click.

I struggled not to express my surprise. Her office was as messy as the rest of the house was clean: the perimeter stacked floor to ceiling with banker's boxes, shelves overstuffed with binders and loose paper, books lined up doubly, books behind books. No photos of her family, unlike my father's room. In the wastebasket, a rotting sandwich.

Her desk was bare. She had swept off what was on it. On the floor was a twin mattress, thin and sagging from use.

Jenny returned Nico to me and retreated, aware she didn't belong here. I placed him in his bouncer, pushed a pacifier into his mouth. I shut the door.

"Middleport," it said, in her penmanship, on the side of several of the boxes. I had been born on Long Island but was too young when we moved to remember anything about it. The binders and notebooks bore a sailboat logo that seemed familiar to me. Had I seen it before? I opened folder after folder, studying their contents. I realized: It had been emblazoned on the side of the Maiers' sailboat in the Hamptons, identical script that said "The Beacon." There was an agitated, swirling feeling in my stomach. What did this mean? Had my parents worked with Otto Maier? If so, why had they kept this from us?

I remembered the difficulty I'd had conceiving. When I'd told my mother it was due to chromosomal abnormalities, she had seemed shaken but not surprised. When she had met Nico for the first time—could my memory be trusted?—there was wonder on her face. Ping's letter flickered into my mind: *I wonder who else you have harmed along the way.*

I called Matthew. He picked up right away.

"Hi," I said.

"Are you okay?"

"I'm okay."

"How's your dad?"

"Not great," I said. "He's not himself. He was really rude to Jenny."

"I'm sorry."

"It's not your fault."

I was shaking and was certain he could hear it through the phone.

"Is something wrong?" he asked.

"Listen," I began, "I need to tell you something—"

The wall clock stopped then. It was midnight. Time dilated and my body numbed. In the past, when these pauses had happened, they were out of my control. I was unable to pull myself out of the protracted moments—like being too little, too weak, to lift myself out of a swimming pool. I would think and think and time wouldn't pass.

But this occasion was different. Time's passage was in my control. I could keep the second hand where I wanted. With time extended, I could turn over every possibility. I could determine the right thing to do. All the time in the world—it had the ring of luxury. But considering every option, feeling the past and imagining the future at the same time—it was a burden. It overwhelmed me. What would I do? How could I leave? But how could I stay?

We couldn't raise our son with these people. They couldn't be trusted. But what was so evident to me, Matthew might see differently. Could he leave his comfortable life behind? I'd been without money and could do it again. All I wanted was our family, together and unharmed. He had changed his name to distance himself from his family. But he had never completely removed himself from the comfort and entitlements of being a Maier. For as similar as I'd often felt we were, we saw the world differently. He would see this differently.

I let time begin again.

"What is it?" Matthew asked.

Nico gurgled, the pacifier released to the floor. Now he squirmed and scrunched his face—about to cry.

"Never mind," I said. "I need to feed Nico. I'll see you soon. Everything's fine."

What could I remember? I thought for an eternity until a memory came. I must have been three years old, in a white-walled room with bright lights, like a doctor's office. "Hold still," my mother said. My mother was telling me it wouldn't hurt if I just held still. I didn't know what they were doing to me, but I remembered Otto—I remembered him now—wearing the same silver glasses, watching. He didn't scare me but my mother did. I was afraid of her.

PART TWO

Nick

CHAPTER 1

2021

EVEN THOUGH HE DIDN'T have a license, technically, and I didn't have a permit, Timothy was teaching me to drive in his dad's pickup truck, in the parking lot of what used to be the Kmart.

Behind us, the pickup bed was covered with a tattered blue tarp. Whatever was underneath made a terrible noise whenever the truck lurched. It was nothing fragile, Timothy assured me: wood, tools, bags of concrete. His father was a sculptor whose pieces looked, to me, like stacked trash. But every noise filled me with dread.

"Try it again," Timothy said. "Think *elegance*. Like, fucking . . . *ballet*."

He shifted us into first. I inched my left foot off the clutch, moved my right foot off the brake and onto the gas pedal. But already I could tell the effort was doomed.

There was the familiar, terrible convulsing of the machine's mysterious innards grinding to a halt—stalling for what must have been the hundredth time. Timothy ran his hands through his hair. He was losing his patience and trying not to show it.

"You're too nervous. Nothing that bad will happen."

"Shouldn't I learn on an automatic transmission first?"

"Beggars can't be choosers, can they?"

The beggar was me, and no, I could not. The matter of my driving was an ongoing debate between my mother and me. But "debate" suggested I had a say in the matter, when I did not. I'd been forbidden from getting my license. The topic wasn't up for discussion. My mother thought sixteen was too young. Eighteen would be a far more reasonable age, she said. I found this unreasonably cruel.

"I think you're releasing the clutch too fast."

"Fuck you."

"Well, try it again. Don't be nervous."

What a thing to say. How convenient it would be, if I could turn nervousness off, like a switch. I loosened my grip on the steering wheel and did what Timothy said—released the clutch slowly, eased onto the gas—listening for the moment when the engine caught, and this time the truck sputtered to life: I was driving.

"Now depress the clutch and shift into second."

"Depress?"

"It just means *press*, you idiot."

We were flying now. Unfortunately, we were also quickly running out of parking lot and headed toward the darkened Kmart, empty of everything except for the shelves, like it had been raided in a movie about the apocalypse.

"Brake! Brake!"

I accelerated by mistake, taking us over a cement wheelstop. A log fell out the back. We hit a concrete planter of ragged Queen Anne's lace. The flowers shook at the impact, white blossoms shuddering onto the hood.

Later, Timothy called. His father, seeing the dented bumper, had only laughed. I felt a twinge of envy. "My dad," Timothy could say so casually, without any fanfare at all.

Driving was part of the plan, because escape was part of the plan. Our lives would be unrecognizable in a few years, Timothy and I were sure of it. College was our ticket out. We pictured it as nothing short of paradise. In college we'd live our lives the way we wanted to live them.

Our island was so knowable: thirty-seven square miles of Douglas fir and ponderosa pine and Sitka spruce, with their mossy arms raised exuberantly and madly upward, like conductors before orchestras. The smell of molding trees, the misty rain, the dampness that I felt inside, which required a well-made fire in the woodstove to crackle dry. And then the perfect days, when the sun sliced through, when a whale breached off the shore. It was a beautiful place to grow up, but I didn't know it then, having had nothing else to compare it to. We were stranded here, kids without agency. And last year, as sophomores, we'd been doubly trapped because of the pandemic. It was hard to love a place you didn't choose.

At Timothy's, after school, I was Genghis Khan and he was Napoleon. He was dominating, which was how it always went. It was his PS4, and he'd had more practice conquering landmasses.

"You know it's pronounced *Jing-gis*," Timothy said, not taking his eyes off the screen. "In Mongolian."

He was two months older than I was—sixteen where I was fifteen. He liked to act as though in those extra months he'd experienced far more life, and was qualified to bestow an elder's wisdom upon me. If it came up in school, in history, Timothy would say *Jing-gis* when not even Mr. Cooke would, and everyone would snicker. It was like how he insisted on pronouncing *gyro* correctly when no one else did, not even the island's gyro shop owner, who was not Greek. It made him sound like the asshole he occasionally was.

Timothy's living room was sunny and warm, unlike ours. I preferred being at the Beckers' to freezing at home. In addition to the PlayStation, they had a big TV and a coffee table cluttered with magazines—what a normal kid's house was, at least I imagined. At home we didn't have a TV or Wi-Fi. Unlike every other junior I knew, I didn't have a cell phone.

"Your generation is addicted to those things," my mother had said when I'd last brought it up. "You'll have plenty of time to be addicted when you're older."

"I'm going to be absurdly behind, technologically speaking," I protested unhappily. "I'm going to be thirty and falling for online scams. It'll be so embarrassing. And then you'll feel sorry you were ever like this."

She wouldn't budge. The desktop computer my mother had reluctantly purchased for remote learning sat unused now in the living room. She had canceled our Internet service when we returned to in-person classes.

When I was at Timothy's she didn't care. People assumed he was a positive influence, but his politeness was an act he put on around parents. My mother had no idea what a devious piece of shit he could be. My personal theory was that it was because he had been born on September 11 and was never allowed to be happy on his own birthday.

Usually, only Timothy's father was home. His mother commuted to Seattle for work and his older brother was in college, at Reed. After school, we sat in front of the PlayStation with crackers and cheese.

"Is this wholesome?" Timothy's dad asked.

"It's wheat," Timothy said. "So . . . yes?"

"I meant your game."

"Sure," Timothy said. "We're learning geography."

His father shook his head. Every day, they did this dance: mild disapproval to punctuate the fundamentally laissez-faire attitude Timothy's father held. The games were allowed because our grades were good. Timothy was a positive influence on me at least in that sense. I was a straight-A student because Timothy was; I was a National Merit Scholar because Timothy was.

After Timothy won, which he did every afternoon, we put on one of his father's records to study to. It was old-man music we groaned about and would never admit to enjoying, even though secretly we did: Creedence Clearwater Revival, Bob Dylan, Smokey Robinson. Timothy and his father spoke teasingly, with affection. When I felt envy rising up, I tamped it down.

My mother never talked about my father, and Timothy liked to interrogate me about it.

"Don't you think that's weird?" Timothy asked me now.

We had our calculus homework spread out before us, and Hall and Oates sang about a rich girl.

"I wish you wouldn't do this."

"He doesn't even send you birthday cards. Isn't that what deadbeat dads do at least, like, occasionally?"

"Quit it, please."

"And why don't you look Chinese—like even a little bit? What if there was a mix-up at the IVF place?"

"You try talking to my mother."

"The fact that you don't know his name is absurd."

He reached over and drew an X over one of my solutions with his chewed-up pencil.

"That's wrong, by the way."

"Thanks."

"You could do one of those DNA tests. Where you spit in the tube?"

"Cool, yeah. I'll just reach in my wallet for two hundred dollars."

"We could get jobs."

"Sure. Okay."

"Don't you want to know if you're even Chinese? What if she's not even your mom?"

It was something I'd wondered myself. Why didn't I look Chinese? My hair was blond, and my eyes were blue, and I didn't resemble my mother at all. But genetics could be weird. A few years ago, Timothy had shown me a picture on Instagram: A Chinese woman had posted a photo of herself with her white husband and her pale baby. "I've always wanted a blue-eyed baby!" read the caption. It was depressing, like she was saying Asian babies were worse. I had seen pictures of twins who looked as though they were from different families: one with red hair and pale skin, the other with dark skin and hair. I assumed that was what had happened with me: some bizarre accident of genetics.

Timothy had no idea what it was like to be in my family. He believed a conversation with my mother could be reasonable or informational. But I knew it wouldn't go any differently from the conversations we'd had in the past. I'd been eleven when I last broached the topic of my father. She didn't let me see her cry, but later, I heard it through our thin walls, muffled and alien. My ordinarily unflappable mother, who never cried. I had no desire to ask her again.

"Ask her," Timothy said. "I'm not giving you any more driving lessons if you don't."

"You're an asshole, you know that?" I said. I knew I wouldn't hear the end of it until I agreed. "Fine, I'll ask."

Home was a six-minute walk from Timothy's, so I always left Timothy's exactly at 5:54, because six was when my mother got home from the day care. Timothy's neighborhood was regular two-story houses; from there, the houses shrank the closer I got to home. Between us was a small graveyard, marked with mossy stones. Most of its inhabitants had died young in the 1800s, which was oddly reassuring to me.

Their ghosts were babies, and babies most likely didn't know enough to be vengeful.

It was late September, and the nights were cooling, the sky darkening earlier. A neighbor's dog barked ferociously, a sleek black Doberman named Hannibal, who hated us. Timothy might have shouted, "You don't have to bark at us: We're carbon-based life-forms!" Or "You don't have to bark at us: We're Eukaryota Animalia Chordata Mammalia!" But I said nothing, walking as fast as I could past the mean dog, worrying about how I would bring up the subject of my father with my mother.

Approaching home—single story, covered in cedar shakes, weathered by the rain—I saw the windows were dark, meaning my mom wasn't back. I turned on the lights and shivered. Our house was always cooler than the outdoors, defying the purpose of a house. I started a fire in the woodstove: torn cardboard over balled newspaper, kindling, and the live oak I'd chopped two summers ago. I'd been making fires since I was nine. It blazed orange, flames licking the glass of the door like it was candy.

It had always been the two of us. Whenever we met anyone new, I received bewildered looks when I introduced her as my mother. No one questioned or looked askance at Mary Johnson, who had a Korean face and two white parents. Mary had been adopted from an orphanage in Seoul when she was three and was the only other Asian person on the island, aside from my mother and me.

I heard the jingle of keys, and my mother entered, dark hair swinging into her eyes, arms full: yellow flowers, pizza boxes, a shopping bag hanging from her wrist. I hurried to help her.

"I think it was my turn, but I wound up getting your favorite *and* my favorite," she announced. "No such thing as too much pizza. Could you put the ice cream in the freezer? And set the table?"

She cut the ends off the flowers and stood them in a vase. I set the table and filled water glasses for us. She accepted her glass and swallowed her lactose intolerance pills.

"How was school?"

"Fine."

"Timothy?"

"We're good."

"What's wrong, then? Did you not want the pepperoni?"

"No, I did. Thanks."

It was impossible to think thoughts around her. She knew me too well.

"My sullen teenage son."

We sat, selected our slices. I already knew how the conversation would go. It would be better if I got it over with. I closed my eyes and spoke.

"Can you tell me about my father? Not necessarily, like, right now, but—"

"Nick, honey, we've been through this."

"I just thought, because I'm older—"

"We left on bad terms."

"But why? Why did he leave?"

"Well, actually, we left. I left with you. He didn't want to come with us," she said at last, with finality. "I'm sorry."

I gazed at my pizza. An urge came over me to start crying. It was weird that I felt self-conscious in front of my mother. At one point in my life I had done nothing but cry. I had steeled myself for this outcome, had suspected the conversation would go this way. Yet here I was, disappointed.

"Could I at least know his name?"

I was angry but tried not to show it. It would make the evening unnecessarily difficult. My mother would encourage me to talk about my feelings, when they weren't exactly complicated: I was frustrated with her.

"Do you want ice cream?"

When I said nothing, she stood to fetch bowls.

"I'm sorry, Nick. I wanted to protect you. He didn't want you to go looking for him, and I promised you wouldn't."

"He could have changed his mind, though. Right?"

She shook her head, casting loose strands into her eyes.

"No."

The conversation was over. There was no one's face I knew better than my mother's. I could recognize expressions in it, the same way I could tell the moment when the madrone or oak caught fire by the shades of blue and orange. Her expressions were slight, but I grew up reading them like a language: the way she looked to the side when she was uncertain, or her eyes widened when I said something that interested her.

She knew my face, too, but it had changed in ways hers had not. Where the lines in her face grew more pronounced, my face changed, year after year. She was constantly having to learn a new language.

I'd always felt the responsibility of being her entire world, and when Timothy and I talked about college, when we fantasized about it, the pressure of being my mother's precious only son was what I wanted to escape, too.

I found myself growing angry with my father, this stranger. How could he have made a judgment about me before even knowing me?

She kissed the side of my head, lightly, like it was fragile, like I was a lightbulb and pressure would be dangerous.

"You look a lot like him," my mother finally said. "Like, really, a lot."

She laughed sadly and set the bowl of ice cream before me.

"Matthew. That's his name. Okay?"

CHAPTER 2

TIMOTHY'S FATHER ASKED AROUND and found us jobs with Farmer John, who lived on the inlet and grew oysters. Even before the pandemic, no one saw much of him. He was widowed and kept to himself. At the market, he always bought a bachelor's quantity of produce: a handful of string beans, a single onion. At one of the stands he was given loose cloves of garlic—not even the full head. When we were kids, he had frightened us: pale, gangly, with dark hair, like a vampire. Although I guess if he ate garlic he wasn't a vampire.

After the conversation with my mother, relayed to him in its entirety, Timothy, undeterred, doubled down. We would get jobs, which would pay us, and with that money we'd order DNA tests, with which I would seek out my estranged relatives. It still seemed like a waste of money, but it was impossible, arguing with Timothy.

John wore brown Wellingtons, a rubber apron, and a cheerful plaid shirt, which somewhat diminished the vampire vibe. He peered, amused, at us.

"You boys can be here by five A.M.?" he asked, not concealing his doubt.

We swore to him that we could.

"Do you know anything about oysters?"

"We're willing to learn, sir," Timothy offered in his suck-up voice.

John had a closetful of boots in all sizes. We found pairs that fit us and followed him to the shore. The tide was high, so we kayaked out. He pulled bags of oysters from the water and showed us how to sort them, separating them according to how fast they grew. All of them were the same species, the exact same kind of oyster, but some grew faster than others, for no discernible reason. I was a head taller than

Timothy, six feet and taller than everybody in school, and we made an odd pair. I slouched, and my mother was constantly—annoyingly—reminding me to stand up straight.

"Not bad," John said after our first morning. "You know, I could pay you in oysters. Best in Puget Sound, in my humble opinion."

"Just the money, please," Timothy said.

After work Timothy drove us the five minutes to school. He only had his permit, but the drive was down a single road and his parents didn't see the sense in waiting. Like his parents, Timothy abided by rules only when he could comprehend their purpose.

Second period was AP U.S. History, and Timothy, a day into the semester, had already lodged a complaint about the lack of coverage of the Sqababsh, who'd been the original inhabitants of the island. The point of AP history was to prepare for the national exam, Mrs. Healey explained, and it was doubtful the Sqababsh would be on the national exam. Timothy had a counterargument ready about the importance of *actual* U.S. history, and all our classmates snapped their fingers in agreement. Everyone was eager to join in a conversation about colonialism and white supremacy when not everyone had done the assigned reading. The risk of being one of Timothy's teachers was that there was always the chance Timothy might hijack a conversation, not unlike a terrorist on a plane headed for the World Trade towers.

"The colonizers had to insist so vehemently on their right to the land because the right itself was so shaky. The shakier the claim, the more aggressively they asserted it."

Mrs. Healey thanked him, relieved he was at least addressing, in some oblique way, the material at hand.

Often, I had to protect him, soften what he said, explain he hadn't meant the thing he had said in the brusque way he had said it. Classmates and teachers tensed when Timothy talked to them, bracing themselves for some contrarian comment. I could sense them relax when I cut in. Frequently I felt fed up myself. I wished we were like everyone else: that we had girlfriends and after-school activities and played pickup basketball with the other guys our age. But Timothy hated basketball, which he was bad at, and loved PlayStation, which he was amazing at. He genuinely enjoyed studying.

Why can't you just be normal? I sometimes thought. *Life would be easier if we were both normal people.* But then he did something thoughtful, or generous, in characteristic Timothy fashion, and I would feel so proud that he was my best friend and no one else's.

When we were nine, Timothy got new roller skates as a birthday present. I didn't have skates of my own. So Timothy suggested we each put one skate on. We skated around haltingly, arm in arm, a slowed-down three-legged race on wheels. It was possible back then: We were the same size until seventh grade, at which point I grew taller.

We never said *best friend.* It was embarrassing to say. We were each other's only friend, would be the more accurate way to put it.

⌒

We pooled our earnings for a DNA test. I protested: It wasn't fair that Timothy's money should go toward a test for me.

"I promise you, it'd be wasted on me," Timothy said. "I already know I'm Jewish."

"What if you're secretly Chinese? And we're brothers?"

Timothy snorted. "Just pay me back when you're rich."

Timothy gave our cash to his father in exchange for the credit card.

"You're not doing anything illegal, are you?"

"Obviously not with a credit card."

We used Timothy's mailing address, to keep it from my mother.

A month later, it arrived, the box bearing a colorful pattern—twisted ladders of DNA. Timothy cut open the shrink wrap with his house key, and out fell three plastic tubes—saliva receptacles. I spit into them, then slid the tubes into the prepaid envelope. The results would take another month.

On my way home, I stopped by the post office. It was strange to imagine a mailperson unknowingly carrying around my saliva. Instead of dropping it into the blue mailbox right away, I stood beside it, clutching the envelope. There was a trash can nearby and I had the impulse to throw the envelope away. This had been Timothy's idea, after all. I could pretend it had gotten lost. Did I actually want to know? But I felt guilty: We had spent two hundred dollars on these plastic tubes in my hands. I held my breath and dropped it in.

Timothy lasted another week at John's farm before quitting. He missed sleeping in. Without Timothy and his car, I had to take the bus from home to the farm, then to school after that. Every morning, I fell asleep in calculus, and Timothy would have to explain it to me in the afternoon.

I stayed. I liked being paid, and the physicality of the work. One of my jobs was beating the oysters with baseball bats, so their shells would chip and grow in a curved cup shape. It was what restaurants preferred, because the curved shells were easier to hold.

I even liked feeling a little bit miserable, my hands reddening and numbing. The discomfort was mine and no one else's—not my mother's, not Timothy's, either. In the mornings, John and I watched the sky shift, to pink, then blue, or more often gray, which was how it stayed most days, beyond the trees, silver as a shell. The world always seemed to be ending, not even in one specific way but all the ways: climate change, gun violence, war, coronavirus. In the quiet mornings it didn't matter: The world would go on without us. My hands remained icy through calculus.

John explained that oyster farming was actually one of the most sustainable means of seafood production. Oysters filtered the water, controlled algal blooms, sequestered carbon. That felt good, like at least my job was better than flipping burgers, which some of my classmates did. It seemed depressing, supervising pucks of beef as they went from icy and pink to brown, knowing that beef production was one of the leading causes of greenhouse gas emissions.

John's wife had died three years ago. The land he farmed had been his family's for generations. And before that, Native people had harvested oysters here. He showed me the middens they created: mounds of bleached white shells bigger than my bedroom and older than John was. An oyster formed itself from its environment: pulling calcium carbonate out of the ocean, creating its own shell.

Fridays were paydays. I paper-clipped the checks to my calculus notebook, and after three weeks, I had enough to order another DNA testing kit for Timothy. It arrived at his house one afternoon.

"This is pointless," he said, "but I'm touched."

"You're welcome," I said.

He dutifully mailed his saliva.

I'd insisted on waiting to open my email until he got his results, too. His email arrived two weeks later, with an identical subject line, unassuming and chipper: "Learn all about you!" Both our inboxes were open now, tabs side by side on his web browser. Timothy wiped the dust from his laptop with a sock.

"Ready?" Timothy asked.

"Not really," I said. I pushed the laptop toward him. "You look first."

Timothy announced the results: I was German, English, and a tiny bit Swedish. And I was 50 percent Chinese. I had cousins in China and in the northeastern part of the United States. I had "relatives" on the website, but no one closer than a third cousin. Timothy tried not to appear disappointed by the lack of interesting information.

"You could message them," Timothy said.

"The random cousins?"

"Why not?"

"What could a third or fourth cousin possibly tell me?"

A page predicted information about me: hair brown, eyes brown. The predictions were disappointing—entirely wrong. My hair was blond, and my eyes were blue. Other facts, though accurate, were trivial: I liked cilantro. I had an athletic build. My earwax was waxy. I was likely to not be lactose intolerant. What had we paid for?

Timothy was, as he'd suspected, 100 percent Ashkenazi Jew. His hazel eyes and dark curly hair were correctly indicated. We laughed, to conceal our disappointment, and agreed that this had all been a waste of money.

CHAPTER 3

AT THE CHRISTMAS TREE farm I sawed down a small, elegant spruce, with the branches spaced out on the trunk, narrowing to a single point. Every year my mother insisted I help decorate it. We hung golden tinsel and lights and ornaments, which were mostly crafts I'd made in school: serious photos of me at various ages, fabricated from Popsicle sticks and macaroni. The effect was that our tree was a bizarre shrine to me. I imagined aliens arriving and deciding I must have been an important god.

One December, a few years ago, when I was thirteen, we'd had the Beckers over for dinner. I'd built a fire, and my mother had cooked a feast: a lamb roast, lentils and soft eggs, a salad with lots of different kinds of leaves. "It's so cozy in here," Mrs. Becker had exclaimed upon entering. "These wildflowers! You need to teach me how to decorate." Then came the compliments about the food. "This dressing! I need your recipe." "You're lucky, Nick," Timothy's father said, turning to me. "You get to eat like this every day?" My mother had smiled, accepting the compliments, but I burned with embarrassment. The Beckers were just being nice about our too-small home, and she couldn't even tell. *Cozy* struck me as a bad word.

There was excitement about Christmas this year, that everyone could now celebrate with their extended family after last year's isolation, when we could not. But last year hadn't been different for us, and this year wouldn't be different. Small Christmases were the only ones I'd known.

My mom's rules about Christmas presents were: one present only, and whatever we got the other person had to be free. It couldn't have been purchased with money. In years past, she had given me: play-lists, exceptions to rules, a hand-bound book of my favorite bedtime stories. I'd picked flowers; I'd cooked her dinner. It was my mother's attempt to instill in me a sense of anti-materialism, even though it didn't do away with my desire for a PlayStation. By now, I was used to it. When I was younger, the envy was overwhelming. Sometimes I wondered: Would I be a different person if I'd had my classmates' towers of presents?

On Christmas Eve, her gift for me appeared at the base of our tree—a wallet-sized box, wrapped in paper. Definitely not a PlayStation.

Hers was a field trip, I told her. Not far. I would direct her there. Early Christmas morning, we departed. I looked at my mother's profile while she drove: Her ears were pierced, but I'd never seen her wear earrings. In the car I could smell her cherry ChapStick.

"What?" she asked, glancing at me, smiling.

"Nothing," I said. "We're here."

John, in his familiar brown boots, waved as we pulled up. The sky was my favorite color: pink silver, only at the bottom, like fabric that had been dipped in punch. He gave my mother a tour. He laid the tiniest oysters, resembling pebbles, in the palm of her hand. Even smaller ones were indistinguishable from grains of sand.

"So they feed themselves?" my mother asked.

"They pull what they need out of the water."

"And what does Nick do?"

We all laughed. John explained the sorting and beating I did. In fact, the first oysters I'd hit with bats had grown to full size and were now in a tank of circulated ocean water, awaiting their fates: to be transported to Tacoma, then Seattle, to be distributed to restaurants. John pulled one of those sacks from its tank.

Effortlessly, he demonstrated shucking, plunging the blade into the hinge and twisting. The oyster's body glistened grotesquely—a living, quivering thing.

John passed it to me. I handed the halved oyster to my mother.

"You don't want it?" she asked.

I still hadn't tried an oyster. They frightened me. John joked that I was a more trustworthy employee this way.

"Next time," I said.

She tilted her head back and swallowed.

I tried my hand at opening one; it was more difficult than John had made it seem. These were the same shells I'd beaten with a bat through the fall, chipping away at them so they'd grow smoother curves. Doing that, it was easy to imagine I was swinging away at a bag of rocks. But the act of shucking was unavoidably violent: forcefully prying apart this living creature that wanted to stay closed.

"Here, let me," my mother said. She surprised me, popping it open easily.

John walked to the water and returned with quarter-sized oysters I'd never seen before.

"Native oysters," he said. "The water used to be filled with them. Until they were overharvested."

"By people?" I asked.

"It's always people. There's a group of us trying to rehabilitate the population."

He shucked the tiny oyster, passed it to my mother.

"It's okay to eat them?" I said. "I mean, if you're restoring them?"

"It's a balance." John looked to my mother, like I was too young to understand.

The oyster was flat and small in her palm, like a stone for skipping.

"It tastes like pennies," she said, eyes closed, savoring.

At home, she made hot chocolate to warm us up, the way that I loved. I could never get the ratio of cocoa to milk right when I did it for myself.

I opened the gift she'd carefully wrapped, a small box that might hold a necklace. Inside it was a slip of paper that said *January 5, 11:00* A.M.

"It's an appointment," my mother said. "For the DMV. To get your permit."

I threw my arms around her—catching us both off guard.

"Maybe I've been a little too tough," she said. "You'll be a good driver."

"Better than Timothy."

"It's not even a contest. And, besides, I'd love a chauffeur."

She let me drive her car to St. Anthony's, where we volunteered every year, spooning Christmas lunch onto paper plates. I did the mashed potatoes with an ice cream scoop and she lifted the thick, dry turkey slices with tongs. There were always a few men who paid particular attention to my mother, who said "Ni hao" or "Konichiwa," or mentioned they had an Asian girlfriend once. I felt protective of her. I tried glaring at them, but even though I was tall for my age, I was not exactly intimidating at sixteen.

In the afternoon she made popcorn, and we smuggled it into the island's lone movie theater, which was screening its annual holiday-themed movie. Last year it was *While You Were Sleeping* and this year it was *Die Hard*.

Every Christmas I couldn't help but wonder if other families, gathered, were better at this. If other families, I mean, were better at being families.

I didn't hear the phone ring while doing the dishes. Afterward, I noticed the answering machine, blinking red.

"Hey, it's me." Right away I could hear, in Timothy's voice, some difference in it. He had something to tell me. "Merry Christmas," he added distractedly.

I hadn't seen Timothy all week, which was rare for us. I'd been working overtime, helping John with his New Year's Eve orders.

"How's it going? We watched *Die Hard*."

"People always call *Die Hard* a Christmas movie," Timothy said. "But arguably it's a Hanukkah movie. About persistence in the face of oppression."

"Yeah, okay. We saw it for the Hanukkah reason."

Timothy inhaled loudly. "Come over tomorrow? There's something you should see."

"What is it?"

"Just come over."

At Timothy's house, it was Mrs. Becker who opened the door, surprising me. She was usually at work. Even in her sweatpants and loose T-shirt she was pretty, like she belonged in a romantic comedy. Her light hair fell to her shoulders.

"You're so tall now!" she said to me. I could feel my face redden.

Behind her, beside an elaborate, sculptural silver menorah, a Christmas tree was dressed exuberantly, in blue and white lights, with gifts mounded beneath it.

In his room, Timothy was stretched out on his bed, laptop on his chest.

"Dude," he said, handing the laptop to me. The window was open to my email inbox.

"You have a new DNA relative!" the subject line said.

This new relative and I shared fifty percent of our DNA, the email said.

This new relative was my father.

It didn't say his name, only that he was forty-nine and lived in New York. I could hear my own heart pounding in my ears; my insides felt tight. I slammed Timothy's laptop shut.

"Fuck, right?" Timothy said.

I stood and began to pace, clutching the laptop, warm against my chest.

"You have to message him."

"I don't know."

"Come on, you have to. Do you want me to?"

"No way."

"Give me that." He motioned for the laptop.

"I could wait?" I continued pacing. "See if he sends me a message first?"

"But this was the whole point."

There must have been fear on my face, because Timothy's tone softened.

"It'll be okay."

I sat down beside him. I put my head in my hands. He elbowed me gently.

I surrendered. I handed the laptop to him. He typed like a lunatic, faster than anyone I'd ever seen.

"It's done," he said.

"What did you say?"

"That you're sixteen years old, and live near Seattle, and you want to talk."

"And now what?"

"Now we wait."

At home my mother was pulling clothes out of the dryer. She set my things to the side in a heap—I was responsible for those—and folded her own.

Why hadn't she ever remarried? There were seashells perched on the bookcase and I tried to remember where they'd come from. I thought of her pierced ears, the lack of earrings. All the versions of her that preceded the one I knew.

"When did you get those shells, Mom?"

"What shells?"

I gestured to the bookcase.

"It was at a beach in Oregon, I don't remember the name. You picked them out."

"I did?"

"You were small. You probably don't remember."

"I don't."

Beside the shells was a baby food jar of pressed four-leaf clovers. There were at least twenty of them, flattened like confetti. I held up the jar.

"What about these?"

"I've been collecting them," she said, "over the years. You found a few of those, too."

She stopped folding and turned to me.

"All these questions! Are you okay? Did you have too many snacks at Timothy's?"

"Just tired."

After dinner, I excused myself to call Timothy.

"Did he respond?"

"Not yet."

"This was a terrible idea."

"Dude, it's only been two hours."

I hung up. My palms were sweating and the phone was slick where my fingers had been. I wiped it off with my T-shirt.

Each day, before calculus, I asked, "Anything?" and he shook his head. I checked in the library between classes. Nothing. I shouldn't have let Timothy send the email; I was angry for letting myself be pushed around by him, as always. Whoever my father was, he wanted nothing to do with me, like my mother had said.

CHAPTER 4

DECEMBER BECAME JANUARY. Enormous Christmas trees, stripped of their glamour, lay on their sides like drunken men.

Spring was subsumed by the SATs. Timothy's colorful leaning tower of softcover prep books, with their bold capital letters on the spines, grew by the week. Timothy hid PlayStation games in his online book orders. We practiced taking tests—Timothy's idea of fun—and would grade each other's. Between tests, we played the new games. He was trying to distract me from the fact that my father had not responded to me, and I appreciated it, even though all this was his fault in the first place.

Meanwhile I pretended I couldn't have cared less. I wanted to spare Timothy's feelings, lessen his disappointment. He'd wanted so badly for me to have answers. This was what love had always been for me: denying your own reality in order to protect another person.

"Do you ever think about going to prom?" I asked.

We were in Timothy's father's pickup truck. On the way to the SATs, we'd stopped for breakfast burritos from the not-Greek gyro shop. They had been wrapped too loosely. Scrambled eggs, surfing watery salsa, escaped from the top and sides.

Junior prom was in early May. But kids had already begun to ask one another in absurd, theatrical ways: bunches of balloons, grand declarations in front of entire classrooms.

"It's like you don't even know me," Timothy said, indignant.

The two of us lived on a different planet. What would it be like to have a group of friends? To have a party-sized number of people available to hang out with you on a moment's notice? To get drunk at parties? That was always how it was in the movies. I'd only ever had Timothy.

He'd used the entirety of our napkin supply, leaving me with nothing to wipe my hands with.

"What you should be doing," I said, "is using the tortilla as an intermediary napkin. A tortilla is basically a napkin. Or just use the napkin at the end."

He rooted around in the glove compartment and found me a packet of tissues.

"You aren't even curious?"

"Curious about prom? Not really. You are?"

"No," I said quickly. "It's just a question."

Timothy had never expressed interest in anyone at our school. It was something we didn't talk about, as though he was above it. But wasn't he at least thinking about it?

I didn't tell him about my crush on Wendy Perez. She didn't have her own laptop, either, so we were always at the library together, using the shared computers.

"How's your calculus?" she'd asked me the other day.

I fell asleep every day in class, but I said, "It's okay."

"I might need some help," she said.

For some reason I said, "Amazeballs."

"Cool," she said.

I turned my attention back to the computer and hated myself. Who said that? I had never said *amazeballs* in my life.

Life would be different if I were Wendy's boyfriend. I would get invited to parties. But then who would Timothy hang out with?

The SATs were held in a high school on the mainland with high ceilings, a stark contrast to our crumbling building, with the roof that leaked, and pots that caught the rain and made *dink dink dink* noises while we wrote our essays. The school had a woodshop, a pottery studio, a lap pool. In a place like this, I thought, you could be smarter without even trying.

The classroom smelled like graphite from sharpened pencils. Between Timothy and me we had probably taken two hundred tests, but I couldn't help being nervous. If I had any shot at going to the same school as Timothy, I would need a score that was very close to perfect.

"Just do your best," my mother had said in the morning. Even college was optional, she insisted. "You don't have to go to college just because everyone else is." Often she said this when she noticed how late I stayed up to study. What mattered was that I found what I loved to do, she said. At some point. There was no rush when it came to that, either. I appreciated what she was trying to do—other kids' parents pressured them to fulfill their own forfeited childhood dreams—at the same time it annoyed me. It *did* matter to me. I wanted to do well in the conventional ways—having no other metrics, not knowing how else to measure myself.

"Can I see your phone?" I asked Timothy while we waited for the other students to take their seats.

I opened the browser to my email. Wendy had emailed. The subject line said "Calc help :-)." And right below the email from Wendy, meaning it had come earlier this morning, was an email from the DNA testing company saying I had a new message from "Matthew."

"Time to turn off your phones," the proctor announced, glaring at me. I returned it to Timothy.

The insides of my stomach lurched, like there were sharp things in it. When I reached into my backpack for my water bottle, I saw that my mother had slipped a granola bar into it.

I tore the test from its flimsy plastic, fretting. What did the message say? I could imagine its contents: *How dare you reach out? Don't contact me again.*

The proctor paced the aisle to deter cheaters. She called "Time" exactly when I was filling in my last bubble. I looked to Timothy and knew from the big grin on his face that he had done well. I wasn't sure about myself.

"I need your phone again," I said to Timothy as soon as we were outside.

"What's going on?"

Nervously, I kept typing in the wrong username and password. It was like being in a dream, technology failing. "Login error," it kept saying, until at last I managed it. He apologized for his delay in getting back to me. My message had come as a surprise. He'd been given the test as a gift and not expected any interesting results. His name was Matthew, and he was so pleased to make my acquaintance.

Mr. Becker told us to be good. He was leaving for the lumberyard. Outside was blooming: the rhododendrons erupting into color, the bare-branched trees acquiring new green. We sat inside playing our brand-new PS5.

Since making contact, Matthew and I had sent emails back and forth: He lived in New York, he worked for his family's foundation and was in venture capital, investing in startups. I told him about high school, the SATs, Timothy. I sent him photos of myself as a child. I didn't include any with my mom. He didn't mention her. In one of his emails, Matthew asked for Timothy's address. The next day, the PS5 arrived, along with a boxful of games.

We wouldn't know our test results for two to four weeks. This was life now: waiting. Waiting for the six months between my permit and being able to take the test to get my driver's license. Waiting for test results. Waiting for next year. Next year, we'd wait for college acceptances.

The pickup pulled loudly out of the driveway. A few minutes later, we heard it return. Maybe he forgot something. But then the doorbell rang. Timothy and I looked at each other. No one ever rang the doorbell. The delivery people always left packages by the door and gave a quick knock. Nothing ever got stolen in the neighborhood. Timothy got up to see who it was.

"Hey, Nick," Timothy called to me. "There's a dude here who, uh, looks a lot like you."

He was dressed in a button-down shirt, nice slacks, gold watch. He wore a surgical mask. He gave a small wave.

"Hi," I managed.

Half his face was obscured, but it was clear he had my eyes. Or rather, my eyes were his.

"Hi," he said. He held out his hand for a handshake. "I'm Matthew."

"Nick."

Timothy reached his hand out, too.

"I hope this isn't weird," Matthew said. "I was in the neighborhood."

"It's definitely weird," Timothy said.

None of us said anything for a moment. Timothy said, "Would you like to come in, Matthew? I can offer you Dr Pepper or organic ginger soda, and our finest assortment of instant noodles."

Matthew towered over Timothy. That he was my father was so obvious. His hair was the exact color mine was, his lashes long like mine. When he stroked his jaw nervously, I saw his hands were mine, too. I had typed so many sentences to him, but in person I couldn't think of a single thing to say. My stomach hurt and my throat felt dry. I was afraid that if I spoke it would come out as a croak.

He was in town for business, he explained. He spoke quickly—flustered, too. He apologized for not messaging beforehand. It was unlike him to be spontaneous in this way, but he had been in Seattle, and he had Timothy's address because I'd given it to him, for the PlayStation. Getting to the island wasn't exactly a casual trip from Seattle, but I didn't mention it.

He couldn't stay long but wanted to say hello in person. Timothy fetched the soda, and Matthew and I stood in silence while he did. I worried that if I said something wrong he might decide he was justified in not having been in touch with me.

"Any news about the SATs?" Matthew asked when Timothy returned.

"We'll find out next month," Timothy said, handing the glass bottle to him.

Matthew took the soda with his left hand. I was left-handed, too. He removed his mask and tipped his head back to drink it. Timothy watched, stunned, marveling at the resemblance, I knew, because I was marveling, too.

I couldn't go straight home. My mother would know something was the matter. I stopped by the market for a sharp cheddar she liked—a prop, an excuse—and bought myself a Gatorade. Orange was the only acceptable flavor.

Before leaving, Matthew had given me his business card and said that he'd love to take Timothy and me out to dinner the next time he was in town.

It was past six but I didn't hurry. I sat on the curb to drink the Gatorade. I removed the card from my pants pocket. I stared into it, as if a hologram might appear from it, like Princess Leia. The business card was heavy, made of thick card stock. The text said Matthew Allen Maier of the Maier Foundation. His number and his email. We'd been messaging through the DNA testing website. I hadn't known his full name.

Mrs. Hayward, my second-grade teacher, stopped outside the store, holding two bulging bags of groceries. I startled and returned the card to my back pocket. I helped her load her groceries into the back of her Subaru, where a big white dog stared at me.

"How's your mother?" she asked.

"She's well."

"You know those aren't good for you," she said, gesturing to the empty bottle I clutched. "The artificial coloring."

"Don't tell my mom," I said, and she winked.

When she was gone I pulled the card back out of my pocket and memorized the email and number before throwing it away.

My mom was most likely at home by now. She would be in the kitchen, starting dinner. If what she said was true, and he hadn't wanted to know me, why did he seem to want to know me now?

Her hair was in a messy bun on her head, a pen above her ear, the word *flour* written on the back of her left hand. I searched her face for what was mine.

"What? Do I have something on my face?" She swiped at it, smearing white on it.

"Well, now you do. Come here." I wiped her face with my sleeve.

She grasped handfuls of greens and transferred them to a pan. Our hands were nothing alike, whereas our hands had been identical, Matthew's and mine. My mother's fingers were long and her nails were oval; ours were square.

She hummed a song to herself while she cooked, and now, when I didn't recognize it, I wanted to know where it was from. It was a kind of jealousy, or suspicion: Who were you, before me?

She'd said he hadn't wanted to see me, to know me, and yet he had shown up here. Their accounts differed. I should trust her over him: She was my mother, she was no stranger. *He* was the stranger, but our likeness made me feel as though I knew him.

She brushed the hair from my face with her "flour" hand, kissed the side of my head.

"My son," she said admiringly.

The Halloween I asked to be a peacock, she covered my face in shimmering blue-green eyeshadow and fashioned me an extravagant tail from real feathers, so a hundred eyes trailed me to trick or treat. She comforted me after a kickball smashed me in the face and humiliatingly left spots of blood on the linoleum as it bounced away. She laughed only a little before getting on her hands and knees to clean it. She was my funeral director, gathering around the toilet whenever my pet fish perished. She packed the best school lunches.

And she had her million rules. She was so strict about certain things and permissive about others, and I couldn't understand the underlying logic. Sometimes I hated being her only child, the object of all her attention. Having to eat dinner together every night. She made me feel guilty if I skipped it. She wasn't normal and so I wasn't, either. I resented that part the most.

But I knew she was trying her best, especially on her own. I couldn't have asked for a better mother, and yet I was asking for— I couldn't help wanting—a father, too.

CHAPTER 5

WHAT I TOLD MY mother was that I was spending the night at Timothy's. It wasn't not true: I *would* spend the night. What I didn't mention was that, before that, Timothy and I would meet Matthew in Seattle, at a restaurant he recommended in Ravenna. I think he invited Timothy because he could tell I would have been uncomfortable, alone with him.

It was Timothy who researched Matthew. He presented his findings to me like a school report, with sources and everything. My father was Matthew Maier, of the Maier family, meaning the multinational pharmaceutical company.

"As in disgustingly rich," Timothy had said.

Matthew himself didn't appear to be involved with the company. He was absent from the website. In the past he had worked in investment banking, and now he was in something called venture capital, which Timothy explained to me. His most recent success was investing in a startup that created rapid-result tests for viruses.

Then there was the Maier Foundation, the family's charitable nonprofit, founded by Matthew's grandfather to distribute the family's gigantic fortune. The Maiers donated to arts organizations: museums, theaters, inner-city arts camps. They founded charter schools. They offered scholarships to promising minority students in STEM and funded scientific research. Their website was mostly white space.

"So is he, like, a good guy or a bad guy?"

"Hard to say one hundred percent," Timothy said.

Among what he discovered was a *New York Times* wedding announcement for Lily Chen and Matthew Allen at the family's compound in the Hamptons. My mother looked happy, less tired than she always did now—her hair a deeper black.

And Matthew had another son. His name was Samuel, and he was two years younger than I was. From his Instagram and TikTok accounts, I saw that he looked nothing like me. He was stocky with dark hair.

Timothy let me use his phone to check Samuel's social media accounts, and I availed myself of that—more often than I would like to admit. He posted constantly. A selfie with a large, spotted fish he'd caught. A selfie at a Nets game, enormous paper Pepsi cup in hand. A selfie with friends on a yacht, the sea in the background, the phone reflected in his lenses.

I wondered what I might have been like had I grown up in New York with Matthew as my father. If I'd have a girlfriend by now. If I'd party on yachts. If I'd be less scared of certain things that reliably scared me: Wendy, for example.

I'd considered asking her to prom. We'd been studying together, meaning I tried to explain limits and infinity but wasn't sure what she got from it. But I was embarrassed for even wanting to go, because Timothy found it "offensively fatuous." I couldn't be sure how she felt about me, but I was sure she wasn't *repulsed:* She did want to study calculus with me, after all.

But then, in calc, Greg asked Wendy to be his prom date in front of the entire class. I let that be my decision for me—I wouldn't go. Sometimes it seemed like there was a script that everyone else was following that hadn't reached me and Timothy. Prom without Timothy would have been awkward anyway. I hardly knew my classmates. I was relieved but disappointed, too.

I wondered if anybody, presented with a yacht on which to party, opted not to board it and chose to stay home instead, playing video games with a friend like Timothy.

The restaurant was dark, like it wasn't even open. Matthew was seated at the table and stood when he saw us. He reached out to hug me, briefly and awkwardly. He hugged Timothy, too.

"Did you find this place okay?"

"We took a Lyft from the ferry," I said.

I hardly ever came to Seattle. I'd been here on school field trips, but my mother made it only once or twice a year, to buy Asian groceries. We rarely went to restaurants. Being waited on made her uncomfortable.

Matthew ordered for us: a salad, steak that was pink in the middle, french fries that had been fried, the menu said, in duck fat.

They were the best fries I'd ever eaten: crisp and browned on the outside, deeply salty, soft and hot on the inside.

"How many ducks do you think it took to make this many fries?" Timothy asked.

"A lot," I said. "A whole flock?"

"A raft."

"What?"

"That's a group of ducks. A raft. It's a flock of seagulls." He broke out into "I Ran" and shimmied with his shoulders.

"You're like brothers," Matthew said, amused, and it made me think of Samuel.

The fries were gone and Matthew ordered more.

"How'd you do on your SATs?" Matthew asked.

We reported our scores. Timothy had gotten a perfect 1600, like we knew he would. I got a 1500, an even split between the sections.

"You could take it again," Timothy said, disappointed for me.

"I'm good."

Matthew congratulated us and clinked his wine to our water. I felt pleased to have impressed him. I wondered how our company compared to his real son's.

"Where do you think you'll apply? For college?"

He ordered all the desserts on the menu for us to share: a berry thing, an ice cream thing. He tried each dessert in measured spoonfuls and I mimicked him. I found myself wanting to please him, make him laugh or nod in agreement.

"We don't know yet," I said quickly. I hated thinking about it: the likelihood that Timothy and I would be separated.

"Nick's mom wants him to stay in Washington," Timothy added.

"Oh?" Matthew said. "Is that what you want?"

"I haven't really thought about it," I lied.

Timothy excused himself to the restroom.

"I was thinking you could come see me again tomorrow," Matthew said at last. "Just you. If you're comfortable with that."

I would have to think of another excuse for my mother. It wouldn't be hard, but the thought filled me with some dread: the lie after lie. I couldn't say why, but lies seemed less immoral when spaced out.

"Yeah," I said. "I could do that."

"What'd I miss?" Timothy asked, taking his seat, eating the last of the melting ice cream in a single bite.

What I said was that I was going to a party. My mother was happy to hear it, because I never went to parties.

"Have fun," she said, overly eager. All of it embarrassed me: her excitement, my lie.

Matthew and I were seated side by side at the bar. Behind it, a man shucked oysters.

Without Timothy to fill the silences, it was much quieter. We were both quiet people, it turned out. Every question I thought I might ask him—mentally I'd run through the list on the way here—now seemed childish.

The restaurant was crowded, exactly the sort of place my mother would never go. Matthew read aloud from the menu, asking what I might like: razor clams, mussels, whole fish, scallops? I didn't want to say I didn't know what half of what he read was and told him to decide.

"Have you ever had an oyster?" he asked.

I shook my head.

"You can't live here and not eat oysters."

I hadn't told him about my job with John, at the oyster farm. It hadn't come up. In our messages I hadn't mentioned it, and I didn't now. I didn't know why I didn't. It would have been a topic of conversation. But I had the impulse to keep some information from him—to keep it for myself.

He ordered two dozen, and then, seeing my wary expression, added oysters Rockefeller—cooked ones—in case.

"That's a lot," I said nervously, and he chuckled.

"Don't worry. It's okay if you hate them."

They arrived on ice, on a single silver platter like a pizza tray. The server pointed out which were which. They all came from Puget Sound, inlets I recognized the names of: Totten, Eld, Little Skookum.

Matthew picked one up and tipped it into his mouth. I took a long drink of water. I didn't want to seem like a chicken in front of Matthew, but I remained terrified of them: slimy, jiggly, and so *whole*. A complete creature you slid down your throat.

"How's the driving practice going?" he asked.

"You don't have to do this," I blurted.

"What's that?" he asked.

I looked down at my hands. I was confused by my internal state: I had wanted to know him all my life, and now here he was. I could sense I was about to cry and held the tears back.

"I don't want you to feel like you have to do this," I said. "Out of, like, obligation or guilt. Or whatever."

"Nico, this isn't obligation."

"Nick."

"Nick," he corrected himself. "I'm so glad you reached out," he said. "I'd love to keep getting to know you. If that's okay."

"My mom said you wanted nothing to do with me."

"She said that?" He sounded surprised.

"Yeah."

I turned my focus to the oysters. I picked the smallest one. People were so intent on getting me to eat oysters for some reason. I had to get it over with. I doused it in Tabasco. The liquid pooled in the shell, like a red-rimmed eye. I shut my eyes and poured it down my throat, trying to chew as little as possible. I swallowed.

"I never said that. I promise."

I reminded myself that I hardly knew him. Still, I found myself trusting him over my mom. His face was so like my own that I believed, correctly or not, I knew it. In the newspaper wedding announcement she had looked so different. I tried another oyster, with lemon this time. It tasted sweet and oceany. I could see the appeal. I reached for another.

CHAPTER 6

SENIOR YEAR HAD STARTED when Matthew came to Seattle again, meeting with the CEO of a company that made lab-grown seafood. I picked him up in Timothy's father's truck. He smiled when he saw me pull up to his hotel, the Toyota wheezing behind a sleek black limo. In one hand he held a white shopping bag.

"Nice ride."

"It isn't mine."

"Sounds intense back there."

"It's art stuff, supposedly."

He held his phone in his lap so I could hear the GPS directions, the voice of an Australian woman. The parking was valet, and the boy who took our keys had to ask around for a fellow valet who could drive stick.

The hostess led us to our seats: plush velvet chairs, purple like thrones. Women sat with stools at their feet, their purses resting on them—stools specifically for purses. The menu was entirely pastas so at least the words were mostly familiar. My plate arrived—a heap of noodles and mussels. I took a bite. It was better than any pasta I'd ever had.

"It's hand rolled," Matthew said.

"What?"

"Fresh. Not from a box."

"It's insane," I said, which pleased him.

"Where are you thinking of applying?"

"I don't know yet. I was going to apply to Washington State. Maybe UBC?"

"But what do *you* want?" he asked. "Not your mom."

I'd never let myself say it out loud and was almost afraid to.

"I want to go where Timothy goes."

I couldn't remember what had led Timothy and me to become friends in the first place. Was I even capable of making another friend? I didn't think so. As exciting as it was, the prospect of college was scary, too, and I didn't want to do it alone.

"Which is?"

"He's wanted to go to Princeton since forever."

Matthew nodded. My food was gone from my plate and he was still taking bites from his own. He ate so much more slowly than I did.

After dessert, he reached into his bag, which had been sitting on the floor behind him. He held out a wrapped gift. I opened it carefully.

Inside was a box, a picture of a laptop on it. Silver, thin, fancier than Timothy's. My mouth fell open. I shook my head, pushed the box toward him.

"I can't take this."

"How are you going to write your college applications?"

"Your son should have this."

I'd never brought up his son before. But he seemed unsurprised by my question and laughed softly.

"Trust me, he's got a laptop. Several, in fact."

"It's too much."

"Really, it's nothing."

"Thank you."

I rewrapped the box as best as I could. How would I hide it? In the truck, I found a thin King County Library tote bag. The laptop was slightly visible through it.

It was nearly ten when I got home. My mother was wearing a sweater in the too-cold house, legs curled up beneath her, reading a thick paperback on the couch, colorful plastic flags sprouting from it—pages she'd noted and wanted to remember. Something was baking: The kitchen was warm and smelled like vanilla.

"Where were you off to?"

"I helped Mr. Becker pick something up," I said.

It wasn't untrue. Before meeting Matthew I had helped Mr. Becker pick up redwood from a table maker in Seattle; it was why I had his truck.

"You're such a good boy," she said, and drew me into a hug. "I raised such a good boy."

I stiffened. The laptop was in the bag, slung across my shoulder. She wrapped me in her arms and kissed me on the side of the head.

Slow down, I said to my heart. In biology we'd watched an animation of the organ: It looked tortured, writhing with every beat. It was so weird, that a heart could just go on beating—the same one—for years, until it stopped.

My mother could have reached over, glanced into the bag, but she didn't. She closed her eyes when she hugged me and didn't notice it.

"I baked cookies," she said. "Chocolate chip, with those discs you like."

"They smell good," I said. They were my favorite. She made them with big chocolate discs instead of chips. But I wished she hadn't. I wished she had somewhere else to be instead of at home, baking me cookies.

She offered me one and I forced it down, even though I was full.

Hiding the laptop from my mother was easier than I thought it would be. It stayed in my backpack, and at home, I never used it. I used the Wi-Fi at school, or at Timothy's.

Hiding the meetings with Matthew—he visited every month that fall—was as easy. My mother respected my privacy—rarely entered my room, out of caution or embarrassment. I was responsible for washing my own bedsheets since becoming a teenager. I used that trust to lie to her, constantly. It was a perfect ecosystem in which my lies could flourish—the way mushrooms popped up at the shaded bases of trees, especially after storms. I justified the lies upon lies by reasoning that she had been the one to lie to me first.

One night we sat in Matthew's hotel room—he only had an hour this visit, between meetings—and I told him that Timothy was planning to apply to Harvard, Princeton, Yale, and Columbia. I was considering applying to those places, too. But the applications were expensive, sixty to a hundred dollars each. And I hadn't told my mother I was considering them. I already knew she would balk at the cost, at the distance.

I sat on the unused extra bed, drinking my ginger ale, which came with a lemon twist, so it resembled a real cocktail. Matthew seemed distracted. His wedding ring clinked against his glass, and he drank his Manhattan faster than I'd seen him drink anything. He reached a hand into his pocket and passed it to me: a credit card.

"For the application fees," he said. "You should apply where you want to."

I ran a finger over the raised lettering. The name on it said "Nico Maier."

I should consider using his last name for the applications, he went on. Fair or not, he'd heard that qualified Asian students had a harder time of getting into these schools. With a last name like mine, my less-than-perfect grade point average and SAT score, did I really stand a chance? I lacked extracurriculars; my only foreign language was Chinese. They might think I was dull, that I lacked personality. He didn't mean that crudely; it wasn't a judgment on affirmative action. He was just repeating what he'd heard. Admissions officers tended to view Asian students as less well rounded.

When I didn't say anything, he said, "Don't decide yet. Just think about it."

The next week, at home after Timothy's, I was surprised to see a man in a branded polo shirt kneeling by an electrical outlet. He said he was installing the Internet. On the kitchen table, there was a rectangular black laptop with a bow stuck to it. It was an older PC, with shiny keys that told me it had been used before. My mother must have saved up for it for months.

"You'll need it for your college applications," she said.

She reached into her purse and took out her credit card, pressed it into my hand. For the application fees, she explained, echoing my father, not knowing it.

I hugged her tightly so she couldn't see my face. I wondered if she could feel my guilt, like a fever.

"I'm sorry. I've been too old-fashioned," she said when we pulled apart. She squeezed my hand, smiled with pride. "You're old enough now."

CHAPTER 7

MY FIRST COLLEGE ACCEPTANCE came from UW Tacoma. The campus was only an hour away, and if I went there I could even live at home. My mother proudly printed out the email and affixed it to the fridge.

I hadn't told my mom that I'd applied to the same Ivy Leagues Timothy had—fees I'd paid for with Matthew's credit card, instead of hers. I doubted I would get in, in which case I never had to tell my mother I'd applied in the first place. I was most likely going to a state school, anyway. Every day, we compared inboxes.

On the day Timothy got acceptance emails from all the Ivies— Harvard, Yale, Princeton, and Columbia—there was nothing in my inbox, no rejections or acceptances from any of those schools.

"You'll get yours soon," he said. "I know it."

I doubted it. I didn't have enough extracurriculars. What looked more likely was exactly what I'd known would happen: that we'd wind up in colleges across the country from each other. Timothy would make East Coast friends and forget all about me.

He tried not to bring up college too much, because I was waiting on word from the schools that he'd already been accepted to, but he couldn't help it, couldn't contain his excitement. I encouraged him; I didn't want him to have to lessen his joy on my behalf.

He couldn't make up his mind. He'd dreamed of Princeton, but some days he thought Harvard or Yale might be a better fit. He talked on and on, and I wanted to be happy for him but only began to feel sorry for myself.

———

The emails arrived all at once. Harvard, Princeton, Columbia, Yale. They were all acceptances. "Dear Nick Chen Maier," all the letters began.

Timothy congratulated me, thrilled, but I could tell that he was surprised. I was, too. Neither of us had expected that I would actually get in. I'd doubted I would be admitted to any of these schools, let alone all of them.

When I forwarded my mother the letters, I deleted the "Maier" from my name.

"You applied to Harvard?" my mother asked, quietly, not able to hide her disappointment.

"I only wanted to see if I could get in. You know, Timothy's always wanted to go to Princeton. I thought it wouldn't hurt to apply."

"Those schools are very expensive, Nick."

"There's financial aid," I lied. "They're offering scholarships."

"Scholarships to Harvard, Princeton, and Yale," she said, repeating my list. I didn't mention Columbia. "I *am* impressed. I wish you could have told me, though."

I apologized.

After the first lie, others had followed—necessary to support the first. I'd lost track of everything I'd said to her, but it was easy to be consistent, because all of it was in service of the thing I could never tell her. I was no longer a boy without a father.

"Don't rule out the West Coast schools so quickly, okay?" she said.

I promised her I wouldn't, even though, to be honest, I already had.

⌐

"Look at you two," my mother said.

My mother hardly ever left the island and was out of place at the airport.

It was Timothy's idea that we should go on a college tour, visiting schools before we settled on one. We'd watched campus tours on YouTube, but they weren't very illuminating. The decision was huge: It would dictate the next four years of our lives.

Between us, we had saved enough for an East Coast trip. I had money from working at John's, and Timothy's extremely frugal grandmother had recently died and left him some money. He didn't tell me exactly how much, but when I asked if it was enough to buy a car he flinched and said yes.

Timothy's parents thought it would be a good experience. My mother wasn't as crazy about the idea but allowed it. I assured her that I was considering Washington schools. I couldn't tell her the truth, not yet.

It was so dishonest, I'd complained to Timothy. She insisted that she wanted me to choose for myself. Yet it was obvious she wanted me to stay nearby. She hid this poorly.

"Parents are clueless," Timothy had said. "Not to stereotype moms, but I think moms, in particular, are terrible liars."

We'd be visiting Princeton, Columbia, Yale, Harvard, but I didn't tell my mom about Columbia, which was where Matthew had gone. I was being paranoid. But I didn't want her to know I would be in New York. We planned to see Matthew there.

"We'll be safe, I promise," I said.

"Sure you will." She smiled. Her eyes were wet. "Take care of him!" she called to Timothy, who tipped an imaginary hat.

Inside the airport, at the self-check-in kiosk, I turned around to see if my mother was still at the curb. She was. It reminded me of my driving test. "Knock 'em dead," she'd joked, and the DMV employee had raised his eyebrows. "Not literally. Don't do that." She had watched as I pulled the car from the DMV parking lot, and when I returned, she was waiting in the exact same place, as though she hadn't moved. I felt prickles of guilt all over my skin. Here, again, she sat in her car, watching, maybe believing if she looked long enough I wouldn't disappear.

In Newark, Timothy gestured to the duty-free and said, "Alcohol."

In advance of our trip, Timothy—evil genius that he was—had made us fake IDs using a color printer and laminating machine. We didn't party with our peers, but some afternoons we drank Timothy's dad's Modelos while playing video games—never enough that he would notice them missing. But we fully intended to get wasted on our college tour. It was part of figuring out the correct college culture, went Timothy's reasoning.

Our IDs were Florida driver's licenses. My license said I was Nick Maier, twenty-one years old. I gasped, seeing it. He used a photo I'd never seen before: In it, I looked serious—mature even. Our birthdays were the same except for the birth year, and our street addresses were the same, relocated to Tampa, zip code 33610, in case the bouncer tried to quiz us. Timothy had heard of fakes being lost that way before.

We strolled the aisles of perfume and located a cheap bottle of whiskey. I brought it, cradled, to the register. But the bored cashier asked for my ID in a cursory way and didn't even compare the image on the card to my real-life face. He put the bottle into a duty-free bag, passed it to me like it was a baby with a diaper that needed to be changed, and returned to his game of *Fruit Ninja*.

We stepped into the night, exhilarated. Timothy ordered an Uber. Osmaan would be driving us to Princeton in a blue Toyota Sienna.

"You do long drives often, man?" Timothy asked Osmaan.

It was such a weird thing to say. I hated when Timothy added *man* to the end of sentences. I was embarrassed for him. But Osmaan seemed not to mind the question.

"Not often, man. But it's good once in a while. The stop and go—traffic in the city—it's not so nice. Where you boys from?"

"Seattle," I responded.

I should have asked him another question after my rote reply, something to draw Osmaan into conversation. I knew what I was supposed to do at the same time I didn't know how to do it.

"Is it that obvious we're not from here?" Timothy laughed. He was more adept at dialogue. I always assumed that the other person would rather not talk.

But Osmaan returned the laugh and said he'd always wanted to go to Seattle, and maybe he would someday.

"Where are *you* from?" Timothy asked, and then they started talking about Somalia, where Osmaan was from, about which Timothy knew a surprising amount.

Osmaan's face opened up when he talked to Timothy. He smiled a big smile, he called him "man." I said nothing. I wished I had Timothy's social ease, always having a response to what people said, being able to say something that would encourage them to talk further. While it was true he frustrated our teachers, they at least treated him like an adult.

There were things about Timothy I wished would rub off on me— most of all his ease in who he was. He never seemed to experience the uncertainty I felt constantly. It was as though he'd emerged from the womb perfectly secure in who he would be and what he was capable of, like a giraffe that could stand an hour after being born.

We stepped out of the Uber, to air that was cold and sharp as ice water. Something electric sparked in my chest. Here we were, on our own, actually doing what we had dreamed of, our parents a country away. And yet I was still the kid, following Timothy around. It was Timothy who spoke to the man checking us in at the hotel front desk, amused to see two teenage boys. I registered the drop in Timothy's speaking voice, to communicate that we were grown-ups.

I ventured out to the hallway ice machine. When I returned, ice in hand, Timothy, in a white terry robe, had arranged himself across the bed, propped up on one elbow, faux seductively. We burst into laughter. I put the other robe on, over my clothes, placed a couple ice cubes into the heavy-bottomed glasses from the bathroom, and poured us drinks.

It was exhilarating to be here, making our own decisions, as though we were already beginning our new lives. It was dinnertime in Washington and my mom was home, alone. I tried not to think of it: that my freedom meant her solitude. The whiskey was harsh and chemical, noticeably bad, even to me. But because we were here, it seemed the best thing I'd ever tasted. We luxuriated on our own queen-sized hotel beds in our absurd, billowing terry robes, stretching across the divide to pass the whiskey back and forth, topping ourselves off generously, growing giddier.

"Have you told your mom about your dad?" Timothy asked.

"No fucking way."

Something had happened between them that I might never know. I couldn't understand how they had come together, in what universe, under what circumstances. They seemed as different as two people could be.

"Well, what do you think?" Timothy asked. "What do you think happened?"

"I don't know."

"Don't you *want* to know?"

Of course I did. But this was probably the main difference between Timothy and me. Where Timothy asked questions, seeking answers, I was the rule-follower who didn't probe too deeply, because I worried about what the answers might be or, more likely, that answers didn't exist at all.

"That's your dad, you know."

"What?"

"Matthew. On your fake ID." Timothy was slurring now. "It's an old passport photo I asked him for."

I pulled the card from my wallet and regarded the image on it. It was true. The person in the photo resembled me but wasn't me. His forehead was slightly larger; his eyes were a slightly lighter blue. Even I had mistaken him for myself.

I woke up with a shudder. The clock said 2:02 A.M. For a moment, I didn't know where I was or how I had gotten there. Timothy stirred.

"You okay?" he murmured.

"Yeah," I said, remembering, relieved to hear my friend's voice.

I went back to sleep and had a nightmare in which a man collapsed to the ground, hands at his heart. The phone in my pocket wouldn't let me dial 911; the numbers weren't numbers, exactly, and the call wouldn't go through. I woke up gulping for air.

I looked at the clock again, expecting it to be morning, but it still read 2:02. I got up, went to the bathroom, splashed water onto my face. I was sweating from my temples and my head was pounding. It was probably the alcohol; I wasn't used to it.

On the bedside table, the clock's second hand stayed arrested: For as long as I watched, it didn't move. I hated when this happened to me. It had happened before and my skin always felt weirdly numb, my vision slightly blurred at the sides. I couldn't say why or predict when; it seemed to happen randomly. During these episodes, I felt trapped. Finally the minute changed. I opened my laptop, the laptop my father had given me, to search for an answer.

Everything was the same as when I'd googled this before: articles that tried to explain why time felt so slow at a traffic light, while the years could seem to fly by. Posts about time passing faster as you got older, about the timelines of heartbreak and grief, about slowing the process of aging. Time could seem to pass more slowly in novel situations, I read. Maybe that was all this was. Here I was, after all, in a novel situation.

The results grew further and further away from my original question: "Will my grief ever go away?," "Animals that live forever," "ten ways to stop an anxiety spiral," "For The First Time In Forever Lyrics from Frozen." I took deep, slow breaths, the exhales longer than the inhales—tip two for stopping an anxiety spiral.

But on page eleven of the search results a post in a forum, dated 1999, caught my eye: *Does anyone ever feel like time gets stuck? I have these moments when time won't move. A minute lasts forever.*

The post went on to describe what I felt exactly: how time stayed completely still. My thoughts raced when I was trapped in a moment like this one. They accumulated like Tetris blocks, unable to be cleared. Afterward, checking the time, I would see that no time had passed at all.

There were no responses to the original post. The thread had been archived, and the username had no identifying details, besides *TimelessinNY*. The user hadn't posted anything else.

Searching the Internet, time had resumed, and flown. Now the clock said 2:59 A.M. I closed the laptop.

When I woke up it was morning: 9:39.

Timothy had flung the curtains open. He was already dressed—knit scarf, hands in his trousers, dressed the way he always did, like a nerd straight out of Harry Potter. I knew he must be hungover from all the whiskey we'd had, but he was putting on a good show of vigor. He'd made coffee in the hotel's pot and extended the paper cup of brown sludge to me.

"You sleep too much," he said, shaking his head.

A shuttle bus took us to campus. Entering through the iron gate, we were a world away from the highway where our hotel was, everything green grass and stone.

"What we should do," Timothy said, "is go to the admissions office. Sign up for a campus tour."

"Why do I need a dad when I have you?"

He swung his backpack at me. Princeton had been Timothy's dream school since he was seven, so his excitement was obvious, buzzing in the air between us. He pulled out his phone.

"This way," he said, not looking up from it, beginning to walk.

He navigated right into a student, who was staring into a phone himself. The guy's math textbook fell to the ground, along with Timothy's glasses. I bent to pick both up.

"Hey! Watch where you're going," said the guy, whose main attribute was that he was tall—as tall as I was. He wore a white backward cap that his longish blond hair came out the sides of.

"Yeah, you too," goddamn Timothy said.

I watched the blond guy bristle, like an antagonized wolf. He took a step closer.

"Hey," I said to the guy. "He didn't mean anything, man. We're in high school. We're just visiting. It was an accident."

He turned to consider me. I gave him an apologetic expression.

"Where you visiting from?" he asked.

"Seattle," I said. "We're checking out campuses. Looking for the visitor center, and got turned around." I chuckled to convey our foolishness, our harmlessness.

"It's just over there."

I thanked him. Acknowledging that he was the more senior and we were subordinates was the best way to get out of this situation, I thought.

"Sorry about that," he said to Timothy. "Wrong foot, bad day. I'm Joe." He reached his hand out for us to shake it. Timothy shook it without a word, not accepting the apology necessarily.

I spoke again, so Timothy wouldn't interject with something that ruined the progress I'd made. For once, I was the authoritative, mature one. I was saving him, instead of the other way around.

"Hey, Joe," I said. "What do you think we should do while we're here? We're trying to get a feel for things."

Joe liked being consulted.

"Check out the gym, for sure. The dam's pretty cool. . . ." He trailed off. "Actually," Joe said, looking to me. "There's a party at my eating club tonight. You should come." He appeared proud of himself for remembering this.

"Sure," I said. I gave Joe a pat on the back because he seemed to want that. And then: "Thanks, man. That's really generous of you."

"Give me your number. I'll text you the address."

"I don't have a phone, but—" I nudged Timothy to hand his over. Joe typed his number into Timothy's contacts.

"Our parties slap." Joe grinned now, playing host. "Get ready."

Once Joe was gone I touched Timothy's still-tense shoulder. "You okay?"

"That guy was such an asshole," Timothy said, scowling.

"It was an accident."

I was proud of myself for garnering us a party invitation. But Timothy's excitement dissipated with the encounter, his mood changed. The tour took us inside classrooms and dorm rooms—grand buildings so unlike anything in Washington. But I could tell Timothy's fantasy of Princeton began to dissolve—replaced by a reality that disappointed him.

CHAPTER 8

TIMOTHY LEANED AGAINST THE window, eyes closed. The bus from Princeton to Manhattan was cheaper than the train by ten dollars. I opened my laptop, pleased to see there was Wi-Fi.

The night before, after putting Timothy into bed post-party, I'd emailed Matthew. *Excited to see you!* I wrote, then deleted. I settled on: *Looking forward to seeing you tomorrow.*

We'd gotten separated at Joe's eating club. When I found him upstairs, Timothy was at one end of a Ping-Pong table, half a dozen athletes at the other. Picking a fight with the pack of them was not a good idea, but he was too drunk to understand that. What seemed clear was that he had outstayed his welcome, but in classic Timothy fashion, he had no desire to go. The more they wanted him to leave, the more belligerent he got, the more firmly he insisted on staying. The situation was like one of those Chinese finger traps you got as prizes at the arcade. Timothy had explained it to me once: Baffling as it seemed, it was a basic property of a helically wound braid that it lengthened and narrowed like that.

There was no reply from Matthew, only an email from my mother, asking about the trip. I tried not to feel disappointed—it was morning, and I'd sent the message to him so late last night. To my mother, I wrote that we were doing great, omitting the whiskey we'd drunk, the beer pong commotion. Instead I told her I thought Princeton felt like another planet. We would be going to New Haven, I wrote, and though it was technically true, we were headed there eventually, I didn't mention that, before that, we would be spending two nights in New York.

"How are you feeling?" I asked Timothy.

Eyes closed, he waved me off with a hand. With the other hand, he clutched a paper barf bag.

From my seat, I refreshed my email. It was embarrassing, to feel the hope rise up and then, immediately, evaporate. A big part of adulthood seemed to be checking email repeatedly.

Traffic stalled as we approached the city. The bus crept along one small heaving gasp at a time. Out the window, the skyline was unreal, like a movie poster—something I'd seen in so many photographs, it looked fake.

It was afternoon when we arrived in Chinatown. The sun hung severely in the sky over us, like a malicious cartoon sun. We were shoved along by people eager to be off the bus. New York made sense as scenery, a skyline outside a window. Thrust into the middle of it, the city was a shock: how dirty it was, the smells of car exhaust and boiled meat.

In our dark hotel room, the only window faced directly onto an exercise studio, people extending themselves in what looked like medieval torture devices. Dark stains on the patterned carpet resembled inkblot tests. Timothy pulled the shade down, collapsed onto his chosen bed, shut his eyes, and within seconds was snoring. Sitting in the darkness beside a sleeping Timothy, I opened my laptop again, to refresh my email. Still nothing from Matthew.

I left the second hotel key card on the pillow by Timothy's head and ventured out. On the street, Chinese women were selling foreign-looking fruits and shouting at the other Chinese women who were unwilling to pay the full listed price. I bought a couple waxy clementines, their leaves and stems still on them.

I missed my mother but couldn't call from here. She would know, somehow, in her telepathic Mom way, exactly what I was keeping from her and where I was.

Back in the hotel room, Timothy sat upright, though unmoving—wearing sunglasses, so I couldn't tell if he was awake or asleep. He'd opened a single shade so the room was no longer pitch-black, which was, at least, progress.

"Are you human again?"

He didn't respond right away. I wouldn't have been surprised to find out that Timothy was an alien, sent from another planet to push our civilization along.

"We have to go," I said.

There was still no email response from Matthew. But we had made a plan, weeks ago, to meet at the fountain in Madison Square Park, so we took a cab there. At the fountain, we waited. We stepped aside for tourists taking pictures. We searched for Matthew among the people passing through: men in suits walking briskly, joggers huffing to their own soundtracks, dogs searching for the ideal place to relieve themselves. Over and over, I circled the fountain. We'd planned to meet at five, which came and went. It was five-fifteen, five-thirty.

"He's probably stuck in an important meeting or something," Timothy said.

He sat on the sidewalk, legs extended before him. I stayed standing so Matthew would spot us easily, even though I was tired, too. The lights on the Empire State Building blinked on. Then it was six, six-fifteen—still no Matthew.

"He could be swamped with work," Timothy said, noticing my disappointment. "I'm sure there's a reason. Whatever. We'll still have fun, okay?"

In the morning, I woke to Timothy saying "Fuck" in front of the mirror, his shirt off and his pants pulled partway down. There were raised pink blotches all over his back. I looked down at my body— marked, too. My skin felt hot and tight, like it might come off as one piece, as a dry shell.

"Bedbugs," he said. "We can't stay here."

He had an aunt who lived in a rent-controlled apartment on the Upper West Side, where we could most likely spend the night. She was often out of town; her girlfriend lived in Rhode Island. I freaked out at him because he hadn't mentioned her in the first place.

"You're bringing this up *now*?" I was stunned. "*Fuck* you."

"She's kind of . . . I don't like asking her for things. Let me call her."

"Unbelievable."

He phoned her from the bathroom. I heard his voice shift into a respectful tone, unlike the way he spoke to me.

"She says she's out of town and we can just ask the doorman for her spare key."

Next door was a souvenir shop, and we bought tourist T-shirts and shorts to change into. At the corner laundromat we put our clothing into the dryers at high heat. Everyone on the Internet said we should throw our luggage away, so, reluctantly, we transferred our clean clothes into plastic garbage bags. I folded each of my shirts before putting them in the garbage bag, which Timothy made fun of me for.

Miserably itchy, we made our way north holding our bulging white bags—strange Santa Clauses in New York—emblazoned apparel. We bought plasticky subway cards at the Canal Street station. I swiped mine like I saw everyone else doing and kept getting error messages, the turnstile unmoving, Timothy on the other side, until a woman, fed up, swiped it for me. It let me through on her first try.

We got on the subway: first a dirty one, before transferring to one with slick light blue seats and working lights that told us that we were at Eighty-sixth Street. When we emerged from the underground tunnel, it was as though we had been teleported to a different world. These were the New York buildings that people inhabited in the movies: clean and multistory with uniformed doormen, awnings outside bearing names in cursive. White people entered and exited, arms looped with shopping bags.

I refreshed my email inbox. Nothing from my dad. Another email from my mom, telling me that she'd gone for a walk that morning and found a litter of new kittens at the base of our neighbor's pine tree. The neighbor was trying to persuade her to keep them. There was a photo attachment: They lay in a towel-lined milk crate, orange and black and brown, like a variety box of donuts, eyes closed, small bodies piled on top of one another, seeking warmth, or maybe not seeking anything at all, not yet.

The door opened to a living room of stuffed chairs, some torn at the arms so the cotton batting was revealed beneath, and a coffee table piled high with magazines. When I riffled through them I saw that some dated back to the 1970s—half a century. The kitchen was stacked high with take-out cups, mugs filled with ketchup packets. A cat might have lived here once—there were toys strewn about—but nothing appeared to, anymore.

I would take the stained couch and Timothy his aunt's bedroom. We didn't have to speak to understand that we were in agreement: We would spend as little time here as possible.

Timothy ordered us breakfast sandwiches from a deli downstairs. We sat to eat them on a bench in the median area dividing Broadway, cars speeding past us on both sides. Pigeons encircled us, waiting for our castoffs. Matthew was here, only across the park.

"You know," Timothy said, "it's not a secret where he lives. You've seen those pictures."

Nearby, a man was crushing aluminum cans rhythmically, one by one. I threw my wrapper, globbed with excess orange cheese, into the trash.

"I'm not showing up without an invitation."

"You're his son, though."

"Just fucking drop it," I pleaded. "Please."

He dropped it—a minor miracle.

We visited Columbia—tall columns and a million steps—but it was hard to get enthusiastic about it. The whole time, I couldn't stop thinking that Matthew was so close. Why didn't he want to see me?

"Look," Timothy said, and pointed up. A black-and-gold plaque on a building said "Maier Medical Library."

Afterward we got watery hot dogs. At the Museum of Natural History, we read informational placards about taxidermied animals. Near the polar bears, a boy clung to his father's neck, weeping. His father's neck was slick with tears. Under their fur, the signage said, polar bears have black skin. Considering the human-sized dioramas, I wondered how it would look, the diorama of my own life. Re-creations of Sitka spruce and western hemlock, needles and spruce cones scattered on the museum floor. Me with my backpack heading to school for the day, and my mother in the doorway behind me, hair long and black.

Timothy could tell my spirits were low. He didn't bring the topic of Matthew up again.

"Let's have something good for dinner," I said, holding up the credit card that Matthew had given me.

I pictured him, at a future date, looking at the statement, noticing the New York charge. Realizing how close we'd been. Then again, did he even look at statements? *Fuck it*, I thought. The anger felt like heat in my chest. *Fuck him*.

CHAPTER 9

WE WERE TIPSY ARRIVING in New Haven. In the bar car of the Metro-North, the bartender had considered our IDs with skepticism before deciding what the hell and pouring us plastic cups of rum and Coke anyway.

Timothy's GPS instructions took us past wig and cell phone shops, and long blue buses sighing passengers onto the street. I pushed my father's credit card across the front desk at the Omni. He hadn't responded to my text messages, my phone calls, my emails. He could pay for this, too.

"We have a suite available," the front desk clerk said.

"We'll take it," I said.

It was triple the size of our Chinatown motel, with two queen-sized beds and a view of the New Haven Green. Timothy fell asleep easily, as he did, but I lay in bed, staring into the orange black of my closed eyelids, thought after thought rising like zombies in a video game. Foolishly, I'd fantasized about New York: Matthew showing us around, me deciding on Columbia. How stupid of me, to have hoped for all that.

My mind refused to stop humming. I grabbed the plastic hotel key card from the nightstand and put on my fleece pullover. A walk, I hoped, might fix me.

The night manager nodded at me as I passed. He'd been streaming a TV show on his phone and turned it facedown, acting as though he had been standing watch, as if I cared. Of course he was bored.

It was two in the morning. Kids not much older than me were out, stumbling home. One group of girls wearing short, sparkling dresses and smeared eye makeup, talking and laughing loudly, walked in my direction. They giggled at the sight of me, and I felt like a child in my flannel pajama pants, printed with candy canes, purchased by my mother on sale after Christmas. As they moved past me I noticed something shiny fall and make a sound when it hit the ground. I bent down to pick it up. It was a bracelet with tiny charms on it.

"Hey!" I yelled after them. "Somebody dropped this," I said, holding it up.

One of the girls stepped forward to claim it. She looked mixed-race, Black and Asian, maybe. She was wearing purplish lipstick and dangling silver earrings. She was beautiful, and when I realized my mouth was open, in a doglike way, I closed it.

The girl took the bracelet from me, touching more of my hand than she truly needed to. Deftly, she clipped the bracelet back on, and it jangled, sliding down her wrist.

"Thanks," she said, smiling. She didn't seem drunk up close. They only seemed drunk in their pack.

They began to walk away and I hurried to say something.

"Do you go to college here?" I called.

"I do. Do you?"

"I'm visiting schools," I admitted. "I don't know where I'm going."

"Cool. Good luck."

Silently, I reprimanded myself. Why did I offer the fact of my being in high school so readily?

"What's your name?" I called out.

"I'm Miranda. Thanks again for this." She held up her wrist. Her bracelet made a lovely sound. "See you around."

In bed, I lay awake, charged with new emotion. Like that, my many thoughts of Matthew were replaced—crowded out by Miranda and the fraction of a second I felt her hand on mine. It wasn't only that she was pretty. She was someone completely new—someone I hadn't grown up with on the island, knew nothing at all about. Who was she? I had to see her again.

Both of us slept in, till noon. It was a short walk to Old Campus, where Yale's freshman dorms were. Here the paths crisscrossed neatly, creating tidy triangles of green, bronze statues punctuating them. The trees were dignified and shapely, so neat in contrast to our disheveled trees at home, dropping all their needles, their bark bursting through as though bubbling from a cauldron. At home, the Douglas firs and western hemlocks wore deep brown bark that ran up the trees in strips. Ferns burst from their bases. It was only after seeing the trees here, I realized, that I could describe what home was like.

Students tossed Frisbees and walked on ropes tethered between trees. They weren't much older than us, and yet they lived here, unsupervised.

We were startled by the sound of church bells ringing. It seemed to be coming from a spooky-looking tower, like a home for a sentient gargoyle. A familiar song began to play, rendered in bells: "Like a Virgin," taunting me.

On the other end of Old Campus, I spotted her: She was sitting at the base of a dark statue, peering down at her phone, thumbs moving quickly. Miranda. She was wearing shorts that showed off her long brown legs, a sweater. Her brow was furrowed, like she was solving a math problem.

"That's Miranda!" I said to Timothy, forgetting he hadn't met her.

"Who?"

"Hey!" I called to her. "Are you following me or something?"

I was trying to sound playful, but as it came out of my mouth it sounded accusatory. This happened when I was nervous. Timothy stared at me like I was insane, like he couldn't believe I was talking to a real human woman this way.

She looked up from her phone. Smiling to see me, she slid it into her purse. "Creepy."

She stood, brushed the grass off her knees, which had little indents in them. I needed to ask her something to keep her from leaving.

"Do you know where we could eat around here?" I blurted.

"You know," she began, "I bet I could sneak you into the dining hall."

I didn't consult with Timothy before nodding.

We followed Miranda to a dark-paneled room with high vaulted ceilings like a church. The stained glass cast gem-colored light on the diners, who seemed oblivious to the beauty of it all. The food was copious: a cereal bar; a salad bar; a table full of dessert, Jell-O and cupcakes, a carafe of sprinkles. At least twenty types of salad dressing.

"The food smells better than it actually is," she said.

"It doesn't smell good," Timothy commented dourly.

All the dining hall workers were Black, catering to the young students of all races.

"Income equality is really bad in Connecticut," Miranda said, addressing my thoughts. "The richest people make, like, fourteen times what the poorest do. It's pretty fucked up." She glanced around. "I don't know if I can get you in today. Too much surveillance at the moment."

"Can we buy you lunch?" I tried. "Somewhere else?"

Out of the corner of my eye I could tell Timothy was resisting an eye roll. I was not very smooth.

She considered this for a moment. "Well, why not? I'd love an excuse not to eat here."

I admired Miranda as she held the laminated menu; her bracelet slid down her wrist.

"I don't know why I'm even looking at this. I always get the same thing. Here. You can't go wrong with any noodle."

Miranda handed the menu to me and touched my hand in the process, though she definitely didn't have to.

She pulled her hair back. Her eyes were so dark they were almost black, like metal, like the shells of the oysters at John's farm.

"It's not, like, *real* Chinese food," she said. "Compared to Seattle."

"We're not really from Seattle," Timothy said.

"My dad's Chinese," Miranda said, "and he hated this place."

"My mom is Chinese," I said.

"For real? You look *hella* white." She asked Timothy, "He's actually Chinese?"

"He's half Chinese," Timothy said. "His mom's Chinese."

The tea arrived in brown plastic tumblers. Timothy ran his fingers over the pebbled plastic and agreed, "He looks hella white to me, too."

Timothy finished his Singapore mei fun in minutes. I tried to pull him into our conversation, but my attempts were in vain, and he never engaged. I knew Timothy so well. He was impatient, he wanted to go.

She told us about her classes. She was majoring in sociology. She was a DJ at the radio station, she wrote for the Arts and Entertainment section of *The Yale Herald*, she was a cofounder of a feminist magazine.

I was close enough to see that she had light freckles on the bridge of her nose. My insides felt cold, like yogurt.

"Could we see your dorm?" I asked.

I didn't know how or why I was being so forward. Timothy wore a look of incredulity. He'd never seen me this bold.

"Understanding a university's dorm life is crucial in making a decision, I'd say," Miranda answered, more at Timothy than at me. She could sense his impatience, too.

We followed her back to Old Campus. The bathrooms were all-gender. A student wearing only a towel and flip-flops scurried back to her dorm room. It was strange to think we would spend four years of our lives showering in shoes.

"I'm heading back to the hotel," Timothy said, barely concealing his annoyance. It was our trip, and I was clearly besotted with this interloper. "Thanks for the noodles."

We watched him trudge off. I hoped he wasn't too mad; I would make it up to him later.

"Your friend is sweet," she said.

"He's sweet but nuts."

"It's nice when boys have close friends."

I reddened.

"Don't be embarrassed, you nerd." She pushed me playfully on the shoulder. "I mean it. It's nice."

She took me past the repertory theater, to the library, to a few of the lecture halls. Above the door of one was a golden plaque that said "Maier Hall."

"Hey, do I smell like Chinese food?" she asked.

She leaned forward, motioned for me to smell her hair. I did as instructed. I had to be honest: It smelled like flowers, but also unmistakably like Chinese food.

"Damn it." She laughed.

I was stupefied to be here, smelling this beautiful person's hair in the state of Connecticut. My whole life in Washington seemed very small, already receding into the past. I could have fit my entire life, until now, into a snow globe in my hand. My disappointment in Matthew still pulled at me, insistent. But her presence required all my attention: Looking at her, I could think of nothing else.

"What do you think? Do you like it here?" Miranda's eyes sparkled.

"It's amazing," I said, honestly.

A green Bible was tented open on Timothy's chest. On TV, a corpse had been freshly dragged out of a harbor: pale, swollen, lips permanently purpled. He didn't bother to greet me.

"Don't be pissed," I said.

"I'm not."

He stared straight into the television. The response wasn't convincing.

"Well, great, then."

He changed the channel to some kind of competitive cooking show: a close-up of a chef's sweaty forehead as he intently, urgently diced, transforming a curvaceous pepper into squares. Timothy kept his eyes fixed on the television and I stayed standing by the door.

"Let me buy you a drink," I tried.

He followed me to the nautical-themed bar I'd noticed nearby, on College Street. The neckless bouncer sat at the door on a plush stool and took one look at Timothy's ID before shaking his head.

"Let's see yours," he said to me.

Dutifully, I handed it over.

"I can't take these, gentlemen."

He put the cards in his pocket.

"We need those!" Timothy protested. "They're our licenses!"

The bouncer chuckled. He took out a pair of scissors and cut each card cleanly in half before returning the pieces to us.

We trudged in silence to the hotel room. Now I had fucked up a second time. Timothy swiped sullenly at his phone instead of speaking to me. A few minutes later, he stood and put on his coat.

"I'll be back," he said.

"Where are you going?"

"Just out."

He slammed the door, leaving me alone. His revenge, I thought.

At least the minibar was on Matthew. I unscrewed the tiny cap of a bottle of Bombay Sapphire and downed it—disgusting. The cooking show Timothy had been watching ended, and another began. On it, bakers competed to make cakes that resembled other objects, like suitcases or toilet paper.

Two and a half hours later, Timothy returned. He was utterly wasted. I was wasted, too, but I could tell that somewhere, somehow, he had managed to get far more drunk than I had. He'd temporarily forgotten that he was angry with me. I was relieved, because he could really hold a grudge, and now he seemed to have forgiven me. We began to discuss our trip.

"Princeton?"

"I fucking hate Princeton," Timothy slurred.

"Columbia?" I thought of Matthew, bitterly.

"I wasn't that impressed by Columbia."

"And what about Yale?" I asked hopefully.

"Seems fine," Timothy said. "I don't know yet."

He knew how I felt about Yale. He had seen it on my face. We changed the subject. Timothy reached over my bed for the remote and switched off the TV. He propped himself up on an elbow. He smelled different to me. Where had he been? I unfolded my pajama pants, put them on.

"Have you ever wondered," Timothy asked, "if you're a little repressed?"

"Is this about the fact that I fold my clothes?" I shook my head. "It's good to fold your clothes."

"You're really attractive, you know that?"

I laughed. "Yeah, right."

"No, you are. You act like you don't know it, and maybe you don't. But it makes your life so easy and you don't even appreciate that."

Timothy was staring at me. I coughed, uncomfortable.

"Let's talk about something else, please. You're being weird."

He uncapped the Pringles tube from the minibar—an eight-dollar tube of chips Matthew would be paying for. He was so drunk. He didn't know what he was saying.

"Your parents. There's another interesting topic that you have heretofore failed to probe. What is their deal? And could you be the heir to some insane fortune?"

"Have you forgotten," I said, annoyed, "that my father doesn't fucking care about me?"

Everything I'd feared had turned out to be true: Matthew had made contact out of obligation, only after I'd initiated. When it came to actually seeing me, where he lived, that was a different story.

"Listen," Timothy said, so serious it freaked me out a little. "Your dad, he's not just, like, a regular venture capitalist. His family has had wealth in this country forever. A century." He extended the tube to me. "*Your* family."

"He's not my family." I shook my head. "My family is my mom. If he's my family, why'd he disappear? Again?"

"You're being a fucking idiot," he said. "Be hurt if you want to. Sometimes I think you like it, being sad. It gives you, like, a personality. But this is your birthright. Life isn't fair. You happened to be handed the long straw, the long end of the stick. You could be cashing in, and instead you want to languish on the island with your antisocial Chinese mom?"

I didn't say anything at first. He was being so mean.

"You act like this is up to me. That's not what I want, either," I said. I moved closer to him, to pry a mini bottle of Jack Daniel's from his hands. He'd had enough.

"What, then?"

"I want my *own* life. Not theirs, whatever their bullshit is. A life that belongs to me."

Timothy laughed, like he couldn't believe me.

"Nobody gets to have that. This is, like, the closest possible thing. A life uninhibited by any obstructions—the paths are all clear for you, Nico Maier, free of potholes or brambles. It's the luck of the draw, whose baby's mouth the silver spoon winds up in, but that's the way things are. You're the baby, if I'm not being clear."

It hit me, then. I almost laughed with how obvious it was. I had been accepted into these colleges because of my last name. The library at Columbia, the lecture hall at Yale. Were there professorships at Harvard and Princeton, named for the Maiers? I hadn't gotten in because of my good grades, because of my fascinating essay on oysters.

There had to have been large donations made. God, Timothy was right, I *was* a fucking idiot.

"Fuck you. Why do you look so sad now?"

Then he leaned over and kissed me on the mouth.

It was a shock. I had never kissed anybody before. There was no distance between us. I could make out Timothy's hard-on, pressed against me. Entwined with the surprise was horror, even though I didn't want to feel it.

Through his slightly fogged glasses, Timothy looked at me expectantly, drunkenly but lovingly, as though this had been a long time coming.

I kept my body very still.

"You didn't tell me you were—" I began to say, stopping before the word *gay*.

Timothy's expression darkened. He shifted, putting space between us.

"You never asked," he said. "You say you're my best friend, but it's like you don't even pay attention. Obviously I'm gay."

"Do your parents know?"

"They've known since I was ten."

"I—I'm sorry. I don't . . . I don't feel that way about you."

Timothy laughed—armoring himself again. "Feel what way? I don't feel any way about you, Chen."

Then he grabbed the empty ice bucket and threw up into it.

We brushed our teeth side by side, as we had every night. We turned off the lights and lay in our beds. I couldn't sleep but I kept very still. I knew he couldn't, either.

In Cambridge, we were sober and quiet with each other. We wandered around redbrick buildings that all seemed like places where you could sign the Declaration of Independence. We bought logo-less backpacks from the Harvard bookstore so we wouldn't have to travel home with our garbage bags of clothes.

Despite our spirits it was obvious, touring the campus, how much Timothy liked it here, how he even looked like he belonged. That evening, he declared he was going out.

"Can I come?" I asked.

"No," Timothy said. "I mean, it'd be weird for you, I think. I met him on Grindr."

While he was out, I roamed the square alone and found myself in church for some reason, watching evening Mass from the back pew of St. Paul's. I hadn't paid attention, Timothy had said, and he was right. Somehow I was self-absorbed without even knowing who I was, or who I should be—an exasperating combination.

In the morning, packing for our flight home, Timothy struggled to zip his pack. It bulged with its contents.

"When did you buy more clothes?"

"I didn't," he said innocently.

"Let me."

The zipper seemed stuck. He hadn't bothered to fold any of the clothing, which seemed to me, immediately and apparently, the problem.

"Nope," I said. "Just fold this shit, come on. It'll take five minutes."

I shook the clothes out and began to help him fold.

He *had* gone shopping. Somehow without my noticing, Timothy had bought a sweatshirt that said "Harvard" on it. We'd sworn not to make any decisions about schools before we discussed them. I didn't mention it, just folded it and tucked it into the backpack. Once all the clothes were folded, it zipped easily. I resisted the urge to say "I told you so."

At the front door, two kittens—one orange, one black—greeted me before my mother did. They were as small as coffee cups, mewling and wiggly, knocking blindly into my shins with their heads. From behind them, my mother emerged, and hugged me like she'd been told I would die soon. She didn't let me go until I said, "Mom." Once, I would have told her everything.

She picked up the black kitten and handed it to me. Cradling it, I could feel its bones beneath its fur. It looked up at me with watery green eyes and let out a helpless noise.

"I think they prefer being spoken to in Chinese," my mother said. "They also prefer to drink water out of wineglasses."

"Did you name them?"

"I was waiting for you."

"What were you thinking?"

"Bacon and Eggs? Bugs and Bunny? I told you I needed your help."

"What were your parents' names?"

An expression of surprise crossed her face. Immediately, she gathered herself.

"May and Charles," she said.

What she'd told me about them, I could hold in one hand: that they were scientists, they had immigrated from Hong Kong and, before that, Beijing. They'd never told her much about themselves, and so she hadn't had much to tell me. She wished she'd asked them more, before they passed.

"This one looks like May," I said, picking the orange one up.

She gazed up at me with crusted round eyes.

"Hi, Charles," my mother said to the black kitten. "You are so small," she said, in Chinese. She had sent me to Chinese school as a child and had learned along with me. But because she'd come to the language later in life, her tones would always be wrong.

The kittens tried and failed to leap onto the couch, so we lifted them up. We sat side by side, as a kitten fell asleep on each of our laps, rendering us immobile.

"So," she said. "How was it?"

There was no better listener than my mother. She could hear in between words; it was as though she could hear more frequencies, like a wolf. I told her about the bedbugs but transposed them from New York to Princeton. I'd really liked Yale, I told her. She murmured her encouragement, even though I knew it was still there, her desire that I stay closer to home.

I wanted to tell her about Timothy—unburden myself of what had happened—but for some reason, I couldn't. I couldn't form the sentences. When she ran out of questions, and me things to say, we stayed sitting, our thighs touching, as the cats slept, keeping watch—silent sentries.

An email arrived from Matthew.

Nick,

Please forgive me for my silence, and for missing you and Timothy during your New York visit. It has been a difficult time with my son Samuel. We had a scare. He nearly overdosed. His mother and I drove him to a rehab center. It was terrible of me not to get in touch, but my appointments went out the window that day. I hope you can understand.

I'm terribly sorry for not writing you sooner. It's been a difficult month, to put it mildly.

How are you doing? Will you tell me about your college tour? I realize the tuition for these East Coast schools is sizable, perhaps more than has been set aside for your education, but please don't let that be a factor in your decision. You should consider your college education paid for. Let me know what you decide. I hope you choose an East Coast school, and I get to see more of you soon. My deepest apologies, again.

All my best,
Matthew

I read the email once, then again. It was a legitimate excuse, and I was relieved he hadn't blown us off for something trivial. Yet I couldn't help but think: Samuel was Matthew's real son, and here was proof of it.

I was unknown, a private fact—and this was a good thing, I told myself. It was the best of both worlds: I was unknown, yet I was afforded privileges, the biggest one being I didn't have to worry, anymore, about how I would pay for college.

And yet, I wondered what I actually meant to him. He said he wanted to spend time with me. But did he? If I ever overdosed, if I acted up, it wouldn't be Matthew who drove me to rehab. His spending time with me was contingent on my being perfect. He didn't need another fuckup son.

He was giving me the money only out of guilt, or obligation. It was me who'd gotten in touch with him, not the other way around. He'd claimed differently, but of course you would when face-to-face with the person you had intended to abandon.

I typed my response:

Hi,

Thanks for writing. I figured something happened, it wasn't a big deal. I'm so sorry to hear about Samuel. Is he doing better now? That sounds like a really hard situation.

I don't really know how to say this, so I'm just going to type it all out really fast and hope it comes out right.

Regular people know what they want, like Timothy. They have feelings and impulses and they act on them—or so I assume. I search the Internet for "how many slices of pizza is it normal to eat."

I know I take life way too seriously—for anyone, but especially a teenager. It's embarrassing. When I met you I felt relief. Here's a person like me. Everything, going forward, would be okay. I would know how to live my entire life. That things wouldn't have to be so weird and hard for me, like they always are, because you existed: someone who had done this all before.

According to my mom it's okay to be different. It's something she's said to me all my life, that there's no such thing as normal. I want that to be true, but I don't think it is. She's someone who's different herself, no question, but her way of being different is different from mine. She doesn't understand me, not the way you do.

You know, when you took me to that restaurant, with the oysters, I didn't tell you what I learned from my job, farming oysters. That they have three-chambered hearts and colorless blood. They breathe via gills. They have two kidneys and a nervous system. It's kind of amazing, to be able to hold all that in the palm of your hand. That's what I was thinking before I ate that first one, with you.

I get that it's complicated, our situation. It's confusing. Maybe even unprecedented! You have a real family, and I just showed up. I caught you by surprise and that wasn't really fair, I'm realizing now. I just wanted to let you know how much it meant and means to me, knowing you. Obviously I love my mom, but when I met you, things finally made sense. Haha—no pressure, or whatever. I don't want you to feel any obligation to keep me in your life. I know you have your real family.

Thanks for the offer to cover college. Timothy and I decided to go to Yale. It's not something we could afford otherwise. I'd have to get a couple full-time jobs. Imagine anyone looking at my résumé. I don't know if they have oysters there.

Nick

I reread my email. It was mortifying, too nakedly emotional. He didn't want to hear so much from me, not really.

I deleted it.

I was sorry to hear about Samuel, I wrote. I hoped he was okay now. I was going to Yale, and that was where he could send the money. I said thanks. I signed my name.

It was so stupid of me, believing he wanted a relationship. When he already had a real family. I could use the tuition money, that was true. I didn't want to refuse that. But I would destroy the credit card, and that would be that. I wouldn't contact him anymore.

Timothy wanted Harvard, but I wanted Yale. Before, I might have changed my mind to agree with him, but now it was the other way around. I said that I preferred Yale, and there was no argument: He yielded. So what if I'd gotten in only because of my last name? I'd lived my whole life as a Chen, not a Maier. It seemed only fair that I take this one privilege.

Matthew emailed again: He'd loved his experience at Columbia. Was I considering it? It would be an opportunity to spend more time together. He was articulating all the things I had once longed for him to say, but now it was too late. Samuel was his real son, and I was his charity case. Columbia was the last place I'd go.

Timothy and I never talked about what happened in the hotel room in New Haven. We couldn't. The rest of senior year, our friendship proceeded as usual. I didn't stop going to his house after school, but neither did the incident make us closer, like it might with girls, or I imagined it could with girls. Then again, we were already so close.

To my mother, I kept insisting I was considering state schools until I couldn't any longer. I knew how much it would hurt her, my leaving. Without me she'd be alone. I would be abandoning her, when she would never abandon me. Yet I knew she wouldn't stop me. It was what she'd always said: My life was my own. My choices were mine to make, even when they were the wrong ones. When I was seven, she'd let me eat Lucky Charms until I was sick, vomiting a pastel rainbow, magically delicious.

I would always feel guilty toward her. Was *guilt* the right word? I just mean there could never be a righting of the scales. Why did parents perform all these un-repayable acts? Was it because they felt guilty for bringing us here in the first place? It was a chain of guilt, like daisies, unbroken.

How could I say that I was afraid of who I'd be if I stayed? If I didn't leave, I would stay trapped in a life as small and static as hers.

When my mother said that Yale would be expensive, I told her I got a full scholarship.

I'd been telling her lie after lie, and now I watched as she lied to me. She was happy for me, she said, she was proud. She was a terrible liar.

It was my idea to host a graduation party. I wanted to see how it might feel: the sort of normal high school thing Timothy and I never did. Our parents were surprised—it seemed out of character for two kids who hadn't ever been interested in group activities, not even prom—and threw themselves enthusiastically into the planning. I suggested the seafood restaurant in Seattle that Matthew had taken me to, which Timothy's mother was familiar with. She complimented my taste and insisted on footing the bill. To my mom, I acted as though it were Timothy's idea. I never stopped to consider what I had begun doing: lying casually, taking advantage of other people's desire to please. It was a power I'd never wielded and now wanted to test.

The night of the party, our families carpooled to Seattle together. Timothy's dad drove us in their minivan, a dusty, decades-old Nissan Quest. Everyone's cars were so old. How hadn't I noticed before? When we parked, it was between a shining Tesla and a BMW.

Our classmates arrived one by one in their nice clothes, looking disconcerted, childlike. The cool kids weren't cool out of their context, and I watched as Timothy enjoyed this new dynamic. They were deferential to him, to us, the party throwers. We would be going to Yale while most of our peers would remain here, starting community college.

I could feel the moment Wendy appeared. She wore a dress with cherries on it, lip gloss that made her mouth look plastic. After prom, Wendy and Greg had started dating, and she traded my calculus tutoring for his. "This is so fancy," she said, wide eyed, and I shrugged, like it was nothing. I had her attention, and I enjoyed that. Across the room, Greg noticed us, and began to approach, wanting to claim or protect her; I enjoyed that, too.

My mother held a glass of champagne. She seldom drank. She laughed generously at jokes—jokes that weren't even funny. She touched the tops of people's arms as they talked. On occasion I caught her staring at me, with love in her expression that was a little too much to bear.

She was staring, again, when I tilted my head to eat an oyster. When I looked back at her, her face had lost its color. Her expression said she didn't know me at all, yet recognized me completely.

CHAPTER 10

WE DECIDED THAT SHE wouldn't come with me to Connecticut. I assured her I'd be okay, that I would call her with my new phone as soon as I got there. The decision was made early, and then, as the day of my flight approached, we couldn't remember who had suggested it originally, and regretted it.

My bed had a plastic feeling. I hadn't thought to bring bedding, though now that seemed obvious. I had not brought anything that parents were probably supposed to remind you that you needed. I felt a wave of sadness, missing my mom.

A skinny kid with tall black hair entered the room and introduced himself as my roommate, Amir. I'd taken my sweaty shirt off to switch into another, and because I was shirtless we both blushed, me more obviously than him. I rooted around my duffel bag for a plain T-shirt.

"I have spares," he said, looking to my empty closet. "Hangers," he added, in case it wasn't clear.

Amir's parents poked their heads into the room, took one look at me, and ducked out quickly, thinking I hadn't seen them. Amir and I exchanged looks.

"They're shy. They're nervous around Americans."

"I'm half Chinese."

He considered me.

"Cool."

"Where are you from, again?"

"Texas."

"You don't have an accent."

"It comes out when I'm drunk," he said, shaking his head.

In addition to hangers, Amir had brought ample supplies of all the household goods a dorm room of collegiate men would need, and insisted on sharing them with me. His electric kettle; his mini fridge; his iron; his bed raisers, square blocks you could use to raise your bed—he'd brought eight, just in case; and his hampers. Multiple hampers for whites, darks, and linens, he explained. Proudly, he unwrapped eight pint glasses etched with the Shiner Bock logo from their tissue. Eight was ambitious, I thought. I could picture Amir, at home in Texas, imagining the party he would have in college, eight fellow students each holding one of his Shiner Bock glasses filled with chilled brown beer.

When his parents returned, they shook my hand, pleasantly, though they still didn't speak.

"We're going to get an early dinner," Amir said. "Do you want to join us?"

"I'm gonna unpack," I said.

This was a lie and Amir knew it. He cast a pitiful glance at my things.

"Suit yourself. See you later, roomie!"

I looked out the window—the side of it, so they wouldn't see me. Downstairs, outside, Amir's parents transformed: They spoke loudly to him in another language. They shouted, and he shouted back. I knew that, even if we lived together for the next four years, he would never shout at me. This tone of voice was reserved for family. They disappeared from view, shouting the whole way.

We were an American family, my mother and I, and yet it wasn't American, I thought, for her to love me as much as she did. Was it Chinese? It was some synthesis of the two—elements brought together, combined to form a new compound. So often I felt it was a burden, to be loved by her. Yet, here, without her, I missed her.

The dining hall workers were on strike. They marched in navy polo shirts, chanting along with a gravelly-voiced woman with a megaphone. New students walked past them with their plastic tubs of essentials, looking apologetic and lost. Idly, I wondered where Miranda was.

The university had given us vouchers to be redeemed at local restaurants and businesses because the dining halls were closed. At the convenience store I exchanged a voucher for a bottle of juice—

350 calories per serving, the label said; it was two servings—and a tub of hummus, a watery bag of baby carrots, and a block of cheddar cheese.

With my new cell phone, I called Timothy. He'd changed his voicemail message. What used to say, "Yo, leave a message," now was his full name, enunciated and professional, asking would you please leave a message.

"Hey, it's me," I said. "I'm here. Just wondering if you are, too. Okay. Bye."

I called home, but my mother didn't pick up, either. I left a message: "I made it. I'm alive. I guess I was supposed to bring bedding?"

Where was Timothy? I imagined him settling in, his bed made by now, his personal fridge well stocked. He was probably with his parents, having dinner. Maybe his mother had even invited his roommates to tag along.

A half hour passed, and neither Timothy nor my mother called me back. Then an hour, then another. I tried to read the course catalog but couldn't focus. The room was too hot.

I made myself a loose pillow from a sweatshirt. In the morning, I would take the bus to the mall to buy sheets. It was eight-thirty, earlier in Washington—too early for bed. I was exhausted from not having slept on the plane, but it was the kind of tiredness that felt shot through with nerves.

I slid my thumb across my brand-new phone. With it, I could look up the answer to any question in the world. And yet what I did instead of filling myself with all the world's available knowledge was constantly refresh my email inbox. I scrolled social media: People posing artificially. Food. Everyone dancing, for some reason.

As a child I had learned the names of trees and birds and reptiles from paperback field guides. Now I could take a photo of anything—a beetle, a shrub—and be informed, within seconds, what it was. There was no need to wait or write down a question for later. It was a paradox: Though the results came quickly, hours passed easily this way.

When Amir returned, I pretended to be asleep. I heard him step into the room and notice me. On tiptoe, he changed and crawled into his bed. His nose whistled while he slept.

————

Timothy was letting his hair grow out and it suited him: It was wiry and wild, like Einstein's. We were in Commons, the enormous dining hall lined with stained-glass windows. I hadn't seen him since we'd arrived.

"I'm trying out vegetarianism," Timothy said when he saw me glance at his plate.

It was all vegetable sides: roasted cauliflower and potatoes, a spinach salad, a little dish of cottage cheese and mandarin orange segments. A chicken leg sat grotesquely on mine.

"One of my roommates published a research paper in *Science* as a junior in high school. He was *sixteen*."

"Damn. About what?"

"Something about fish pigment. And my other roommate, Mehmet—he tested out of Chinese. He learned it on his own, from YouTube and books. Now he's starting Japanese."

Timothy rambled on ecstatically. He was trying out for an a cappella group, and I tried to hide my hurt: I had never heard him sing.

"Are you going to take Cancer?" I asked.

"I can't. Computer science is then."

"Oh," I said, trying to conceal my disappointment. We'd planned on taking Cancer together. We wouldn't have any classes together if he didn't.

"What are you going to do?" Timothy asked.

"What do you mean?"

"Like outside of classes."

I started cutting into the chicken with my knife but stopped. The skin sagged, like loosened pants sliding to the ground. It had transformed into an unappealing thing that I didn't want to eat anymore.

"I'm not sure yet."

The truth was I couldn't begin to think of extracurriculars. Though it had only been two weeks, shopping for classes, I already felt behind, like there weren't enough hours in the day to study. The other kids, kids who'd gone to private school, seemed to already know what was being taught. I thought the point of classes was to learn, but for some of my classmates, it seemed the classroom was a place to show off what they already knew. I was envious of the ease with which Timothy fit in. I'd suspected it, but already it had become clear: I wasn't smart enough to be here. I didn't say any of this to Timothy—didn't want to bring his mood down with my own challenges.

His excitement felt like a wall between us, distorting everything he said. I struggled to listen.

I'd thought transporting me to another setting was all that was needed to render me normal. I'd failed to consider that I might be the same person here.

It was always me who emailed Timothy, to ask if he wanted to get a meal. "Of course!" he'd write, but then he would cancel when something came up: a practice, a meeting, a deadline.

Timothy joined an improv group. I attended their first show. I laughed only at Timothy's jokes because, I was proud to see, he was the best. I watched him sing a cappella. He'd made so many new friends.

Over trays of food at Commons we would try to catch up, each glossing over things that had tormented the other over the hour or day or week, falling short of being able to communicate our own realities.

When we did manage to see each other, we'd be interrupted by Timothy's new friends: the same private school kids who terrified me in my humanities classes, always beginning conversations I didn't know how to participate in. What did he see in them? I quietly seethed, but it was obvious: These were the people Timothy was always meant to be friends with. Not me, the person he'd had no choice but to be friends with when we were children.

"How do you know each other?" his friend Simon asked, once.

He posed the question with a smirk, like, how could I possibly know his brilliant friend Timothy? We were different species: Simon in his V-neck cashmere sweater, his boat shoes without socks. In my logic class, he talked constantly. "It seems to me," he always began his comments. Whenever he spoke I felt a flood of resentment.

"We went to high school together," Timothy replied, at the same time I opened my mouth to say, *He's my best friend.*

In November, while crossing the courtyard to the library, I saw Timothy walking arm in arm with a young man—older than we were, maybe a sophomore or junior. He looked as though he had grown up on the East Coast, had gone to Exeter or Andover. By now I knew these names and I knew the types. He was handsome, as tall as I was, and the same color blond as me—dulled by the winter.

I watched as Timothy's companion squeezed his arm playfully, gave him an affectionate peck on the cheek. In response, Timothy took the blond's face in his hands and kissed him passionately. They separated, clasped their hands together, and walked out of view. Neither Timothy nor his companion noticed me. I felt a pressure in my ribs, then; I couldn't comprehend the emotion. Desolation? All this time, we had been growing apart, but now it was definite: Timothy was no longer mine.

CHAPTER 11

I WAS STRUGGLING IN every class and told my mother so. We decided I wouldn't come home for Thanksgiving. This year, the holiday coincided with my birthday.

The dining halls and most restaurants were closed, so I ordered takeout from the Chinese place Miranda had taken us to. That had been less than a year ago, but I felt like a completely different person.

Campus was eerie, empty. Snow began to fall. I remembered, as a kid, seeing snow for the first time—my surprise that snowflakes actually looked as advertised. I'd expected they would be like the sun: drawn one way in childish pictures but more boring in real life. Now I held an enormous snowflake on my cold pink hand and admired the intricate points of it. It began to melt immediately. I wondered if Timothy was home in Washington, if he'd brought his boyfriend.

In my reflection, I saw that the snow had collected in my hair and stood attentive, sparkling, aging me.

After I stopped responding to Matthew's phone calls and emails, they began to dwindle. But he still wrote, on occasion. There was an email from him in my inbox now:

Dear Nick, happy birthday. Eighteen! That's a big deal. I hope you're enjoying school. New Haven isn't very far from New York. I'd love to see you. Are you angry with me? If you are, please let me apologize in person.

I deleted the email, like I'd deleted the rest of them.

I kept checking my texts to see if Timothy had written. Nothing. It was the first time he'd ever forgotten my birthday—he always made fun of me for being younger than he was, even though it was only by two months. What did it say about me, that I could only understand myself in relation to another person? Alone, I was a blank.

My mother called. "Happy birthday. How are you celebrating?"

"I got noodles," I said. "And I'm studying, I guess."

"You could buy a lottery ticket. But no cigarettes, please."

"It's okay if I get addicted to gambling?"

"I have a feeling you won't. Have you checked your PO box? I sent you cookies."

"Thanks. The post office is closed today. I'll get it on Monday."

"They'll be stale. I should have timed it better."

I looked forward to it not being my birthday. Why did it have to be such a big deal? I said goodbye to my mother and turned my attention back to my textbook but couldn't focus. In the common room I pulled a blanket over myself and streamed TV on my phone until I fell asleep. This was my eventless life, without any people in it.

In the morning, the world outside was blanketed in white.

Between Thanksgiving and Christmas I stopped being able to sleep. It seemed unbelievable, that I had ever managed it before. I would wake up thinking it must be the morning, that I'd slept all night. When I looked at the clock I would see that only a minute had passed, time trapped, the way it had been that night in Princeton.

Schoolwork was impossible. In my cancer class I learned that cancer resulted when genes that regulated cell growth and differentiation were mutated and caused a series of downstream effects in cells—chain reactions. Initial errors compounded into unmanageability. This could have described my performance in school. *Initial errors compounded into unmanageability.* It didn't matter how much I studied, how hard I worked on my papers. I was unqualified and now, on top of that, sleep deprived. I couldn't retain anything and my mind felt like Swiss cheese.

I staggered from class to class. The snow soaked through my shoes, so it felt like walking around in soggy loaves of bread. The fleece pullovers I'd worn in Washington were insufficient here.

Amir recommended a doctor who prescribed me Klonopin. Even when doubled, when tripled, it did nothing.

In the dining hall, I noticed a flyer for a sleep study at Yale New Haven Hospital. I took a picture of it. Maybe they could tell me what was wrong.

The room was sparse, like a hotel: patterned bedspread, flat-screen TV, a window overlooking the green, with people, like Sims, crossing it.

A woman attached electrodes to my body, to my legs and chest, near my heart, my head. She positioned a plastic tube near my nose.

"This is a lot."

"I know, I'm sorry." She was sympathetic. "It's to measure your movement."

She left, and the doctor entered. He looked young, and it made me distrust him. What could he know? He sat in the chair beside me.

"Can you tell me what you're feeling?"

"It's like time gets stuck," I told the doctor.

"Do you have more trouble falling asleep? Or staying asleep?"

"I don't know," I said, impatient. "It's both. It's a pause. I want the night to be over, but it won't end."

I tried to explain. Every night I stared at the clock and found it wouldn't move. When I was trapped in the moment I felt filled with a dread that I would be this way forever: I would be eighteen, twenty, thirty, forty, living useless lifetimes in the hours between sleeping and waking. He listened with a blank expression, not writing anything down.

In the morning, he returned to my bedside. The results were encouraging, he said. I was sleeping more than I'd suspected. I didn't have sleep apnea or restless leg syndrome. Everything appeared normal.

"You could probably use more sleep, but what you're getting isn't bad," the doctor said. "It's true that you're waking in the night, like you say, but it looks like, cumulatively, you're doing okay."

"Could it have to do with my circadian rhythm?" I asked. "Could I have some kind of disorder?"

"It's possible," he said, in a way that I knew meant he wasn't really considering it. "A disorder of that kind is fairly rare."

I never understood when doctors dismissed possible diagnoses because they were rare. Even if they were rare, someone had to have them, didn't they? Why couldn't it be me? The doctor's face was doughy, with bored green eyes behind round glasses. He looked at his clipboard, not at me. I had the desire to punch him.

Being a doctor immediately ennobled a person. But not all of them were noble, obviously. This one seemed like he was probably a bad father or partner. *You shouldn't be allowed to be a doctor if you aren't a good person*, I thought. For certain professions it should just be a rule.

"Have you been treated for depression?" the doctor asked, and when I didn't respond, he added, "That seems to me like it could help."

❧

The door was propped open, and kids spilled out onto the stoop to smoke, despite the unpleasantness of the weather. Another group, wearing parkas, passed a plastic bottle of Everclear.

"Hey, man," a parka'ed body called out, by way of welcome.

"Keg's in the kitchen," someone else said.

An invitation to a house party on Edgewood had trickled down to me via an older girl in my philosophy seminar. She flirted with me despite the fact that I never said anything intelligible.

The party was well under way. I had gotten into the habit of arriving to parties late. If you timed it right, when people were drunk but not too drunk, a late arrival made communication easier. Everyone would be eager to hold court, to take on the conversational burden, and all I would have to do was stand and nod. People called me quiet, inscrutable, and that was fine with me. There was no shortage of opinions here; I didn't need to have another.

I filled a cup with beer, drank it immediately, and dispensed myself more. I searched the room for the girl in my class who had invited me. She was in the corner of the kitchen, her face very near a boy's, likely uninterested in being interrupted.

Weeks ago, at a dorm-room party, I'd had my second first kiss and lost my virginity in the same night. I drank warm screwdrivers mixed by the girl whose party it was. Her name was Liz. Her suitemate cut lines of coke with her Yale ID, neat rows on the back of her iPhone. When she looked up, I saw she still wore braces. She handed me the rolled-up bill, and I took it.

Liz sat attentively beside me on the futon, webbed her hands in mine. She kissed me, her mouth tasting of vodka—or was I tasting my own mouth? It was my first kiss, aside from Timothy's. "Follow me," she said, and led me to her bedroom.

I'd stopped contacting Timothy, and he never reached out to me. How unfair it was, that I missed him. He could forget me so easily, when I couldn't remember myself without him. In all my childhood memories, he was there—impish, curious, driving me to try things I never would have without him.

"You don't have a roommate?" I asked.

"She's indisposed," Liz said, nodding in the direction of a girl, wine bottle in the crook of her arm, asleep in a beanbag chair.

Her bedroom was identical to mine, two extra-long twin beds pushed against opposite walls, but with feminine flourishes. She guided me to one of the beds—pink bedspread, ruffled pillows, a stuffed anteater. I sat politely on it.

"What do you want me to do?" I asked.

She moved my hands, positioning them inside her thighs, beneath her skirt. She pressed her own hand to my erection and, into my ear, said, wetly, "Anything you want."

In the living room: a velvet couch, butterfly chairs, a scuffed-up rug, shoes shoved in a corner—a hasty attempt at cleaning. All the regular adult things that existed in houses, but not cared for in the proper ways. These were philosophy majors: I heard someone mention Kant, a slurred argument about deontology. I doubted I would stay very long.

I returned to the kitchen for a refill.

"Nick," a familiar voice called out.

Miranda's hair was pulled back from her face. Huge golden hoops in her ears, so all of her was shining. Her eyelashes looked heavier. When she gave me a hug, her cool earring touched my cheek.

"Long time, stranger," she said.

I'd seen her at Commons on occasion, eating with her friends. She never noticed me. Rarely in groups did you notice those who were alone. It only worked the other way around.

Just then, a boy emerged behind her. A man, more like. He was tall and built. He wore skinny black jeans and a plain white shirt, fit tight, that showed you exactly the shape of his chest. His hair was buzzed short, and his skin was deep black.

"This is Isaiah. My boyfriend," Miranda said. "Isaiah, this is Nick. Nick's a first-year."

"Cool. Hey."

Isaiah shook my hand. He asked where I was from, what I was studying, how I'd found school so far. Certain people seemed like they knew exactly what paths they were meant to take, and Isaiah was one. Once in a while, people interrupted to touch him on the shoulder, to say hello. It was apparent he was the sort of person other people tried to impress, never the other way around.

"How'd you two meet?" I asked.

"Hm," Miranda started. She pressed her fingers to his upper arm, as if to say, *Tell the right story.*

"She stalked me," he said, leaning in conspiratorially.

"Like followed you around?"

I looked at her. She reached out to squeeze his neck and didn't return my gaze.

"Something like that." Isaiah laughed in this easy, disarming way. I could see why she liked him—why anyone could. "Showed up to all my games for some reason."

I was used to being the tallest in a room, but Isaiah was taller than I was. Beside him, I must have looked sallow, exhausted. All night I'd found it difficult to follow the threads of conversations, and I was finding it hard to follow now.

Miranda watched me with a concerned expression. From the purple bags beneath my eyes it must have been obvious how poorly I'd been sleeping. I asked what they were doing for winter break, and Isaiah said they planned to see Miranda's family in Oakland.

"We should probably go," Miranda said to Isaiah, then to me, "Tests tomorrow. Responsible thing to do, and all that."

He nodded obediently.

"Good to meet you, man," he said, shaking my hand, as though I needed the assurance. He was right, I did.

Miranda gave me a hug and a kiss on the cheek. Her hair smelled like strawberry shampoo. I almost sneezed; it tickled.

"Take care, Nick," she said.

CHAPTER 12

"YOU LOOK SO TIRED" was the first thing my mother said, concern in her voice. She stood in the doorway of my dorm, wearing a knitted hat and scarf of matching, multicolored yarn. Winter break had begun, and my roommates were home with their families.

When I told her about my insomnia, she insisted I shouldn't travel. She said she'd come to New Haven. She would rent an apartment near campus so we could spend Christmas together.

She held a thick winter coat in her arms, a shopping bag revealed to contain a hat, gloves, and a down comforter. There were things my mother knew without my telling her.

Using our hot plate, she made Chinese soups with roots and berries, concoctions that had specific medicinal purposes, and tasted of ginger and earth.

She asked me, gently, what was going on. I confessed I was lonely, that Timothy had new friends. It had been a mistake that I'd been accepted, because I wasn't smart enough to be here. On top of that my mind was playing tricks on me: There were moments that time felt stopped.

"What does it feel like?" she asked gently, interested.

I couldn't stay asleep, I told her. I would wake up trapped in a moment. It was as though time had dimensions, width and length, and where most people perceived time's length, I could feel the width of it. The doctor had said it was depression.

"I'm sorry I ruined Christmas," I said.

"You're my Christmas, okay?" She frowned. "You being okay— that's all I want. Tell me more about how it feels."

It was as though a minute stalled; time wouldn't budge. A feeling of drowning, in a pool, unable to save myself. My mother listened.

Finally she said, "I have it. I have what you have. I know exactly what you mean."

She described the watery edges of vision, the feeling in her skin. No one else ever understood what she meant when she tried to describe it. But she'd learned to live with it. There was a way of resting into it—a relaxing. I could prolong an hour to linger in it, only for myself, in my own mind. She explained how I could release the moment, too.

"But why? Why are we like this?"

"I don't know," she said.

I could sleep through the night again. The circles beneath my eyes faded and disappeared.

It happened as she said: I could experience time at a different rate from how it passed. I used this ability to study. In extended time I was able to grasp concepts I hadn't been able to before, spending minutes instead of hours in thought. I was no longer pressed for time.

I received A's on my exams. I raised my grades. Was this ethical? It wasn't exactly cheating. I wasn't a genius like so many of my classmates were, so it was only fair that I had this.

Why were we like this, my mother and I? I read scientific papers about internal clocks, trying to understand what we might be experiencing. All organisms had molecular clock mechanisms and circadian cycles: Our biology kept the time. But nothing I read explained our particular condition.

The school year ended. I flew home. At the airport, I saw that my mother's face seemed to be broadening—not that she was gaining weight, but her features were changing: Her eyes were narrowing, her cheeks flattening.

"What?" she said, staring at the road ahead. "Why are you looking at me that way?"

"Sorry."

She could see the judgment in my eyes. It felt like a failure on my part, that I couldn't hide it better.

"How were finals?"

"Can we talk about it later, Mom?"

"Fine. Okay."

I took my phone out of my pocket and scrolled: friends' vacations and dinners, graphics about police brutality, raccoons joyfully eating watermelon. I could feel her eyes on me, judging my phone use. It was irritating.

Into Tacoma, over the bridge, she didn't ask questions. We sat in silence, making our way onto the familiar green of the island. Silently, she pulled into our driveway. Our house looked like gingerbread, molasses brown and crumbling.

My bedroom was unchanged except for the dust that had gathered on my speakers and participation trophies. Dust was dead skin and hair and clothing fibers, among other things, and I wondered if it was my old skin—shed by a previous version of me—that had collected here, proof of my disintegration. Or was it my mother's skin that had found its way in? The cats were grown now, full-sized cats who regarded me with indifference, except when they wanted their faces scratched.

"You know what I forgot?" my mother said, poking her head into my room. "Olive oil. And soy sauce. Would you get some for me? Not the low-sodium stuff."

At the grocery store, Timothy's father gave me a lingering hug and patted my back. He was wearing sandals and I couldn't help but stare at his big, misshapen toe, with a dead purple nail. He told me that Timothy had gotten an internship at a pharmaceutical company doing vaccine development in the Midwest, where he was probably, at this very moment, syringing viruses into chicken eggs.

"What are you majoring in?" he asked.

I'd decided I would double major in molecular, cellular, and developmental biology and philosophy. Maybe it was petty, but I wanted to show them: the teachers and classmates who had thought me incapable, like Timothy's smug friend Simon, a philosophy major, who only seemed smart because he'd been assigned relevant reading at Exeter. I could read those texts, too.

"I hope you boys are taking care of each other out there," he said. "You're a long way from home."

The part of his shopping cart where a baby would go was filled with packaged organ meats. They were for the dog they'd adopted once Timothy left home. She was old and Timothy's parents cooked all her food.

"We are," I lied.

At home I told my mother that I had run into Timothy's father.

"How's Timothy doing?" my mother asked.

"I don't know," I told her honestly.

She nodded, unsurprised. She knew these things happened, that people drifted apart. It was what made her different from Timothy's father, from many of the people who lived here: her realism, their idealism. Our white neighbors had sought the island's isolation and thought of themselves as outside the mainstream. But they didn't see how central they still were—how the world revolved around them. My mother never described herself as an outsider, she just was one—that was obvious to me. From the perimeter, she could see what was invisible to everyone in the middle.

She took the oil from me, uncapped it, and tipped it into a pan. She slid the onions from her cutting board into it and they sizzled.

"What's the new place like?" I asked.

She was downsizing, moving to an apartment complex a few miles away. The onion scent filled the room. The new apartment had an exhaust fan, so it wouldn't always smell like cooking. Would her belongings fit there, transplanted? The antique rocking chair, the cast-iron pans? I wasn't sure if I'd miss this place.

"Well, it's new," she said. "So . . . less defunct."

"You're saying that like it's a bad thing."

"It *is* a bad thing. But the new place has heating. Hard to muster up the energy to make a fire for just myself. Without my darling boy."

Watching her cook, I tried to imagine her in her new home: bright white walls, a dishwasher, a roof that didn't leak. I hated myself for thinking what I was thinking—that I didn't want my life to resemble hers. Maybe loneliness was in our genetic makeup, though, and no matter what I did, who I met, I would always be alone. After we ate, I did the dishes, running the water as hot as I could, so hot that it burned, and my skin went pink.

In the weeks that followed I helped her pack. I retrieved waxed boxes from the grocery store. Their sides were printed with anthropomorphic produce, dancing artichokes and asparagus from California.

I emptied my old bedroom mercilessly, throwing out old binders of schoolwork, filling garbage bags of clothes I'd grown out of to take to the Goodwill. In my mother's donation bag I found two identical silk dresses: one black, one blue. They were fancy, and I had never seen her wear them.

Around my mother, I made an effort to be the same person I had been before, even though we both knew that I wasn't. In the year that had passed, I had met people she hadn't, sat in lecture halls learning history, philosophy, biology. Our vocabulary was less shared than it had once been. I was undergoing a change, being molded by other forces. Or maybe it was my own arrogance, to believe that only I had changed, and my mother hadn't.

Before I packed them, I flipped through old photo albums. My dark-haired mother, crouched down to secure her small blond boy, our backs sprayed in the mist of a waterfall. My hand held protectively on the pocket of my corduroy shorts. I remembered what I was guarding: a small blue rock my mom had given me. I imagined the albums winding up, one day, in an antique shop. The future people wondering who my mother and I were to each other. She'd been my entire family. It was as though she'd grown me in her hand. Yet I wondered: What would it have been like, to have a father, too—the storybook family?

I took out my wallet, extracted the halves of the fake ID that Timothy had made. I had a new fake now—a better one, Maryland— and no longer needed Timothy's, flimsy in comparison. I studied the photograph. This was Matthew, Timothy had said. I remembered his last email, which I'd deleted without responding to: *please let me apologize.*

I held the half of the fake ID with his photo next to photos of my mother and me. It was a way to imagine what it might have been like. Matthew, beside us, at the Grand Canyon; Matthew's hand in my small one, on that trip we had taken to Yosemite, all of us minuscule against soaring redwoods. My mother's face embarrassed me. In the photos, you could see how nakedly she loved me. Love exposed you like a cooked fish, the skin peeled back.

CHAPTER 13

IN THE DINING HALL, we sat at the large polished table. After every holiday there was the obligatory catch-up. When we saw one another next it would be as though we'd never left. Nothing could be said that would adequately capture the time that someone else had spent apart from you. My suitemates had done internships in New York and Chicago. Amir had taught English in Korea.

"What about you, Nick?"

I spent the summer at home with my mom, I told them.

"Awww," everyone said.

"And you grew a beard!" Colleen said. "I like it. Can I touch it?"

I leaned my head obediently over and let her run a hand along my jaw.

"It's softer than it looks," she said, and then everyone started grabbing at my face, issuing verdicts.

Colleen was cute. She had big stunned eyes and cheeks that were always perfectly flushed. Like most of us, her day-to-day uniform was a hoodie, but underneath her breasts were round and amazing. She was in engineering, one of few girls, and it was guaranteed plenty of her classmates lusted after her, too.

When we were gathered like this, around the dining hall table, I wondered how many of my peers were, like me, the products of in vitro fertilization. They all seemed so perfect, like they had been invented in a lab. A few of them had. At one point we had been blastocysts, chosen for our health. Sometimes I spaced out and pictured us as embryos. In amniotic sacs, cells multiplying by the day, tiny curled seahorses.

After the summers were accounted for, we moved on to other subjects: our new dorm rooms, an email from the dean about cultural appropriation at Halloween, which members of the animal kingdom had big butts. One of us occasionally got up to get seconds or dessert or cereal, or to refill a Nalgene bottle with juice.

The dining hall numbers dwindled. I felt a hand on my shoulder, and there was Miranda, with her dark eyes that caught mine. Like that, she had all my attention.

"Hey, you."

Colleen watched us with fascination, a false smile fixed on her face. Aware that whatever interest I might have had in her had, within seconds, vaporized. I hoped it wasn't obvious, my powerlessness before Miranda. She was a junior and exuded confidence.

"Hey," I said. In my surprise, my voice sounded pathetic—higher pitched than I meant it to. "Everybody, this is Miranda. Miranda, everybody."

She sat down at the table with us.

"Y'all have the best food," she said.

There were murmurs of agreement, as though we could take credit.

"How do you know Nick?" Colleen asked politely.

Miranda looked from her to me, me to her—her assessment was quick.

"He stalked me," she said.

I shook my head. "She stalked *me*," I said, a little too vehemently. "You can't trust her. You just met her."

"I don't know, Nick," Amir said. "You seem way more like the stalking kind."

Miranda laughed, touched Amir on the arm. "Thank you."

He brightened like a bulb. She had that effect.

"For real, though," Miranda said. "He found my bracelet."

Miranda held up her wrist, jangling the bracelet in the process.

"It was from my dad, actually," she said, looking at me. "I don't know if I ever told you that."

I shook my head. She hadn't.

"My dead dad," she elaborated.

No one knew how to respond to that.

"Shit," she said, noticing the time on her wrist. "It's been a pleasure, guys, but I have to go."

She stood, then seemed to have an idea.

"Wanna come with me to buy some used textbooks from a Craigslist rando?" she asked. "You could protect me in case he's a serial killer."

She was standing very close and I was holding my breath. I exhaled.

"You'd protect me, I'm pretty sure," I said. "But yeah."

I stacked my tray on hers and returned them both. I felt conscious of every move I made, feeling her eyes on me. I could feel my dining companions watching, too.

"Colleen's pretty," Miranda said, once we were outside. I wasn't sure how she wanted me to respond.

"Yeah," I said. "She is."

Was that what Miranda wanted to hear? She typed an address into her phone.

"Oh, shit, he's at East Rock," she said. "The Craigslist guy."

The address was a mile away. "You don't have to come if you don't want to." Lightly, I wondered if all she'd wanted was to separate me from Colleen.

I shrugged. I wasn't going to abandon her now and she knew it, so the mentioning was more of a formality. I would follow her anywhere.

We navigated to the address, but what we expected to see—some crumbling shared student house—was instead a neat two-story home surrounded by hedges groomed into roundish shapes. On the porch, terra-cotta planters brimmed with red-orange geraniums.

When the door opened, it wasn't a student but a man in his fifties, wearing wire-rimmed glasses, with a book in his hand.

"Professor Robison," Miranda said, startled.

"Ms. Lee," he said.

He seemed unsurprised. He must have known it was her all along. He'd seen her email address though she hadn't seen his, which had been anonymized by Craigslist. Had he expected her here alone? It was strange if so.

She held up a twenty-dollar bill. He handed two books over to her—in the exchange, dust plumed in the light—and pushed her hand back.

"You know, you're doing me a favor," he said. "Keep it."

"You were selling it."

"I have a lot of books," he said. "I'm always having to get rid of them. Would you like to come in?"

"This is Nick," she said. "Nick, this is Professor Robison."

"It's Bill. Please call me Bill, Nick," the professor said.

He maintained a smile on his face, as though nothing were out of the ordinary and he'd expected to see me, too. He moved a stack of books from the coffee table and gestured for us to sit. There were Tiffany lamps and large, dusty-looking rugs, and a grouchy, long-haired cat that sat on an ottoman like a sculpture. In the corner was a child-sized play kitchen. An egg Velcroed to a pan. He wasn't acting very fatherly.

"Wine?" he asked Miranda.

"Sure?" She caught my eye and shrugged.

He took two crystal glasses from a hutch of carved, dark wood and poured red wine for Miranda. We said nothing, only looked, wide eyed, at each other.

He handed a glass to me without asking my age. Miranda began to say something, then stopped. Neither of us bothered to correct him. In silence, we accepted the glasses.

They began to talk. I couldn't stop watching her: her hand moving through her hair, brushing it to the side; her hand bringing the glass to her mouth, pink with her lip gloss, then lowering it, letting her grip loosen. I wanted to hold it. Her eyes grew glazed with the wine.

"I don't know," Miranda said. "I think I'd rather have people try to be good rather than not try at all."

"But each of us thinks of ourselves, and our actions, as being more well intended than others," the professor said. He looked to me. "Nick, have you taken much philosophy? Have you read any Kierkegaard?"

"He's in science," Miranda said.

"I'm actually double majoring in it," I clarified to both of them. " 'We live forward, but understand backward.' Isn't that Kierkegaard?"

The professor clapped his hands together, delighted. "The very one."

He was possibly high. I noticed a jam jar full of weed on the kitchen table when I went to the bathroom. I wondered where his family was, if he had one—the kids who flipped pretend eggs.

———

Outside, the sky was beginning to dim. We were there for almost two hours.

"What was that?" I asked, once we were a few blocks away.

"I think he's harmless. He's just lonely."

"That's cool? Getting your students drunk?"

I was somewhat drunk myself.

"We're adults, aren't we? Anyway, thanks for *protecting* me." She smiled, amused at how riled up I was. "My hero."

"That's not what I mean. Would you have stayed, if not for me?"

"I stayed because of you," she said.

"That's confusing," I said quietly. More to myself than to her.

"Well." She looked at me. "What do we do now? Will you buy us more wine?"

The books were in her purse; the yellowed edges frilled from the top like a wild oyster's shell.

"I'm younger than you."

"Yeah, but . . . they'll sell *you* wine. Trust me."

She waited for me outside the wine shop. She hadn't told me what to buy but I didn't want to spend too much time considering it, not wanting to appear suspicious. The store was small, with shelves labeled with handwritten recommendations, like at a bookstore, except that here I didn't know what any of the words meant. I determined that the cheapest bottles were on the bottom shelves.

Miranda laughed when she saw me emerge with a jug. She put it into her tote bag, which now bulged with the wine and books. She balanced the strap on my shoulder. Then she broke into a run. I had no choice but to chase her.

"Where are you going?" I called, and she only motioned: *Come on.*

I followed her up East Rock's wooded trail. The climb winded us, so we didn't speak. Robins paused in the middle of the road, then bounced out of our path. A woman on a bicycle beside us, pedaling slowly, called out: "We'll make it!" The rocks were covered in graffiti, as though tattooed. In yellow, the words "I hate vandalism."

We reached the summit as the sun was setting. It smelled like cut grass, crushed clover. Darkness was moments away but here, for now, was light: The sky was pink as a cheek and the park had emptied and the air had cooled. We could make out Long Island, across the sound. A single woman stood with her large black dog, so dark it was featureless, like a hole cut out of a picture.

Dandelions grew between the bench slats. Miranda unscrewed the wine and took an unwieldy swig of it. She wiped her mouth with the back of her hand. She handed me the jug and watched me take a drink. She had this expression on her face, like she was trying to figure something out.

"What?" I asked.

"Nothing," she said, and looked away. She rubbed her hands across her upper arms.

"Are you cold?"

I pulled off my hoodie. It was filthy. I wore it all the time and never remembered to wash it.

"Such a gentleman," she said, but didn't object, neither to the gesture nor the garment itself. She tugged it over her head. "But now you're cold," she observed.

"I'm fine," I lied. The hairs on my arms were standing; goose bumps gave me away.

"You don't have to be macho around me."

"I'm not being macho."

"You are," she said, laughing. "You're being macho."

A cool breeze blew, and I drank more wine. It was warm going down, and that helped.

"Come here," Miranda said. "Don't be stupid."

She slid closer to me, wrapping me in both her arms, which were in my hoodie. It was weird, like I was giving myself a hug.

"Better?"

"Better."

I wanted to kiss her so badly. It seemed impossible that a feeling like this wasn't obvious, wouldn't be broadcast from my skin to hers.

I had innumerable questions: What did I like and not like, who I was, the kind of person I was going to be—all of these were mysteries to me. But this wasn't: I wanted this person before me, and nothing had ever been clearer.

The sun had set. The wine was half gone.

"What?" she said, raising an eyebrow. "I'm getting a vibe from you, Nick."

She was still wearing my sweatshirt. I pulled her to me. I wanted to stay here forever. In the next moment, she could push me away, flee, never speak to me again. I kissed her.

She surprised me by kissing me back, with a force that suggested that she might have wanted this, too. She pushed her body against mine. Time wanted to fall away but I fought to keep it still.

She pulled away and looked at me, eyes wide, guilty, and said, "I'm with Isaiah."

We made our way down the hill, without speaking. At the entrance to her dorm room, we lingered, kissing again, my hand beneath my own sweatshirt, on the small of her back, on the place her ribs curved; her hand clasped behind my craned neck. When I tried to maneuver her toward the stairs she stopped me.

"No, Nick," she said, shaking her head. "I can't."

"Please."

"I have a boyfriend. Remember?" She said it softly, as though she were reminding herself, rather than me. A student brushed past, pretending not to notice us. I wondered if it was someone who knew her, who knew Isaiah. "Just let me think, okay?"

When I said nothing, she repeated, "Is that okay?"

Miranda returned my sweatshirt to me. It smelled better now that she had worn it, her scent layered with mine.

On the walk home, the chill was sobering. A streetlight flickered, yellowish white and eerie. A group of pale bodies streaked past me.

"Niiick!" a naked person yelled as he raced by. I squinted at the bodies, blindingly white.

By the time I realized it was Timothy, he was already gone.

Amir wasn't home when I returned to our room, beaming stupidly to myself, the happiness a foreign sensation. I wanted badly to tell someone: An impossible thing had happened, my life was changed.

The moment I plugged my phone in to charge it, it rang. It was my mother.

"Hey, Mom."

"Have you been drinking?"

"A little," I confessed.

"You left something here."

"I'll get it when I'm home next, Mom. I—"

I was eager to tell her about Miranda. She would be pleased for me.

"It's a driver's license," my mother said, then. "At least, I think it's supposed to be."

No, I thought. I'd put it away, hadn't I? I opened my wallet, pulling all the cards from it, frantic.

"Nick Maier?" my mother said, very evenly.

I didn't know what to say. I was frozen, crouched beside the electrical outlet.

"When did you meet him?" she asked.

I was drunk and couldn't think things through enough to fashion a lie. I told her the truth. I told her about the DNA test, about meeting in high school. My confession was met with silence.

"Hello?" I tried.

"You kept this from me."

My hand that wasn't holding the phone was a fist. I unclenched it. She had no right to be upset. I had done what any normal person would have. I was drunk, and the words—accusatory, righteous, furious—poured unfiltered from my mouth.

"How can you say that?" I raised my voice. When my suitemates returned home they would be able to hear me through the walls, but I didn't care. "You were the one who lied to me first."

"That's not true. You can't listen to what he says, Nick. He's—"

"He never said he didn't want to know me. *You* did."

"It's more complicated than that."

"He wanted to know me, and you kept him from me."

"That's not what happened, Nick."

I didn't tell her that I'd stopped answering his calls, hadn't spoken to him since starting school. I didn't tell her about his real son. Let her think we had a relationship, that our bond was close, and I was having the time of my life here, with him, on the East Coast.

"You ruined my life, Mom."

I was shaking.

"What, Nick? What are you saying?"

Only a moment ago, I'd been delirious with happiness. It was like the happiness had vaporized and reassembled into fury. I felt blind with it, as angry as I'd been happy a moment ago.

I unleashed every grievance I ever had: not having Internet, not having a phone, all my mother's stupid rules, imposed on my entire childhood for reasons that made no sense at all. As a result I was a weirdo, I didn't know how to have friends, I would never be normal.

"You ruined my life. You controlled everything about it until I had nothing left."

"Nick." She was concerned now. "What's this about?"

"Why couldn't you let me be a normal kid? Instead you had all these stupid rules."

"No, that's not—" she protested. "I wanted you to choose everything for yourself. To have *real* choices." She was crying now, and the sudden, familiar impulse to comfort her came over me.

"How was that my choice, not having a father? I don't know how to be, or who I am. I don't have any fucking friends. I'm a freak of nature and I—"

"You're my son. Not his, okay? I can explain all this if you'll just—"

"Why couldn't you just let me be normal?"

"Nick. *Please.* I wanted you to think for yourself. I wanted you to want what you actually wanted. 'Normal' isn't even . . . there's no such thing as normal."

I heard the front door close. One of my roommates was home. I lowered my voice.

"Don't call me again."

"Nick, don't. Please. Let's talk tomorrow. You're drunk."

"Fuck you," I said, and hung up.

CHAPTER 14

I DIDN'T HEAR FROM Miranda the next day, or the rest of the week. My mother left messages that I deleted without listening to. My shock and regret hardened, like clay, into rage.

The green of the trees browned; the air cooled. The libraries, like cathedrals, took on an eerie quality. I resolved that I wouldn't need anyone. Not Timothy, not Miranda. Not my mother or my father. If loneliness was in my DNA, as I suspected, maybe it meant I had an adaptation others didn't, like the first frog that blended in with its environment and avoided being eaten. Except my adaptation was that I needed no one. I wouldn't need anyone.

In the artificial coolness of the gym, I resolved to have a body without any softness in it. I would be invincible—armored and unbreachable. The repetition and mindlessness reminded me of oyster farming—the satisfaction of those early hours in the water. For months, I exercised and studied. My chest and legs bulked and hardened. My exams and essays were returned to me, always A's.

Often, Isaiah was in the weight room, too, arms and temples glossy with sweat, like a plastic action figure. I could picture them together—he and Miranda—so easily. I felt sick, physically ill with desire—powerless, unable to exert control over the situation. Knowing that the person I wanted, more than anything, was with someone else and wasn't thinking of me the way I thought of her.

He gave me a small nod. I didn't know if he remembered that we had met at the party on Edgewood. But I could tell he didn't know Miranda and I had kissed. She hadn't told him.

I wiped down the bench. I checked my phone and saw that I had a missed call from Miranda. I stared at it for a moment, not quite believing. Then I hit the call button.

"Hello?" she said. I was still clutching my sweat-soaked shirt. "Nick? You there?"

"Hey," I managed.

"What are you up to tonight?" she asked, so coolly and casually she almost convinced me that nothing had ever transpired between us, that we'd recently seen each other, that we were casual friends.

Isaiah walked past me to the showers, just then, towel at his waist. It had been four months since that night on East Rock.

"Nothing?" I'd promised to study that night with a roommate; it didn't matter.

There was a screening of *Only Angels Have Wings* at the Whitney, she said. Would I go with her?

"Sure," I said, in disbelief.

"Cool. It's at seven. I'll see you there."

And that was all. The phone showed how long we'd talked: thirty-five seconds.

She was waiting outside the Whitney when I arrived. Bundled in a huge coat with fur on the hood framing her face, like a lion, looking minuscule inside its mane. And like that, my longing returned—electrifying. I had tried so hard to squash it but was helpless to now. Her lips were shining, glossed, flecks of glitter on them.

"Have you seen this?" she asked as we walked toward the entrance. Her boots made a crunching sound over the gravel. I shook my head.

"It's the best," she said, lifting the hood from her head. Could she really have called me after four months just to show me a movie she liked? I wanted badly for her to say more: to tell me she wanted to be together. She was being so nonchalant, as though we'd seen each other yesterday. And yet I couldn't be frustrated with her. I was only grateful.

We found seats. She leaned to show me the miniature bottles of Maker's Mark she'd stowed in her gloves.

I stole glances to watch her watching Jean Arthur, whose character was named Bonnie Lee, a showgirl passing through a South American trading port—a "Ms. Lee," just like Miranda. The Ms. Lee beside me laughed with her eyes closed, with her perfect head thrown back. The Ms. Lee in the movie gets entangled with Cary Grant, an air-freight pilot wearing extremely high-waisted pants.

The pilots make impossible decisions with coin flips, surrendering their lives to chance. In the final scene, Jean Arthur asks Cary Grant if she should stay—in other words, with him, in this trading port—or board the boat that will return her to New York. Cary Grant says he'll flip a coin; heads means she should stay. He flips; the coin says heads. Ms. Lee protests: She doesn't want this decided by fate. "All you have to do is ask me," she says. Then she turns the coin over in her hand and sees that it's double-sided: heads on both sides. He's asked her to stay, without saying it.

Afterward, outside, we were pleasantly buzzed from Miranda's secreted whiskey. She drew her hood back over herself; it was cavernous. She peered at me expectantly—I could see how much she wanted me to love the movie, too.

"You were right," I said. "The best."

She'd reapplied her lip gloss in the bathroom, and I wondered if it was for me.

"Miranda," I said.

"I know," she said. "I'm sorry."

It was winter now, unequivocally. Her *sorry* was visible—an apologetic puff that appeared in the air between us, before disappearing.

Don't say you're sorry, I thought. I didn't want her to have anything to be sorry about. What I wanted was simple: for her to want to be with me.

I touched her cheek, the down of it. She flinched a little. Her eyes, staring up into mine, looked wet. I bent to kiss her, and she let me. She kissed me back. There was a snowflake on her eyelash; snow had started to fall.

Miranda shook her head slightly. She leaned in to whisper into my ear. Her breath had mint and whiskey on it.

"I guess we're doing this, aren't we?" she said.

"Yes, please," I said.

We spent almost every night together. Her window was drafty—the radiator hissed hotly and ineffectually from the other side of the room—so we stayed in bed, under colorful quilts sewed by her mother, thinned from use.

Sex with her was different than it had been with anybody else. I didn't need to be drunk. I didn't have to keep myself from having thoughts, as I did with other people. What we were doing made sense to me; we made sense. Afterward, she would turn onto her side, bending her lashes against the pillow. Nothing had ever felt as right as being with her. I was who I was and she loved me.

I loved her without makeup. I loved the way she ate incredibly fast, as though some predator were coming for her food. I loved the nights we lay around in Korean face masks, terrifying ourselves and laughing through the cutouts.

"Earth to Nick," she sometimes said to me. "You're not here. You're in your head."

"Where should I be?" I'd ask.

And she would take my hand in hers: warm, physical, alive.

"Be here," she'd say. "With me."

It was easy to adopt Miranda's passions as my own. So much was enraging once you bothered to pay attention. On the news it was always hurricanes, earthquakes, heat waves, fires. Everything getting worse: inequality, corruption, racism. White supremacists were feeling threatened, lashing out, believing themselves to be the arbiters of who were and weren't real Americans, conveniently forgetting that they themselves occupied stolen land.

We went to protests and demonstrations: Black Lives Matter, Stop Asian Hate, climate change, prison abolition, reproductive rights. On Saturdays, we took the bus to the correctional facility in Bridgeport, volunteering with an organization teaching incarcerated men how to read. On Sundays, Miranda would begin to make pancakes and abandon them midway. I would finish griddling the batter, ladling it into elaborate shapes. We got into fights and made up in bed. For the first few months, when we went to parties, she introduced me only as Nick, a friend. Maybe I was imagining it, but her friends regarded me with amusement. Like I was a new puppy received at Christmas— a creature that a child might grow tired of. I wondered if it was because I looked white. It was so obvious, to date a white boy. It disappointed me, but no matter: I'd waited so long, and I could wait longer.

At a St. Patrick's Day–themed party she wore a hunter-green dress that I wanted, only, to take off. Everyone looked foolish wearing green—including me. And yet we did; no one didn't need luck. The room was festooned in tinfoil shamrocks.

"My boyfriend, Nick," Miranda introduced me, at last. I loved hearing it from her mouth.

"So your mom raised you," Miranda said, late one night.

We were in her bed, which had so many more pillows than mine did.

It was during nights, lights off, that I could tell her more about myself than I'd shared with anyone. I told her about my upbringing, the lonely Washington island I grew up on, about having Timothy as my only friend, about my mother's solitude. How I'd wished, more than anything, to be normal. She listened, kindly and intently. With her I could unburden myself of everything—almost everything.

"Where was your dad?" she asked.

"New York," I said into Miranda's neck. We'd gotten back in touch in high school, I said. I didn't tell her that I'd stopped responding to his calls, that he had a legitimate son who wasn't me.

"Maybe we could see him? When we go there."

She'd landed a summer internship in Manhattan. I'd been reading a textbook in her bed, highlighter in hand, when she shrieked at the news—it was the job she'd hoped for—and bounded into bed with me. I'd streaked her arm with neon.

There was more I could tell her. And what a relief it would be, to have someone know me completely. I felt the words form. I hadn't known my father growing up. My mother had lied about him. I had a half brother. That was my family.

"Yeah, we could," I agreed.

Miranda found a summer sublet in a shared apartment in Carroll Gardens, above a running shoe store. Our roommates were older than we were—one was even in her thirties—adult women with real jobs. Our room had the only access to the fire escape, so the roommates passed through it, stepping onto our frameless mattress and out the window to smoke. It smelled permanently of cigarettes.

She left me money for groceries, which was sort of humiliating. I cooked dinners that would be waiting for her when she got home from her internship. She fawned appreciatively, even when the recipes weren't successful.

Some nights she texted to say she wouldn't be back for dinner. She was getting drinks with her new coworkers and I shouldn't wait up. On those days I put the meals—quiche, spaghetti, congee—in the roommates' rinsed-out take-out containers so she could bring them to work for lunch.

It was easier not to spend money when you were alone. I took long walks and returned damp with sweat. At the public library, I read newspapers alongside white-haired men in pilled brown sweaters, who asked if I was finished with each section. My father was nearby, I kept thinking. But he was busy with his real son. He didn't need to hear from me.

On the Fourth of July Miranda and I sat, legs outstretched, by the East River. We drank bad sake and chased it with potato chips.

"I don't actually like fireworks," she said. "So many other things are better."

"What? That's crazy. Name one thing."

"Easy. The moon." She gestured to it—full and glowing. "The moon is better than fireworks."

"Our Chinese ancestors are rolling over in their graves."

"But think of it. A world without fireworks, or gunpowder."

"Dogs wouldn't freak out every Fourth of July."

"We'd spend all night looking at the moon."

"Do you know about Chang'e?" I asked.

"No. Tell me."

"She lives on the moon," I said. It was a bedtime story from my mother. "She was married to Houyi, a skilled archer. There were ten suns in the sky, back then, and Houyi shot down nine of them. She stole the elixir of immortality—in some versions it's a pill—and flew to the moon to escape being caught."

"Why did Houyi shoot down the suns?"

"I don't know that part. He was being thoughtful? It was so hot, in those days. So he's the reason the planet's, like, even inhabitable. Either he was super considerate—"

"—or it was toxic masculinity. He shot them down just to prove he could."

I kissed her. Her mouth was salty and sour from the salt-and-vinegar chips; it almost hurt. She pulled away.

I half listened while she talked about her job. Was my father nearby, looking at the same erupting sky?

"Earth to Nick," she said.

"Sorry."

"I said, do you want to get sushi?"

I must have winced at the word *sushi* because she added, "On me."

A pause, then: "Maybe you could get a job?" Miranda suggested, very gently.

CHAPTER 15

IT WAS BUSY THAT NIGHT. That I'd been hired was a stroke of luck—my perfect timing. I walked into the restaurant, résumé in hand, at the same time the bartender stormed out. He bore more than a passing resemblance to me. We could have been actors, auditioning for the same role. Danny, the manager, asked when I could start, and I replied, "Whenever you want. Today." It was the right answer.

When he walked up to the bar my heart turned leaden, immovable, like it had fossilized. He asked for a scotch and soda, and when I asked what kind of scotch he said, "The best you've got."

Of course he would come here, of all places. I recognized his face from the hundreds of photographs he'd posted online. They were taken from more flattering angles, but still I recognized him.

"Your ID?" I asked—I was terrified to ask.

He wore an impatient expression, as though the question were an imposition; reached into his wallet; handed the card to me. He watched as I glanced at his New York–issued driver's license, which said he was Samuel Maier, twenty-one years old. I knew, for a fact, that he was younger than I was. Seventeen. He'd had an expert ID crafted—the best that money could buy, I supposed.

My hands shook as I poured our best single malt. I wondered if he noticed, and then I decided that of course he didn't—he had no reason to care, or to give me a second thought.

Samuel was wearing a navy-blue suit, in a slim fit—an attempt to look grown-up. His dark hair was trimmed neatly—the haircut looked fresh—and gelled into submission.

He watched me while he took a sip, as though ready to throw it in my face if it wasn't to his expectations. I turned my attention to the bar and wiped it down with my rag. When I looked back up, he nodded.

"It's good. What do I owe you?"

"Thirty."

Now his eyes were fixed on me, as if he was trying to place me.

"Do I know you?"

"I'm new here."

"I feel like I know you. What's your name?"

"Nick."

"Nick. Did you go to Dalton?"

I shook my head. He slipped me two twenties.

"Keep the change," he said.

"Sam," someone called to him—a young man whose face was covered in painful-looking pink acne. He'd also made efforts to look older: His hair was slicked back and his watch was heavy on his wrist.

"Sorry I'm late, man."

Samuel turned to me and fished another two twenties from his wallet.

"He'll have one of these, too."

I made change and set the tips aside. They were guided to a table. I didn't notice them leave. Maybe my head was down, maybe I was making a drink. We were in the weeds for a few hours. Likely he'd left during one of those hours and I'd missed his exit. But I felt, the whole night, the way I did when I spoke in class. My heart at a gallop. My hands were clammy handling the glasses.

"You okay?" asked Harriet.

She'd been kind to me, helped me through my first weeks, when everyone else looked at me skeptically—doubting that I would last.

There was more cleanup than usual. We had to stay an extra hour. Everyone complained about it, but in a good-natured way. The others brightened when I made out the tips: We'd had our asses kicked but made a killing, at least. I poured everyone shots to celebrate: bourbon that Danny had set on the bar for us, reward for a night well done. Everyone, with a few drinks inside them, loosened up. Harriet asked me for two shots of tequila instead of the bourbon, which she didn't like.

"I don't care if that makes me uncool," she said.

She undid her hair, which she typically kept coiled in a bun but released, fell all the way down to her waist. She tipped each shot into her mouth, one after the other, quick and natural. She was always watching me. I'd heard she was a writer, and that made me nervous. What did she know about me? Whatever the insights were, I wanted to know them. She was always observing and had a memory that defied how much drinking the servers seemed to do. She never had to write orders down. When I was around Harriet I thought about the future even as the present was happening: what she'd remember about who I was, maybe better than I'd remember myself.

She licked the tequila from her lips.

"You're in college, right, Nick?" Harriet asked.

"Yeah."

"Let me guess. Columbia?"

"Yale."

"Where are you staying?"

"Carroll Gardens," I said. "With my girlfriend."

"Cute," she said.

She stacked her tequila glasses neatly, pushed them toward me.

I wondered how old she was. My guess was thirty, but I wasn't good at guessing these things.

"You did good, kid," said the server I'd overheard, the week before, saying I was inexperienced. He needs to speed up, his conversation partner had said. But at least he looks the part.

By now I knew his name was George—everyone called him Georgie, but I was still too new and called him George.

"I'll be honest. I didn't think it was possible. But tonight? Tonight you were on fire."

I felt something like pride rising up. Noticing that, George cut in.

"Don't let it go to your head," he added.

George was middle-aged, in his fifties. He'd been at the restaurant for years: a lifer. He had a round face, with one of those beards that fanned out, and didn't have the mustache part. He was improbably cool—not exactly good-looking, but charming, with a pleasant face and shiny, rosy cheeks. There were tables that asked specifically for Georgie.

"Can you make me a Manhattan?" he asked.

"Coming right up."

I rubbed the orange peel against the rim of the glass like I'd been taught, poured whiskey and vermouth and bitters, and stirred. I loved the music of the bar: the ice and the glass and the spoon, clinking. I stirred it for a moment longer than I needed to, before I added his cherries—I knew, had heard, that he liked two.

"Mm," George said as he sipped. I felt another swell of pride at having his approval.

On the subway car home, it was only me and a sleeping man who had his rucksack hugged to his chest and a cardboard sign that said "My life is a fucking pain in the ass." Beside him was a plastic water bottle, with what looked like a mint sprig in it. I saw movement: the fins of a goldfish. What I'd mistaken for mint was an aquatic plant.

The tips were in my back pocket: a good sum of money. It would go toward rent; I was also saving up to take Miranda to the restaurant. But I could spare some. I put two twenties in his lap, pinned it under his sack.

It was four in the morning by the time I got home, but Miranda wasn't there.

Now that I had a job, we were always missing each other. I was asleep when Miranda left for work; she'd be asleep when I returned.

It was a Monday, my day off, and I wanted to surprise her. I bought two veggie burritos and followed an employee into her building. It smelled like coffee and new furniture.

She wasn't at her desk. Instead of texting her and ruining the surprise, I waited in the high-ceilinged lobby, beside a fiddle-leaf fig plant. I recognized one of her coworkers, Zoey, who brought me a can of barely flavored sparkling water.

Five minutes passed, then ten, then thirty. The foil-wrapped burritos cooled in my lap. Finally, I heard the sound of her laugh—bright and clear, her real, genuine laugh. She was in the lobby, standing with a man. Her laughing stopped when she saw me.

"Nick."

It wasn't happy, the way she said it. She wasn't pleasantly surprised to see me.

"I thought you might want lunch," I tried.

"I'm sorry, honey," she said. "I just got back from lunch."

"Okay," I said, at a loss.

"This is Eamon," she said. "He works here, too."

Eamon shook my hand. He was Black, shorter than I was, wearing a cardigan, thick glasses. He looked like someone who hosted a podcast.

"Do you have time to hang out?" I tried.

"I'm sorry, baby," she said, reaching up to kiss me on the cheek. "I have so much work to do. It was sweet of you to come by, though."

I didn't know what to say to that.

"I'll see you at home, okay?"

She waved, disappeared behind the closing elevator doors. I wondered what she had said to Eamon about me. She'd never mentioned him.

August came. The city sweltered, reeked, but to me it hardly mattered. Work was an alternate world of dark wood and cooled air and women with rings that tapped against the glasses I passed to them. I'd grown good at bartending—I could tell by the way people lingered—and that filled me with pride.

I'd saved enough to take Miranda to dinner at my restaurant. I knew the wine list, now, like I knew the cell cycle. I could afford a bottle, and it didn't even have to be the cheapest. With my employee discount we could feast. I knew, now, to be embarrassed about that first jug I'd bought. Now I could taste the differences between Sangiovese and barbera and gamay because I'd practiced with Georgie.

I looked forward to showing them off: Miranda to my coworkers, my coworkers to Miranda. I felt so proud being able to say, *This is my girlfriend.* She wore a necklace that made me want to touch her collarbone, and the charm bracelet from her father that slid down her wrist when she held the glass that Georgie refilled with water. The smile that lit up her face when she met them—I loved seeing them receive it. It made a person feel chosen. It was Georgie who waited on us, and he charmed her in return. I could see why he was so many diners' favorite.

Our entrées arrived: osso buco, immense with its bone, on a circle of polenta; pappardelle Bolognese. It was all very good, and I wanted her to effuse, but she didn't. She didn't eat in her typical way—quickly. She cut the meat into smaller and smaller pieces. She told Georgie everything was delicious, even when I knew I had eaten the lion's share. I had saved up for so long to bring her here. I knew Georgie was watching and hated to think Harriet was, too.

"Is it okay?" I asked.

"It's good," she said, not convincingly.

I took a deep drink of the wine Georgie had selected for us. She kept her head down. She pushed her plate away, most of it uneaten, the charms hitting the plate and table and making a sound.

"Did you want dessert?" I tried.

"Nick," Miranda said.

No, I thought.

I wished time would stop. I wanted to keep her from saying whatever it was she was going to say. I must have already known what it would be.

"I think we should break up."

I didn't respond. Another sip of wine.

"I think we should break up," she repeated.

"I heard you," I said, "but I don't understand."

She lowered her voice. I knew Harriet was watching, even as she didn't look like it. This was one of her gifts: to keep tabs on everything happening around her.

"I don't think this is working."

"I didn't know anything was broken," I said, my voice getting louder. "Shouldn't we talk about this first? Shouldn't we have talked about it?"

"We're talking now."

"This isn't talking."

"Have you ever been broken up with, Nick?" she asked gently. "I don't have to give you a reason. It's not working for me. That's it."

"Is this because of Eamon?"

"It doesn't matter. It has nothing to do with you."

She wouldn't meet my gaze, and this made me angrier and louder. I'd never raised my voice to her before. I'd been so worried what Harriet and Georgie thought, but I had drunk enough not to care.

"Did you cheat on me?"

I sloshed more wine into my glass. I could feel Georgie hanging back, wanting to pour it for me but knowing not to approach.

"Fine," she said, quietly, to compensate for my volume. "It's about Eamon, okay? But we didn't do anything. I wanted to end things before we did anything."

I seethed. I didn't believe her. Already I'd drunk the bulb of wine I'd poured.

"Please don't make this harder than it already is."

"Don't turn this around," I said, "like you're the hurt one."

"I do love you."

Her eyes filled with tears, even though this was entirely her fault. She didn't have to do this. Why was she doing this? My chest felt like it was being crushed, an aluminum can. I hated her, suddenly.

"So this is your thing, I guess?" I knew I should stop. I knew I shouldn't finish the sentence, that the next thing I said would be ruthless and couldn't be unsaid. "Leaving people when you meet someone new."

"That's just mean, Nick," she said.

She blinked, and tears ran down her cheeks. An hour ago I would have comforted her, and now I was unmoved.

"Can you go?" I asked. "Just go."

"Nick."

"Dinner's on me," I said, as coldly as I could manage.

With her napkin, she wiped the wetness from her face. The black smudges transferred to the stiff white napkin. She stood and gathered her purse.

"I love you, okay?" she said. "But I can't be with you. You don't even know how to be with you."

And she was gone. I remained at the table. My coworkers kept refilling my wineglass, and I heard myself rattling on to them, making grand, nonsensical pronouncements about I don't know what, about love. As though I knew anything at all. It wasn't my shift, but I tried to be helpful. I tried to bus tables, clumsily. When I saw the tickets pile up I jumped behind the bar and filled wineglasses. The wine splashed onto the sleeves of my shirt.

An order came in for a hot toddy and I filled the glass with water. But the glass had been cold, and the water was hot, and the glass shattered, dramatically. Pieces flew everywhere.

"Hey, it's okay." Harriet was behind me.

She put her hand on my back, but I barely felt it. Georgie materialized with a broom and began to sweep.

"Just sit," Georgie said, sounding protective and exasperated all at
once. He positioned me back at the bar. He slid a plate of spaghetti
and meatballs in front of me, speckled green with parsley, and tucked
a napkin into the front of my shirt. I scarfed the spaghetti, sobering
only slightly. The world swayed around me. Harriet came up beside
me, touched my hand.

"Stay at my place," Harriet said.

She had a studio apartment and a pull-out couch. It would be
no trouble, she insisted, because she was heading to her boyfriend's
anyway.

She gave me her keys and address: a studio in Little Italy. I stumbled there. I made the pull-out bed for myself. I turned on the TV
to drown out my thoughts; on the news, another mass shooting. It
occurred to me I hardly knew Harriet. We were work friends, but that
was all. I saw her every day, and on some occasions we drank together,
but I knew nothing about her real life. I didn't know if she had siblings; I didn't know if her parents were alive. She had a collection of
Russian nesting dolls on the TV console.

On my phone, I opened my email and tapped compose. I typed
"M" then "A" into the recipient field—it autofilled to Matthew's email
address. Emailing him was the last thing I wanted to do, but I didn't
have much of a choice. I described my situation: I had been living
with my girlfriend, and she had just broken up with me. Now I had
nowhere to go. Did he have a place where I could stay, for the final
few weeks of the summer? I thought of what Miranda might have
said—such a privileged, rich-guy move. But it wasn't like I could keep
displacing Harriet. A hotel room would have cost more than I made
at the restaurant. I sent the message and turned my phone face down.

Minutes later, my phone dinged. It was an email from Matthew,
giving me an address in the West Village—an empty apartment where
I could stay. All I had to do was go to the building and ask Mario, the
doorman, for the key. He could come by around six to say hello, if that
was okay?

CHAPTER 16

THE APARTMENT WAS IMPERSONALLY furnished, like a location for a photo shoot. In the kitchen, a knife set without a cutting board; in the bathroom, no shampoo or soap but a large bottle of conditioner. The only houseplant was a lone purple orchid. I wondered how it stayed alive.

Promptly at six, Matthew rang the doorbell, though he must have had a key.

"You're taller," he said, at the door.

"I don't know about that."

He stepped into the apartment with some unease.

"Did you used to live here?" I asked.

"I did," he said.

He touched one of the orchid's leaves and left a clear streak where his thumb took the dust off.

"School's good?" Matthew asked.

"Better now."

"You have a major now?"

"Biology. Minor in philosophy."

"Sounds like a handful."

"To be honest, I don't have much of a social life."

He laughed, a little sadly.

"I worry we're similar," he said.

I felt a prickle of pleasure, hearing him say this. I longed to know why we were similar, or how.

"Why did you stop answering my calls?" Matthew asked. "My emails?"

"You were busy with Samuel," I said. "I didn't feel like I could."

"Nick." He looked at me. "You're my son, too."

"But he's your real son," I said softly, half wanting him not to hear me.

"You're my son, and he's my son," Matthew said. "Okay?"

I stood to fill glasses of water, needing to do something with my hands.

"Why did you leave us? My mom and me?" I asked, my back turned to him.

There was a long pause, as though he were listening for what to say. As though someone else were in the room—an invisible person, feeding him lines that weren't on my frequency.

"It was your mother who left." He put a hand on the back of his neck. "Please, believe me, I wanted to know you."

"So it was her decision."

"It's not so simple. She was upset, and she had every right to be. She had good reasons for leaving. You should talk to her about it."

"We're not speaking."

He walked to the orchid and plucked off two shriveled flowers. He sat back down beside me, the flowers closed in his fist.

"You should talk to her, Nick. She's your mother. And she's a good one."

"Well, I'm not going to do that. So you'll have to tell me."

Matthew couldn't meet my eye. He opened his hand, looked at the dead orchids in it.

"Your mother—she uncovered something that had been kept from us." He hesitated before continuing. "Your mother's parents knew my father. They worked at an institute funded by my family."

"You didn't know this? When you met?"

"No. We didn't. They kept it a secret from us." He continued to stare at the orchids as he spoke. "Your grandmother and my father worked on gene therapy—you would understand the science better than I do. They developed an experimental treatment, which they gave to your mother. Their goal was to eliminate genetic diseases passed on by one parent. It didn't go as they planned and, later in life, left your mother unable to conceive naturally. She hasn't told you any of this?"

I shook my head.

"Your existence was only possible through in vitro fertilization.

With you, they attempted the therapy again, and this time, succeeded. In fact, it worked better than they thought it would. You carry both of our DNA, but with my genetic contribution emphasized. Your mother's had been compromised by the earlier treatment."

"And that's why I look like this."

"That's right."

"So my mom was angry with her mother. And your family. For what they did to her. And me."

Matthew stood to throw the flowers away.

"She told me I had to choose," Matthew said. "Between my family and the two of you. I didn't think I had to. I didn't see why our lives couldn't just continue, why she couldn't stay. There was nothing to be done."

"But she wouldn't."

"No, she wouldn't."

I thought of the times I'd played *Dungeons & Dragons* with Timothy, our unsatisfying games of two. Who you became, what powers you possessed—it was a roll of the dice. But my grandparents had seized the dice for themselves, wanting to roll them. I resembled Matthew because of what they'd done.

My mother hadn't told me any of this. She had kept it from me. Whatever had happened to her—to us—it wasn't right. But I agreed with Matthew. Nothing could be changed. Why did she have to punish me, too? Where was my choice in this? I didn't ask to be born, but here I was, anyway. She could have just stayed. Instead, she had done to me what her mother did to her: She'd made a decision for me. She hadn't given me a say in the matter.

"It wasn't that we didn't want to be together," Matthew said. "I wanted to be your father. I still do. Will you let me do that?"

"You don't make any sense together," I blurted.

"Oh," Matthew said sadly. "We did."

Junior year began, and I missed Miranda. My life, which had seemed so full with her in it, now was empty again.

Of course I slept with other people. With other girls, I thought of Miranda: her cold cheeks and ears, her wrists, the coolness of her bracelet's charms against my chest. Inevitably she would be the person I measured everyone else against. When girls kissed me, when girls took me home—I didn't say no when I should have.

I tried to remind myself of the things about her that had frustrated me. She didn't know what she was feeling or wanted from me until she was in the throes of the emotion. Often, she was moody, unpredictable, unable to articulate why she felt the way she did, because it came from some deep, submerged part of her. One moment we'd be laughing together and the next she'd be furious at me. She had been charmed the first time I spoke Chinese at a Chinese restaurant, but on a later occasion she rolled her eyes and said, "Don't be a cliché of a white guy speaking Chinese," to which I argued that I was a Chinese guy speaking Chinese. Once, I'd confessed how ill-equipped I felt in my philosophy section, especially when it came to sharing out loud, and she was in one of her moods. She turned to me, exasperated, and said, "You know, you look like you belong here. You look like you've belonged here for hundreds of years. Yale didn't really start admitting Black folks until 1964. Women until 1969."

Later she would apologize. She knew I felt out of place, regardless of how I looked, and that was valid, too. But I never said anything like that to her again, knowing what she believed about me. I kept my feelings to myself.

I had sensed her frustration with me, my lack of clarity: I didn't know what I wanted to do, who I wanted to be. I agreed. I wanted to know how, and who, I should be; I was trying to figure that out, but she wanted me to know already. *This is just another thing I can't talk to you about*, I thought. *The same way I can't talk to you about my family.* She wanted me to be someone I wasn't: Isaiah, who was in law school now. Eamon, with his social justice podcast, determined to make the world a better place. She never said it, but I knew she wished I didn't look so white.

I stood in line at the Dunkin' Donuts, at the train station, going to New York to see Matthew. I needed coffee, and was considering a cruller. I saw her in my periphery right away. There was no missing her: her hair, the way she moved. I bought the coffee and not the pastry, and walked in the direction she'd gone. Like a dog, all I needed was the suggestion of her, and then I could follow—a useless sixth sense.

She boarded the Metro-North. She slid into one of the vinyl seats, leaned against the window, and was asleep. She lifted her head as we pulled into Grand Central. I followed her. She got on the 6 train, took a seat next to a small, grandmother-age woman who was peeling an egg. At Canal Street, she gathered her purse and hurried off. I was heading uptown. But at the last moment, I slipped through the closing silver doors. It wasn't so much a decision as it was a pull, like a magnet. I followed her.

She pushed through the turnstile. She was gathered into the current of mostly Chinese people, and I followed close behind, though not too close. I was more noticeable than I liked here. She stopped in front of a shop where a Chinese woman stood with her arms folded, looking cross. T-shirts hung from the store's rafters, printed with Jim Morrison and Che Guevara and Lady Liberty. There were lanyards and key chains and mini-flashlights, and cheap-looking luggage that smelled powerfully of plastic. The woman nodded slightly, and Miranda nodded in return. She approached a gate beside the store, pressed a button, spoke into it. The gate buzzed and Miranda opened it—a familiar gesture for her. It slammed hard behind her. The woman in front of the store made a disapproving noise at me as I lingered. *Was I going to buy anything?* I apologized in Mandarin, catching her off guard. I bought a key chain that looked like a tiny license plate. "New York Nick," it said.

From inside the store I saw Miranda reemerge, grinning hugely. I knew this smile, because it had once been reserved for me. She held hands with Eamon.

Eamon looked the part of her boyfriend—nothing like me. He was well-dressed, nothing fancy but put together. His hair was clipped close to his head. They even looked alike, with smiles that mirrored each other's.

CHAPTER 17

"I FORWARDED THE E-TICKET to you," the email from my mother said. "You don't have to stay the whole time. But please come home. We'll talk. I'll explain everything. I miss you."

In my inbox: a plane ticket that would take me home to Seattle. I moved my mouse over the two emails—the e-ticket and my mother's message—and selected them both. I pressed delete.

She had had her chance to explain herself. She'd had my whole life and had never told me the truth. My anger at her calcified.

Another email, from Matthew, asked about my plans for Christmas. He would be in New Haven and would love to see me.

"Sure," I typed out. "I'll be here." I pressed send.

CHAPTER 18

SENIORS CALLED IT THE T, short for Tomb. There were fifteen of us, in total—tapped juniors to replace the senior society members—and on this night the fifteen new members and fifteen outgoing seniors gathered for dinner. It smelled the way it did at St. Anthony's at Christmas, like long-cooked cafeteria food. We stood around holding non-alcoholic punch. Skull and Bones was a dry society. Introductions were made and the names left my mind immediately.

Hanging in the portrait hall of the T were Bonesmen of the past, all of them white men whose faces blurred into one. Amid the former presidents and senators was a painting of Otto Maier. I'd never met him. He was my age, and the resemblance was unmistakable—between him and Matthew, between him and me.

Timothy stood against the portraits—completely still, like he was one of them—with a neutral expression I couldn't read. He broke into a grin when he noticed me. We embraced.

"Thank God," he said. "I'm relieved to see you."

"Same."

We didn't speak about the time that had passed between us. For some reason we didn't have to. There was nothing that needed to be said.

Conspiratorially, he pointed out the other juniors: the captain of the football team, the editor of the school paper, a chocolate heiress.

A senior in a navy Yale hoodie shook our hands in congratulation. "What's up," he said to Timothy and me. He told us that being part of the Bones was the best experience of his life, before making his way toward the heiress.

"Too bad for him," Timothy said to me, low so no one else could hear. "Best experience of his *life*? I mean, come on."

I heard her bracelet before I saw her. But I knew it had to be her, and it was: Miranda, greeting her friends. She was a member of Skull and Bones and she hadn't even mentioned it the entire summer. She said her hellos. It was so hypocritical. For all she railed against the patriarchy, the powerful, here she was, happily a part of it. Justifying it to herself in whatever way. Timothy put a hand on my arm and said, "Easy."

She couldn't have wanted me here. She must have voted against me. The longing I had felt so recently transmuted into anger. We were given a tour: the portrait hall, random literal bones, a room of plush chairs where we'd be telling one another our stories next year. On one wall hung license plates that bore the number 322. If we saw license plates with that number we were encouraged to steal them for the collection.

I took a seat far from hers. Dinner was out of a Norman Rockwell scene: Salisbury steak, mashed potatoes, greens streaked with cream. I was unable to make small talk and I let the conversation, led by Timothy, happen around me. Miranda, at the opposite end, laughed with her society friends—last year's football captain turned toward her, rapt. What a phony she was. She tried to catch my eye; I felt her, trying to catch it.

We drove to the Hamptons with the windows down, Timothy and Timothy's new boyfriend, Saul, who was a couple years older than we were—in the school of management—and Megan, a tennis player I was seeing on and off. Saul drove us in his hatchback: a tight squeeze, with Timothy sitting shotgun, playing Bach the entire drive, arguing with Saul about Handel. They argued relentlessly about things that didn't matter, which I thought boded well for the relationship. Their arguments were trivial, easy to recover from.

The address Matthew had given me took us past a gate, past an even green lawn and a fountain. Matthew and Otto sat in rocking chairs on the porch.

We were clowns in a clown car: four adults emerging from a too-small vehicle. Megan fit right in, with her expressive, big green eyes, pearls around her neck, and pink polo shirt the color of cut grapefruit. In fact her family had a house like this, I knew, in Rhode Island: enormous and perched high on the rocks overlooking the water, signs on the gates that said "NO TRESPASSING."

Introductions were made. Otto's hair and glasses were both silver. He was a mirror image of his portrait. He spoke to me warmly, and yet his gaze unnerved me, as though he were assessing me. There was so much I needed to ask him.

"How was the drive?" he asked.

"Argumentative," Timothy responded for me, noticing my nervousness, and we all laughed.

We moved as a group. In the kitchen, we drank glasses of unsweetened iced tea. I never really understood the point of iced tea, which seemed worse than water. In each of our rooms—one for Timothy and Saul, one for Megan and me—was a panoramic view of the Atlantic. We played a game of touch football, then tennis, which Megan creamed us in. We lay stretched on the beach. Timothy was the only person who could read tomes while sunbathing. While the rest of us grew sleepy in the hot sun, he held up a thousand-page historical novel.

For dinner, the chef laid out grilled prawns and corn on the cob that we ate messily, butter dripping down our arms.

Megan and I fucked in the pool house, and she gasped quietly when she came. She gave astonishing, luxurious blow jobs, sometimes insisting on them, as though she kept an orgasm ledger in her head. We spent mornings with our legs wrapped around each other. Her hair stayed sticky from the salt water. She was beautiful, but I knew she wouldn't be anything to me—that we wouldn't mean anything to each other, in the end.

On our last morning, Matthew announced he would take everyone sailing. We filled a cooler with champagne and bottled water, wrapped flutes in linen napkins.

"Is Otto going?" I asked.

"No," Matthew said.

So I stayed behind. I waited in the kitchen for Otto, nervously refilling my cup with coffee, which increased my nervousness. He smiled, seeing me. We hadn't ever been alone together.

"I hoped you would stay," he said. "Let's have a chat."

I nodded. He gestured at me to follow him to the living room. I didn't sit beside him. I remarked on the weather, unsure of where to begin.

Finally, I asked, "Why did you do it?"

"There it is," Otto said. He had politely listened as I commented on the clouds. "We had the best of intentions, please believe that. We wanted to eliminate genetic disease passed down by one parent. We were so hopeful. It meant we could ensure healthy lives for those who were doomed to unhealthy ones. Can you understand that?"

I didn't respond.

"We gave the therapy to our children, your mother and my son Thomas, because we had faith in it. We believed it would improve their lives. If it had succeeded as we intended, your mother would have never known. Perhaps Thomas would still be alive."

Otto paused, collecting himself.

"When your parents were trying to conceive you, it was our second chance. An opportunity to finish what we began. We wanted to make things right. And it was a success. Here you are." He smiled then, and touched my shoulder.

"So it worked. It works." My coffee was cold now. I drank it anyway.

"Not only did it work, the results were beyond our wildest dreams. You took after Matthew so utterly. You are living proof that we can change outcomes, for the better. No one needs to suffer undesirable heritable diseases."

What he said made me feel special. My existence was proof that fates didn't have to be inevitable. How many lives might be changed because of me, my life? I had wanted to do something worthwhile, and here Otto was telling me I already had.

Matthew gave me a set of keys. I came back to the Hamptons with Timothy and Saul, and Timothy without Saul. Each time, I brought a different girl. Whoever it was—whatever girl—was irrelevant. We would swim and we would sail and we would play tennis. She would wear borrowed tennis whites, never asking why there were clothes in her size in the guest-room dresser. I attracted, like a bright bulb to moths, those who thought they could mend what was broken in me. I began to recognize the breakups before they happened. She would summon me, tears in her eyes. A litany would be voiced: I was distant, incapable of intimacy, closed off. To me it felt like the opposite: There was so much inside me it was overwhelming; I didn't know how to begin to communicate it. They asked what I'd always wondered about myself: What was wrong with me, that I was incapable of closeness?

On a day in spring, before finals, I came alone. Otto and Matthew were sitting together on the porch when I pulled my borrowed car into the driveway. The sight was striking: two lean figures, like different versions of the same man. And I was the third, resembling them uncannily, too.

"Why isn't Samuel ever here?" I asked.

"He's with his friends," Matthew said.

"He prefers their company," Otto added.

A deer had fallen into the pool. It was grotesque, getting it out. It took the two of us, Matthew and me both, to lift it. Animal services came to pick up the bloated corpse. Cleaning the pool, I found an earring, a golden clover, that I put into my pocket. It was four leaves—lucky—the logo of a jewelry company that rich girls wore. It could have been Megan's, or Clara's, or Molly's.

We sat in the sun beside the pool and watched while men drained it. I couldn't stop thinking about the drowned deer and how it must have felt, in its last moments, trapped in the water, a completely wrong atmosphere.

The pool was refilled, rechlorinated. Matthew swam laps. He seemed thinner; I could make out the curves of his ribs, like prison bars keeping the soft things inside. His skeleton would outlast his tissues and skin, possibly survive several geologic eras. The mounds of bleached shells at John's oyster farm had been there for thousands of years. Matthew emerged from the pool, the hair on his legs pasted to them. I so rarely saw his legs, and noticed that his knees were knobbed, turned in—the same way mine were.

We sat at a small round table, outdoors, the three of us. My family had never resembled me and now it did.

Seeing each of them was like looking into a funhouse mirror, but instead of making me fat, or thin, or broken up like a cubist painting, I was aged by decades. In that moment Otto and Matthew didn't seem to me like separate people, but like my future selves.

I'd wanted to be normal—it was what I'd once shouted at my mother. With them I finally was part of something, exactly in my place. It alleviated the dread in me. This was my family.

"You'll work with us this summer?" Otto asked. "It's quite a good fit: Your interest in the sciences. Your language skills. It would be an honor to have you."

Matthew had told me that he and Otto once had a difficult relationship. But Matthew saw, now, that he had meant well. Otto had wanted to spare his son—Matthew's brother—pain. It didn't work then, but it could now. Here I was, the living proof.

I'd wanted to do something—to be someone. I didn't want to be like my mother, running from what she was afraid of. Matthew and Otto were trying to change lives, change the world. Through science and technology, the foundation's mission was to help people everywhere live healthy and productive lives. I could be part of that.

It was pleasurable, hearing us referred to as a group—like having a drink that bloomed warmly. I thought of Samuel. I wondered if he even knew about my existence. He wasn't here, and without him, I could so easily think of them as my father, my grandfather. Mine alone.

"Yes," I said. "Yes, of course."

༄

It was the same city, but I was a changed person in it: someone who could navigate the subway system, who walked quickly, unfazed by odd happenings. It was strange, how used to it all I now was. How, at Matthew's condo, I greeted Mario by name. How, when he asked questions about my life, I could respond with questions of my own: how were his wife, his child, the new one on the way—a girl, this time.

How the apartment no longer stunned me with its dimensions, even though it was triple the size of the one I'd shared with Miranda and her roommates—bigger than any living space in New York should rightly be; how I could sprawl out on the couch without feeling like I wasn't supposed to be there. How quickly, I just mean, someone can get used to things.

One night I went to my old restaurant and sat at the bar. Miranda was here, somewhere in the city. She'd always planned to move to New York after graduation. Now she had another reason to: Eamon.

Georgie and Harriet were delighted to see me. Harriet placed an old-fashioned before me, made by the new bartender. He wasn't as good, she confided. They insisted I didn't pay, and I left double what the drink cost in tips.

The foundation's many projects included vaccination campaigns; addressing health inequities; screening against diseases in utero, like Down syndrome and spina bifida, in poorer nations; and more. Finally I was doing something worthwhile. And my coworkers were remarkable people. Our debates and discussions struck me as more consequential than the ones we had at school, arguing about long-dead philosophers like Hume and Bentham. My coworkers ranged in age and upbringing; the scope of what we talked about felt bigger. It wasn't theoretical. Some of their projects wouldn't come to fruition for another twenty or thirty years, if that. I admired their patience, their commitment. I wanted to be like them.

With the Maiers, I could do more than Miranda, with all her lip service. I thought of my mother: We volunteered every Christmas, serving food to the same forty men, year after year. It wasn't enough. Our generation faced so many threats, and it was urgent we do something of service. Working with the Maiers, I finally would.

There were two types of people, from what I could tell. In the first group were people who felt like they had to earn their existence. The other group took life less seriously. I envied the second category but couldn't help that I was a member of the first.

Two weeks into the job, Samuel started, too.

He walked in breezily. He was familiar with the building's layout, having been brought here as a child. He held a Danish in a paper bag, taking bites of it with nonchalance, not even asking if he could. The crumbs fell to the carpeted floor and he didn't notice, or maybe didn't care. On my first day, I'd eaten a granola bar in the bathroom.

I was on my way to his office—to Matthew's office—when Samuel stepped in my path. Did he recognize me from the night I had served him scotch? I wondered what our father had told him.

Samuel stood before me, wiped the pastry grease from his hand onto his pants. I could feel myself flinch at his carelessness. He probably sent everything to the dry cleaner. I ignored dry-cleaning tags and never washed my single suit.

"You," he said, and put out his hand to shake mine. "Hey. I'm Sam."

Samuel—Sam—placed his black leather messenger bag on his desk. He was assigned to the cubicle diagonal to mine. I was six inches taller than he was, a full head and shoulders. We couldn't see each other when we were sitting down—this was a relief—but when I stood I could see his dark hair, his pale part, over the partition.

He was about to start his freshman year at Penn and would be interning with the foundation's PR team. I tried making small talk. It was a middle-aged thing to do—remarking on the weather—and he didn't bother dignifying my attempts with responses.

I began to come early to work, to miss Sam before he arrived. I put on my headphones, so he wouldn't talk to me. But he always sought me out.

"Doing important work, are you?" Sam would say. There was a current under whatever he said to me, live like a wire. All I needed was to avoid activating it.

He was easily bored. He was given tasks that he grew tired of quickly. From nine to five he harassed his coworkers, daring them to find his jokes unfunny. They always laughed uncomfortably.

Day after day, Matthew remained cloistered in his office, door shut, his secretary stationed outside like a bodyguard. On occasion he requested me, but I hated being summoned. Sam was always watching. Once, accidentally meeting his gaze, I saw it clearly: the anger that I had been invited, and he had not.

Sam wasn't a hard worker. Matthew said this to me with disappointment. We were in his office, and he spoke quietly. Sam was interning here only because he lacked other options. He was irritable and wasn't personable—somehow both lazy and aggressive.

"We spoiled him," Matthew said to me, as though I would understand, as though I weren't also his child.

Nervously, I looked to the closed door. Sam had seen me enter the office, and I didn't want to stay long. I wanted it to appear as though it were just a routine check-in, nothing special.

"He's young," I said quickly. "People change."

Matthew had never introduced me as his son, not to anyone in the office. He'd never spoken to Sam and me together, like we were brothers. And yet there was nothing that needed to be said. Our resemblance was obvious—unmistakable.

It felt unfair, that through no fault of my own I was the son Matthew preferred. I hadn't sought the role. What I wanted was to work in peace. I would have happily been anyone else, without any special accommodations, out of Sam's watchful gaze.

CHAPTER 19

IN LATE SUMMER, the office was sparser—people on vacations. The few who were present high-fived Sam, gave him slaps on the back. He'd just made a television appearance on a morning show, announcing a new scholarship program that would send DC's poorest STEM-oriented students to college.

Sam was still wearing his TV makeup. His suit was tight and fitted, and I could feel the heat of his body through it. He kept glancing at Matthew's office door, which stayed closed.

He announced that we were going to lunch to celebrate. We asked Matthew's secretary if he could join us. She apologized. Matthew was occupied, with meetings scheduled for the rest of the day.

"Could he cancel his lunch plans?" I asked her quietly. "It would mean a lot to Sam."

"I'm sorry," she said. "He can't."

At the restaurant, Sam ordered two bottles of the most expensive Napa cabernet on the menu. One coworker, realizing this would be a feast he wouldn't be financially responsible for, ordered surf and turf—lobster and filet mignon—and everyone else followed suit. I could see Sam straining to be happy, resolving to himself that he wouldn't let our father's lack of approval detract from his pleasure.

Back at the office after lunch, we were all tipsy. Matthew remained behind his closed door, inaccessible. Again, I saw Sam look to it. Through the glass door, our father held a phone to his head, high-rises behind him, reflective and iridescent as mother-of-pearl. He must have known we were outside, looking in. I could see how the lack of acknowledgment destroyed Sam, how all he wanted was to please. And how Matthew's withholding eclipsed his joy.

"We're going out tonight," Sam said to me. It wasn't a question.

He called it celebrating, but it was something else. Sam was bellowing, demanding we all keep up with his drinking. Fear of him sobered us. He slurred pronouncements about each of us and we were expected to laugh at his every joke, even when we were hurt by them. I had a pretty face and no personality, for example. One by one our coworkers quietly peeled off.

By midnight, it was just the two of us. We'd wound up at the restaurant, my restaurant, because Sam wanted the steak frites. I'd been counting his drinks and lost track. I'd stopped at three, knowing it would be left to me to get him home. I excused myself to go to the restroom and found Harriet holding a bouquet of smudged wineglasses, each with a slanting pool of liquid at its base, ruby and gold. I asked her to make Sam's drinks weaker, and to give me club soda dressed with limes, faux gin and tonics.

Sam downed his weakened scotch and soda in two swallows.

"I heard a rumor you grew up poor," he said.

"We weren't poor. Middle-class, I guess?"

"Tell me about your science bullshit," he said, leaning forward. "I'm kidding, I'm kidding. Seriously, I want to know. What do you do all day? Chinese stuff?"

"Working with the Beijing team, yeah."

"Because you speak Chinese."

"We're working on vaccines. The idea is China could be a global partner in making inexpensive vaccines for developing nations. So we're better prepared for the next pandemic."

"Planning to save the world, huh?" Sam smirked.

He was making me uncomfortable. Sam never looked at me and now he met my eye challengingly. If I was honest with myself, he was right to suspect that I thought I was better than him.

When the check came, Sam slid it to me, wanting to be cruel, knowing I couldn't afford to be as cavalier with money as he could. It came to nearly four hundred dollars for weak drinks and club soda. I must have looked stricken, because Harriet, observing the encounter, took my credit card and handed it back to me uncharged, the tab comped, the receipt reduced to zeros.

Sam's favorite dive bar was two blocks away and he careened to it. On the sidewalk, giggling girls made way for him, and in response, he flashed his oily grin in their direction.

A champagne-colored Camry was parked on the street. It had a California license plate, 322 in its sequence—the Skull and Bones number. The plate holder said "Botany is bitchin."

"I need this," I told Sam.

I kneeled and unscrewed it quickly, letting the screws fall to the ground. I tucked the plate beneath my armpit.

"Oh shit." Sam laughed. "You're more fun than I thought."

A cop on the corner, dressed in blue, was busy pressing a man against the hood of his car. He didn't notice us.

The bar was dim, thick with bodies, and smelling of tomorrow already—the spilled-beer scent. Beneath our booth, though not as discreetly as he thought, Sam took out a legal pad and cut lines of coke onto it with his false driver's license, the same license he'd shown me last year—the one that said he was twenty-four now. He was eighteen.

He looked like a child. Bartenders must have known to just go along with him, with whatever he wanted, because he was rich and, more important, irresponsible. He would buy expensive drink after expensive drink, even after the point where it didn't matter—when he would have drunk anything, didn't appreciate anything top-shelf.

"Let me buy you another," he said.

"Just water."

"Come on, man."

Already it was clear he wouldn't take no for an answer. I shook my head and he set the bourbon before me. He drank his drink in one swallow and set the glass down loudly, wetting my hand with stray drops from it.

"What's it like?" Sam asked. He leaned back into the booth and crossed his arms.

"What's what like?" I repeated, confused.

"Being the favorite son. Seems nice."

"That's not—"

"Don't act like you don't fucking know it."

You're the one who had him, I wanted to argue. *You got a whole life with him.*

Sam sucked up half the coke and was now handing me his rolled-up bill with an expectant expression. I did the coke and downed the bourbon.

"Come on," he repeated, impatient. "It's like he needs proof that I'm worth it."

"Worth what?"

"I'll never be good enough for him. He thinks I'm a waste of fucking, I don't know, oxygen."

His eyes were bloodshot, marbled with red. His voice had a wobble in it, like he was about to cry.

"Sam, he loves you," I said.

"You know what?" Sam said. "Fuck him." He never said *our father.*

All he'd wanted was approval, and it had been withheld. How could I explain to him that I expected nothing, and was happier for it?

At last call, after more bourbon, he gave me a drunk's hug, tight and sweaty.

"Thanks, man," he murmured. "You're all right."

I put him in a cab home. License plate under my arm, I walked to the office instead of the condo—it was closer, went my muddled logic—and fell asleep at my desk.

I woke up, drool puddled beneath my chin. I ventured out to buy a coffee. It was acrid in my throat. The world spun slightly. I was still drunk.

When I returned, I found Samuel at his desk, with a blank look on his face, gray-purple bags beneath his eyes. The sun hadn't fully risen. Underneath the fluorescent lights, Samuel's dark hair glimmered. I gave him a pat on the shoulder; he barely registered it. Though he had a hand on his mouse, the computer's screen was dark: It had gone to sleep.

I sat to answer emails, struggling to form sentences. Sam was silent in his cubicle. Coworkers filed in, continuing small talk they'd started in the elevator on the way to the office, chuckling. Then the tapping of their keyboards began, every day the same bizarre music.

How many words per hour were we all writing, I wondered, and what for.

"No, no, no," I heard someone say. Then: "Nick, call 911."

It was Ray, his face drained of color.

"What's going on?"

"Call 911 *now*," Ray repeated.

I did as he said and handed my phone to him once the operator began to speak.

A small crowd had gathered at Sam's desk. I stood. There was Sam, collapsed over his keyboard—a string of gibberish on the open email. There was an empty pill bottle beside him, a few of the pills scattered on the desk, caught between the keyboard keys, round green seeds.

"He's not breathing!" someone cried.

"No," I said, disbelieving. "No, no, no, no. Fuck, Sam. You fucking idiot."

I took Sam's hand. It was warm, but so limp I almost immediately dropped it. I could sense Matthew's gaze on me. EMTs rushed in, lifting Samuel onto a stretcher. My coworkers watched with hands over their open mouths. Matthew looked to me and shook his head, as if disappointed.

I thought of Otto's attitude toward Sam: one that had mocked him, lightly. Was it anyone's fault, that Sam was like this? Was Sam himself to blame? Did it even matter, whose fault it was? I wanted to shout at my father. *All Sam needed was you.*

"Are you coming?" the EMT asked Matthew. "You can ride along in the ambulance. But we have to go now."

"I'll be right behind you," Matthew said.

The ambulance siren wailed, loud, then fainter.

Matthew returned to his office and shut the door.

PART THREE

May

CHAPTER 1

2030

IT'S SAD THAT I'M DYING, but why doesn't it work in reverse? Do you ever think, how sad it is that when I was alive, you weren't yet born? All those interesting years you missed out on.

It was during those years, before being your mother, I'd discerned my meaning, my purpose. I was to change how life could be. I was to make the unjust just—to right what began wrong. Apart from being your mother, it was my life's mission. You might not believe that—that being your mother was my other great work. But it was always both, I swear to you: the work and the love hand in hand.

Late last night I called you from one of the city's remaining pay phones, on the corner of my street. The longing to hear your voice had become unbearable. Two drunk men in synthetic leather jackets—the black flaking from the folds—clutched the necks of green Tsingtao bottles and tapped urgently on the glass. My heart sped; I heard the frenzied beat of it in my ears. What were they capable of? One shouted in Cantonese, and the other laughed. They wanted my attention, but I wouldn't give it. Before long, they lost interest and staggered away. They called me *grandmother*.

"Hello?" came your voice, through the distance.

By now we have spent more years apart than we have together. I wondered if you would recognize my voice.

"Hello?" you said again, more impatiently this time.

I wanted to say that I was sorry. I wanted to explain my many reasons for failing you. I wanted to insist on the goodness of my intentions: I believed I was doing what was best for you.

Lily, I would say. America was a place that made promises. In America, a farmer's daughter could become a scientist. In America, parents hid their disappointment in their children. But I was a poor actress. Your father said that to me, once. I hid my disappointment without success. I hadn't realized that, as an American child and a Chinese mother, our difficulty communicating would always be insurmountable. But I could have tried harder. I regret it every day.

Your voice traveled through the phone.

"Fuck you," you muttered, before hanging up.

When you are angry, you remind me of myself.

Early in San Francisco, the old women like me are already awake, lifting the lids of aqua-colored bins in search of usable cans and bottles. Ragged men and women without homes sleep on the streets, cuddled with their dogs, whose resigned faces rest on their paws. Officially, it's summer. Here, that means cold. The morning smells of eucalyptus and car exhaust, the sour-alcohol scent of empty bottles.

I stop a young mother, pushing a stroller, about to throw a bottle into the trash.

"May I have that?" I ask.

She looks stunned—startled by my command of English, I think— and hands the bottle to me. It is glass, with rounded shoulders, a vessel for expensive tea. I place it in my wheeled cart.

Hurriedly she pushes her baby away from me. What is it about me, I wonder, that makes her uncomfortable? My age? My apparent poverty? Seeing me, does she worry I'm who she might, one day, become?

Year after year strollers grow more complicated, made of harder and harder plastic, cushioned to oblivion—as though babies could know or care. The complicated strollers are not for the babies, but for the parents themselves. They believe they're making decisions—the decision to "start a family," it is commonly said—when in actuality they control nothing, nothing but the stroller they choose, how much money they spend.

I wasn't any different. I pushed you around the harbor in the nicest stroller we could afford, lined with plaid flannel, even though you were born in June and the flannel was unnecessary, in those first months of your life. I loved that you came in June. *After May*, I whispered to you.

A few blocks away, I notice an identical stroller on the street, a piece of printer paper taped to it: "FREE." It's been marked with neon-green graffiti. I don't take it, of course. I know its value but have no use for it. To someone with no use for it, it is garbage.

You weren't breathing, when you were born.

What I've wondered is if it would have been better if you'd died. I wouldn't have wronged you as I have. I wouldn't have had to make the choices I made.

The umbilical cord was wrapped tightly around your neck. A nurse removed it, and we watched you, awaiting your cry. It was as though you took one look at the world and decided against it. It was a protest in miniature, and it was only a moment—seconds that felt to me like centuries—before you opened your mouth and wailed.

While the nurses fussed over you, I hemorrhaged—more blood than I thought a human could contain. It was everywhere: on my husband, on my lower body, soaked through the hospital sheets and doctor's gown. He tried to act calm—the doctor did—but I could see the concern plain on his face that we might both die, mother and child, and how it would ruin his day.

Life always seemed too short, but now, alone, life seems far too long.

Your son wears a fleece sweater and jeans, with a black backpack—a uniform like all the other young people in this city.

Usually, he's alone. On this day, a young woman accompanies him: a coworker, Asian, wearing the same backpack, with the same bright blue company logo. She smiles broadly at him. Her teeth are small, like baby teeth, which have the effect of making her seem younger than she probably is. She wears pants that even I can recognize have gone out of fashion, and a sweatshirt that's far too big for her. They walk straight to the candy aisle.

"Nerds for nerds?" the boy proposes, and I hear her laugh.

I know he likes gummy candies, but I watch him pretend not to like them, or anything, too much. He's making his preferences less known so that she might express hers.

"I got this, Jess," he says at the cash register, pulling out his wallet. The girl beams, and watches as he taps his card against the reader.

At noon, every weekday, for the past month now, I've made my way from Chinatown to the drugstore near the Montgomery BART station, where the buildings loom gratuitously, sleekly, unlike other buildings in San Francisco. The downtown high-rises remind me of New York, of our time together before you disappeared.

Following the boy, I may as well be invisible. It's no longer surprising that, day after day, no one asks me what I'm doing, with my shopping basket I fill with items, then return to their shelves. All the products are packaged as colorfully as candy: the adult diapers, the cough syrups. Plastic cases trap the toothpaste, lotion, soap. What do they have in common, except someone might really need them? By now I recognize the employees: the Thai woman with the clipped, boyish haircut; the shy Black man in smudged, round glasses, permanent clouds in his vision, struggling to make small talk with the customers. Not once has someone said to me, "Ma'am." Not once has someone asked if I can be helped to find what I need.

It hardly matters, what an old woman is up to. Whereas eyes follow him, as if it's easier, gravitationally, to affix one's attention to the young and beautiful.

People once looked at me the way they look at him, with open and interested faces. It was that way for me, before.

I have come to learn certain facts about him. The biotechnology startup where he works occupies four of the topmost floors of a nearby high-rise. Every day, I walk past the building. Its windows mirror the sky—its blueness or grayness, strewn with clouds, puffy or flat or fast moving. It's confounding; the birds fly into it.

Dead thrushes and sparrows collect at the base of the building, ringing it. Migrants, going north to breed, or south to winter, traveling by night, by the moon and the stars. Mornings, janitors dispose of the winged corpses before the young people arrive for their workday.

With the tower making doubles of everything—double moon, double stars—how are any of us supposed to know which way to go?

On occasion he calls you, leaving work: "Hi, Mom," he says. "Nothing much." Sometimes I am close enough to learn about you both this way, gathering what he says to you into a picture—abstract and incomplete, but something.

In the hair aisle I find myself short of breath. I wonder if the lights overhead are flickering, or if it's in my head. I lean back and the pressure of my body sends boxes of hair dye thudding to the linoleum floor.

I've taken so much for granted. Any organ of my body could, at any moment, cease. I am a collection of cells, and those cells, having divided and regenerated countless times over, are less able to divide and to multiply.

Suddenly, he's there, bent before me, concerned. He needs a haircut. His blond hair is getting long at the sides.

"Are you okay?"

I say nothing. He thinks, probably, that I can't speak English. Let him believe that. I nod. He stares at me longer than he should. His arms extend to retrieve the boxes. The dyes are named after nuts: macadamia, almond, chestnut. He can pick them up faster than I can. For every two boxes I pick up, he returns four. He is so close to me, and I know what he must see. My hair is thinned—white as cotton. His eyes are blue like the bay and his eyelashes are thick and curled, like a baby's. Like his as a baby.

I nod again and smile, to indicate I'm okay. I say nothing. His friend stands at the entrance, observing. Assured, he goes on his way. It would be odd to stay longer with me. Before he goes, I see him turn around, to look at me one last time. Out of curiosity or concern, I don't know.

He is not at the drugstore the next day, or the next. For a week, he doesn't appear when he usually does. I worry I've lost him. Now that he's seen my face, I'll have to observe from farther away. Unless he's forgotten the old woman in the hair aisle already, which is of course a possibility.

Another week passes. I step outside with my cart to collect items before the trash truck comes. On my own bin, I notice an unfamiliar bottle, perched on the lid, that I didn't put there. There's something inside the bottle. I pinch it out with my fingers. It's a folded photo, one I haven't seen in decades: the lake, the willow, Ping beside me.

I turn around. Nick is watching me, leaned against the wall, arms folded. He gestures to the photo in my hand.

"Is that you?" he asks.

Not politely, not rudely. Of course, even as he asks, he already knows.

"Follow me," I say.

We make the slow ascent—three painful flights of stairs—to my apartment. He stays close behind me, worried I might fall.

My apartment is an embarrassment. There's a smell, like plastic and cooked turnips, that I don't want Nick to think I'm responsible for. *That's not coming from me!* I want to say. Yet I'm not sure what the culprit is. I gesture to him to take a seat at my Formica kitchen table. I clear the paper advertisements, declaring sales on cream cheese and frozen broccoli, that my roommate, Betty, has circled in Sharpie.

Betty is on the couch, asleep in front of the TV. She watches a redecorating show that is always the same: The host seizes a hoarder's house and makes it look, by the end, like a home furnishings store. How long does it stay like a showroom, I wonder, before the possessions accumulate again, like algae covering a pond? Nick watches me as I move around the cluttered apartment—uneasy, tidying.

I brew tea for us: a deep brown pu-erh, earth colored. The teacup appears miniature before him. Hunched over, Nick looks like one of the bears from "Goldilocks." I was always unable to tell that story with a straight face, though you loved it. I would burst into laughter, picturing bears eating congee. He's as improbable as a bear here: this blond, blue-eyed, all-American boy beside me.

Nick drinks the tea in one hot pull, the same way Charles did. I take small, measured sips. Nick's hands remind me of his, too, though in reality, they can't. All of us see what we'd like.

"So you're the mad scientist," he says flatly, without anger. Curiously.

The resemblance to his father is striking. But I can see, too, that in his movements, there is something of you—learned, maybe. The look that he wears now demands to know: *What on earth have you done, and why have you done it?*

I have never spoken of my past to anyone. A part of me wonders: Will I melt, upon speaking it? But I need him to understand. Perhaps, then, he will be able to reach you.

ONE YEAR, FOR MOTHER'S DAY, Lily gave me a watch. She was eight years old. I don't know where she got the money. It was silver, with a small blue rhinestone on the tip of the second hand, like a tiny orbiting planet that traveled clockwise with the seconds. In Chinese, giving a clock is bad luck. It suggests the end. In giving a clock, you're reminding someone of the reality, the eventuality, of their time running out. My daughter, the American girl—of course she didn't know. I thanked her for the gift but couldn't shake my superstition.

Another inappropriate gift: During our first year at the laboratory on Long Island, the board of directors sent us seven pears in a box, arranged upright, green with blushing pink chests. One pear, one chosen pear, was wrapped in gold. Was this pear special? I asked. No, I was told. The golden pear was simply chosen at random. This was a tradition of the company's, dating back to the 1930s, to wrap one lucky pear in gold. I ate the good-luck pear. Though beautiful, it was mealy and overripened and caused me tremendous flatulence.

Pears are another gift the Chinese believe unlucky. *Lí*, the word for pear, sounds like "separation" or "parting." Pears mean goodbye.

Was the gift meant to send a message? I mean it when I say: This box of pears was terrifying. In America, my ambition, like a flame, had only grown. I hoped for more time in this country—this place with its abundant promises. Without time, ambition is worth nothing: It is only frustration. Time was what I wanted, more than anything.

But I should probably start at the beginning.

For certain organisms, it is obvious why they become what they become. Their genetic codes spell out their fates. But it was not inevitable that I became a scientist—or your grandmother. In fact, it was the opposite.

Understand that no one from my village left it. When I think of my childhood, in the southern basin of the Yangtze River, I remember the humidity, the heat without relief. I remember the verdant, vibrant landscape—the green of rice stalks, bamboo and chrysanthemum that grew along the river. But it was a lushness no one had the luxury of appreciating.

If I remember beauty only dimly, it's because it is ugliness I recall with greater clarity. The men in my family were coarse, cruel. My two older brothers tormented me ceaselessly and took pleasure in making my daily responsibilities as burdensome as possible. They put cockroaches in my shoes and dog shit in the water pail I retrieved our water in. They called me hideous and strange. Every day I was first to the paddies, and the last to leave, to avoid them.

It was learned, my brothers' behavior. My father never spoke softly to my mother. I only ever heard him shout. His boys—my stupid, oafish brothers—were his pride. My father rarely acknowledged me, as though I were sick with a flu he could catch.

We grew rice. In every season we had rice of different ages planted. Nearly always, we were harvesting. I looked for the yellowing hulls, stalks bent at the slightest angle. When we harvested, we bent over like rice stalks ourselves. The cold, grainy mud squished between my toes, and not long after getting into the water, the skin on my legs would start to itch. I had no choice but to work, ignoring the discomfort. At least my mind could wander elsewhere. I imagined myself in another place, in a different era. I'd never have had the luck to be born someone else—an empress, or even better, an *emperor*; a man, not a woman—but what if I'd been born *somewhere* else, a place where, whoever you were, you could make your own choices? That was all I wanted. Not a grand desire, just a fair one.

"Someday, you'll do great things," said Kong Tee, and I believed him.

Kong Tee was a painter—the only artist I knew. He had been a childhood friend of my mother's. For this and other reasons, my father despised him. He was a good-for-nothing who hardly worked, my father said. Don't be like Kong Tee, my father warned us children.

A useless man! My brothers, my father's senseless echoes, called him peculiar. But I adored him. No one understood me but him.

What I remember about Kong Tee is his big, wide smile, and thick eyebrows like caterpillars that rose when he was pleased. He smelled of incense instead of the manure we all stunk of.

His hair was full and dense. As a child I poked his paintbrushes into it, trying to see how many could stay. How unlike my father he was. I feared my father and would have sooner leapt into the well than played with his hair.

Kong Tee visited only when my father wasn't home. Like an animal with enhanced senses, I could hear his gait from yards away. He walked differently from my father and brothers, as though he were a different sort of man. I would fling open the door and run to him, eager to see what gifts he had brought me from his travels. Longan fruits came from farther south and were my favorite.

He'd attended Peking University the year of its reopening, after the war of resistance against Japan. He studied with illustrious professors who taught new, mind-opening courses. He was part of massive demonstrations, protesting against the Kuomintang and American imperialists. "No more hunger, no more civil war," he chanted with his schoolmates. He believed that in a new China, men and women could be equals, and that the application of science and logic would result in a more just society. In other countries, he'd seen it. I believed everything he said, because what choice did I have? I was a girl who wanted to be somebody.

It was only later, as an adult, that I understood, from my father's perspective, his feelings of inferiority when it came to Kong Tee. My father was illiterate, and Kong Tee had not only read books but traveled as far as England. As a girl, I believed I was the reason for his visits. When I was older, I laughed at my own foolishness. He had come, of course, to see my mother. They had known each other as children; they were each other's oldest friends. I wondered if they had once been something more. My mother, who was always tired, who acted as though life itself were a burden to be lifted on her back alone, lit up whenever he appeared. Around the time she was married off to my father, Kong Tee had left for Beijing. He had traveled. If he'd seen the world, I wondered, why did he come back to our village? He must have loved her. I felt fortunate that he did, because I was the beneficiary.

He painted calligraphy on delicate paper, made locally from rice, hemp, and mulberry. He gave me books to read, Chinese novels and poetry and translations of Western work—Ovid, Shakespeare, Darwin—that described worlds apart from my reality. Biographies of great men—and they were always men. It was because of Kong Tee that I imagined one day, when I was older, I could do as he did and escape this place. Except, unlike him, I would never come back.

When he was away, I memorized poems, wanting to impress him when he returned from wherever he had traveled to. "While we are in the mood of joy, let us drink!" went one Li Bai poem. "Let not the golden bottle be lonely, let us waste not the moon!" Li Bai wrote a lot about being drunk under the moonlight. This was amusing to me, that writing about being drunk counted as literature.

Kong Tee could be gone for weeks on his trips, gathering inspiration throughout China. This was an artist's task, he explained, to observe. It was an artist's work to be attuned to everything that surrounded him, even when it was easier not to notice—to let suffering define one's life. His paintings were made possible by his travels, of course, to the mountains of Anhui, the weeping willows to the north, the sand and surf in Hainan. Mountains and trees were grander through his eyes. Whenever I grumbled about my youth and immobility, Kong Tee refused to entertain my complaints. You'll miss this place, he told me. If only you could see how beautiful it is. All around us, there were miracles to be witnessed, marvels to be given attention. *Look around,* he said to me. *Really look.*

And for moments, when reminded, I would see as he saw: the dragonflies skimming the surface of the water, wings like alien jewels; the ripening hours before the magnolia or clover burst into bloom, their heavy buds holding secrets before they all spilled out.

I turned thirteen the year Mao's Great Leap Forward began. That same year, my first period came. My mother gave me cloth to catch it.

This would happen every month, my mother explained, unless I was pregnant.

I had already decided I would never have children. What a burden we were on my mother—a burden on my mother, yet nothing to my father. What if my children turned out to be monsters, like my brothers? This was possible; it was in my blood. I would be a childless woman whose dreams were only her own.

Excitement hung like mist in the atmosphere, touching everyone. China would industrialize, under Mao. At last, China was marching forward into the future. We were living through history! What an honor, to be alive at the same time as Mao Zedong!

Mao was one of us: the son of a peasant from Hunan. He had declared the founding of the People's Republic of China when I was four years old. This was the only China I had ever known. To my parents, it didn't matter who was in power as long as we weren't treated badly. Mao spoke of equality, of communal power, which had never existed—could never have been possible—under the Kuomintang or Japanese. The words captivated me; they dripped with promise, dew on new green leaves.

It was foolish, but I thought that meant equality for me, too.

We were tasked with killing: rats, flies, mosquitoes, and sparrows—pests who took food out of our mouths, according to Mao. This gave us children a project to collaborate on—three siblings who otherwise had very little in common. Day and night, we banged pots so the sparrows wouldn't have a place to land and would fall exhausted from the trees.

Flies were more difficult to catch. Smaller creatures felt time pass more slowly, Kong Tee explained to me. A fly could move out from under your swatter because it could see it in motion. A larger creature, a creature like us, perceived time as passing faster. As you got older, time passed faster and faster and faster until, at last, it was over, Kong Tee said. That had seemed so impossible to me. As a child, tortured by my brothers, time felt interminable.

One afternoon, my brothers and I found a sparrow's nest, and an egg inside it, a crack down its center. We could make out a beak: a bird was struggling to break out of it. At another point, we might have helped it. We might have tried to nurse the motherless bird to life with a bit of cooked rice. But now, given our commands by General Mao, the sparrow was our enemy. My older brother smashed the egg, bird within it, with a heavy rock. I looked away, so they couldn't see my tears.

After we crushed the baby sparrow, I refused to continue killing the birds. I begged my brothers to stop killing them, too. My brothers called me a coward, a bad communist, and the worst insult of all—a girl. But it wasn't their fault that they had been born what they were: that a rat was born a rat, or a sparrow a sparrow. As it wasn't mine that I had been born a Chinese girl, in a poor village, instructed by those who were older, who supposedly knew better, to exterminate these so-called pests. Now I wonder if learning to extinguish small lives was a first step toward greater cruelty. Killing sparrows was how it began, how an entire generation developed callousness to the suffering of others.

In the fields, observing the world around me like Kong Tee, I saw that there were more insects than usual. In the end, the "eliminate sparrows" campaign would lead to widespread crop failure. Adults believed they understood the nature of things. The logic went that the sparrows ate our grain, and eliminating them would mean more grain for the people. But that wasn't true: The world was more complex than these men understood. Sparrows ate insects, and without them, the pests came for our rice crop, ruining it. Our already meager yields were worse than they had ever been. It sounds like something from a storybook, but it really happened: Locusts descended, dark and ugly, like a plague instated by a disappointed god.

My period didn't return when my mother said it would. Had my body decided I wasn't a woman, after all? Later I learned that I wasn't alone: My classmates' periods also went missing. We were so hungry that we could no longer bleed.

Kong Tee said I had an artist's temperament, but when he showed me how to dip his fine-haired brushes gently into the paints he'd made from natural pigments—ground stones and barks that created brilliant yellows and reds and blues—my lack of skill was apparent. Patiently, he demonstrated: Certain strokes made branches and leaves, while others made rigid cliffsides.

"What do you mean, an artist's temperament?" I asked. "You can see I'm no good!"

We both laughed at my trees, stiff and unlifelike.

"I mean," he replied, "you're hungry."

"We're all hungry."

He shook his head. "Not here," he said, putting a hand to his stomach. "I mean, not *only* here. You're hungry for more than this," he said, and gestured around us.

"And that means I have to be an artist?" I asked.

"No. What I'm saying is, I can see that you won't be content here."

After the paints were put away, the brushes washed, his words remained. The only biography of a woman Kong Tee had given me told the story of Marie Curie. When she was a student, she could become so lost in her studies that she forgot to eat. When it was cold in the Paris winter, she wore every item of clothing she had. Her health suffered because of the radiation she was exposed to her entire life. What did I care so deeply about that I would forget to eat, that I would suffer for? I knew, even as I articulated the question to myself, exactly what it was.

Where Kong Tee's passion was to observe his surroundings and translate them into his brushstrokes, I wanted to know *why* they were the way that they were. How did a seed know to become a sprout, then a stalk, then eventually rice? How did a sparrow know to become a sparrow? The knowledge wasn't in its mind but in its cells. How had my parents produced individuals as different as my brothers and me? We shared the same dark eyebrows that made us look severe, angry when we weren't, and yet we were as different as people could be. There was a naturalness to how our fates seemed to unfold, and implicit in my existence I felt the challenge: I wanted to do more than what I had been born to, I wanted to escape the confines of our village life—of my lot and luck to have been born to this family. I would not become a mother, a farmer—miserable. I would study as hard as I could. I would do well on the national college examination, I would be accepted into a university, and I would leave.

When Kong Tee stopped painting his landscapes, I should have known, should have been prepared for the worst to come. On the government's orders, he began to paint propaganda. His new paintings were unrecognizable: His landscapes had rarely included people, but now he painted smiling portraits of men and women, fair-skinned girls and boys with rosy cheeks and glossy hair. These were fictional people: full of vigor, aspirational versions of ourselves. In reality, we were hungry; we were thin from the lack of nutrition, skin darkened from working outdoors, and never as happy as the people in the propaganda. They couldn't suffer and stink like we did.

I missed the paintings Kong Tee had done before: the mountains shrouded in mist, the jagged trees. Paintings that lacked people entirely, or that depicted them as insignificant in contrast to the rest of the natural world. His perspective reminded me how vast the Earth was, reminded me that I was a speck, that there was so much more to existence than what immediately surrounded me.

Kong Tee didn't approve of Mao's actions.

"Another harebrained plan," Kong Tee would say, shaking his head.

"Don't talk like that," my mother would whisper.

But he was right. With the shift to communal farming, we grew less food. The so-called Great Leap Forward was a great leap backward, though we couldn't declare that aloud. Famine swept China, like a punishing storm. Secretly, my mother sold our chickens' eggs—careful to conceal it from busybodies like Auntie Siew. It was a capitalist enterprise—forbidden—but because people wanted the eggs, no one ever reported her.

The irony would have been laughable, if it weren't so devastating, if the famine did not kill so many people. Instead of growing rice—which was what we knew how to do, because it was what we'd done for years—men plowed the land in order to plant sorghum.

For weeks, my father and brothers came home covered in dust, their shoes caked in dirt that my mother and I would have to clean. They spent the daylight hours digging graves for the men and women who starved to death: Auntie Chew, who sold us tofu; Tongtong, who had jumped rope with me when we were kids. He was only fourteen.

Aside from the old people, it was the men who died more frequently than the women. It confirmed my belief that women were stronger.

Mao said we would usher in an age of industrialization by making steel. Overnight, backyard furnaces appeared. We collected metal for those furnaces—bicycle parts, knives, tools—searching for shining things, like bowerbirds building nests. The children took turns watching the furnaces, feeding fuel to them. Once we ran out of wood, the men began cutting down trees. With axes, my brothers swung at the same trees we had climbed as children. There was one I loved called the dove tree, because its flowers looked like the wings of doves. I counted the fallen trees' rings, each one a year of life. Many of them were a hundred years old, felled by boys. I wondered how I would look, cut open: Would there be thirteen rings, or thirteen nestled selves?

My mother and I were more alike, I realize now, than I wanted to believe. As a child, she disappointed me: She seemed to me so docile, and so plain. She expressed few opinions and was always deferential to my father. She scolded me for being *too brave*.

But she was brave, in her own way. In addition to the eggs, she kept a hidden stash of rice. Auntie Siew noticed the wok that my mother had and commented about it loudly. Many others had put their woks into the steel furnaces already. But my mother didn't see the point of it. Like Kong Tee, she found the furnaces stupid. She didn't say so publicly—like everyone, she had learned to be careful about what she said—but she never participated as enthusiastically as others did. We needed woks to cook. Despite all the steel being produced in backyard furnaces, it was not clear why, or for what purpose, it was being made.

In the end, my mother was right. The steel we'd made was useless. It wasn't strong or high quality enough to make anything that was needed. It served no real purpose except to waste our time. It angered me, that our oldest trees had been fed to the furnaces, pointlessly.

CHAPTER 3

I HAD TWO SHAMEFUL SECRETS. On the day I turned sixteen, dirty
Mr. Haw stopped me on the way to fetching water. He must have been
fifty years old, ropy with muscle from decades of farming taro, eyes red
with permanently burst blood vessels, like rusted tree roots extending
over the whites of his eyes. He had always looked at me with open
desire, his eyes lingering on my breasts and backside. I found him
repulsive.

It was my birthday, I'd been thinking happily. I was one year closer
to taking the exam—to leaving this place. I was distracted, dreaming,
when he intercepted me. He pressed me against a cold stone wall and
buried his smelly, sour mouth into my neck. I shouted—no one was
near enough to hear me. He put his hands on my chest roughly. His
hands were cracked, and dark dirt filled the cracks, like fractures in
a dish. He was pressed up against me when the sky rang loudly with
thunder, shocking him. The rain started to come down. That day, I
managed to wriggle away. I begged my mother to have my brothers
fetch the water and she shook her head sadly. They would never agree
to it. It was a woman's job.

The second incident, I wasn't so lucky. Nor the third or fourth.
I learned to float away from my body as it was happening. My mind
went blank and my body went limp. I worried I would become pregnant: How could I love a baby that was half him? It's evil of me, but I
would have abandoned it. If I got pregnant I would have no hope of
leaving the village. If there was a silver lining to starvation, it was this:
Perhaps I was spared pregnancy because of it. My hungry body was an
inhospitable home.

My other secret was that I wanted to go to Peking University, as Kong Tee had. I was number one in my class—no great feat, because there wasn't any competition. My classmates, like me, were preoccupied and hungry. School was the last thing on their minds. But I was determined: If I could get away from Mr. Haw, away from my brothers, away from the endless labor, if I could only go somewhere that learning was valued, where I could study in peace, I could flourish—a seed given the opportunity, at last, to sprout.

One book Kong Tee gave me was *On the Origin of Species.* I read it, rapt. China was so large: What changes had taken hold in the many parts of it? How was I similar to or different from someone in the north, who ate wheat instead of rice, or someone from a desert region, who drank goat milk? Our neighbors were Hakka like us. I was curious to meet people from elsewhere.

Each day, after my work out in the fields, I studied for the college entrance exam until early the next morning, only to rise a few hours later. I would have been happy to have thirty-four-hour days.

The days-long exam took place in June. The majority of my classmates didn't bother to sit for it, well aware they wouldn't pass. My father scoffed. What was the point? With my not-bad looks I could be married soon. Until then, I was needed in the fields. My mother, who never challenged my father, argued on my behalf. Let her go, my mother insisted, more fiercely than I had ever seen her. In the end, he let me.

The exam hall was nearly empty, even though there were hundreds of potential students in the province. There were questions about biology, chemistry, trigonometry, literature. There were essay questions. One prompt I remember was: "You are free because you may choose how to cross the desert; you are not free because you must cross the desert either way. Respond to this." I was at a loss, but I remembered reading Karl Marx, who said: "Men make their own history, but they do not make it as they please; they do not make it under self-selected circumstances, but under circumstances existing already, given and transmitted from the past." We made choices in our daily life, I wrote. But countless other things had already been chosen for us.

———

The official was out of place in my village, wearing a uniform with many pockets. I remember the way he walked: pigeon-toed, self-satisfied. He informed my parents that I had been accepted to Peking University, selected to study biology. I would do great work for the party! My brothers were silent and wide eyed around the outsider. After he left, they snickered, bold again. What kind of mistake was this? they sneered. She must have cheated, they said. I didn't care. I tuned out their voices. I didn't have to listen to them anymore.

My life began in earnest when I left home for university. It was 1965. Picture me, with my hair in two long braids, thin from never having had enough to eat.

Beijing was gray: gray stone, gray sky, compared to the vibrant green of home. Gray seemed to me a more reasonable color. Against the cool gray, flowers burst from pots and sidewalks—roses and peonies, densely layered with petals. I wasn't sure where to look, because there was so much to take in. I was dizzy with happiness.

In Beijing, I was assigned to live in a siheyuan with four other girls. The hutong that led to it consisted of many uneven steps, and it took all my focus not to fall on them. As I walked, I felt a mixture of excitement and dread over the miracle it was, that I was even here.

I knew no one in Beijing—certainly no one from my village. Finding my way in the city, I felt loneliness and pride—the gratifying feeling of superiority. I remembered Madame Curie, writing in France: "This life, painful from certain points of view, had, for all that, a real charm for me. It gave me a very precious sense of liberty and independence."

The girls, my new roommates, were in the kitchen, laughing loudly together, when I arrived, holding the bag—an empty grain sack—containing my belongings. The kitchen was warm and steamy. It smelled like white rice. My mouth filled with saliva.

"Oh, she's cute," said one of them, as though I couldn't understand.

"What's your name?" another asked.

I struggled to get the word out. In putonghua, I was Mei.

They didn't have accents, like I did. And they were larger than me, too—their shapes fuller. They seemed to smile more widely. Compared to them, I was a pitiful sight.

Their families were wealthy. This was obvious, immediately. Later I would learn that all were daughters of Communist Party officials. Right away, I recognized them as city girls. They wore clothes that fit well. Their cheeks and lips were reddish with makeup. I must have looked like a child to them. But we were all children.

Our wooden bunk beds were carved with characters from students past. A clothesline hung across the room, the girls' blouses like flags, pretty florals that I envied. My clothes had always been hand-me-downs from my brothers, plain and loose and stained.

Communist officials had seized the Western items belonging to everyone else, and I realized where they had gone: to these higher-up families, and to these girls, who wore pigment on their faces and fashionable clothes.

It had been warm because of their cooking, but soon I would learn that, because we had the eastern building, our dorm would be dark and cool nearly always.

On that first day, they pointed me toward the bedroom I would share with Lanlan. The walls were thin, and I could hear the girls in the kitchen. They laughed; they were laughing at me.

"Don't be mean," I heard Lanlan say.

Tears formed against my will. I tried to hold them back, but they fell anyway.

"Dinner's ready!" Lanlan called to me.

I wiped the tears from my face, forced a smile. It was a feast like I'd never seen. Each roommate contributed a dish she knew how to make. Pork rib soup with watercress. Steamed pomfret with scallion and ginger. White rice. I marveled that all of it was for us. What little meat or eggs my family had was given to my brothers.

The food was salty, sweet, rich. I ate so much that my back ached. The girls spoke with city accents and left food on their plates—more proof they had grown up rich.

Afterward, I washed the dishes. Every last dish had been dirtied. Now I know it was because of their inexperience. Back then they seemed so knowing and so worldly. I was in awe of them.

That first night, uncomfortably full, I lay in bed, awake. Lanlan spoke in her sleep. My ambition, at first so uncomplicated, now was swirled with fear—ink in a bowl of water. I'd been so proud, believing myself to be special—the only student to leave my village—when, compared to these girls, I was unexceptional.

In the morning, I brushed and braided my hair. It was permanently rippled from the braids I wore it in, so I followed the dents. Walking to the campus, I thought of my family. By this hour, my mother would have cooked breakfast. My brothers and father would have eaten first, in silence. My mother always ate afterward and cleaned up after all of them. But my life could be different. Already, it was.

Everyone watched as I located an empty seat and slid into it, trying to make my breath quiet. I was late; I had gotten lost. The chair made a loud noise despite my efforts. I cast my eyes down, afraid to meet my teacher's gaze, for fear that he would take it as an opportunity to embarrass me. Casual humiliation was what I had come to expect from men. But he said nothing. I opened my composition book. My pencil grew slick with the perspiration from my hand.

The teacher was young and spoke impatiently. His hair was gelled and neatly parted, as straight as if it had been drawn with a ruler, exposing a strip of clean yellow-white scalp. His Adam's apple was prominent, as though it might burst through the skin on his throat.

He was describing the solvency of water, its role in the human body. He spoke too quickly, and I struggled to follow. Water has a biological structural role, he explained. Water fills a cell as air fills a balloon. Amino acids, DNA—all these shapes are reliant on water.

"Zhang Mei Ling," the teacher said. At home I was Chong Moy Ling. He looked to me. Here was the humiliation that I knew was coming. "How is your handwriting?" I nodded instead of speaking.

He beckoned, and I approached the chalkboard, feeling my classmates' eyes on me. I wore my brothers' frayed clothes, refashioned to fit me. The teacher handed me a piece of chalk. I was to write notes as he spoke. Eventually, I grew more comfortable. These were facts I knew. I even quietly corrected an error he made—water's point of vaporization.

Later I learned that what had seemed like impatience or cockiness was the teacher's own nervousness. Chen Wen Fong was only a graduate student, thirty years old, a substitute for our actual professor, who was out sick that day. He'd been as uneasy as I was.

———

Every morning Lanlan drew black wings on her eyes like she was an American movie actress. She was the daughter of a prominent party official, and right away, meeting her, I knew she had been spoiled all her life. Others might have judged her for this; I didn't. Instead, I wished I'd had her luck.

"Want to try it?"

She swiped her colors over my features and smiled, pleased with her work.

In the mirror, my own face surprised me. It wasn't the plain face that greeted me every day; it was pretty. Lanlan wore miniskirts and let me borrow one—we were the same size. It was a thin black silk that moved while I walked—even snagged against my rough hands as I smoothed the skirt down. How luxurious it was, the numerous silkworm cocoons that had gone into the making of it. I wore it only indoors, in our room. It would have been too ostentatious outside.

Yet I did want to be looked at. Outside, I wore Lanlan's floral cotton dresses. When I did, I could feel the eyes of both men and women on me, expressions of surprise, perhaps envy. There was a thrill in being noticed by men who did not disgust me.

"Mei is so lucky," Lanlan often said.

I was one of the few girls in my classes. My roommates studied literature and poetry, and teased me for having a bounty of men to choose from in the sciences. From the way they spoke, I wondered if they had come to college only to meet their future husbands.

"It's not like that," I told them.

I didn't need the distraction of a romantic interest. But most of all, it wasn't appealing—the thought of being touched. The truth was I was afraid. When I looked at the boys in my class I could easily picture them transforming into dirty Mr. Haw. I could smell his breath, feel his coarse hands on my chest, mistaking roughness for tenderness. I'd always feared he would tear off some part of me. A breast would thud to the floor, or an ear—detaching as readily as doll parts. I feigned indifference when the truth was more complicated: I was frightened of setting anything into motion that I didn't know how to contain.

Instead I spent hours alone in our shared room, wearing Lanlan's silk clothing while reading the library books that I newly had access to.

I had never seen so many books, on every subject imaginable. It was books, the immense volume of them, that opened my eyes to how little we understood about the world we inhabited: a world that appeared ordinary in its dailiness yet contained mysteries upon mysteries, one door opening onto another.

CHAPTER 4

HOW CAN I DESCRIBE the energy of Beijing, especially compared to my village? The trees planted neatly, the bicycles parked thickly in two rows, the butcher counting change with his abacus, coins and beads both clinking. In the village it was the chaos of familiar people together, orchestrated, by habit, into movements like dance. In Beijing, there was the polite order of strangers. The cabbage heads stacked high at the market and the straight lines we had to stand in, waiting our turn to claim them. The portraits of Stalin and Lenin. Everything ordered and clean—at least in the beginning.

Outside of China, the Americans and Soviets were in a race to send people to the moon. The moon? The same one we saw, hanging in the sky? It was incomprehensible. Space was impossibly out of reach for the Chinese.

What interested me was the opposite: the nearly imperceptible. Biology fascinated me, the astonishing intricacy of who we were born as and became. Invisible codes made us. Our cells carried the instructions with which we formed ourselves.

In the United States, two scientists—one American, the other German—discovered the first codon in the genetic code: the sequence of three bases that coded for a single amino acid. At least in those first years, before life changed, there was the naïve feeling that we, young men and women in China, could do something significant on behalf of our country, something more groundbreaking—more revolutionary—than those other countries' scientists had.

Here in the city I could sense Kong Tee's presence, his experiences infusing mine. At my age, he had protested in Tiananmen Square, demanding an end to Confucian hierarchies. As students we were to be treated the same—whether we were rich or poor, male or female. For the first time, I felt the pleasure of possibility. My life could take whatever extraordinary shape I willed it to. At least, that was what I believed then.

CHAPTER 5

THE TRAIN I TOOK home for Lunar New Year—the Spring Festival, we called it then—was crowded with students doing the same. My mother waited at the station, out of place: She always seemed a little bit lost outside home, without her brood. When I waved, she didn't wave back. It was only when I came closer that she recognized me.

"You look different," she said, in Hakka, trying not to stare.

My figure had grown fuller. I'd lined my eyes with Lanlan's black pencil. I wore one of Lanlan's hand-me-downs, too: a Soviet-style cotton dress, printed with flowers. They weren't flowers that I recognized, but unfamiliar Soviet flowers.

More than physically, my mind was changed, too. Every book I'd read led me further away from her, from the life we once shared.

At home, recent rain had turned the landscape lush. It made me think of Kong Tee and his paintings. I couldn't wait to see him, to share what I'd been learning, to compare notes on Beijing. He would understand in a way no one else would.

My brothers greeted me shyly. Where they might have rough-housed with me when we were younger, they didn't dare to now. Had I really changed so much?

They asked if I had ever seen Mao Zedong. We lived in the same city, after all. I had not. Only in the same posters they saw, where he was smooth skinned, plump faced, the picture of health and leadership.

When I excused myself to study the textbooks I'd brought, my brothers left me entirely alone. It might have been an order from my parents. I'd always resented that my brothers' names meant "clever" and "intelligent," where mine meant "beautiful." It had always angered me. But now I was the clever, intelligent one.

That night, at dinner, my parents and brothers fed me as though I were an honored guest. My mother steamed a precious whole fish, decorated the top in green chives and red wolfberries. A fish was meant to bring good luck for the new year. She made my favorite dessert, sweet taro.

After dinner, my mother and I cleared the dishes. Alone in the kitchen with her, I asked, in a low voice, where Kong Tee was. There was so much I couldn't wait to tell him. I'd expected to have seen him by now, materializing in our kitchen to ask what my mother was cooking, impishly, the way he always did. He would have given us gifts for the new year. I'd wanted him to be impressed by me—how straight I stood now, how grown-up I was, how self-possessed. I anticipated the questions he'd ask, about my classes and teachers and classmates; I readied my answers for him.

My mother's eyes filled with tears. She wiped them with the back of her hand quickly.

"He's gone," she said. "They took him."

"Who?"

My father appeared in the kitchen then, and we stopped talking. He was never pleased when I asked after Kong Tee. But I didn't understand. What did she mean? Who took him, and for what reason?

When I awoke the next morning, it was to the sound of firecrackers, the exuberant cries of schoolchildren in the streets, followed by the shouts of their parents, telling them to shut up. We were entering the year of the horse. I was drawing the pencil across the tops of my eyes, referring to myself in the small hand mirror I now carried, when my mother materialized beside me.

"Wipe it off," she said. She handed me a rag she'd wetted.

"It's only makeup," I protested.

"Do you want them to think you're a capitalist?"

I wiped it off as instructed. In the mirror, I looked unfamiliar again. Or painfully familiar: my face plain and flat as it had always been. I looked like the person I had been before my life had changed, and I didn't like it. I wanted to appear as changed as I felt.

In the afternoon, I helped my mother fold bak chang. She used salted egg yolks and chestnuts in the filling, a scant amount of pork.

But my mother was capable in the kitchen and had always been able to transform meager ingredients into something more. The neighbors dropped by to share what food they had, hoping for her famous sticky rice dumplings in exchange. Now, when I think of it, I realize this was community—this was caring—unlike the so-called communism imposed on us.

Watching my mother fold bamboo leaves, I thought of the ways I wouldn't become like her. From decades of field work she looked twenty years older than her real age, her face brown and deeply lined. Her dominant shoulder sloped more than the other, from years of carrying a basket pole. Around her wrist, her jade bracelet was nearly white. Jade was supposed to protect its wearer and bring luck: The color changed with time and circumstance. That hers had no green in it, was so pale, worried me. It was a sign of ill health.

When the neighbors appeared in the kitchen, they showered me in compliments.

"You look like your mother! So beautiful!"

"No, no, not beautiful," my mother had to reply.

"And so smart! A scholar!"

"In many ways, very stupid," my mother added.

When my mother was given a compliment about any of her children she had to immediately shoot it down, by calling attention to how ugly or stupid we truly were, and then to compliment the speaker's offspring.

She never told me she loved me. It wasn't the Chinese way. She showed her love to me in the way she defended my studies to my father, who would have preferred that I stay home and be married. She showed her love when she scolded me the most harshly.

Once the bak chang were steaming, she turned to me. With some difficulty, she removed her jade bracelet and pressed it into my hand. The belief was that jade should belong only to its wearer—it had a soul and was bound to one person—and so I was surprised when she told me to put it on. I knew that the jade had come from Lantian and that the bracelet had been a gift from my father's family. On me, it was too loose.

"Keep it. Maybe one day it will fit."

"It's yours."

"I don't have the money to buy you one of your own. Better some protection than none at all."

What about you? I wanted to protest, but she was stubborn. Arguing would be pointless. She had made up her mind.

I could feel, without her saying so, that she was proud of me. She was concerned at the same time. Though my parents couldn't read, they had been careful to procure a copy of Mao's Little Red Book. Soap factories had been repurposed to print it, and my parents, like our neighbors, were fearful of appearing indifferent. We had only one small bar of soap that we conserved, and yet we had this useless book of sayings, trite and faux philosophical. My parents had no use for it. If they had actual political opinions, I didn't know what they were. They were careful never to express them.

"Don't worry about me," I said, trying to reassure her.

The regime would always need scientists. Science was needed for progress, to move the country forward and make it truly prosperous. As a scientist, I would be indispensable, advancing China into its inevitable future.

She was silent in response. Already she knew there was no point in arguing with me. I'd always been stubborn, but now I was proud: I could argue circles around her, ferociously, and she didn't bother to argue back. She wasn't educated enough. It wasn't until years later that I would understand that just because I could win an argument, it didn't mean I was right.

There were moments I caught myself watching her, feeling pity that she hadn't been born later, hadn't experienced the freedom I had. My dreams for the future were the engine of my life, and I wondered: Had she ever even dreamed?

At our New Year's dinner, the table crowded with extended family, I wore the patterned dress that Lanlan had given me, belted at the waist to reveal my figure. My niece, my mother's brother's daughter, stood in our kitchen, eating the sticky rice my mother had made. I could feel her eyes on me.

"You look like the girl from the poster," my young niece said to me, admiration in her voice. I knew the propaganda poster she spoke of: It hung in the square, a girl surrounded by roses. The girl's cheeks were as pink as the flowers.

"She means you look healthy," my mother said. It was her way of cutting me down to size. Healthy, when everyone else went to sleep hungry. It was wrong of me to feel beautiful, a propagandist's ideal of beauty, when so many others were suffering.

Despite all my conviction—and conviction was easy to maintain without knowledge or proof—it was my mother who knew better than I did.

The return train to Beijing was crowded with college students. It was a relief to arrive in the city, where I was one of many women wearing patterned dresses. Here I didn't stand out, nor look out of place.

CHAPTER 6

WHEN OUR TEST SCORES were posted, it was always the same: the name Ping at the top, and mine second, no matter how hard I studied. I thought of him as my rival: the boy in the back of the classroom. I recognized him as a fellow poor student from the way he appeared as frightened as I did of making a wrong move. All this, even as he quietly excelled. His hair was a darker black than mine, almost blue, and wavy. No one else in class had curly hair.

He never acknowledged me. We poor students knew who one another were, even without speaking. We sat in the back, wearing clothes that were tellingly threadbare. We avoided one another, hoping we might pass unnoticed if we didn't congregate. A single ant could travel unseen more easily than a colony.

Much later, he would tell me that he was from a village an hour north of mine. His family had raised poultry. On winter nights he kept baby ducks in his shirt as he slept, their soft, new down warm against his chest.

It was inevitable, that he was assigned to be my partner. Ping, who disliked me so much he couldn't even look at me. As though he believed me too stupid and disdained my very existence.

We were to study the lotus and its repair mechanisms. It was a plant both common and sacred, seemingly ordinary—abundant—yet fascinating, our professor explained. Its seeds could survive dormant for decades, even hundreds of years. Its flowers generated heat to attract pollinators. We wondered about these mechanisms, if it might, one day, be possible to splice a lotus's traits with a crop like wheat.

From the lake, Ping and I gathered leaves and buds and pods. The flowers were closed, not yet blooming. He dove to the bottom of the lake to dig up roots.

It was strange to see him in the sun, when all year I'd seen him under the cold, artificial lights of the science building. In its warmth, he was a different creature—more like a boy than the brilliant student I'd supposed him to be, with his long brown arms and thin fingers, grasping the too-large flowers.

Under microscopes we made note of their cells, miniature cinder blocks. A stalk that seemed to us so plain, so inert, in actuality abounded with life—whole cities unseeable on our scale. The leaves were rough because of protuberances, like small hands, that swatted the water away.

We stood green stems in glass beakers. We studied the chloroplasts within the leaves. Like our mitochondria, they contained DNA. Under a microscope, what was obvious disappeared. Even the color green vanished. What seemed obvious to us, to our naked eyes, was anything but. We were blind to so much. It thrilled me: that what was invisible to our eye could be so rich.

I thought of myself as a lotus plant—growing from the dirtiest mud but, in the sun, blossoming, untouched by the mud it originated from. I wasn't ashamed of my upbringing, but I wanted to move forward—away from the past. It was easy, for me, to never look back.

It angered me, to consider what I could have done, how far I might have come, if I'd had the time that my classmates had to spend on their schoolwork. If I hadn't had to help my mother and father in the rice fields or dig for roots when food was scarce. If I'd had those hours, as my wealthy classmates had, I wouldn't have squandered them.

Like me, Ping had had to catch up. He hadn't had the privileges that our classmates had, either. And yet, even as my lab partner, he rarely spoke to me—he shook his head yes or no in response to my questions. He never acknowledged our similarities. I wondered if he thought I would drag him back down into the mud with me.

One afternoon, after our classmates had left for the day, and our professor, too, we stood at our workstations, not speaking as usual. Ping's back, turned, annoyed me. I grew bold. Who did he think he was? Why did he believe himself superior to me?

"Why don't you look at me?" I challenged him. "When you talk, why don't you look at me?"

"Because . . . ," he began.

He tried to meet my eye, but his gaze fell back toward the floor, to my feet. My cloth shoes had once been black but now they were brown, covered in dust, like bread that had been floured.

"You make me nervous."

"How could I possibly make you nervous?" I laughed. "I'm only a girl."

"You're not a regular girl."

"Of course I am. Don't tease me. Do you want me to feel that I'm odd?"

He had tidied up; he walked to the door. Now he did look at me. His eyes were a muddy brown, framed by dark lashes.

"You asked what I thought," he said quickly. "I'm only telling you."

By June, the heat in Beijing was insufferable. In the afternoons it rained, and the sound was like dry rice poured into a bowl. I studied to the sound of thunderstorms. Hours passed like minutes, I was so engrossed in our work. We had narrowed our interest: We would study how the lotus understood time. *Understood* is not the right word—it's a human word. How did a lotus know to open in the day and recede into the water at night? I say *know*—again, the wrong word. Understanding, knowledge—it was what *we* wanted, not the lotus, which only did what it did without our human anxieties.

The changes had begun to become impossible to ignore. Members of the philosophy department put up a handwritten poster that denounced a long list of so-called counterrevolutionary people. We regarded the poster with amusement. We had no idea that, in time, these posters would come to cover every square inch of Beijing.

Every day Ping and I met at the library. Inside, it was only slightly less humid than it was outside. The warm room always smelled of scalp and pencil lead and old books. Against one wall was a glass case, holding carved jade and ivory artifacts. But what captivated Ping and me most was the lotus seed: a beige-brown lump that rested on a tasseled silk pillow. It was said to be magic. It had been carried to the first emperor of united China in the mouth of a dragon, descended from the heavenly realm. That emperor had drunk elixirs meant to give him immortality, but they were full of heavy metals and had most likely killed him.

"Do you think it would grow? If we planted it?" I asked Ping.

"A two-hundred-year-old seed, perhaps," Ping said. "But two thousand?"

When we needed more samples, we visited the lake. Dotting the water were the circles, like plates, of lotus plant leaves. Raindrop-shaped buds held petals that crept closer, each day, to unfurling. As humans we were made of the same stuff, but their nucleotides were coded such that they grew round green leaves instead of our human organs, our beating hearts.

We took turns diving down. Underwater, the plants were taller than we were—taller, even, than certain trees. It was always easier to believe in our own significance, our intelligence that was capable of shaping the natural world, even though I had seen, firsthand, the failure of the Four Pests campaign. To study the lotus should have humbled me, should have put me in my place and made me see how impossible it was to fully understand—how insignificant our knowledge was, by comparison. What could we know? And yet, with the hubris of youth, I thought to myself: *Everything.* Given time, we not only could, we *would*, know everything.

We sat on the rocks, the varied buds spread out before us, like we were women selling them at a market stall. I handed Ping my thin towel. We could measure the sugars in a lotus cell to know what time of day it thought it was. But I wanted to understand the plant's DNA, the very instructions that told it when and how to repair itself—how to bloom and close, how to remain inert for hundreds, even thousands of years. Could we read its DNA, like a language?

"That's impossible." Ping sounded exasperated. "Da hai lao zhen." Like fishing a needle from the sea.

When Ping was lost in thought, he had a habit of tensing his jaw—I could see it, when he was hunched over an exam, or when I said something, deliberately, to provoke him. It was tensed now. I could see its outline on his face and I found myself wanting to touch the angle of it, where the skin met bone, beneath his ear.

He said nothing for a long moment. Unlike me, he paused to think before he spoke.

His quietness gave the impression of his saying very little, but I'd learned he could say quite a lot. When he was younger he had wanted to be a doctor. Now he wanted to be a professor, to spend the rest of his life learning. *Then why is your mind so closed?* I thought, frustrated. I wanted him to agree with me: One day we would read DNA, and understand it.

My frustration solidified into something else, into resolve. I leaned over and I kissed him. He was still damp; he smelled like mud and lake water.

Ping stayed very still. I flushed red with embarrassment. *Too brave,* rang my mother's voice in my head.

He packed up his bag, silently, and left.

My body thrummed with shame, a new engine. It was other boys who had paid attention to me, not Ping. What did I have to go and kiss him for?

In the morning he wasn't in the library. For the next few days, then the week, I continued studying our lotuses without him, measuring the sugars in their cells, exposing them to a range of temperatures. It was unlike him to vanish like this, when he had never been so much as late. I knew, then, that I must have done something truly shameful.

CHAPTER 7

IN JULY, NEWSPAPERS PUBLISHED a photo of Mao swimming in the Yangtze River. In Wuhan, the chairman's small head bobbed, vulnerable. Behind him were his three bodyguards, only their heads visible, too. According to the newspapers, he'd broken speed records. It couldn't possibly have been true. He was seventy-three years old.

Ping was the person I wanted most to talk to—the only person I could speak honestly with. With everyone else I had to layer in false excitement, declare that the news was amazing. What a vigorous leader we had! But Ping was avoiding me. It was my fault for ruining what existed between us. I was too brave, like my mother always said. It would do me well to be less brave.

I found him crouched by the lake, fumbling with a spoke of his bicycle wheel, clearing willow from it, the long branch like a necklace of narrow green sickles. Two weeks had passed. Ducks quacked nearby, amiably, as though they recognized him.

Ping peered up at me. The bicycle, which leaned against a tree, was a woman's bicycle. I wondered if he had a sister, if this might be her bicycle. We hadn't spoken about our families—not yet. In Beijing I was my own person. At home, I was seen only as part of a unit, one of my family. It was a relief, to forget about them. In forgetting, I could feel less guilt for having abandoned them.

Don't say anything, I thought. *Don't ruin things further between us.* But I couldn't help myself.

"You didn't have to run away," I blurted.

He said nothing. He brushed leaves from the bicycle seat.

"I'm sorry," I added, wishing I knew what to say to make things right.

Still he didn't respond. He placed the branch to one side, the spoke now clear of debris. He stood.

"We can pretend it didn't happen," I said, desperate.

I looked beyond him, to the lake. Sometimes I wondered what lived inside—what monsters. I was a scientist and didn't believe in monsters. But I couldn't help it: I was never fully able to abandon the Chinese beliefs in ghosts and ancestors. Or forces like luck, which I believed in, despite myself. I believed, that is, in a lack of it. I had never in my life felt lucky. The communists had told us that there was nothing to believe in—it was why they destroyed our old gods—but belief couldn't be discarded so easily, on command.

"Let's swim," Ping said suddenly—after all I'd said. I tried not to look disappointed. "Like Mao," he added.

By the way he said it, with amusement in his voice, I could tell he didn't believe it, either. Mao hadn't broken any world records. He was an ordinary man. I'd heard rumors that he invited young women into his bed, several at once, believing that sex would prolong his life. They went willingly. It reminded me of the emperor and his elixirs. Every powerful man, possessing everything already, wanted the thing he couldn't have: time.

Ping took his shirt off, tossed it onto a rock. I felt, in my chest, the familiar feeling of desire: an electric ache. A line ran down the center of his chest, down his abdomen. My ears burned. He leapt in before I said anything, splashing me as he hit the water. I looked to our left and right to see if we were being watched.

"What are you waiting for?" he called up to me.

He wasn't wearing his usual serious face. In the water, he appeared at ease—at home. His village was surrounded by rivers and lakes. Swimming, he wasn't the shy boy I'd first met in class.

I took off my outer layers of clothing and followed.

The cold water made me gasp. The ducks approached, tilted their heads, wonderingly, before paddling away. We raced. He was the stronger swimmer. But I was more stubborn. When he grew tired, I pushed myself and overtook him.

Afterward we floated on our backs and watched the clouds move across the sky. Underneath its expanse we could picture ourselves anywhere. Not in this country, with its limitations. Lying on the water, I felt not only outside of space but outside of time.

Around us were the lotus pads we had grown so familiar with. The flowers had finally bloomed—blush colored with golden centers. It was only an invisible code that had instructed them to become what they now were. It felt, to me, that this moment was inevitable, that our own invisible codes had brought us here. It confused me, this flush of happiness, when I had thought of myself as destined, permanently, for grief. We'd mourned the loss of so many people during the famine. In the years to come, we would lose so many more.

I didn't want to leave. If I could have halted time, I would have: I would have remained in this moment for as long as I could—for my entire life.

Ping lifted himself from the water and offered a hand to pull me out. Hours must have passed, because the sun was setting, the sky a painting. Backs to each other, we said nothing as we pulled dry clothes over our wet bodies. A breeze blew then, chilling me. I crossed my arms to warm myself. Noticing, he reached out. The heat of his touch on my arm was a shock. Then he kissed me, so lightly it seemed it might not be happening. And that was all. He mounted his bicycle and was gone. He left a lotus blossom in my hand.

At home, Lanlan was in the kitchen, hand-washing her undergarments in our small sink. The sulfurous odor of boiled cabbage wafted in from the canteen downstairs. Once, she'd looked so glamorous; now she was plain. Like all of us, she'd stopped wearing makeup, fearful of seeming like a capitalist. Her pants were like mine, cut off at the ankles.

"You're wet," she said to me flatly.

I wanted to tell her what had happened with Ping—at last I had news of my own!—but when I looked into her face, eyes cast down and concentrated on the basin, I saw that she was holding back tears.

"Are you okay?"

"They arrested my father," she said. "Those bastards."

He'd been accused, by his colleagues, of being a traitor. There was no trial, only the accusations. He was thrown in prison, and neither Lanlan nor her mother could visit him, or they would be accused, too. He must be hungry, she cried. He must be lonely. She twisted the water from her socks and I helped to pin them on the clothesline, where they dripped loudly onto the floor.

"He'll be released," I said, though of course I didn't know. Angrily, she wiped the tears off her face.

She led me firmly by the hand into our shared room. On her bed was a heap of random objects: a ceramic jar painted beautifully with a unicorn, pairs of socks that bore brand names. She began rummaging through my things. She pulled out the miniskirt and colorful Western dress she'd given me in our first year. The pair of high heels, the tube of lipstick.

"You need to get rid of these."

"But I like them."

"Don't be stupid. You'll be punished. And your books."

She reached under my bed, where she knew I hid my books. She held up the Shakespeare, the Dostoyevsky, the Camus. The biographies of American scientists, with their improbable stories of rising from poverty, defying odds to accomplish remarkable things.

"Let's go."

Arms full of books and clothing, I followed Lanlan in a march back to the lake. Only an hour had passed since I'd been there with Ping, but it was night now: a menacing dark, moon shining weakly behind the clouds. Over my prior happiness, I adopted Lanlan's fear.

We threw the objects in. The dresses fluttered down, like women ending their lives. I'd never seen Lanlan this way, so frightened. When we'd first met she was so carefree, in the way only a rich, spoiled girl could be. And now she gazed out at the water, watching the items sink, one after the other, with an empty look in her eyes that seemed already resigned.

"Your bracelet," she reminded me.

I touched my wrist, my mother's bangle. No, I couldn't. It was all I had of her.

"My mother gave it to me," I protested.

"And my father is in prison."

She was being stern with me, in the way that friends on occasion must be, and I was grateful for her care. And yet I couldn't toss the bracelet into the lake, not yet.

"I just need a moment. Go home, Lanlan."

"You'll get rid of it?" she asked me skeptically.

"I will. I promise."

I watched her walk away, her shoulders slumped. It was a new posture for her—she had never slouched this way.

I squatted. With a sharp stone, I dug a hole. In the lake, the lotuses swayed, my witnesses.

I slid off the bracelet and dropped it into its grave. I thought of the lotus seed at the library, encased in glass. This was a bracelet and not a seed; it wouldn't sprout. Once I had filled the hole, I marked its location with four smooth stones. I put my hand to the earth and promised I'd return.

It was my first time in love, and the intensity of my own emotion felt foreign to me—dangerous, bound to implode. Had I ever felt so happy? That my happiness was tinged with the fear that it would disappear was, I would understand only later, central to the thrill of love. Accompanying that was another fear—Lanlan's fear, of what was happening in the city, in China—far larger than us, and our lives.

Our professor had given Ping, his star pupil, a set of keys that unlocked classrooms in the biology building. One key opened up the storage closet, crowded with broken furniture, dusty boxes of glassware, stained lab coats—the detritus of students past. Another key accessed the roof: a flat concrete expanse with vents spiraled like snail shells.

"We shouldn't be here," Ping said.

He looked to his left and right, behind him, nervous we might have been seen. I closed the door behind us.

"Where better to be?"

"You're too brave." He shook his head, echoing my mother without knowing it.

On the roof, we sat, legs outstretched. Etched into the metal were lovers' names: who had loved, or still loved, whom. I ran my fingers across the characters, warmed from the sun, imagining who might have once been here. Others had had the same idea. There was nowhere else to be alone.

I rested my head in Ping's lap and looked toward the clouds. Shapes drifted by, amphibious: a newt with a curled tail, a frog.

"I'll be Madame Curie," I told him.

"You're in the wrong country for that," Ping said, shaking his head.

"Where should we go?" I asked.

"Where should we go," Ping repeated, trying out the sound of *we*. He didn't want to seem too pleased. The wind whipped around us. My hair caught in my mouth and I pulled it out.

"France?" I asked. "America?"

"How is your English?"

"I would learn, certainly. How hard could it be?"

"And how would you get there?"

He didn't bother to hide the skepticism on his face. Already, it was a face I'd come to love: dimples that appeared like commas on his cheeks, curly hair that was unruly at the sides, eyelashes that, enviably, were longer than mine. His features were a language, telegraphing what he thought: It would be easier to be reborn and experience another lifetime than to escape this place.

The sky was orange now, a clementine's peel. Because I couldn't see any of Beijing, there was the same feeling, looking up, that I had floating amid the lotuses in the lake, that we could have been anywhere. He touched my hair in the soft way that only he touched it, and the sensation sent a current of energy up my spine.

"A balloon," I joked. "A hot-air balloon."

"In that case," he said, smiling, "I'll ride a dragon."

Had I never felt at ease before Ping? This was how it felt to be with him—a deep sigh of comfort. Until now, belonging had meant a denial of myself—a flattening. With Ping it was different. I could be who I was, however imperfect. My brothers' voices rang in my head, trapped like an echo in a cavern: I was *hideous* and I was *strange*. But Ping called me beautiful, called me brilliant. He wouldn't turn away. Instead he turned toward me, like a plant toward the sun. He knew me, even without my explaining.

We spent nearly every evening on the roof, discussing the dreams we didn't dare tell anyone else, watching the sunsets and the green- and gray-clad figures congregated below.

We talked about DNA, about its spiral-staircase structure dis- covered by James Watson, Francis Crick, and Rosalind Franklin. It thrilled me to think that, in the future, DNA could be read. As Chi- nese we knew thousands of characters; we could learn DNA, which seemed almost simpler. Four nucleotides encoded the information that resulted in who we were.

Rice had been recently hybridized—sterile rice fertilized with pollen from another variety—and this resultant rice was better than its individual parents, which were susceptible to pests and disease and rot. What about traits that *we* had been born with? Were they traits that could be changed?

What had life been, before him? It hardly mattered. Love was indistinguishable from possibility. With Ping, I felt more than the sum of my parts—that I transcended my status—as a girl, as one of seven hundred million people.

When I dreamed at night, it was of the double helix and its ele- gance, like a ladder I could climb to somewhere—anywhere—else.

While a revolution happened all around us, it was in love that I felt most that I was experiencing it—revolution, I mean. The feeling that, together, the two of us could change the world.

CHAPTER 8

THREE RED GUARDS JOINED us in the siheyuan, already cramped with five girls—lured by the promise, made by Mao, of free travel and accommodations. Red Guards began flooding into Beijing, and we university students had to share housing with them. We welcomed them, tentatively. They were children, ages twelve through fifteen, wearing uniforms of boxy jackets and loose pants, each with short hair, because braids were feudal. They rarely bathed, and stank as a result. They wore their clothes day in and day out, and shared the same thin quilts, brown with sweat and age.

They were fundamentalist in their beliefs. You couldn't even find common conversational ground in talking about something neutral, like what we wished we could eat, because it would have seemed ungrateful.

Food grew scarce again. The cafeteria served sweet potato leaves, dank and slimy, and steamed cornmeal buns you couldn't look too closely at or you would find mold.

If the Red Guards felt any hunger or suffering, they didn't mention it. They seemed not to experience emotions in the same way the rest of us did. There was nothing they would talk with excitement about except for their love for Mao or the revolution.

Young girls held rifles as casually as they might have once held schoolbooks. The city transformed. Red Guards tore flowers from their beds, smashed pots theatrically on the ground. Flowers were bourgeois. Windows were broken and left unrepaired.

Our siheyuan fell into disarray. Our communal latrines overflowed with too much excrement—the foulest stench. In time, impossible as it seemed, we grew accustomed to it.

———

One morning I was surprised to see my young niece, the one who had said I looked like the girl in the poster, standing at my door.

"Ah Yoke!" I said. Had she come to visit me? A strip of red cloth encircled one of her arms, even though I knew she wasn't an official Red Guard. Their armbands were silk while hers was a crude cotton—too big. It had been pinned to fit.

"Hello," she said without smiling.

"What are you doing here?"

"Waiting for my friends."

I spoke in Hakka, our language. She replied in her accented Mandarin.

"But in Beijing?"

"I'm here to see Chairman Mao."

My new roommates emerged: stern girls also wearing red arm-bands, and coats they never washed. She left with them, without even a wave goodbye. Maybe she didn't want to show favoritism, which was counterrevolutionary—a bourgeois tendency. Still, it hurt me.

I was eight years old when she was born: old enough to change a diaper, my mother said, and so I did, though poorly. She had stayed for a spell with my family, when her parents were being questioned about their affiliation with the Kuomintang. For that year I read her bedtime stories, and my parents, worried she was too thin under their watch, gave her our best food. My brothers never harassed her.

Her face was changed. She'd scowled, refusing to smile at me. As though she had metamorphosed from silkworm to moth, winged and white.

Ping and I sat on the street by the herb shop and stopped talking to listen to the radio broadcast. The Central People's Broadcasting Station was Beijing based, but my mother, father, and brothers—along with the rest of China—would hear the same news I did, from a loudspeaker in their market square. The "news" was often not news at all but sayings from Mao. If it was music, we were to break into a rehearsed, identical dance. "No matter how close our parents are to us, they are not as close as our relationship with Mao," went one song.

Dangerous counterrevolutionaries were among us, the radio announced today.

"As if we have the energy to be counterrevolutionaries," I said.

Ping's eyes darted nervously, surveying our surroundings.

"No one's here."

"The shopkeeper," he said.

Inside his store, the shopkeeper was busy, moving a gray powder from one glass jar to another.

"You need to be more careful, Mei." Ping shook his head.

Ping told me about Wang Rongfen, a German-language student, who wrote letters to Mao denouncing what was happening in China. Rongfen was the same age we were. Attending a rally in Tiananmen Square, she was alarmed: The fervor and language reminded her of what she'd learned about the Third Reich. She wrote four letters to Mao, not expecting responses, but hoping for them. *What are you doing? Where are you leading China?* she wrote. For that, Rongfen was imprisoned—given a life sentence for asking questions we harbored, too.

The latrines were filthy—the city swelling, destructing—and yet what I remember about September is the weather—beautiful—and how the birds sang. Despite the ugliness that grew inside so many, unfurling like seeds, being in love enveloped us, a soft armor, as though we were hidden, together, in the center of a flower's closed bud.

Outside the bubble of my subjective bliss, China was changing. Liu Shaoqi, China's president, had been jailed. At the university, whole departments were being shuttered. Professors and public intellectuals were replaced by those who could reeducate students. At first it was the history and literature and philosophy departments—their teachers torn down, denounced, humiliated. It seemed impossible that the revolution could come to us. We were scientists, and science was necessary. And me? I wasn't careful until it was too late.

On the roof, the sun setting, I stroked Ping's tense back with my fingers.

"Professor Wu is worried," Ping told me. "He's being investigated."

"But the party needs science," I insisted. "For progress."

"There's no logic to it, any longer." He shook his head.

While we kissed, my hands fell to his belt. When he stroked my breasts, beneath my shirt, I froze. I longed for him—the longing bore into me, a deep ache—at the same time my body remembered fear. I thought of Haw—how disgusting it had been to be pressed up against him, his hot sour breath, and the roughness of him. This was different, and yet it was also the same.

Ping saw me hesitate. He removed his hand. I swore to him that I was ready—there was a quiver in my voice even as I said it, unconvincingly—and he heard it. He stopped.

"It's okay," he said. "Let's not rush."

"But I'm ready," I insisted. I wanted to be with him; I was eager for it. It was my body that remembered and hesitated.

"We have time," he said.

I protested—I was ready—but he repeated himself. Another time.

That night, quietly so as not to wake Lanlan, I touched myself, imagining it was Ping's hand and not my own. When I gasped, she turned.

The next evening he waited for me by the roof's entrance. He led me up the narrow stairs. He'd spread out a blanket. Around it, in small cups arranged erratically, were gardenias. He'd been tending to a plant that the Red Guards hadn't yet destroyed. He held a small bouquet to my nose and I inhaled its distinctive fragrance, like nothing else. We would make a new memory, he explained. It would supplant the old one.

I took his shirt and pants off, and laughed a little at the sight of him, looking vulnerable: his lanky scholar's body, cross-legged. The sun set around us, casting warmth onto his flesh—drowning him in gold. The gardenias were all I could smell. He asked what I wanted, and his cheeks flushed when I pulled him close and said I wanted him.

Ping and I descended the stairs, hungry from missing dinner. Usually, leaving the roof, the building would be completely dark.

But on this day, our classroom was brightly lit. Someone else was here. I recognized Wen, the teaching assistant, by the top of his head—his hair no longer gelled but neatly parted. He was tidying, gathering documents, throwing others into a trash bin. Wen noticed my hand entwined with Ping's and understood our relationship right away. We released them. He pretended as though he hadn't seen.

"They've imprisoned him," Wen said to us sadly. "Professor Wu. They're seizing the building for a cowshed—they'll hold prisoners here. I wouldn't come here anymore."

Ping thanked him and turned to leave. I followed. Wen reached out to take my wrist.

"Be careful, Mei," he said, quietly, into my ear. "You're not careful enough."

Wen had been a student during the Hundred Flowers Campaign and had witnessed his professors, who had been encouraged to speak up, air their grievances about the party. Not long afterward, Wen witnessed these same outspoken people punished for their views, sent to the countryside or to gulags, or worse. He knew better now than to express his opinions too strongly. At any moment, the winds could shift. A harmless statement made on one occasion could be used as evidence on another.

"Be careful," Wen repeated, more urgently. "Don't be too outspoken. You're a poor actor."

Wen was right. The next day, our remaining classes were canceled. Professor Wu had spoken out against one of the factions and been imprisoned. Wen was tasked with being one of the watchmen.

Outside the science building, Red Guards, laughing with one another, threw things into a bonfire, so large and animate it seemed sentient. It was as though they were feeding a monster: books and papers and even chalk went into its ravenous red-orange flames. One of the brown file boxes belonged to our classroom. I remembered that I had written, onto the corner of one notebook page, in a rare moment of frivolity, *Mei loves Ping*. The smell was revolting—burning plastic, chemicals, worse. I can vividly remember the stench. The jubilation on their faces.

What wouldn't the Red Guards ruin? They disdained the past;

it was meaningless to them. They possessed the certainty that comes with being young. I'd heard of them raiding homes—seeking out paintings to ruin and porcelain vases to smash. I could understand the impulse. I, too, had once resented the rich people who could own such valuable objects while others went hungry.

And yet I would have been content to covet them. Instead, the Red Guards declared it all garbage. Casually and carelessly, they destroyed history itself. I thought of the artifacts at the library, the ones Ping and I admired. They were proof that hundreds of years ago, thousands, people like us had lived. In the future, people like us would live deprived of these connections to the past.

"Everyone has gone mad," Ping whispered. He wanted to assure me, though of course he had no idea how anything would turn out. "They'll come back to their senses."

But I wondered: Could this be who they—we—really were?

I woke to a loud, desperate shriek. Our young roommates held Lanlan's arms and hair and wound fabric around her wrists, binding them. I recognized the pattern of the fabric—small yellow flowers, shreds of Lanlan's own clothing. She looked to me tearfully.

"What's happening?"

"She's a capitalist roader—leading others down a capitalist road! She should be punished."

"No! She's—" *She's only a girl*, I wanted to say. But we were all girls.

One of the Red Guards glared at me: Did I want to be next?

The Red Guards had taken great pleasure in punishing the sons and daughters of former officials. Cutting them down to size, humbling them. The power structures had been upended, and they could punish people who had once made their own lives difficult.

It took four Red Guards to drag her by the legs, writhing, out to the cobbled square. They'd tied her hands and gagged her, so she tried to keep her head lifted. Her head hit the stones and made sickening sounds, like she was a sack of grain being dragged and not a person.

I followed them, not too closely behind. The fear was sour in my stomach. A crowd—gleeful, unruly—had amassed in anticipation. They shouted generic insults. A scowling girl with shorn, short hair put a cap on Lanlan's head, then looped a placard around her neck. "Capitalist," the sign said. They untied and ungagged her and forced her to hold her arms outstretched behind her, like the wings of an airplane. Her mouth was stuffed with stones and shoe polish. Girls marked her face with confiscated lipstick. A boy, wearing a shirt with his sleeves rolled up, poured black paint on her head, and she struggled to breathe. It was smooth as oil; it pooled beneath her.

It didn't escape anyone's notice that I wasn't shouting along. I could feel their glares. Instead, I stood unmoving—stunned. What could Lanlan have done to deserve this? Her arms, still extended at her sides, shook with exhaustion. I tried to picture the happy girl I had met, who had loaned me clothing like a sister would, when the others had teased me. Maybe that was her crime—her happiness, her kindness. Ashamed at my own helplessness, I walked until I couldn't hear their shouts anymore, or Lanlan's cries. Once I was far enough away, the mob's chants fainter than the birdsong, I wept.

Looking at my roommate, Betty, I think of Lanlan: I wonder where she is, if she has grandchildren, who she wound up marrying, if she is still alive. Betty is an ABC: American-born Chinese. She picks up an apple from the counter, rinses it, and bites into it. That's how you know. I would take it and cut it into slices, put it on a plate. See if anyone else wanted some, too.

Not to say that Betty hasn't faced hardship or discrimination in this country. I know she has. But most people in America, those who are fed and clothed and housed, can choose what to care about. From your comfortable position you can decide if you want to know about people in Syria or Myanmar, with the flip of a television switch.

It was my idea, to save the objects in the case—to reach them before the Red Guards did. Ping tried to talk me out of it—how was this any different from stealing?—but in the end, not wanting me to attempt it alone, he agreed.

It was satisfying, the glass shattering beneath my hammer. I understood how the Red Guards could find destruction pleasurable. There was a clarity when the glass broke, like the ringing of a bell.

We wrapped each of the objects neatly in newspaper, printed with propaganda about how it had been a record-breaking year for grain. We hid them inside a lift-top desk in the stacks. But with the seed, I hesitated. It was not apparently precious. It required explanation. In ten years—twenty, thirty—when the objects were retrieved, would it be obvious what it was? I held it in my hand. It was so plain: browning, inert. Smaller than a fresh seed, shrunken with age. Given years, would it shrivel into nothing?

"Put it here," Ping said. He held out a lacquer box. "Hurry. What are you doing? What are you waiting for?"

A light came on. A voice called out: "Who's there?" Footsteps came closer.

We left by the rear exit, running as fast as our legs would carry us. By the lake, we caught our breath. I opened my palm. The seed was still in my hand. To Ping, I said it was an accident. I almost believed this myself. But the truth was I'd wanted it. Even as I insisted I didn't believe in magic, I wanted it. I brought it to my mouth and swallowed.

Each day I obediently attended my political classes and repeated slogans: *To rebel is justified. Purge bourgeois thinking. Destroy the four olds: ideas, customs, habits, and culture. Work hard. Work harder.*

Meanwhile, anger roiled in me. How could "communism" look like this? Like chaos, like the worship of one individual? I tried not to show it, remembering Wen's words: that I was a poor actor. In the mirror, I practiced a flat expression of indifference to the constant, ubiquitous cruelty. Why was I immune to the fervor? I was older than these children—less impressionable. But really, the reason was selfish: Instead of being in the laboratory with Ping, we recited slogans. What a waste.

CHAPTER 9

THE BANDS OF RED on their arms came into focus first. Then their scowls. Six girls surrounded my bedside, and my niece was one of them.

"Ah Yoke," I said, turning to her. "This must be a mistake."

"Don't speak to her!" another Red Guard shouted—the one in charge. Her armband was unfrayed red silk.

"Ah Yoke!" I tried again.

She said nothing and wouldn't meet my eye. Three girls seized me. Behind my back, Ah Yoke and a comrade tied my wrists together with rough twine. When I tried to wriggle loose it bit into the thin skin there.

They forced me to stand. It was a girl who held the gun, frowning to appear threatening, but so young. I followed them outside, where a crowd had already collected, awaiting me.

A placard was placed around my neck, a paper hat on my head. Ah Yoke still hadn't spoken directly to me, but she was the one to put the hat on my head. She threw liquid onto my face and it stung my eyes. It was a dark, smelly urine, and I wondered whose it was. I had taught Ah Yoke to read. I had taught her to use chopsticks. When my mother wanted to slaughter her favorite chicken, I had begged for the chicken's life. She was allowed to live another month, and Ah Yoke carried her around, doting on the creature as though it were her baby.

One of her friends smacked my face with a wooden plank. I could hear the crack coming from inside my own head; I saw the splatter of red that gushed out. I remembered the way I'd exited my body during encounters with Mr. Haw and did the same now. A tooth came loose in my mouth, and I spit it onto the ground. With my tongue I tried to staunch the blood that flowed from my gums.

Afterward, when I crumpled to the ground, the crowd dispersed—uninterested now. I heard a distant voice shout my name. And then Ping was there, holding me.

"Your shirt," I said. My blood soaked the white of it.

My vision was bleary, but beyond him, I noticed a poster I had never seen before. A girl smiled slightly, eyes cast to the side, holding golden wheat. She wore two black braids and a smile on her face. Her cheeks were a rosy pink. "Work toward the communist goal" it said. I knew, at once, that the poster had been painted by Kong Tee. It wasn't just that this girl looked like me. She was me.

One of my two front teeth had been knocked out. Several others were badly chipped. I was in pain, but the reason I wept was not because of that. It was my own vanity. Twenty-one years old, and already I was no longer beautiful.

We lay outside, in the alley behind the storefront of a sympathetic shopkeeper. A crate served as a pillow for my head. The shopkeeper gave me a cloth and a tin can of water to clean up with, and warm rice wrapped into cloth to press against my injuries. He left the items beside us and ran back inside, afraid to be caught and punished himself.

"You can't even look at me," I said.

"That's not true," Ping protested. "You're as lovely as ever. You're more distinctive this way."

I wasn't in any mood for joking. I had taken my name—which meant "beautiful"—for granted, even scorned it. I believed I could change my own circumstances with determination and intelligence. What a fiction. For as much as I claimed appearances didn't matter, of course they did. It was obvious: Beautiful people were treated more kindly.

"Have you made your wish?" Ping asked.

"I'm saving it," I quipped, "for an even worse situation."

He held me. He risked his own safety by sympathizing. What if he was seen?

"Do you still want to marry me?" I said. "Even like this?"

A curl fell into his face, and he ignored it. He took my hand in his. It was rough like mine.

"Of course. We have our plans, remember." He tried to buoy my spirits. "We're going to be famous husband-and-wife scientists."

"Do you think I could wish for that? That we close our eyes and wake up famous married scientists?" I mused. "Anyway, how is that possible, if you haven't even asked?"

"Then I'm asking you now," Ping said. "Will you marry me?"

While dancing in groups, while being photographed, we were to smile. To show how wonderful it was to be Chinese! I see it on television today: the Chinese in New China singing songs about their great country, men and women and children wearing ear-to-ear smiles, the apples of their cheeks artificially flushed with peony-pink powder. I wonder, What do they really feel, despite appearances? Missing my teeth, I no longer smiled or laughed. Was it because I no longer smiled or laughed that I never felt happy?

My wounds had only just healed—a cut had solidified into a white scar at my hairline, above my ear—when all the university students were rounded up to go to the countryside, to learn what was more important, Mao said, than any of our texts: how to work the land. We were to learn from the peasants; we would be reformed through labor. "We, too, have two hands, let us not laze about in the city," an editorial said. "The intellectual youth must go to the country, and will be educated from living in rural poverty."

Red Guards herded us to trucks. We piled into the back, like livestock. We sat with heads down, arms around our knees. Our stench was that of exhaust and body odor. Ping gripped my hand.

For hours, we traveled, feeling every imperfection in the road. Our bodies were pressed so tightly together that our backsides and legs and even ribs ached. The truck slowed, then stopped. A guard motioned for several of us to come down—Ping among them. I didn't release Ping's hand. But the guard shook his head and pointed with his gun; back into the truck I went.

We continued on. Ping grew smaller and smaller against the backdrop of green. I tried to memorize the road, the path to his village. But was it two rights and one left, or one right and two lefts? We passed lakes and streams, and the landscape changed from green to yellow. I was deposited, with several of my classmates, at a crumbling house in a dry field. This was Hubei Province, where we would farm wheat.

The peasants showed us how to do the work of slicing the wheat stalks and baling. My classmates were ineffective: their pale students' bodies trying to perform the labor that the peasants had done for their whole lives.

I was accustomed to hard work. The skin of my hands and feet was already thick from my childhood spent in the rice paddies. If only I'd been taken south, I might have been planting and harvesting rice—something I knew how to do. Instead I did a mediocre job of the wheat.

Nights, we slept beside one another on the cold ground, letting our neighbors' bodies warm us. Falling asleep, I thought of Ping. I missed him terribly. I could hardly remember who I had been only a year ago: the hope-filled person. Here, scientific discovery could not have mattered less.

My mother's bracelet was still buried by the lake. In the hurry, I'd forgotten it. The only person I knew still in Beijing was Wen. I wrote to him, telling him where to find it: by the lake, at the base of the old willow, marked by four smooth stones. I wasn't certain I could trust him, that he wouldn't report me. But I had caught him looking at me on more than one occasion. I remembered his face when he had seen Ping's hand in mine—the concealed jealousy—and knew that this was something he might do for me.

Months passed before I received a letter from Ping. He was ten villages away—twenty kilometers to the northwest, where the climate was cooler and they grew tea leaves. He'd found a place where we could meet—between us, along the Han Shui River. We would meet on a night when the moon was full and would light our way.

On that night, I waited until the others fell asleep. I brought a jackknife, not that it would have protected me from much. Wild pigs watched me, their eyes shining like longan pits.

He was waiting where he said he'd be, tinged yellow by the moon.

"Why are you crying, silly?" he said, laughing.

We didn't have long together. Our days began early. We held each other and willed the sun not to rise.

Our dreams had tightened. We didn't aspire to change the world anymore. We wanted, simply, to be together.

"We could swim," Ping said.

I shook my head. We would never make it. So many people hadn't. First, we would somehow have to wend our way south. And then there was the water itself, filled with sharks. Even a strong swimmer would take at least four hours to get across Deep Bay. A weaker swimmer could take eight. We were both strong swimmers, but it would be cold. On top of that, boats patrolled the bay. The risks were too numerous: being caught, being eaten, dying of exhaustion. I'd heard stories of corpses that washed up on the shore of Hong Kong—people who'd died of exhaustion or had simply given up.

"We have to try," Ping said.

"Is it better to be alive like this or to be dead somewhere along the way?" I asked him. I genuinely wondered. My bravery had dried up and fallen off, a husk.

"I'm not alive here," he said. "And I don't think you are, either."

We made a plan, encouraged by the warming days. Next week, we would meet at the river. We would hitchhike our way south. And then we would swim.

It was an impossible plan. Success would mean defying so many odds. Yet the more I considered it, the more convinced I was we had to attempt it. If we died, we died. Books had filled me with romantic images of lovers dying, entwined in each other's arms.

I hadn't yet made my wish. What if I could wish for our safety— our freedom? But there was no such thing as magic. Could I really entrust our lives to a seed?

Wen stood beside the farmwife, so clean in contrast to her. As always, his neat white part. Frowning, she beckoned me to him, then left us. He extended my mother's bracelet to me.

"Thank you," I said. I was touched that he'd come. "You got my letter."

Wen looked as youthful as ever. He hadn't been taken to the countryside. He was still at the cowshed, a prison guard. Why hadn't Wen been relocated or punished, as a scholar himself? Was it that he had said the right things to the right people, or that he was older, or innocuous enough? I didn't know why some fates were different from others. Had he eluded persecution because, as a guard, he persecuted others? I couldn't begrudge him this. He was doing what he needed to survive, and I could understand that, of course. Yet it left an unpleasant taste in my mouth.

"Leave with me," Wen whispered. "I have a plan."

"Leave the village?"

"Leave China."

I shook my head. "It's impossible."

Here was another naïve man. He hadn't been through what I had, and it was easy to dismiss him. The skin of my hands cracked and stitched itself together only temporarily, before tearing again, bleeding at the seams. His hands were pale and free of calluses. He had always been a scholar, a rich boy. I wanted to laugh. What could he know?

"It's possible," Wen said.

He had a plan. In one week, if I met him at the abandoned mill, a truck he'd hired would be waiting for us. I held back another laugh. It was the same day Ping and I had agreed to meet. The journey would be long—twelve hours south.

"And what then?" I said, challenging him. "We swim?" I made no effort to disguise my skepticism.

I thought of Ping, treading water amid the lotuses in the lake, so at home. His face in a blossom, inhaling. His lips against my neck. Thinking of his body pained me physically. I remembered that I had once felt pleasure but couldn't remember the contours of it. My heart was so broken, I felt that at any moment it might stop pumping. And yet it continued, unfairly, a blithe biological function. Of all people, I understood this.

I hated that I had ever been so close to Ping, to now be without him. To have watched him breathing, asleep, overwhelmed with fear that one day his breathing might stop. If I had never touched his body I wouldn't miss it like I missed it now.

"We'll take a boat," Wen said. "It's already paid for."

He promised no harm would come to me. He would see to it. His face was pleading and open. Wen was a brave man, but he was brave in proportion to what he had experienced. He had suffered—all of us had—but he hadn't suffered the way Ping and I had.

"Thank you for the bracelet," I managed to say. He had, after all, come all this way to give it to me.

The days, fully accounted for by our work, passed too quickly. At the week's end, I still didn't know if I would walk to the river, where Ping would be waiting, or meet Wen at the abandoned mill. Ping and I had imagined our futures so vividly. What would a life with Wen be like? When I tried to imagine it there was only blankness. I hardly knew him.

I had the suspicion that each person was allowed only a bit of ease. There was a limit to fulfilled desire in a life. Of course I hadn't been to America. I wasn't aware that certain people lived extravagant lives—with no end to their wanting, never punished for it. But I didn't know that yet.

As I worked, slicing wheat stalks, I fretted. Time was passing too quickly, and I didn't know whom I would choose. The sun progressed across the sky in its impartial arc. It dipped below the horizon and painted the bottoms of clouds in lavender.

I'd been so careful not to wish anything, not to even entertain a wish. But my wish surfaced, then, overwhelming: I wished time would stop. I needed more time to make my decision. It was an inelegant wish, formed from desperation.

In that moment, something strange happened. Time expanded, dry rice that swelled with water. Was I imagining it? The world stopped but my mind persisted, recalling memory upon memory. My childhood: A dog's pink tongue on my hand. A classmate playing a lively song on a homemade flute. Climbing the dove tree, with its profusion of birdlike blooms. Then, Beijing: The fragrance of gardenias; the clear, catching sound of Ping's laugh; the flutter of his lashes against my skin. I thought of Wen, our last conversation before we'd been taken to the countryside.

"Where are your parents from?" he'd asked, and I told him. "Do you have brothers or sisters?"

"What is this? An interview?" I teased, and bumped his elbow with mine.

"I'm curious. You seem . . ." Wen thought for a moment. "You're a mystery. It's like you came out of thin air."

I remember how pleased I was to hear this. I would have liked to have come from thin air. It was the future that compelled me, not the past.

I tried to picture Ping and me, swimming in the cold, dark water. Overwhelmingly, the odds were that we would die. It was as foolish as putting four bullets in the chambers of a gun, pressing it to Ping's head, and pulling the trigger. And then holding it to my own head. It was only with Ping I entertained dreams. Alone I was completely practical. It made no sense, to kill the both of us. If I chose Wen we all might live. It would hurt Ping, but at least he would be alive.

Dinner that night was flavorless radishes and cabbage, damp and bitter. I ate as much as I could, knowing I needed the strength for the journey ahead. I stole bruised fruit from the pigs.

He was there as promised—a truck beside him, headlights off. When he saw me crying, he took my hand. I felt how soft it was against mine. We took our place beneath rough burlap that smelled like dirt and manure. Beside me, Wen snored. I tried to will time to pass, but it wouldn't.

It was morning when we were dropped at the bay. Wen had made an arrangement with a skilled sailor. I didn't understand how he had so much money, where he had hidden it, how he still had it.

The sailor reminded me of my own brothers. A sour odor emanated from him, as though, instead of blood, it were vinegar that ran through his veins. He wasn't a decent man who wanted to help. He was only interested in the money that was promised him.

Wen admitted he didn't know how to swim. We wore dirty life vests. Patrol boats surrounded us, dotting the ocean, shining beams of light that crisscrossed around us. Again, a part of me hoped we would be caught. I would deserve that punishment. I closed my eyes, breathing in the fishy smell of the life vests and the sailor's fermented stench. Land seemed impossibly far away.

CHAPTER 10

SLOWLY, ONE BY ONE, my senses returned to me. First, the colors: the blues, like robins' eggs. When night fell, signs announcing dance clubs and diamonds blinked with frantic lights. Until now our lives had been brown and gray, army green and China red. Hubei had been the yellow of wheat stalks, the blue black of dark nights. But Hong Kong was a place run on money. Colors and lights competed for your attention, for the contents of your pocketbook.

After the sights came the sounds: the honking of cars, the laughter of children, the clanging of pots and pans as the food vendors washed their dishes in tubs on the street.

And finally, the scents: the snack vendors' bubbling oils; the ocean odor of the fishmongers, who unzipped mackerel and croaker down the length of their bellies, releasing organs that stank in the heat. It would have been foul to anyone else, but because it wasn't China, it was as pleasing as perfume.

We rented a small room, lying to the landlord that we were a married couple. In those first days and weeks, I was wary as a cat and Wen was cautious with me—gentle.

I couldn't shake the feeling of being watched. I saw judgment on everyone's faces: They were ready to denounce me. But of course no one ever was. Men and women walked around with their minds awash in their own private universes of concern, unaware of what we had recently survived.

Wen took to Hong Kong immediately. I soon realized that the Wen I had known in China was a different man entirely, one who had diminished himself to elude suspicion. Here he was boisterous—even flirtatious. He picked up Cantonese with ease. He stayed out late with new friends to drink and play mahjong. His eyes followed the women walking in the street, who wore tight dresses that displayed the curves of their hips—beautiful dresses that made me wonder about Lanlan.

I should have basked in the freedom, too, drunk it up in the way Wen did. But the freedom disoriented me, made me dizzy. Where was the brave girl I'd been? Many days, I stayed inside, unable to merge with the thrum of people outside. These were Chinese people, too, but we had nothing in common. They were unafraid—wide open.

Cantonese gave me trouble. Its similarities to Hakka should have made it simple for me to learn, but I kept mixing up words. I'd thought of myself as adaptable—I'd spoken Mandarin in Beijing—but learning Cantonese was, for some reason, a different story, as though I were being asked to evolve from sea creature to land animal.

I found work in a plastic flower factory, where my Cantonese didn't have to be perfect and where I could keep my mouth—with my broken teeth—closed. The colored plastic made flowers that would be fashioned into jewelry or décor. I brought a bouquet home to brighten our small apartment, and the vibrancy of its colors—yellow and orange and pink—existed at odds with how I felt.

Alone, I watched our television, which Wen had won gambling. I remember, one evening, watching the news of Apollo 11, Americans landing on the moon.

I was amazed to hear a mention of Chang'e, the Chinese goddess. As a child, during the Mid-Autumn Festival, my mother had told me her story. "It seems she was banished to the moon because she stole the pill of immortality from her husband," mission control told the astronauts. Chang'e was banished, but her husband missed her: He left out fruits and cakes, and it was why we did the same every autumn. I always wondered if it was meant to be a cautionary tale. I would have happily stolen immortality, too.

"You might also look for her companion, a large Chinese rabbit," NASA added. "He is always standing on his hind feet in the shade of a cinnamon tree." "Okay," one of the astronauts said, either Buzz Aldrin or Michael Collins. "We'll keep a close eye out for the bunny girl." Mission control chuckled in response. For them, it was a punch line. The men were exactly who I pictured when I imagined Americans, white men who looked like they ate meat at every meal. They wore small flags—red, white, and blue—on the sleeves of their space suits.

Nights, Wen climbed into bed, reeking of smoke and alcohol, making the mattress creak. He would speak Cantonese to me, forgetting I was struggling to learn, while I feigned sleep, unresponsive.

On one of these nights he reached for me, stroking my side. I stiffened. I wasn't ready, I told him. I could feel an anger emanating from him, thorny in its silence, that he had waited long enough. It had been a year in Hong Kong, chastely sleeping side by side. He had been patient, hadn't he? But he was begrudgingly respectful. He turned over in bed and fell asleep—snoring loudly, it seemed, to spite me.

I was grateful—I was. Wen had risked his own life to bring me here. But silently, I grieved, mourning not only Ping but our dreams of the future. Had he tried to swim? I wondered if he'd made it. I hoped I would see him on the street, at the same time I didn't: What would I say? How could I beg forgiveness? It was not only grief but shame, knotted together, like a mass of mucus I couldn't cough up.

When Wen reached for me the next night, I didn't refuse. I put a hand on his back, felt the sweat collected beneath it. He pressed his mouth to mine. He tasted of beer and smoke and sharp onion. While he touched me, I thought of the men on the moon, who had walked its gray surface. They had even given it a name: Tranquility Base. I imagined myself there, in the silence and expanse. After Wen orgasmed he collapsed onto me, and the weight of his body, his lungs against mine, almost stopped my breathing. He smelled so different from Ping. Every part of him was different.

At the factory we made false roses, daisies, and chrysanthemums, which people bought to put on top of gravestones: flowers that would never brown, or droop, or need replacement. But how could false flowers be a worthy gift for the dead? When they were neither living nor dead, but manufactured.

We made lotus blossoms that women wore on brooches. I knew exactly the flowers that came from our factory and noticed them pinned proudly on lapels all over the city. The plastic felt so different from the flower's real silkiness. After Ping and I had considered the plant so closely, these were a far cry.

———

My coworkers readied themselves to go on strike. Their wages had been reduced, and they were unhappy with the British government. They picketed for communism. "Why don't you join us?" asked Ngah Oi, who worked beside me in the assembly line, making sure the petals weren't bent. I shook my head; I couldn't. I had once been so brave, but fear was part of me now—a grafted branch. It felt like a trap: If I did anything wrong, I would be punished. While my fellow workers picketed, I counted petals, I removed excess plastic with my fingernails. I didn't believe in communism, anyway. I couldn't understand their dissatisfaction. My coworkers didn't realize how good they had it. It was greedy of them, to want more.

From time to time bodies washed onto the shore: men and women who had tried to swim from China, who hadn't made it, the skin on their chests torn from the oyster beds. I was always afraid to walk along the water, afraid I might see Ping's face on one of the corpses.

My coworkers picketed, and soon, the riot police arrived. Protestors were arrested, far more were injured. Angry men and women flooded the streets of Hong Kong, impassioned by injustice. Signs were hung, and I shuddered to see them—familiar red-character signs that said "Stew the White-Skinned Pig" and "Down with British Imperialism." I would have liked never to see a sign again. The protests came to a boil and then, as quickly as they had come, they died down. It was the same story as always: The powerless were no match for the powerful.

I braved the meat market to buy pork for a dish that Wen liked. I stood in the crowd of women, assessing the meat, trying to choose the right shoulder—streaked with the perfect amount of fat, not too little, not too much. I felt a strange sensation in my skin—foreign, yet familiar, somehow. My vision grew hazy, and I blinked in an attempt to clear it. It stayed foggy at the sides. When I pointed to the piece I wanted, the butcher seemed to freeze, his mouth open, the spittle arrested in an arc. Gold capped his back teeth, slick with saliva and light. His cleaver was aloft at the moment time halted. Standing before him, I wondered if my grief had driven me to insanity. Had I died, was this what death was? Standing immobile in front of a butcher's stall, for the rest of eternity?

After a long, unmoving moment, time resumed its regular pace. The butcher handed me the bagged hunk of flesh and my change— bright red blood across Queen Elizabeth's profile.

"What are you standing there for?" he asked, impatient. "Stupid woman," he muttered, shaking his head, returning to his carcasses.

Trembling, I stepped aside. This had happened before. It had been this way on the night I'd decided on Wen—as though time had paused. But how could that be?

The years passed like hours. At least, it seems that way, looking back. Wen got a teaching job at the university; I finished my degree. Wen asked me to marry him—officially. All this time, we had been presenting ourselves as a husband and wife.

The year was 1974. Wen received word that the son of his parents' friends had immigrated to the United States. He worked at a research laboratory in New York where jobs awaited us, if we wanted them. It was the right dream, with the wrong man.

We were married on a day in October—a small, rushed ceremony. Wen's parents attended, but mine couldn't leave China. I didn't have friends, so it was Wen's gambling buddies who celebrated with us afterward, with cold beers and, later, baiju. He was too drunk to make love that night and I was grateful for it.

In the morning, we flew to America.

CHAPTER 11

THE LIGHT WAS DIFFERENT in America. That was the first impression. It was a saturated hue, golden as the yolk of a good egg.

At the airport, to the man holding the stamp, considering my passport, I made a face to match my photo: the same polite, closed-mouthed grimace.

I could not have imagined a place like this: from the height of the ceilings to the variety of people, light and dark skinned, holding multicolored leather luggage sets, as though there were red, yellow, and blue cows here.

"Follow me," Wen said.

He affected confidence, but it was obvious he was as intimidated as I was. He tilted his head back to consider the signs, which were large and numerous, pointing in every direction. It was plain on his face—how lost he felt. We followed a sign with a picture of a suitcase.

"Stay here," he commanded.

"Don't leave me!"

He shook my hand from his arm, exasperated. He walked—the only Chinese man—toward an information kiosk, holding a note that bore the address of our new apartment.

Men, women, and children looked searchingly for their loved ones. They beamed with broad smiles when they caught sight of the person they were awaiting. American faces seemed to me so different from Chinese ones. Americans wore uncomplicated expressions.

Before me, a woman paused. Tall, decorated in pearls, her blond hair neatly cut. She wore a bright skirt suit set—a flight attendant. Her face resembled a fine porcelain plate, like her skin could shatter.

"Are you lost?" she asked kindly.

My English was nonexistent. I smiled with pursed lips and nod-ded, not knowing what to say. I gestured toward Wen, who stood at a kiosk, shaking his own head at the man he struggled to speak to.

"Your husband?"

I nodded, knowing that word, at least.

Her eyes fell near my feet.

"Is this your bracelet?"

She held out my mother's jade bracelet, which must have slid off. It looked greener here.

We arrived past midnight. The address matched a box-shaped building of discolored brick. On the corner a convenience store's shingle winked anxious yellow light. A twenty-four-hour laundromat loudly tossed clothing. I had never seen a dryer.

Wen knocked. It was obvious the man who opened it had been sleeping. Sullenly, he rubbed his eyes. Wen handed him the envelope of American dollars that was our rent. Without speaking, he pressed two keys on a ring into Wen's palm and closed the door.

Our apartment, adjacent to the landlord's, was up a narrow set of stairs that creaked, thick with accumulated dust and hair. It was a room, nothing special or American about it. We hadn't thought about furniture, so we were relieved to see a single mattress on the floor.

Every surface was covered in dust, and the toilet was ringed. I tried to remind myself that this—all of this—had been my aspiration. Tomorrow would begin the work of turning this empty, dirty room into a home.

I scrubbed the bathtub with my hands, running the water as hot as I could manage. I locked the door; I'd never locked a room before. The appeal was immediate: The room was now mine. I removed my clothing and climbed in, enjoying the heat of the water.

"Will you come to bed?" Wen knocked impatiently. The door shook.

"In a minute," I called out, and sank deeper.

In the morning, there were brown marks at the foot of the bed, where my damp feet had left impressions, like birds' footprints in wet sand.

Wen ventured out to buy groceries. At home, cleaning mold from the refrigerator, I began to weep. Wen would be home any moment, and I knew that if he caught me crying he would be irritated.

The food he returned with was strange: Rice that came in metallic pouches, already cooked. Cans containing soup that did not match the photos on the labels. A bottle of wine, for some reason, when we didn't have a tool to open it with. He dug the cork out in bits with his house key.

"Are you just going to watch me?" he asked, not bothering to hide the displeasure in his voice.

"I don't understand why you would buy that. Instead of real food."

He opened the wine brutally: the cork half chipped out, the rest pushed down. There was a mug in the cabinet, left by the previous tenants. It was thick rimmed, the kind used in diners for coffee, I'd later learn. Wen poured wine into it, a cup for only himself.

Angrily, I took the wine bottle and drank directly from its mouth. I wanted to spit it out immediately: It was foul, bitter yet sweet, with bits of cork in it. But Wen was watching me challengingly. Staring directly at him, I swallowed. I lifted his heavy mug to my mouth and drank, in enormous swallows, until all of it was gone.

Yang wore small spectacles and his hair in front trimmed very straight. The laboratory, one of several, looked out onto the sparkling water of the harbor, which reflected the trees clad in their fiery, autumnal foliage.

With Yang, we would be studying viral DNA—simian virus 40, called SV40. While he gave us a tour I held my breath, afraid that if I inhaled it would all dissolve, like a dream. The lab itself was cramped and cluttered, dustier than it should have been. But to us it was a heartening sight. Inside Yang's laboratory we felt at home, among the microscopes and centrifuges, the beakers and solutions, with this man who was Chinese.

Seeing us, his team smiled kindly. Wen introduced himself as "Charles," in English, surprising me. I wondered how long he'd been thinking of that, wanting to call himself Charles. Where had he even encountered that name—the name of an English king? From Mei, I became May—a month in spring, a season of rebirth and renewal.

Yang was an ideal lab-mate: unfailingly in good spirits, never cross. Together, we spoke Mandarin. He assumed the role of our guide, having lived in America for several years already. On occasion Yang would go on pilgrimages to New York City and bring back feasts from Chinatown. Unlike Charles, he knew exactly what to buy.

While we worked, Yang liked to play the radio. Joyful songs, songs about love. They weren't government broadcasts, they weren't propaganda. But later I would realize that, in truth, they were. They were propaganda for a kind of life that I did not yet know how to lead.

We rode the bus to the laboratory, a half-hour commute each way. In the winter, I pictured my organs freezing, smallest to largest: gallbladder, kidneys, heart. Still, I had it better than some of the people who took the bus with me each day: hunched, dirty, burdened. I hadn't expected so many poor people in America. The houses closer to the laboratory were what I had pictured this country to be: large, pristinely painted, with many windows. Even their mailboxes were larger than average, as if rich people received more mail.

There was one house in particular I admired, near the harbor, with green shutters and a weathervane on its roof. A chicken's silhouette pointed in the direction the wind blew. I imagined a brick fireplace inside, a roaring fire meant to keep us warm, not make steel. Beside it, a well-stuffed armchair, where I could read my books. Where did I get that image? Probably a movie—it was nothing I'd ever experienced before. Inside the house with the green shutters, I imagined my own office, with a door that would close, and lock.

Imagination was pleasurable, because reality was difficult. Buying groceries, once, the cashier was so impatient with me she took my pocketbook and counted out the bills herself. I learned the American phrase *time is money*. Lawyers and doctors charged by the hour. Time was a commodity, like gold or corn or beef. Time could be carved up, like cattle, into cuts: into tasks and plans, into weeks and years. The tenderloin was the prime of one's life. I marveled at the abundant beef at the grocery store: red flesh pressed against plastic, a sticker that marked it as USDA select, choice, or prime. It was so like America, to make every part sound appealing, even though "select" was the worst cut and "prime" was the best. What part of my life was I in? Had the prime of it been used up?

One of Mao's numerous slogans was: "The times have changed, and men and women are the same." But Wen—*Charles* now, he insisted I call him Charles—retained old-fashioned beliefs about husbands and wives. As the only son in his family, he had been treated like a prince, and expected the same treatment from me. I was responsible for the household work, on top of my work alongside him at Yang's lab. When I asked him to clean, he did so only half-heartedly. If I asked him to take the laundry to the laundromat—downstairs, hardly a burden at all—he complained. Maybe he believed his calling to be higher than mine, his thoughts to be more important than my thoughts; most men did.

He made efforts, but always in ways I didn't care for. Our first Valentine's Day in the United States, he brought home a dozen roses, deep red. I wanted to tell him that he shouldn't have spent the money—what a waste it was—but I held my tongue. In the cold apartment, the petals swiftly grew limp. They blackened and fell from their stems.

Day in and day out, I smiled my closed smile and tried my best to be pleasant. On nights he wanted to make love I was sure to insert my diaphragm and make appreciative noises beneath him. I reminded myself to be grateful. We had left China thanks to him; we were here thanks to him. And he did try. He did want to make me happy.

The worries of the past had been lifted. And yet I felt weighed down, whenever I raised a hand, a leg. I felt waterlogged with sadness, anger, loss, self-loathing. I couldn't say which. Did everyone feel this heavy?

What if I had never left China and I hadn't left Ping, if I had believed, wholeheartedly, that love was enough? What then? Would he and I have been happy? Would happiness be the question? Having no precedent, I didn't believe that love was a sturdy-enough scaffolding to a life. Between my parents there had been none. With years, love grew complicated, burdened; it faded with washings, like dye from cloth. For a woman, as with most things, love was bound to be worse.

Why didn't I choose him? It wasn't that I was afraid of discomfort. I'd grown up a peasant; I could withstand difficulty. But in choosing Charles, I had made a wager. With Charles, I could have the life I sought. And I was right: With Charles, I had wound up here, doing work that was bound to be important. No, it didn't make much sense, that I despised and thought so highly of myself at the same time. How tangled it all was! The more I hated myself, the more I needed to prove my extraordinariness. I was Chang'e: Seeking the elixir of immortality, I was banished to the moon.

CHAPTER 12

YANG'S HOME WAS ONE of the storybook houses: painted a clear, untroubled white, with a gabled roof and stubbornly cheerful flowers in the planters on the porch outside, hanging on for life before winter.

"This is the address?" I asked Charles, and he nodded.

It was Yang's wife who opened the door, smiling with her vibrant lipsticked mouth. She was pretty in a tended-to way. Her features were pleasant enough, but her beauty came from the attention she must have paid herself: Her skin was clear, her fingernails painted the pastel pink of baby clothes, and her hair shone, elegant—wound into a spiral at the nape of her neck, an object of art. Yang had told us she was from Shanghai but nothing else. I held my breath. I hated the smell of lipstick; to me, it smelled of cruelty. I remembered, too vividly, the blood-colored slashes the Red Guards had marked women with.

I never imagined Chinese people living inside such a house. Immediately I felt the envy rising in my throat. You envied what you felt was possible. I'd never thought living like this was within reach, but now I saw that it was.

Yang's wife said we could leave our shoes on, even inside. Charles obliged, following, complimenting her on the décor, while his shoes brought what was outside in. I couldn't bear to do it. I took my high heels off and left them by the door. They looked lonely, the only shoes there. My stocking feet were cold against the floor.

On the table, a Thanksgiving turkey rested—enormous, browned skin, the size of two motorcycle helmets. Next to it was a pink ham, glossy with burnt sugar. I had never seen meats so large—this quantity for so few people.

We sat: Yang, his wife, our two American coworkers from the lab,

Francis and Jacob—two single men without families I found difficult to tell apart, with their glasses and brown hair. The conversation
swirled and I struggled to understand it. Even though there were more
Chinese than English speakers, it was English that was spoken at the
table.

Wen's English was awful, but it was better than mine. He laughed
when everyone else laughed, and I did the same, despite not understanding the jokes. After dinner, Yang's wife brought out a dark
bottle—port, she called it, setting it down on the table—and a round,
crisscrossed dessert she said was apple pie. I tried only a bite of pie, a
sip of port. I had never tasted so much sweetness.

After the slices of pie were eaten and the port drunk, our American coworkers stood and thanked the Yangs for their hospitality. I
stood, too.

"Wait." Yang touched my arm. "Sit."

"More pie?" his wife asked, and I shook my head.

They were still speaking English, though they didn't need to. The
Americans were gone.

"What's wrong?" I asked, in Chinese. Always, it was my first
question.

"I'm leaving," Yang said. "To California. Berkeley. There's an
opportunity for me to lead a lab there."

"Congratulations," Charles said, in English. It was one of the
words he knew; he wanted it said to himself. He still nursed his glass
of port and held it aloft, clinked it against Yang's.

I tried to smile, but my mind flooded with worry. "When?" I asked.

"At the end of the year," Yang said, in English. "After Christmas."

"And what about us?" I asked. "Your lab here?"

I hadn't been careful. I'd let myself feel attachment, feel happiness, only to be disappointed again.

"There are new donors. Interested in funding cancer research,"
Yang said, again in English. "They will be retaining some scientists."

"Who are they?" I asked, in Chinese.

"You'll have to learn more English," Yang responded, for the third
time in English—gently, but admonishingly.

I reddened but pushed. And if they didn't want us?

Our work visas would expire, Yang said, at last shifting back to Chinese. We would have to return to Hong Kong.

Practicing English, I could hear words clearly in my head—*thank you, please, sorry, forgive me*—but when I tried to speak, they emerged from my mouth sounding completely different.

I struggled to say the word *Charles*. Why had he chosen such a difficult name?

We tried to speak English at home. We did our best, addressing each other haltingly. *What would you like for dinner? Can you pass the salt? The television is too loud.*

When we fought, we reverted to Chinese, so that the insults could fly more freely. This particular winter—the uncertainty of our futures hanging over us—we fought constantly in our cold apartment, with its broken radiator. We could hear the neighbors' television programs through our walls—the nasal voices of their children's cartoon heroes—so there was no doubt they heard us, too. Our kitchen crawled with mice who shat on our counters, who left only their tails, curled like question marks, in the traps we laid out for them. Entitled American mice.

The thought of being sent back terrified me. To Charles it didn't matter. He could live in America or in Hong Kong. He tried to be optimistic: In Hong Kong, we could resume our lives. We could start a family. I hated Hong Kong, I said. I didn't want to start a family.

Our arguments ran along the same lines. I called him stupid; he called me worthless. If he were more like Ping, I thought, if he were brilliant, there would be no question about our status: The new donors would ask us to stay, to lead a laboratory. On occasion I caught Charles staring at me wonderingly. Did he ask himself why he had gone through all the trouble of pursuing me? Why had he paid for my passage? Why me, of all possible women?

"Why did you bring me here?" I would shout.

"You're such an ungrateful woman!" he shouted back. "Do you want to be in China?"

"Maybe it would be better to die in China," I said, "than to live like a rat here."

I didn't mean it, of course. Despite the many flaws of our circumstances, despite my complaining, coming here was the best thing that had ever happened to me.

The English word *harbor* described the body of water we saw from the institute—tranquil, protected in part by land. But *harbor* also meant "refuge," a place of safety. Many English words, said in identical tones, had more than one meaning. This harbor, which had been my harbor, was at risk of evaporating. The prospect terrified me. I wanted to stay.

It was four American men who came to Yang's lab to meet with us—the tallest men I'd ever seen. Two looked to be in their thirties or forties, with golden hair; the other two were in their seventies, white haired with lined faces. We had decorated the lab for Christmas. Taped to the walls, festooning our stark equipment, were shining garlands and ornaments.

I smiled with my mouth closed, my lips covering my flawed teeth. There was power in being a woman—attractive—but I was only so when I kept my broken mouth closed. I didn't know if these men were the donors themselves—deciding how and on whom to spend their money—or if they were representatives. Either way, we needed to impress them.

"It's wonderful to meet you," one of the younger men said to us. He wore silver glasses over his light eyes. "We've heard a little about you from Yang. He speaks highly of you." I liked the man's voice: There was gentleness and openness in it—a curiosity about what we might say.

In his own slow English, Yang described the work we did, making an effort to emphasize how talented we were, what diligent workers we were.

"Do they speak English?" one of the older men asked Yang. He kept his arms folded across his chest, indifference obvious. Unlike the first man, this one was closed, uninterested, dismissing us already.

"We are learning," Charles said, in English. "We want very much to learn."

"What about her?" They looked to me.

"I can learn English," I said quickly, in English. I heard the irritation in my voice and I hoped they couldn't detect it. Charles would recognize it.

"We are . . ." Charles cut in, worried about what I might say, on impulse. "We work hard. We work very hard. English . . . will be no problem."

"The Chinese do work very hard," one of the older men agreed.

"Aren't we here," I said, impatient now, "to talk about biology?" I stumbled over the words, but the men nodded.

We spoke to Yang in Mandarin, and he translated. He described our interests—the leaps we had made while working together, studying SV40 and its DNA, how it inserted itself into a host genome, how it replicated. One of the older men spoke, and Yang translated for Charles and me. They intended to fund research that had practical applications—that would address diseases, like cancer.

"Will you ask them what they believe will be possible?" the young, light-eyed man said, looking to me. "If they were to speculate on the future of genetics."

I noticed Charles open his mouth to speak and rushed to answer first. I spoke quickly to Yang, who translated.

We were living in a special time, I said. I believed in the comprehensibility of the human genome—especially with the promising advances in computing. Gene mapping seemed to me imminent: In the not-so-distant future we could know precisely the regions that encoded for biological functions. Restriction enzymes had recently been discovered—enzymes that could cleave DNA. This meant that, at some point in the future, we would be able to edit it: the very code of life.

When I finished, all the men were staring at me. Had I been speaking too quickly, or for too long? The dismissive older man had uncrossed his arms and now looked to me wonderingly.

The young man said something rapidly to Yang.

"They'd like to hire an English teacher for you," Yang translated.

"Does this mean they want to keep us?" I asked.

"You'll meet again. You'll talk again," he said. "Then they'll decide."

Darkness has fallen without our noticing. Betty's shoes and purse are gone. One of the table lamps glows orange; Betty must have turned it on. She'll play blackjack late into the night, as she tends to. I don't know how she has the energy for it. Does she believe she'll strike it rich? Even though she hasn't gotten lucky yet?

"It's late. You should go home," I tell Nick. "We can pick up another day."

"It's fine. I have a toothbrush in my backpack." Often, he loses track of time and spends the night at work.

We decide he'll stay overnight on the couch, though he's too tall for it. His office isn't far. I give him my blankets, keeping only a bed-sheet for myself. There is so much I'd like to ask him, but why should he answer? I must tell him about my life before I can expect him to tell me about his.

In the morning, Nick holds his ID card to the low glass barrier and the doors part. He rides the elevator—mirrored gold, making him look like an Oscar statue—to the twentieth floor.

"Hey," Nick says to his coworker Jess, who stands by the snack counter, eating a protein bar, foil slack at its sides like a banana's peel.

He's sure to stand on her left side. Born partially deaf, she can't hear from her right. He wonders if Jess can tell that he's wearing yesterday's clothes. But there's no indication she notices or cares. He likes this about her: her obliviousness to clothing, her lack of judgment over physical appearance.

"Hi, I was just thinking of you. Did you have that sample for me?" Jess asks.

Her glasses are smeared and Nick wonders how well she can see out of them.

"Yeah. It's in the walk-in."

"Levi asked about you this morning, by the way."

"What for?"

Nick pulls up his calendar, on his phone. Has he forgotten a meeting?

"No, he's just . . ." She crumples the wrapper. "He wants to talk to you about something."

"Great."

"Don't take it for granted, being the chosen one."

"I'll recommend you for the position."

"Ha!" Jess says, then lowers her voice. "Well, you should probably find him before he pees his pants."

Nick takes the elevator up another floor and knocks beneath the placard that says "Levi Rathbone, founder and CEO."

"Nicky!" Levi calls. "Come in."

His feet are on his desk, the soles of his sneakers clean, the shoes pure white—they can't possibly have been walked in—and his phone is in his hand, a colorful game on the screen that Nick knows is a knockoff version of *Settlers of Catan*, called *Colonizer*.

"Jess said you wanted to see me?"

"My *man*." Levi keeps his voice upbeat, but there's worry beneath it. "Close the door behind you, will you?"

Nick closes it.

"How was your weekend?"

It's actually Thursday. Levi is bad with dates. *I followed my long-lost Chinese grandmother to her apartment, and she's telling me her life story*, Nick doesn't say.

For the last four years Nick has been working in epigenetic pharmacology, on therapies for heart disease, macular degeneration, lung cancer.

He accepted this job in large part because he wants to prove he can do good, on his own, without the Maiers. Sam is dead. Sometimes Nick visits his Instagram page, where, beneath his final post, a sinister raven on a power line, are comments and emojis, teary faces and hearts. Nick isn't in contact with the Maiers. He no longer wants to resemble Matthew and Otto, men who intend to reorder the world—have the wealth and power to do so—and yet, along the way, have lost their compassion.

"What are you doing Thursday?"

Nick doesn't respond right away. If he hesitates long enough, he knows Levi will continue, and he does.

"I need you to have lunch with me. And an investor. I know I don't always come across as . . ." Levi laughs. "Let's just say I know my weaknesses. You've got a better face for persuasion. And you've got that philosophy thing going on."

Levi can come across as brash, insensitive, tactless. He's aware of these impressions he gives, so Nick is often roped into outward-facing tasks like this—to be Levi's face and his charm. It's his least favorite part of the job. Sensing Nick's hesitation, Levi continues.

"I know we seem really successful from the outside, but . . . we're running out of funds. If this doesn't work out we're going to have to downsize, let lots of folks go."

"How much trouble?"

"This stays between us, but it's pretty urgent. We have six months left, if that."

A model of a heart sits on Levi's desk. Nick touches the heart's cold plastic and it falls apart, each of the chambers. Beside it is a framed photo of a twentysomething Levi, holding a baby—his niece, now a teenager. Nick has met her at the office on a few occasions. Levi spoils her: a car, a clothing allowance, all from her uncle Levi. In the photo, the younger Levi is elongated, thin, and already balding. The Levi sitting before Nick wears a full head of transplanted dark hair.

"Come to lunch with this guy. You're better at making things sound, I don't know. Fucking *noble*."

Levi empties a clear vial of liquid into a glass of water—his unapproved longevity therapy—then drinks it in a few quick swallows. They'll find out if it works in fifteen, twenty years, maybe.

Levi is often frustrating—few CEOs in the Bay Area aren't—but he is, beneath the bluster, a decent person. At least, this is what Nick tells himself. That Levi is in this line of work for noble reasons. His niece was born with a heart defect—an issue with a valve—and his father died at age fifty-five. Genetic therapies might have saved his father; they could still give his niece a fuller, healthier life. At the job interview Nick said, for some reason, his dad was dead, too. It was something they bonded over.

Whenever Nick thinks of Matthew now, he feels a tug of wanting to prove that he's better off without him. Even more than that: The world would be better off without its oligarchs. And yet here is their company, needing money again. He thinks of May, where she left off: meeting the laboratory's new funders. He hates that this is how things are, how much money science requires.

"Yeah, okay," Nick says, finally.

Nick takes the BART from Montgomery to Twenty-fourth Street. He lives in the Mission, on Shotwell, in a four-bedroom flat on the third level of a Victorian built at the end of the 1800s. He's in need of a fresh T-shirt. Also, a shower.

In the Mission, a woman taps his shoulder and holds up pink roses. "For your wife?" she tries. "Only five dollars." The flowers seem resigned. If no one purchases them today they'll wind up in the compost bin.

Only Nick's filmmaker roommate, Al, is home, holding a large jar at an angle, tenderly straining the strings from his homemade kombucha.

"Are those for me?"

"For *us*." The flowers droop in the drinking glass Nick releases them into. A few petals flutter to the counter.

"Where've you been?" Al asks.

"It's kind of a long story." Nick accepts a glass and drinks: It is unpleasantly warm, acidic and bracing. Nick downs the whole glass quickly and wipes his mouth with the back of his hand.

"More?"

"I'm good, thanks."

"You dating someone?"

"Like I'd give you the place to yourself."

The phone in his pocket buzzes. It's his mother. Nick retreats to his bedroom, front facing, with enormous bay windows, hundred-year-old curved glass. He pays more rent than his roommates—his salary eclipses theirs—so they insisted he take the largest bedroom, which is also sunnier and warmer than the rest of the flat. The Victorians liked their homes dark.

"Hey, Mom."

"Hello, son."

"What's that sound?" Nick asks. There's a strange sound, like rocks pinging against glass.

"You're going to make fun of me." His mother laughs. "But I'm setting up one of those 'guess the number of beans' jars for a contest at the hospice center. For the visitors. So I need to actually count them out first."

"You can count while talking to me? Isn't that hard?"

"I'm only organizing them into piles of ten."

"What do you win?"

"I need to figure that out. A jar of beans isn't very alluring, is it?"

As his mother speaks, Nick wonders if he should mention May. "Hello?"

"Sorry. What was that?"

"I said, are you making time for friends?" his mother said.

"What friends?"

"You've got plenty. What's his name . . . Al?"

Al is sitting on their stoop with a glass of urine-colored brew and his vape pen, exhaling clouds. A man in tight shorts Rollerblades past, his husky racing gleefully alongside him. Another man, wearing skinny jeans, holds a tote bursting with curled kale, and another bunch in both his hands, a bride with a bouquet.

"Al has real friends who aren't me, Mom."

"How's Timothy?"

"Timothy's good." How funny, Nick thinks sometimes, that Timothy is still his best friend. And yet he doesn't wish it were different, anymore.

"Remind me what he's doing lately?"

"Literal rocket science."

"Of course he is. How's work? What's Levi making you do?"

"Somehow he's burned through all the money again."

"You know, you don't have to work so hard."

"You can say that, Mom," Nick says with a sigh, "but I still will."

How can he explain to his mother that he does, in fact, have to work so hard? He can't exactly see another way to be. Besides, what's so bad about not having a social life, or being consumed by work that aims to make the world a fairer place? Otherwise, what is he, besides a waste of space, consuming resources while the planet burns? Nick is envious of people who don't feel this pressure—people with weekend plans and work-life balance, people who think he should probably lighten up. At the same time, if he's being honest, he judges them, too.

He decides he'll tell his mother about May, but not just yet. They say goodbye.

He showers and stuffs his backpack with a change of clothes. Near the BART station, the same woman tries again to sell him roses.

In Chinatown, his grandmother is waiting.

CHAPTER 13

IN DECEMBER THE RADIO played only Christmas music—the same songs over and over. I loved the sound of the Ronettes harmonizing, except when Charles ruined it by singing along. He was practicing his English, he protested. I should have been practicing, too.

Not long after our meeting with the men, we began to hear the sounds of construction: the sounds of the laboratory changing. A cement truck sat parked permanently outside, its drum spinning. Day and night, we heard the destructive, shrill sounds of construction. Yang played the jingling music to drown it out, and the effect was a cheerfulness tinged with menace.

"My name is Fiona."

Our new English teacher was Chinese, from San Francisco. She was in her twenties, and wore blue jeans and kitten heels. She was American but spoke some Cantonese.

"That's a beautiful bracelet," Fiona said to me. "Is it real jade?"

"My mother gave it to me. I don't know." I touched the cool stone. I didn't know if it was real.

"I could have it looked at, if you like."

"Thank you," I said.

I slipped the bracelet off and gave it to her. She held it in her hand. Only a moment passed before I reached for it again.

"Actually, that's all right," I said. "Even if it isn't real—it doesn't matter to me."

"Suit yourself," Fiona said, smiling.

With her help, and my diligence, my English improved quickly. My progress eclipsed Charles's. We learned that for certain words, the meanings changed depending on where you put the stress: *de*sert and de*sert*. We practiced the letter R. *Rainbow, rarity, rot.*

We practiced the written word. In China, I had been discouraged from using my left hand to write with and was trained to use my right. In America, it didn't matter. I wrote English with my left hand, which I preferred.

Our lessons covered what it meant to be an American. In American households, they watched hours of television. In America, families ate large amounts of meat and overcooked vegetables until they were soft all the way through.

Where I was better at the language, Charles took to being an American immediately. Greedily, he watched TV. He took delightedly to the new American foods we ate: rich, without flavor, tasting of chemicals. I learned to make meat loaf and Charles devoured it, the crusted top of too-sweet ketchup. We had all been thin in China. But Charles had grown in Hong Kong, and now, in America, he expanded even more in size.

Not only was it important to speak English, Fiona explained, it was important to speak without an accent, so as to be taken seriously. I watched *Gilligan's Island* and *I Dream of Jeannie* and *The Brady Bunch*, and before I learned what the jokes themselves meant, I learned the cadence of a joke, how people's faces and voices changed when they expected you would respond with laughter.

We listened to *A Christmas Gift for You*, which had songs by the Ronettes—my favorite. Fiona told me that the Ronettes were Chinese: They had a great-grandfather who was Chinese. They were proud of it. They drew wings on their eyes to look more Chinese, the way I once had—wings so our eyes could fly.

Many years later, I would learn that Ronnie Spector was kept as a prisoner in her own home. She tried to escape but didn't succeed. Hearing that, I felt sorry for her. She'd become a star, in spite of the color of her skin, and yet even with all the money she had, she had been trapped. Wealth gave the impression of transcending status, but it was only an impression. In the end, she was a woman. In the end, she looked the way she did.

———

Yang left that winter. Our place at the institute was still uncertain. Another meeting would determine if we stayed, or if we would be asked to leave.

To the meeting, I wore my new winter coat of black wool. I liked the way it gave me sharp shoulders and made me resemble a shadow. I drew lipstick onto my mouth—ignoring what the familiar scent made me remember, ignoring the feeling of terror it instilled. In my purse was my Chinese-English dictionary.

In the dark auditorium, waiting for us, were the same men we'd met with before.

Charles spoke confidently in his imperfect English. I watched the men nod to his assertions. I had coached him in what to say: We would continue to study tumor-causing viruses, using restriction enzymes to dissect DNA sequences in those viruses. The hope was to identify genes likely to cause cancer and those that suppressed it. This would be a significant step toward understanding and, ultimately, treating cancers.

My husband was presumptuous, overly confident: What advertised him as an authority actually made him, in my view, a lesser scientist. Science required a sense of openness to being wrong: uncertainty over its opposite. They saw competence in Charles, because they knew the story of him. They were familiar with the narratives of men like him, confident men who announced their own importance, while they underestimated me.

The youngest man—the one with blue eyes and silver glasses—spoke to me instead of Charles. I liked him.

"I hope this doesn't sound strange," this man said. "We need to know that your loyalties are with us. And not to China."

As he spoke he noticed my mother's jade bracelet on my wrist. I tilted my arm so that it slid down, so that it would be obscured by my jacket sleeve.

"We can't go back there," Charles said. "We don't want to."

I spoke up. "China is not my home. We want to be American. We work hard. We will work harder than any scientist here. We can promise you that."

The group of men looked to me, startled.

"Your English," the young man said. "It's much better."

"Thank you."

"It's remarkable. Really, I've never heard such improvement in so little time."

"I work hard," I repeated. "As I've said."

"We need to know you won't take these findings back to China."

"No, sir," I repeated, more firmly. "We may look Chinese, but we have no loyalty to China. We want to be American."

The young man smiled.

"You can call me Otto," he said.

CHAPTER 14

CONTRACT SIGNED, AGREEMENTS MADE, I could hardly believe what followed. We were moved into a home paid for by the new donors. It was the home I'd admired—weathervane and green shutters, two stories tall, in a neighborhood so quiet all you could hear were birds. We'd had to acclimate to the unceasing noises from the laundromat—a twenty-four-hour cacophony of water and air—and now we had our own washer and dryer, in a garage that had room enough for two cars. When the laundry spun, we didn't hear a sound. And in our new house, we could control the temperature. Inside it could be as warm as the summer, even when it snowed outside.

Upon entering the home, you saw a grandfather clock with a swinging golden pendulum, like a tonsil. It chimed, assertively, every hour. The house came fully furnished: a TV on a wooden shelf; a radio; bookcases that held dictionaries, biographies, an entire shelf devoted to encyclopedias, which held information on every subject imaginable. An ample bed with six pillows on it, as though we were three-headed monsters. I'd imagined a fireplace and there it was, a soft armchair beside it. Most excitingly, the door of my office locked.

I was taken to the dentist, a clinic that was small and beige and smelled of mint. I was ashamed to open my mouth, even in front of a professional who had seen countless mouths. On the ceiling hung a poster of evergreen trees and purple mountains, dusted with snow. "SUCCESS," the poster said. "It's never too late to be who you might have been."

The dentist reshaped my broken teeth and put in a false tooth to replace the missing one.

It was as though we were being sent into space, on some kind of physical mission. At the doctor's, we underwent medical examinations. We were X-rayed. We gave urine samples. We were vaccinated. The institute maintained a genomic database, and dutifully we submitted our genetic samples to it.

I swore to myself I wouldn't get used to anything—would never let myself grow too comfortable. At any point, they could take our home away. Our employment. Even my teeth. But I couldn't help myself: On evenings, home from the laboratory, I stood in the foyer, watching the assured ticking of the clock, and felt the unfamiliar swell of hope.

Officially, it was Charles's lab. Of course it was. He was ten years older, with more experience. That was fine with me. What was in a name? What mattered was that our new lab was outfitted with expensive, brand-new equipment, including the most advanced electron microscope, which would be operated by a talented new technician. Charles and I worked happily.

The few other foreign scientists at the laboratory stuck together—eating every meal together, sharing housing. I understood why: In conversations, the Americans spoke endlessly and brashly, and never listened. But I saw how that limited the foreign scientists. Even if they were doing better work, they weren't esteemed in the same way their American colleagues were. So I didn't align myself with them.

Instead I spoke only English and sought Otto's company. At the cafeteria, we informed him of updates to our work. Otto and I sat side by side, because he was left-handed, too. Sometimes it felt as though we were on the same team, interviewing Charles. We lifted our forks, compatibly, as though in a dance.

The word *fortune* meant "chance" or "luck," but its other meaning was "a large amount of money." The same word could have completely unrelated definitions—I knew that now. A bat was a piece of wood used to hit a ball and also a winged creature. A second was a unit of time but it also meant coming after first. But *fortune* did not strike me as completely arbitrary; these differing meanings seemed entwined. It was fortunate for one to have a fortune. You never described someone as fortunate who was penniless. Yet I remembered Lanlan, whose family's fortune had resulted in her punishment. It was a misfortune to have been wealthy, in that era, in that place—fortune marked you.

I wondered, especially when I looked at Otto, if fortune was always good fortune. Maybe there was an amount of money that was as unfortunate as poverty could be.

It was an inspiring time to be in the field: Foreign DNA had been introduced into a mouse's embryo, creating the first transgenic mouse. Insulin was on its way to being synthesized. DNA sequencing methods were becoming faster. We started using the fluorescent dyes that are used today. And I could hardly wait for the years to pass, for technology to advance, for us to learn which regions of DNA coded for which functions and traits.

With Otto, I felt my bravery returning. Speaking with him reminded me of the conversations I'd once had with Ping, except where Ping was doubtful, Otto wasn't. One day, we would be able to read DNA, like a book. One day we might even be able to rewrite the book, or at least make important corrections. There was so little I'd gotten to choose in my life. I didn't get to choose the fact of my being Chinese, the fact of my being a woman. But what if we *could* choose? It was a question that hummed, always, in the back of my mind.

Charles wanted a family, but I didn't want to be a mother. I had known this since I was a girl—had seen the way my mother's time belonged to everyone but herself.

"We should start trying soon," Charles said to me.

It was something that Charles and I argued over, often.

"Every woman wants to be a mother," he said when he wanted to wound me. "There's something wrong with you if you don't. It's biological."

Why did he want a family? He believed it would grant us legitimacy. He believed it would knit us together, make us a real American family.

In the kitchen, Charles sat placidly in front of the coffee he'd never drunk in China and now drank regularly. I liked the smell of it but couldn't stand the taste. The day's newspaper was spread out before him. He looked to me, suddenly.

"Mao is dead," he said, handing me the paper.

"Mao Zedong Dies in Beijing at 82," the headline announced. The article compared him with Chin Shih-Huang, China's first emperor, who unified China in 221 B.C. It could have been propaganda from Mao himself.

The cause was a heart attack. He'd fallen into a coma, and his organs had failed. His body was embalmed and brought to the Great Hall of the People, on the edge of Tiananmen Square, so mourners could pay their respects. I thought of all the care that was being paid to his body, in contrast to the mass graves that we'd had to dig during the famines. Why was this corpse more precious than others? There was a photo of Chinese men and women, somber, wearing black arm-bands, yet I wondered what they truly felt—if they might feel relief.

How had one man done so much damage? That was power, that one person could wield so much influence over the lives of strangers. I wondered if he suffered, in the end. Is it evil to say that I hoped he'd suffered?

That day, Charles could do no wrong. The hours passed pleas-antly. Charles may even have whistled. When our workday ended, he turned to me, eyes bright.

"Let's go to a restaurant," he said.

Since we'd come to America, we had never eaten at a sit-down res-taurant. It had seemed impossible, for two people like us to do such a thing. But tonight we wanted, without speaking it aloud, to celebrate.

There was an Italian restaurant on Main Street I had always peered into the windows of. Men and women sat happily before plates of pasta, their faces—like clowns', with overly expressive features—lit by candles, drinking wine and laughing, elbows on the red-checkered tablecloths.

Tentatively, Charles pushed the door open, and its bell jingled. A man in a black vest led us to a small table. We knew the word *spa-ghetti*. When we tried to order one plate to share, the server shook his head. One order per person.

"And anything to drink?" the server asked, looking to Charles, who looked to me.

"Wine?" I said.

"We'll have wine," Charles announced.

"What type of wine?" the server asked.

"Port?" I tried.

"I don't recommend port with your meal," he said. "Red wine? White wine?"

"Red," Charles said.

The expense felt illicit. The wine cost nearly as much as the food itself. The deep purple liquid came in what looked like a vase for flowers, and our server poured it into glasses that I had only seen in movies. When I held the glass I was transported to the lake, with Ping: I had held the lotus buds this same way, cupped in my palm, stem between my third and second fingers.

Gently, afraid to break them, Charles and I touched our glasses together. The noodles arrived: mounds on enormous warmed plates, three meatballs perched on top, and cheese dusted over it. The cheese smelled rotten.

We never said Mao's name. I was still frightened of speaking any word against him.

Our surroundings grew blurred and gilded. Not being a drinker, I quickly grew drunk. The noodles were sour and rich. I cleaned my plate and scraped at the sauce with my fork. Around us, silverware clinked and voices blended together into one unintelligible hum. Our faces flushed pink and we laughed together, enjoying ourselves.

We were the only Chinese people in the restaurant. Everyone ate their noodles, ignorant. They didn't know. A very important man was dead.

Outside, I leaned on Charles—full of pasta, light with alcohol. I did love him—not in the way I loved Ping, but in a different way. It was appreciation, it was familiarity. Thoughts swirled in my mind, wine in a glass, and I resolved to be kinder to him.

Once home, we stood in the darkened hallway. I stepped out of my shoes, one after the other, my arm on Charles's shoulder for balance. I liked the scent of our home. The way Charles smelled—recognizable— was part of it. I tipped my head to regard him: the stubble on his cheeks, the line of his part, which grew wider with age. It was a face I knew so well now, had witnessed in countless configurations.

"You look handsome," I said.

"Do I? You must be very drunk to say that," he teased.

He held my coat while I eased out of it. He helped find the pins in my hair, and once they were out, my hair fell to my shoulders. He kept his hand against my head, behind my neck—firm and warm. I found myself not wanting him to move it. He lifted me to the bedroom. Desire flooded my body in a way it hadn't for years—a way it had never, before, with Charles. It took me by surprise. I'd believed myself incapable of experiencing it. I'd thought that part of me was gone for good—left behind in China, pinned to where Ping was.

It was only afterward, Charles asleep against my shoulder, that I realized: In our urgency, I had forgotten to place my diaphragm.

It was easy for me to forget that I had a body. I often treated it as an inconvenience: something that took up space, that needed to be fed and tended to, but was otherwise a nuisance that experienced hunger, that experienced heat or cold, and was an interruption to my true life, lived in the mind. But now I spoke to it every day: *Please*, I told it. *Please, don't let me be pregnant.* The terror hummed inside me, a trapped and angry bee.

My period was late. It didn't mean anything, I told myself. It could be the stress of worrying. On my lunch break, I went to the institute's medical center. The phlebotomist was a woman who perceived my ambivalence. There was compassion in the way she drew my blood, with pale, knobbed fingers—a lack of judgment I appreciated. A doctor would call with the results.

How foolish I'd been. I hadn't been careful. Charles never was, because he didn't have to be. I, who never let my emotions overwhelm me, had let my guard down this once, had let the wine transform me into someone else, and of course this had happened as a result, as punishment.

I was at the lab when the phone rang.

"Tell me," I said.

Charles was nearby and I didn't want to use the word *pregnant*. I wondered if he registered the quiver in my voice, if he could hear the worry in it. He moved quietly beside me, scratching notes into his notebook. Of course he didn't notice.

In seconds, I would feel relief. It could be that simple. Or my life would be changed.

"You're pregnant," the doctor said.

My heart sank like a stone to the bottom of a lake. Beside me, Charles laughed at someone's joke.

He couldn't know; I wouldn't tell him. He wasn't observant and I was sure he wouldn't pick up on any changes in me. I would arrange to get an abortion, simple as that. He didn't have to ever know.

When we got home, the phone was ringing. Charles answered. I could hear Otto's voice, loud and happy. He congratulated us on the baby.

The cafeteria smelled repulsive to me—sour coffee, toast burning or browning, eggs solidifying into omelets—but I had to eat. I sat with plain buttered toast when Otto and his wife, Naomi, appeared. She had deep brown hair, eyes as green as soda bottles.

Their children—five of them—were in tow. Wearily, she took the seat across from me, keeping an eye on the children at the pancake station, who were entranced by the chef's acrobatic spatula maneuvers.

"How far along?" she asked.

"Thirty-six weeks."

"Let me know if you need anything. Food, baby clothes. Anything."

Naomi spoke softly and slowly—almost musically, to her own private rhythm. I began to adjust the speed and volume of my speech to match hers. In conversation, I always found myself imitating others. I admired that she never wavered from her own pattern. Though she smiled, I could tell she wasn't happy.

Her baby, Thomas, was in her arms. Even so small, it was obvious he took after Naomi: They shared the same round green eyes, the same dark hair. He began to scream. Then her second youngest approached and tugged at her dress, looking as though he wanted to cry, too. She sighed. So many small hands grasped at her—her arms, her breasts, her calves.

"We'd better go." She smiled again—that smile that somehow had sadness in it. "There's always something. You'll see."

"I'll watch the girls," Otto said, and Naomi nodded. She left with the two youngest, the boys, Matthew and Thomas. Otto remained seated beside me, while the older girls refilled their bowls with fruit.

"I'm not ready for this," I said to him.

"You'll love her," Otto said.

We were having a girl. Charles was predictable, conventional: He'd wanted a boy, because a boy would carry on the family name. This was so stupid, I'd always thought. What was in a name? It was only a sound. Silently, men carried on their mitochondrial lineage: information from their mothers, and their mothers before them.

At first, I'd wanted a boy, too. I was aware of how difficult it was to be a girl. But maybe it was just as difficult, or worse, to be a Chinese boy in America—I didn't know. At least this baby would have the luck of being an American.

"You'll see," Otto insisted. "She'll bring new meaning to the work. Before my kids it was theoretical—wanting the future to be better. You know? And now it's real. The work, it's all for them."

He held my gaze, willing understanding between us. He'd been born rich and couldn't know what my life had been like. But he was also kind to me.

"You'll be a good mother," he assured me.

My memory of the birth is gapped like a net: I remember the doctor and his impatient expression, the torrents of blood that spilled from my small, spent body. While I was given transfusions of other people's blood, I listed tasks in my head: What Charles was to do if I died, what Charles was to do if we both died. If I died, I thought, I would deserve it.

Remarkably, we survived. It was Charles who named her Lily. As I've said, I wasn't invested in names. No matter what she was called, she would be my daughter.

When Lily was brought to me, my fears, which had been building like breath in a balloon, evaporated. And love: Had I ever felt it before? It was a conviction that this miniature person, with her tiniest inhalations and exhalations, faint yet fierce, needed to be alive—and close to me—for as long as I existed. It no longer mattered what had come before—my unspeakable past. The important thing was that she would be my future.

Lily made our family complete, as Charles had insisted she would. She was glue, holding us, two mismatched materials, together. Charles was a good father, I had to admit. He was more natural than I was at certain effusive American gestures, readily offering praise and gifts. He was the easier parent to adore, and they adored each other. He marveled over her every milestone: first steps, first teeth, first words.

Of course I was proud of her, too. The institute ran a day care, and I couldn't help but compare her development with that of the other scientists' children. She walked before her peers, then ran. She spoke sooner, more comprehensibly. She asked perceptive questions. She was driven and gifted. It was a harmless egoism, I thought: the conviction she would be exceptional.

We were Americans, so I told her I loved her. My parents had never said the word to me. But even though the words sounded unnatural when I spoke them, I felt them, I felt them, I wanted to make them felt. I held her tightly in my arms, in an impossible attempt to communicate my love to every particle, to the deepest part of her, to every nucleus.

To take care of Lily, Charles and I traded off at the lab. He worked mornings, and I worked evenings. We were rarely there together. For any other marriage, it would have been fatal, but it gave ours a sort of peace, an equilibrium. I had my tubes tied and didn't tell Charles. For as much as I loved Lily, I didn't want another child.

Science requires patience, and I have always been an impatient person. But what I lived for was that private moment, discovering something no one else had. The moment before it is shared with others—when it is a secret, only yours. In that moment it doesn't feel like an accomplishment but a gift from some god. You know the feeling, Nick.

Certain cancers were inherited. As I said, questions of heritability were on my mind: What could we change about our lives? Could we nudge inheritance in particular directions? Over late nights, I came across something by chance: what we know now as imprinting. I observed how one gene could suppress another.

I observed and isolated two factors from tumor cells: imprinting factors. One factor suppressed the expression of paternal genes when I put it into mouse cells in culture. The second factor suppressed genes from the mother. This astonished me. At least in vitro, we could instruct one set of parents' genes to express itself more strongly. This was apart from our stated work. It was my secret, and I told no one, not even Charles.

In the spring of 1981, Naomi overdosed on Seconal. When Otto found her, she was in bed—eyes closed, bedspread pulled over her, peaceful. It hadn't been her first attempt, but this time she succeeded.

Halfway through the memorial service, the Maiers' two nannies took the weeping children home.

Otto thanked the attendees for their condolences. Charles left. He had work to do at the lab. I lingered, counting the pipes on the organ. Finally, the church emptied. I followed Otto outside. The dogwood trees were blooming.

"I'm not sad," Otto said. "I'm angry. I'm so angry with her."

I sat beside him. A squirrel bounced exuberantly up a tree then, at odds with how we felt.

"Why did she want to die?" He spoke without looking at me. "When her children loved her. When I loved her."

"Isn't that strange?" I said. "I haven't felt happiness on many occasions when I should have. Does that mean there's something wrong with me? Or is that normal? And if it's normal, isn't that terrible?"

"Her mother took her own life," Otto said. "It worries me. My children could live perfectly happy lives. Or—*and*. They could want to die, like she did."

Thomas was only half a year older than Lily was—they were both four. But already he seemed like a sad child, a child who was perpetually disappointed.

If Otto had had any wish, he might have wished none of his children would feel Naomi's life-ending sadness. I thought of my imprinting factors. Recently, I had put them in cultured human cells. I was astonished to find that they successfully suppressed the other parent's genes. I'd told no one. It was still my secret.

Outside the church, we sat until the sun went down. We watched the sky shift to purple pink. The air grew cool. I glanced at him. His face stayed dry. He didn't cry.

———

Not long after Naomi's death, Otto delivered bad news: Our lab was being shut down. There was an opportunity for us in Florida, researching fruit and vegetable genomics. The board was displeased with us. We had not made the progress the donors had hoped for, and Charles was angry with me.

"What are you doing all night?" he asked, and I couldn't say.

I had been isolating enhanced mutants of my maternal and paternal imprinting factors that more potently suppressed the other parent's genes. I was exploring what you do today—what your company does, Nick. I was seeking to create an epigenome editor out of imprinting proteins, taking advantage of naturally occurring machinery.

In my mind, questions kept arising: What if Thomas didn't have to inherit his mother's sadness? What if we could tip the genetic scales? What if we could guide inheritance—make it less about the luck of the draw?

The clock's hands moved quickly when I was engrossed in work, and I resented its progression. But one night, a familiar feeling overcame me. My vision fogged at the edges and the clock stopped. I realized that I could keep time still; I could control it. I remembered the night I'd decided on Wen. I remembered time stalling before the butcher, in Hong Kong.

The seed had granted me my wish. I could have asked for Ping, and instead I asked for time. I was ashamed that I'd chosen this over Ping, yes. But if I was being honest, this was my truer wish. It was what I'd wished for all my life. Long before Ping, I had yearned for more time. And now I had it.

I stretched the hours, staying late at the laboratory, turning this question over. I transferred the more potent MIF-1 and PIF-1 genes to polio virus from monkeys. Simian polio could infect human cells without replicating in them, meaning it could deliver the MIF-1, which would suppress the paternal genes, without causing polio. With this gene treatment, we could, potentially, prioritize one parent's genetic contribution.

I shared my findings—my secret—with Otto. We couldn't know it was safe, he argued. But he was as idealistic and ambitious as I was, and I could tell he was interested in what I said. I described the possibilities to him: This proposed therapy could change brain chemistry, personality traits, mental abilities, psychiatric disorders. In Thomas we could deprioritize his mother's genes. Thomas would begin to take after Otto, rather than Naomi. He wouldn't inherit her illness.

And we would do it to Lily, I insisted. We would diminish Charles's genetic contribution. We would guide fate. The effects on Lily wouldn't be apparent, or even discernible. We didn't need to inform Charles—or Lily, for that matter. Often I wondered if I would have been happier, more successful, if I'd been born in America. Lily could live my life, but better. She would accomplish more than I ever had, and would. It was like giving myself a second chance.

The therapy was a simian polio virus, modified with the enhanced imprinting factors. Given intravenously, it would turn off one set of genes throughout the body. Certain physical traits could change: Lily might remain smaller, with her maternal genes prioritized; Thomas could grow taller. Thomas would take after Otto, and Lily would take after me. His eye color could even shift, from green to blue.

This change would manifest, also, I hypothesized, in their handedness. Both children were learning to draw, to hold crayons and pencils. For the moment, both leaned toward right-handedness. If the therapy succeeded, we would observe a change. They would grow to prefer their left hands, like Otto and me. The changes would be mild, we believed. Neither child would need to be informed of what we'd done.

Charles and I moved to Florida. At first, Otto and I kept in touch, reporting on the changes we saw in our children. We were optimistic when both children became left-handed. Hopefully, we observed them. Had we succeeded?

When I received word from Otto that Thomas had killed himself, at only nineteen, I fell into a deep depression. I had failed. We had failed him. Lily had grown up to be so unlike me, she was practically a stranger.

In Florida, I grew four-leaf clovers, hoping for my luck to change. Who had decided clovers with four leaves were the ones that were lucky? Was it because they were rare? There were plenty of rare things that people didn't deem special and instead wanted to stamp out. Variations that we deemed aberrant and thus abhorrent. It was unfortunate for rabbits—their bad luck—when gamblers decided to carry around their feet.

I didn't learn of the relationship between Lily and Matthew until the weekend of their wedding. Matthew had been using a different last name. I didn't know who he was. In the Hamptons, Otto and I spoke, for the first time since Thomas died. What were the chances? They were such different people, we told each other. Their relationship couldn't possibly last. But it did. When Lily struggled to conceive, we realized the therapy had caused it. The X chromosome she'd inherited from Charles had been affected, leading to issues with her reproductive system.

IVF was the solution. With IVF came the possibility for germline editing—an opportunity to finish the work we had begun. What we had attempted, unsuccessfully, with your mother and with Thomas, we could finally make right.

Otto proposed emphasizing your mother's genes. But we couldn't be certain of the integrity of her genome, after the therapy we'd given her. So we had you take after your father. With better technology we were able to edit the regions related to inherited depression, to serotonin and dopamine receptors. We only intended to tip the scales. You have, primarily, your father's genetic contribution, but without his mother's mental afflictions. This time, the therapy worked—far better than we had imagined it could.

What I did was indefensible. Selfish, foolish, dangerous—now I know this. When Lily left with you—in a rush, unwilling to listen to my explanations—I couldn't blame her. She felt betrayed; she swore to never speak to me again. In my guilt, I returned to Tampa, tending to Charles until he passed. After that, I tracked you: to Arizona, then to Washington.

I followed you here to San Francisco, hoping for I don't know what. All this while, I have been trying to compose an apology. I'd only wanted my daughter's life to be better than mine. I see, now, I was wrong, to have tried to mold the outcome of her life, and yours. I wonder if you can understand this: that the way I loved her was different from the way she wanted to be loved. Every day of my life—and there are not many more now—I will regret this.

All I want is to see my daughter. I don't seek her forgiveness; I understand that what I've done is unforgivable. But I am sorry, and I would like to say it to her.

Will you ask her, Nick? Will you ask her to come see me?

Nick placed his hand on his grandmother's forearm. May appeared so defeated, broken by the choices she'd made. He found he wasn't angry. Instead he felt pity for her.

He left May's apartment, slowly descending the dark, steep steps. *The landlord should install some kind of light,* he thought. It wasn't safe for the elderly men and women who lived here. What made the genetic therapies his company was making any different? They *were,* Nick thought. The treatments would spare people unnecessary suffering. And yet, emerging into the light, he found himself shaken.

Once outside, on the sidewalk, he extracted his phone from his pants. He always kept it in the same pocket of this pair of jeans, and there was a white rectangular outline where it stayed, like the chalk outline of a body. He dialed his mother.

"You won't believe it," she said excitedly. "But someone guessed the number of beans *exactly.*"

"Mom, I have something . . ." Nick inhaled, unsure of where to start. "Something happened."

Lily held the phone pressed against her ear as she stood in the communal garden of the apartment complex. Over the years the tending of it had fallen to Lily, and now—under her watch—it bloomed with flowers and native shrubs: dramatic, hanging ocean spray; purple cones of butterfly bush, reaching upward. The other apartment dwellers—young parents and commuting professionals—didn't have interest or time.

"Why not vegetables?" one of the parents asked.

This was a woman who never weeded or organized the tool shed, only offered mildly accusatory questions when she strolled by. Lily didn't have an answer. The flowers *were* useless.

"They're also called sword lilies," an older resident commented admiringly, pointing to a fiery orange gladiolus. And it was true, it looked like a sword, but totally ineffectual.

To Lily, flowers were a marvel. Season after season, they erupted into their astounding array of colors and shapes and scents—brilliantly existing, never considering the question of: What for?

Lily was fifty-three. When asked her age she had to pause to recall it, and it was with surprise she did, each time. On occasion, she imagined the alternate lives she might have lived, had she made different choices: married or divorced, in New York, still dogged by ambition. Or in Beijing, had her parents never fled, dreaming in a different language.

She'd been pleased to enter her fifties. She'd celebrated her fiftieth with friends, a leg of lamb, a case of wine, and in the morning the hangover was difficult, almost delicious. Here was her body—changed. Unlike in puberty, it had grown more familiar, not less.

She had never been comfortable, as a younger person. There was so much expectation placed on the young, who were uniformly full of potential, who could change the world, until they did or didn't. Nobody expected anything remarkable from a woman her age. But she had never wanted to be remarkable.

Her life was small, and rich, and entirely hers. She had Nick. She had the women friends she played mahjong with and fellow swimmers from the pool. Children from the day care, where she worked; patients at the hospice center, where she volunteered.

Once she had believed that connection meant sameness, consensus, harmony. Having everything in common. And now she understood that the opposite was true: that connection was more valuable—more remarkable—for the fact of differences. Friendship didn't require blunting the richness of yourself to find common ground. Sometimes it was that, but it was also appreciating another person, in all their particularity.

She rarely thought of Matthew anymore, even as she saw him in her son's face. She had loved him—of course she had. What if they had truly been able to choose each other? If she had promised her life to him in the orchard, with only the goldfinches as witnesses? But it was all in the past now.

At the hospice center, sitting with the dying men and women, holding their hands in her own, Lily wondered about her mother. If she was alive, she would be eighty-five. She'd told Nick, as a child, that his grandmother was dead. Later, she confessed she didn't know for sure.

As a parent, she had sought to do the opposite of what her mother had done—not expecting Nick to resemble her, not burdening him with her expectations. And yet was she any different? Could love between a mother and child be anything less than completely overwhelming?

"Mom, are you there?"

"Yes. Sorry. I'm here."

Nick's voice traveled over the phone, and he was telling her: She was alive. Lily's mother was alive.

CHAPTER 15

NICK'S BREATH WAS HOT and wet inside his N95 mask. The sky was gray. At the office, the power was out. The elevators weren't working, so Nick climbed the stairs.

Wildfires raged to the north and south: a regular occurrence now, even as Nick wondered what trees were left to burn. Every summer and fall since he'd moved to San Francisco, fires changed the color of the sky. The sun glowed orange, a hot coal. For months at a time his chest hurt with the particulate-filled air.

They were meeting a potential partner today. In the morning, into the mirror, Nick practiced what he planned to say. This merger was important: They needed the cash infusion, first of all. But more than that, it was crucial to the work they were doing. Longevity solutions for European populations were better studied, but there was a dearth of genomic information when it came to other races. Joining with this company would be crucial for equity, for longevity across populations.

May had made a decision that wasn't hers to make. This was her transgression. Yet Nick could understand it—even relate—though his motivation wasn't glory, but progress.

Was it inherited, their compulsion? This shared need to be productive, to do good, to right some wrong? He wanted his life to mean something; he had yet to prove it.

Nick's coworkers sat at their desks, hunched over cell phones, awaiting instructions from Levi, who paced, hands in his jeans pockets, AirPods in his ears, as he cursed into his phone, trying and failing to buy a generator. The main worry was the organ freezers: all the hearts and eyes that would defrost and be rendered useless.

"Don't open the freezers." Levi cupped his hands to make a megaphone. "I repeat: DO NOT OPEN THE FREEZERS!"

He caught Nick's eye. "Nick, I need you."

The potential partner was meant to visit the office, but with the power outage, they'd scrapped that plan and would meet at the restaurant instead. The lights were on in Hayes Valley. At the curb, they climbed into an Uber.

"This guy has some questions," Levi said in the car. "About ethics, you know. We need you to do your Ivy League philosophy stuff."

Levi looked slightly nicer than usual, wearing a V-neck sweater and leather jacket along with his jeans. He pulled a tin of mints from his jacket pocket and offered one to Nick, before putting four in his mouth at once.

"Bottom line, we need this guy impressed."

"What's his background?"

"He seems to have had his hand in lots of things. But finance, in the past, I think."

"This finance guy has questions about ethics?"

Levi chuckled. "Listen. You do this for me, you do your whole charming, I've-thought-this-all-out thing, and he's on board? I swear to God, you can have anything you want. A raise? Anything."

"I don't need a raise."

"That's a first," Levi said. "Well, whatever. We'll cure cancer and shit."

"Mr. Rathbone," the hostess said, smiling politely. "Your guest is already here. Come with me."

Nick and Levi followed her, the sure movement of shoulder blades against her blouse, past the other seated tables. People turned to look at Levi, and Nick could tell he liked the attention. It was the same reason he enjoyed a new hire's first days, when they were in awe of him, before they got accustomed to his omnipresence, in his gray T-shirt and jeans and wool shoes.

Their table was hidden behind potted ficus trees and fiddleleaf figs and nearly private. The investor sat with his back turned to them, and when they arrived at the table, and Levi put a hand on the man's shoulder, he looked up, and Nick saw that the man was his father.

Matthew still looked youthful, but Nick noticed the threads of silver in his hair. He straightened and held out his hand for Nick to shake. Nick kept his face blank and gave no indication of knowing him, and Matthew, following his lead, did the same.

"Nick Chen," Levi said. "Meet Matthew Maier."

Nick and Matthew shook hands cordially. Their likeness was unmistakable. The men sat.

"How was your flight?" Nick asked, like a stranger. "From New York, is that right?"

"Not too bad," Matthew said. "I'm getting to be a good plane sleeper in my old age."

Nick buried his irritation, the hostility that wanted to surface. Levi had told him it was a potential partnership, but if Matthew was representing Maier? That wasn't a partnership. That was a purchase.

"I'm getting older. I want Maier Pharma to not only do good, but to innovate into the future," Matthew said.

Nick gave the spiel Levi expected him to: Why was it that Black and Hispanic firefighters suffered lung cancer at higher rates than their white peers, even though their exposure to toxic substances was the same? Why was lung cancer a leading cause of death in Chinese women, though 90 percent of those women weren't smokers? Inherited genetic variants and epigenetic commands were responsible. Their company was working on epigenetic therapies. The hope was that modifying gene expression could target and eliminate disease.

"We're passionate about affordability," Nick said neutrally—the script he'd been summoned to recite. But Nick hoped he could communicate to Matthew, without Levi's noticing, that he wanted nothing to do with him. He was doing good work without the Maiers—didn't need them or their money. "The hope is that, in a few years, we can eradicate macular degeneration entirely. Not only that, but other conditions of aging. Right now it's only the rich who have access to the best technologies—"

Nick nearly laughed, because the moment he said "the rich" the server placed, on their table, oysters on the half shell, mounded with caviar.

"And importantly, not only in European populations. It's crucial these therapies be accessible and available to all demographics."

"And that's something that Maier Pharma has been involved in for decades now," Matthew said, nodding. "We have the largest database of diverse genomes."

"We're also interested in longevity," Nick continued. "How do you eliminate diseases that come with aging? We're looking into solving the problem of aging itself."

"There's no need to be coy," Levi added. "The bottom line is, we want to extend life spans. If not forever, pretty fucking close to that. Think of the greatest minds of our time—we know that people's best work happens within a certain window. Usually when they're young. But what if we were able to extend that window? Think of the innovation. Think of how productive any individual life could be."

"And again," Nick repeated. "The idea is for this to be an equitable innovation. That's what we're passionate about. Not something just for rich white men—here he held Matthew's gaze—"but for everyone, regardless of race or social standing, to live long and healthy lives."

Levi had picked up his phone. His attention was always flitting, and Nick wondered if it was a way to assert his power or if he had difficulty focusing. It was probably a mix of both.

"Power's back," Levi announced, relieved. It meant the organs wouldn't spoil. "What do you say?" He turned to Matthew. "Have a minute to see our office?"

The employees were back at their computers and in the labs, as though the morning's outage had never happened. Outside it remained hazy and gray, but inside, the air was purified and circulated and it hardly mattered, what was burning elsewhere.

Levi led Matthew to a conference room, and Matthew took a seat in one of the molded fiberglass chairs. Someone offered Matthew a glass of water. The glass was thin, cylindrical, breakable. They broke at least two glasses a week, and Nick always thought, if he were in charge, he'd buy thicker glasses. What was the point of glass so thin, money that shattered so easily?

Employees filed in. They were quieter than usual, wanting to make a good impression on their possible ticket to wealth and to freedom. His coworkers cared about their work, Nick knew, but given the choice between working and not, they would choose not to. They would travel the world; they would buy mansions.

The chairs squeaked with any movement. In teams, they shared their projects with Matthew. After saying their thank-yous and goodbyes, the young people returned to their stations, some to the lab, others to peck at their laptops.

"I'll be right back," Levi said, leaving Nick and Matthew to stand, together, by the elevators.

"If this is what you want to do, I want to support you in it," Matthew said, quietly, to Nick.

"Listen, we can find other investors. We don't need your money."

"But you believe in this? I want to believe in what you do."

"We don't believe in the same things. We aren't alike, you and me."

Levi returned, and they stiffened. He had a T-shirt in his hand. "You're a medium, right?" he said to Matthew. Nick coughed so he wouldn't laugh. As though his father would wear a T-shirt with a logo on it.

"Let me walk you out," Levi said, and he followed Matthew into the elevator.

They disappeared behind the doors. Nick sat in front of his closed laptop, agitated. He was furious with Levi, angry with himself, sick that he had had to speak with this man he had sworn to have nothing to do with.

At the office, Nick enclosed himself in a phone booth. There was no actual telephone in it, but these soundproof pods were called phone booths. It was the only way to be somewhat alone in their open office. He would put in his notice, he thought to himself. If the companies merged, he would leave.

When Levi returned, Nick, still in the booth, pretended to be busy with his computer. Levi knocked on the glass anyway.

"So that went well," Levi said, pleased. "Matthew was very impressed by you. He told me so just now."

"You didn't say it was fucking Maier," Nick said. "You called it a partnership."

"Sure, it's a partnership. Except one partner's enormous and ancient and can fund the smaller partner's high jinks and, like, innovation. Just think of it, Nick. We'll make a fortune. Have way more resources. Hire even more talent—fill out your team. And this is how we get our therapies to the marketplace, obviously. Win-win-win situation. Maybe even another win in there, but who's counting?"

Nick sat in silence. He considered quitting, right then. He refused to work for or with his father. But his projects—everything they'd done.

"Anyway, thanks, man," Levi said. "I owe you one."

BETTY WAS DEAD. I could feel it the moment I stepped into the apartment, groceries hanging from my arms: a void. She lay stiff in her bed, eyes closed. I put a hand to her cheek. It was as cold and inert as a potato.

I called her granddaughter, an attorney who lived in Petaluma with her husband and two young children, and paid Betty's rent each month. Her phone went straight to voicemail, as I knew it would. I left her a message that said only to call me and tried to make my voice sound cheerful, feeling deceptive as I did so.

Betty often complained about her. Whenever Betty needed something, her granddaughter seemed inconvenienced, acted as though Betty were interrupting her very important life. Of course she was interrupting. As people we interrupted one another's lives—that was what we did. If you sought to live your life without interruption you wound up like me: living life without interruption, totally alone.

Last spring, Betty twisted her ankle. She refused to tell her family. She insisted it was nothing major. Instead, I became her impromptu nurse. We both cracked up at my incompetence, before we grew somber with the realization: There would come a day when one of us grew sick, or fell, or couldn't climb our stairs, or we both did, and then what would happen? But here Betty had died on me. It was her way out of being my caretaker, I thought, laughing to myself.

I wanted to tell Betty's granddaughter that it wasn't too late. That I had been like her, once, resentful of any interruptions. Later, I learned that life lay in the interruptions—that I had been wrong about life, entirely.

Betty's printed polyester clothes were piled high on a chair. A dessert plate on her desk had hardened, ruby-colored jam on it. I picked it up to put it in the sink. I closed Betty's door.

On a typical night, we might have shared dinner in front of the television. We'd gotten on each other's nerves, but we'd been friends. Or maybe we were more like family. The last time Nick had come over they had found common ground in teasing me about my dedicated drawer of soy sauce packets and plastic flatware.

Betty had been born in Sacramento and had a perfect American accent with which she spoke too loudly—obnoxiously. In her youth, she had competed in beauty pageants. She'd won Miss Chinatown USA several years in a row, but never Miss America. Later in life her perfect posture began to curve. The photographs that hung in her bedroom were of herself—satin sashes across her chest; perfect, thornless roses cradled in her arms. It was hard to see the connection between the person in the photographs and the body lying in bed.

It didn't seem right to eat anything with Betty here, yet unable to join me.

I'll go outside, I thought. *I'll buy myself a sandwich.*

At times I feel like a bird, trailing in the wake of the younger and faster. I feel my bones losing their density, becoming hollow and avian. Once on the sidewalk I came across a dead green parrot, one of the wild parrots of Telegraph Hill, green like a tropical leaf, with an embarrassed red face. I thought of the sparrows we'd killed as children and I wanted to apologize, but it was too late. I pinched its small body in the claw of my trash picker and moved it beneath a bush.

On the sidewalk, a man with matted hair and a dirty jacket lurched from side to side as though in imitation of a zombie in a horror film. My body flinched. I didn't want to be afraid of him. He was only a struggling person, likely someone whose bad luck had landed him here.

But crime rates were high in Chinatown. Elderly Asian men and women were targeted for vicious crimes, sliced with knives or bludgeoned with heavy objects, blamed for viruses, blamed for the economy, blamed for our foreign faces. We were easy targets: slow moving and trusting. What was it about us, exactly, that brought out this rage? I cast my eyes down and hurried across the street—what "hurrying" means to me now—to avoid him.

———

It was a clear night, cloudless, with a coin-like moon. I went to the Subway sandwich shop, one of the few restaurants that remained open after the tech workers went home for the day. It was me and two Black men, friends dressed similarly, wearing thick silver chains around their necks. One held the door open for me, amusement on his face. My meatball sub was six inches long. It was too much meat for a person like me, but I sat in the park, watching the old men play checkers, and ate it all.

CHAPTER 17

OPENING THE CAR DOOR, Nick held back a grimace. Matthew, even without his suit jacket, was overdressed for the occasion, as usual. Nick wore his regular clothes: jeans, a sweater, a jacket. Practical layers for the Bay Area. It would be chilly near the water.

They were headed to Levi's mansion in Half Moon Bay, his third—or was it fourth?—home, which he'd bought after he sold his first company. He'd purchased it with his wife at the time, who'd become his ex-wife last year. She'd left the Bay Area and given most of her fortune to charity. Levi kept the house.

"Otto died," Matthew said, to the window. "I thought you should know that."

"Sorry to hear that," Nick replied.

Nick was aware. He had read it in the paper.

"Last month."

Nick detected the pain in his father's voice. He could have inquired into it—made a bid for connection—but opted not to.

Outside the congested city, fog enclosed them. They were nearing the water. Did Nick feel grief? Did he feel anything at all? He was related to this man, but he hadn't known him, not really.

The invitations for the party had been electronic: When Nick clicked a representation of an envelope, a card slid out. The faux envelope and card were both fashioned out of expensive-looking fake paper, paper that looked to have texture on the screen.

The RSVPs were hidden, but Nick knew exactly who would be in attendance. He knew not to mention the party to his coworkers, because not all were invited. In fact only a fraction were.

Levi would have invited the youngest and most beautiful of the employees—the ones who would marvel at Levi's wealth and openly express their admiration for him. The invited employees were usually thin, heterosexual, in their twenties, eager to drink Levi's expensive scotch or partake in the MDMA that Nick was sure had been procured for the occasion. Levi had no issues playing favorites. His favoritism wasn't hidden and that somehow made it feel more honest.

The party itself, Nick knew, was for Matthew. Levi wanted him impressed.

Nick heard the driver's sharp, surprised intake of breath the moment the house came into view.

It was an unsubtle, enormous mansion: built of stone, like a castle, the result of some previous wealthy man's hubris. Surrounding it, rows of cypress flamed upward, like trees from Dr. Seuss books. Their car joined a long queue of sports cars and SUVs around the circular driveway.

"Thanks. We can get out here," Nick said. "We'll walk."

"You sure?" the driver asked.

Nick didn't wait for his father's answer. He opened the door and stepped out. Matthew did the same.

They made their way past a marble fountain—Aphrodite themed. Nick moved briskly and Matthew followed. Already, he wished he could shed him.

Inside, the home smelled fragrant, controlled, not like there were a hundred bodies in close proximity, all with their own odors. In the kitchen, a woman in a tight black dress shucked oysters deftly, nestling each small shell into ice on a wooden platter the shape of a boat. Jazz played softly, seemingly from everywhere. Nick recognized some of the paintings on the wall; they were the familiar brushstrokes of the same painter whose work hung on the walls of the office. Levi had a favorite artist: Stanley somebody.

The bartenders were young women, most of them white, most of them blond, wearing crisp, wrinkleless button-down shirts. Precisely three bartenders weren't white, and they were Black, Latina, and Asian, one of each, as if to satisfy some quota. They were all thin, with smooth, clear skin.

Nick could hear Levi's laugh emanating from the back porch, high pitched and grating. He swallowed an oyster and grasped the shell as he made his way deeper into the house, in an attempt to lose his father. Already Nick noticed people gravitating to Matthew—commoners making appeals to a king.

A bar was positioned beside the fireplace and Nick walked up to it. The Asian bartender sliced limes that made slight, satisfying sounds with each cut wedge. Her hair, streaked with highlights, was tied in a neat ponytail. Her cheeks were rosy and there was sweat on her temple from standing too close to the fire. Nick could easily imagine her somewhere else—on the beach, with friends, in a car with the windows rolled down, hair loose and flying, effulgent. It reminded him that it was money that brought all these people, unnaturally, here.

"Hey there," she said, putting her knife down.

"A seltzer, please," Nick said.

"Ice?"

"Yeah."

"Lime?"

"No thanks."

"Freshly sliced," she flirted.

"Sure, then," Nick said, smiling. "Lime."

She handed him the glass.

"Is that jade?" she asked, noticing his bracelet.

"Yeah," Nick said. "My grandma gave it to me."

"I like it."

He slid a couple dollars in her mostly empty glass tip jar and headed in Levi's direction. The sooner he made his presence known, the sooner he could leave. Nick found Levi insufferable in groups. It was only when they were alone that they could have real conversations.

A group surrounded Levi, talking animatedly.

"Listen, we're going to fall behind," a man was saying. "China is building better Americans than we are, and it's because they're unafraid to go there."

"They'd absolutely go there," a woman agreed. No one in the group appeared Chinese.

"We have the technology, you know? If we don't do it, China will."

"What's that?" Nick asked.

"Polygenic screening," Levi clarified. "Are we talking about intelligence? Screening for the smartest, healthiest people? We do it to plants. Why not us? I'm on board. Obviously the history of it has a bad rap. But those people back then were racists. We're different. We're just providing options."

"It's a slippery slope," a short man said. He was bald, completely smooth looking, like a dolphin. Older than the rest of them, but with a stiff face, achieved via Botox, most likely.

"Don't you wish your parents had made you taller?" a woman, his wife, perhaps, teased. She was drinking something with a cherry in it. The cherry fell against her lips, which were caked in cracked burgundy lipstick, as she sipped.

"I mean . . ." The man's face darkened, and he stiffened. "Do I wish they hadn't picked me to exist? I don't find the joke all that funny."

"Relax, Rich," Levi said, putting a hand on Rich's back. He shook the ice in his glass. "We're all glad you exist."

A famous biotech CEO joined the circle—a man Nick knew Levi felt some rivalry toward. His name was Pax, and he was richer than Levi by five or so billion.

"We're Americans. We have freedom to choose where we live, where we work, what we do for a living," Pax said. "What's different about choosing our own health outcomes, or physical attributes?"

Nick watched Levi. He spoke more grandly whenever he was around other CEOs. It made Levi behave like a sea lion whose territory was being encroached upon.

"Even eye color?" Rich's eyes widened.

"Boring," Levi said. "Eye color, hair color, height, gender—those are the basics. But think of intelligence. Even something like courage, we've seen, is inherited. Anger, too. What do we want? Long lives free of disease, right? Wouldn't you choose that for yourself? For your children?"

"I thought you were working on epigenetic therapies," Pax said.

"We are, we are." Levi waved a hand. "That's the plan—eliminating heritable diseases. But after that? You could select for life span. You could give yourself—give your child—the healthiest, longest, most productive life possible."

Nick shuddered. *Healthy, productive*—they were words that the Maier Foundation had used. But everything Levi was saying was to be taken with a grain of salt, Nick thought. It was a puffing up, said for the sake of this rival CEO.

Pax gave Levi a polite, patient smile. He was in his thirties, handsome, with a full head of light hair that looked natural—good genes. Levi was pulled away into a different conversation, and so Nick remained with Pax, with Rich and his wife.

Nick always thought that if Levi weren't surrounded by wealthy CEOs, absorbing unimaginative ideas of success, he would be living a very different life. He wouldn't be in this castle, alone. Maybe his sadness would be more manageable.

Once, after a party at Pax's Pacific Heights mansion, Levi had been so drunk he couldn't shift his Aston Martin into first. No one else there could drive stick, so it was left to Nick to guide Levi by his armpits and drive him, weeping, home.

"There's some truth to it," Pax was saying now. "Birth rates are far higher among people of color. From a voting perspective it's just not equitable."

Nick stared, horrified. The man was going on and on because Nick looked white. He thought it was safe to say all these things.

"If we had the choice," he continued, "plenty of people wouldn't choose to be white. In fact it's offensive to suggest that everyone would choose to be white."

"So true," Rich agreed.

"To me it's such common sense. My wife, you know, she's Asian," the CEO said.

"Japanese?"

"Korean."

"Nice."

"She's brilliant, I'd be absolutely lost without her. We have the tech now to *choose* to have a child who looks more like me than her. Actually, she's really into the idea. You know, she got a nose job, a boob job. That surgery where they give you a fold in your eyelids. How's this any different?"

"Hey," Nick broke in. "I'm Chinese. And even if I weren't, you should be more careful about advertising your racism." He was aware he was burning a bridge, but fuck this guy.

"Nick." He heard his name called, and turned.

It was Jess. He made his way to her.

"Are you surprised I got an invite?" she said. She'd brushed her too-long hair and was wearing it down. She'd put some effort into dressing up: long skirt and pantyhose, though she was still topped in a sensible fleece sweater.

He *was* surprised, but didn't say so. Her face looked different for some reason, and he realized it was because she wasn't wearing her usual glasses: She'd put on contact lenses. And lip gloss. Eye shadow, maybe. The tops of her eyes looked heavy, darker than they normally were.

"I didn't, actually." She leaned toward him, whispering, "I hacked into Levi's computer and found the invite."

She burst into laughter at Nick's stunned expression. Her laugh was compelling, and he joined her. She'd watched Levi type his password from across the room.

"Perks of impaired hearing," she said. "Enhanced attention."

"Impressive," he said. "Hang on. What's his password?"

"Ugh," she said. "It's embarrassing. You don't want to know."

"Let me guess. His own name?"

"*Imtheboss*, all one word. No numbers or symbols or anything."

"You're joking."

"Maybe I am."

He lifted his glass to hers and clinked it.

"Do you think it's a sex party?" she asked, trying to act cool with it, if it was going to be.

"Not at the moment, no," he said. It appeared very much the opposite: Men dressed identically and practically. Lots of vests.

"Are they a real thing?" she asked.

"Unfortunately, yes," he said.

"Is that the investor?" she asked, gesturing toward Matthew, who stood stiffly with Levi now. "You guys kind of look alike." A pause. "Is that racist for me to say?"

Outside, the clouds were gauzy stripes against the black sky, like a chest X-ray. The night could not have been any more temperate, any more ideal. The sea, visible from the balcony, was black and shining. The moon was bright and full. It was a moon wasted on people who were drunk, who were high, looking blearily at one another and not heavenward. The women, dressed more lightly than the men, sat around the fire pit, draped in absurdly soft throws the color of half-and-half. The men who sat with them were overheating, their cheeks red as tomatoes.

In the corner, Jess talked to a man Nick recognized as yet another CEO, who nodded vigorously, interested in her every word. Nick wasn't surprised: She was brilliant. Nick suspected Jess might have a job offer by the end of the night, and it would be Levi's loss.

If we were able to choose who we were, who our children were, Nick wondered, would Jess have been screened out of existence?

Matthew materialized beside him, at the balcony.

"Let's take a walk," he said.

Nick could feel Levi watching. There was a distance between Levi and Matthew that Levi felt he couldn't quite cross. With younger, more profligate investors, a party like this would have done the trick—cemented their interest. Matthew, instead, nursed the same glass of scotch all night. He offered compliments but didn't appear overly impressed by Levi's house, Levi's whole shtick, as others usually were.

"Let's give him the show he wants," Matthew said.

In Levi's sprawling rose garden, Nick leaned to smell a yellow rose—scentless.

"Try this one," Matthew said, pulling down a rose by its collar; it was pink and as big as a dessert plate. Nick inhaled. It was the rosiest rose he'd ever smelled.

Levi was on the balcony, still trying to participate in a conversation, but watching them. When Nick met his eye, Levi turned away, as though he hadn't been looking, even though Nick knew he had. Matthew was the reason for the party.

They chose a path. The house grew more distant, obscured by trees. Nick preferred watching the party happen from a distance, seeing it like a dollhouse or music box, glowing golden against the black sky, like something you could pick up and hold. He knew he shared this preference with his father. Both would rather be the observers and not the observed. But Nick didn't care to know what their similarities were, anymore: He wanted, now, to pursue all the ways he could be different.

Otto had died. Nick wondered how he would feel when Matthew passed.

The house was no longer in view. They were surrounded by hills, dry grass. They'd been heading away from the shore, and now they were on different terrain entirely. Was it still Levi's property? Here ownership didn't matter: It was the sort of wild, untouched landscape that belonged to no one. Amid the grasses, wildflowers blossomed low to the ground, so small that Nick couldn't avoid crushing them with every step.

The moon was hidden now, stashed behind the clouds. Either of them could have pulled out their phone, used it as a flashlight, but they didn't.

"The merger can't happen," Nick said. "You should just go home."

"I'm getting old, Nick," Matthew said. "There's a lot I regret."

"Like what, exactly?" Nick asked—not genuinely, but not coldly, either. He was curious.

"I should have come with you. All those years ago. You and your mother."

"Why didn't you?"

"It was a failure of my imagination. I couldn't picture a different life."

"You mean a life without money."

"I regret it every day."

"So you think this investment, it'll make up for it?"

"Nick, I don't—" Matthew hesitated. "You could tell me. Why don't you tell me, what it is you need from me?"

Nick didn't know, exactly. They walked in silence and found themselves back, again, in the rose garden. Nick could make out pairs of people kissing on the balcony. Inside, the party guests moved like puppets.

"I wish we'd had more time together. I wish I'd been there for you, growing up."

More time. Nick had never told Matthew about May. About the time she'd wished for and that he had. Matthew was rich, had everything he could possibly want or need, had the luxury of more time than most others, and he still wished for more of it, as his grandmother had, as Levi did.

Matthew followed Nick up the stairs. Inside, Nick felt his discomfort return in a flood. The bartenders and servers and most of the guests had gone. Jess was gone. The guests who remained had paired off, their necks craning toward each other. Levi sat on a love seat with a woman Nick took a moment to recognize. Her name was Margot, and she was one of the company's newest hires, working on the social media team.

"Is that a Jackson Pollock?" Nick heard Margot ask.

"It's actually a Pei-Shen Qian copy of a Jackson Pollock," Levi said.

"A Pei-Shen who?"

"Do you know his story? He lived in Queens. He copied paintings by Pollock, Rothko, de Kooning. These Spanish art dealers passed them off as the real deal. He fled to China before he was found out. This is one of his fakes."

"So you bought it for cheap?"

"No, I bought it for a lot of money. It's a real fake, you know?" Levi grinned.

"Didn't he feel guilty?"

"Did he need to? Qian said, 'I made a knife to cut fruit. If others use it to kill, blaming me is unfair.' Classic Chinese inscrutability."

She must have been twenty-two, just out of college. How common this story was, that they were both acting out, as though in a play that had been written for them. She believed herself to have power—attractiveness and appeal. Levi was the wealthy man who found her interesting. There were other stories being told now, an abundance of other stories, and yet this one persisted. Here were two adults making choices. But was it a choice, Nick wondered, when you were told, all your life, before your life, what it was you should want? If Nick was curious about immortality, it was only because he wanted to see whether, if given years upon years, these scripts could change, turn over, and the dominant actors along with them.

———

Levi's favorite lunch place served custom salads. It was white walled and doubly lit—sunlight through the windows, fluorescent lights overhead—and illuminated Levi's chapped lips, the rings beneath his eyes. He couldn't have slept much. Nick had noticed, that morning, that Margot, the social media hire, was not at her desk.

The salads were made in an assembly line. Levi rattled off a strange medley of leaves, nuts, and beets. Curious, Nick said he'd have the same.

"Fuck, I'm going to be honest, man," Levi started, talking over his shoulder to Nick, who slid his cafeteria tray down behind Levi. Nick wondered what news he had to report, what the future of the company was going to be.

"Dressing?" the visored employee asked. Nick could see the tattoo on her arm peeking out from the sleeve of her polo shirt but couldn't make out what it was.

"Southwestern chipotle. And medium," Levi said, to mean he wanted a "medium" application of dressing.

She tossed his salad with tongs in a large metal bowl. There was a rhythm to it, and Nick wondered if she was playing a song in her head. When mixed, the salad was entirely pink from the beets.

They paid for their own pink salads. When the iPad flipped over and Levi signed, he selected "No tip." He must have felt Nick's eyes on him because he said, "Tipping is fucked. How do we even know it gets to the employees?"

"It does," the woman at the cash register deadpanned.

"Sorry," Nick said to her. He left a larger tip to compensate for Levi's.

Levi sat and popped the plastic lid of his bowl.

"So that guy you met with—doesn't look like it's going to go through after all," Levi said. "Thanks for trying. Doesn't matter. We've got someone else."

Levi drove a forkful of salad into his mouth and chewed. Nick had never seen salad eaten so violently.

"It's no Maier, but it's pretty damn good."

Nick put his fork down and sat up straighter. "Oh yeah? Who's that?"

Levi chuckled. His eyes sparkled with his secret.

"He's very interested, personally"—here Levi brought his voice down, in case competitors were here, also eating salad, which Nick thought was unlikely—"in what *I'm* interested in. Very interested."

Nick's mind felt staticky with worry. The restaurant had filled out and they were surrounded, now, by people eating salad: most alone, a few with companions, having conversations in which each waited for the other to finish chewing. Salad wasn't a good food to eat with company. An oily leaf fell onto Nick's sweatshirt sleeve, and when he picked it off it left a darkened spot.

"Is it Pax?" Nick asked.

Levi grinned. "See, I knew you were a clever one."

When he spoke there were flecks of green and pink lodged between his teeth. He leaned back in his seat, pleased. Levi wanted choices—lives to be selected like salad ingredients. The outcome? All men created equal.

"It's the American goddamn dream." Levi laughed, mouth speckled, pleased with himself.

CHAPTER 18

AREN'T WE LUCKY? Our DNA encodes for innumerable possible people, and yet it's you and I who are here—winners in a stupefying lottery. We came at the exact right moment, a blip in the hundred million centuries of the universe: the Earth inhabitable, not yet engulfed by the sun, but not only molten magma, inhospitable to life. The planet cooled and water formed; it was able to hold an atmosphere. And in this place, on this small blue rock, innumerable miracles: redwoods, computers, stingrays, pianos, you and me.

Nick poured me tea and placed, before me, my small bowl of congee with pickles and century egg, its white alkalized to translucent black. I liked to imagine the egg had been laid by an otherworldly creature—that it was the egg of a dragon or a sea serpent. In fact, the reality was magical, too. It had been transformed from a chicken's egg to this.

In the mornings, instead of Betty, I now saw Nick. He never said that he was worried about me living alone, but I knew he was.

Lily didn't want to see me. Nick relayed the news, apologetic. I'd expected this, yet it still came as a disappointment.

The congee was hot, swirled with soy sauce and spicy with white pepper, exactly the way I liked it. Nick stirred his congee idly, distracted. Levi had lined up interest from another pharmaceutical company, and Nick was worried about the outcome.

Nick opened the newspaper to the puzzle page. Lately we did the crossword together. I was good at the long phrases, because I had studied idioms so intently when I had learned English. I could see the shape of a phrase easily.

An American expression that had always been strange to me was "build a life." My life had not been built. It wasn't a piece-by-piece assembly, following a blueprint. Nothing fit together. It wasn't a structure but a heap.

It had been our dream, Otto's and mine: to give our children the best possible futures. But it was a mistake, believing you could choose for someone else, no matter how well intentioned you might be. And what did we choose, really? We were told what to want: Propaganda was universal. Especially in this country, where the propaganda was that there was none—we were free. But were we? When we were made to value certain lives more than others; when we were made, relentlessly, to want more? What if I had seen through it? What if I had understood that I already had enough?

I had something in common with Levi. I had wished for more time, too.

Nick put down his pen. He seemed to realize something as I spoke. Quickly, he took our empty bowls and mugs to the sink, washed them, and put them on the rack. He put on his backpack and kissed me goodbye.

The rain began so lightly it seemed imaginary. Nick ran—he could still make it if he ran.

Matthew was surprised to see his son in the lobby of his hotel. Outside, his taxi was waiting to take him to the airport, return him to New York.

"If you're serious about wanting to help," Nick said, "I have a proposition for you."

Whenever it rained I thought of the mother by the Macy's, and her daughter—their insufficient clothing, their lack of shelter. For days now, the rain had come down, relentlessly. Their hands were always wrapped in each other's. The daughter wore their only pair of gloves. I remembered it exactly the same: All I had, I wanted to give to Lily. It wasn't pity that I felt but envy, that they had each other.

I'd been collecting money from trips to the ATM, withdrawing two hundred at each visit—the maximum. I had two thousand dollars.

The mother and daughter weren't in their usual location. I walked down the smaller streets, down Maiden Lane and Campton, and still didn't see them. I worried.

The rain soaked through my cotton jacket. The mist began, droplets coming down, chilled as ice water. I searched frantically, willing them to be sheltered, safe.

And then, I saw her. She sat at a bus stop, beside her daughter, her head held still. The red plastic overhang gave her a pink cast, as though she sat under a different sky. I wished I could speak their language. I didn't even know what language it was. If I could speak it, I would have asked for her story, and would have listened. Hearing a story—what did it accomplish? Nothing and everything. The bus stop seats were designed to be uncomfortable, so no one would be able to use them to rest on. They flipped over if you lay down. She and her daughter balanced on their seats. A bus stopped and the doors opened and they didn't board.

The mother wore an expression of exhaustion that I remembered so well. She had surrendered: inviting the discomfort, not refusing it. Pain was easier to tolerate when you didn't resist it.

I approached her. She shook her head vehemently to dissuade me from trying to engage her in conversation. I handed her the envelope of money. She looked inside and shook her head again, panic in her eyes, trying to return it. Rain pounded the plastic awning. I pressed the envelope back into her hands and gave her my umbrella, the scarf I wore around my neck. Quickly, I turned away before she could return the items. And guiltily, knowing that it wasn't sufficient. Why was I lucky enough to have a roof over my head, when she and her daughter didn't?

Home was twenty minutes away, at the pace I went. Without my umbrella, my jacket absorbed the rain. I could feel the dampness, soaking like milk through a cake, to my bones. This rain was cold, but it made me think of playing in the paddies, as a child, when my childhood was intact, before the years of hunger. It was always raining. I'd always been comfortable in the rain.

At home, seeing me, Nick gasped. I was drenched from head to toe, shrunken and shaking, a little wet mouse. He wrung out my coat and hung it to dry. He turned the shower on for me, hot. He turned the heater to high. The shower felt sharp, like needles. He wrapped me in a blanket when I emerged.

I felt dizzy, just then, and everything went black.

A knock at the door before it opened, and there was Nick, holding orange flowers to swap out last week's. He placed the flowers at the foot of the hospital bed—gently, as though they might be too heavy. He pumped sanitizer from the wall-mounted dispenser into his palms and rubbed his hands together, counting silently to ten. With my pink kitchen shears, he trimmed the flowers' stems at an angle. He pulled the leaves off—the ones near the base—so they wouldn't rot. I wondered if Lily taught him all this. I often wondered what residue of her there was in him.

"Don't look so serious," I said.

The diagnosis was pneumonia. When I collapsed, Nick called an ambulance. During the ride, I came to and insisted it wasn't needed, but no one agreed. The doctor—Vietnamese, tall for a woman— monitored my biological functions, in case any of them decided to stop. My heart, she said, concerned her. The more I protested, the more she insisted. She was firm with me, behaving as though she knew me. Maybe I reminded her of someone.

Nick emptied the brown water from the vase into the small sink, refilled it with water from the tap, and stood the fresh flowers up. Marigolds, because it was the season: Vendors sold them on the street for Dia de los Muertos. Inside the hospital room it was seasonless, unrelentingly the same temperature: dry, too cold. It smelled of bleach, and of urine—my own urine, I supposed. A friend from Mexico once told me that the flowers' bright color and strong scent were meant to guide spirits to their altars. I wondered who would be guided here: Charles, my mother, my father? Ping? Or was it my own spirit that needed to be led out?

Nick took a seat on the edge of my bed and smoothed the blanket—about to say something, I could tell, but stalling.

"She still doesn't want to see you," he said.

"Did you tell her everything I told you?"

"Everything. Including that you were dying, even though you're not."

"Of course I am!"

"She doesn't want to see you. I'm sorry, Grandma. You know how she is."

"Well," I said. "You're here."

"I am."

"And you're not nothing."

"I hope not."

I touched the flowers he brought. Their petals felt so much like skin. But I knew that their cells were rigid, not round. Cellulose, not what we're made of.

Though no one else could, I saw so much of my daughter in him. He pushed the gangly metal pole of the oximeter out of the way, pulled his chair close, and took both my hands in his. He was wearing my mother's bracelet. I wondered if he could feel my grief, which ran through me like an electric current—like the tingling feeling that preceded tears. I didn't think of him often anymore, but I thought of him now: Ping had always been able to sense that, as though he could feel the conductivity of my skin.

There was a knock on the door, and a different doctor stepped in.

"Hello," the doctor said cheerfully.

She looked from Nick to me, as if trying to figure out our relationship.

"This is your family?" she asked. I wondered if she meant: *Is this your whole family?* Or, *If this is your family—how?* I answered both questions with a nod.

"I'd like to go home," I said.

The doctor seemed surprised to hear me speak perfect English. She looked at her clipboard, trying to wipe the shock from her face— trying to reset it. Her reading glasses sat on the edge of her nose.

"You're not quite in the clear yet."

"I just want to go home."

"Dr. Nguyen was worried about your heart. We worry you could get worse, if you're not under our supervision."

"I'll come back if it gets worse."

She reminded me of the doctor who delivered Lily. The way they both, this doctor and that one, saw me not as a life, but as a potential death. Certain doctors were this way.

"Tomorrow, then," she said. "Let us keep you for one more night." She spoke slowly with me, as though I might not understand English, even though I was speaking it perfectly with her.

"It will be too late," I said, mostly to myself.

"You'll be okay, Ms. Chen. Press the button to call the nurse if you have difficulty breathing." She turned to Nick. "You'll do that?"

He nodded.

In the night, my fever spiked. It reminded me of the heat of the blast furnaces we melted iron in, the smell and smoke and heaviness of those days—unbearable, except, somehow, we bore it.

What I remember is the longing for fresh air. How thoughtless we had been, to believe that trees needed to be useful, or that usefulness was even the point. I remember tearing apart a bicycle. Dismantling a coffin, after the body had been removed and buried boxless. The thoughtless destruction that had happened, in those years, the erasing of who we had been. As though without a past we'd be unburdened, when in fact the opposite was true: In trying to leave the past behind, like a shadow, it followed you.

I fell in and out of sleep. I couldn't get used to the way the hospital smelled, like packaging and cleaning products, an aggressive but failed attempt to be scentless.

In my fevered state, I wondered if I was seeing things. Nick stood before me, his nose and mouth covered by a face mask the color of the sky.

"Are you busting me out?"

"Yes, ma'am," he said. "Let's get you home."

CHAPTER 19

NICK TRIED TO TAKE a personal day, but Levi insisted that, today, every employee come in. He had big news to share. Walking into the office, Nick heard chatter. This was rare—even lunches were usually quiet, people eating quickly at their desks, whispering in the lounge, popping their cans of sparkling water as quietly as they could manage. Jess held a corn-based compostable cup full of champagne. There was color in her cheeks.

"We're celebrating something," Jess whispered. "We don't know what yet. You okay?"

My grandmother is sick, Nick wanted to say. *I shouldn't be here.*

Levi climbed onto a desk, crowded with orange-labeled bottles of champagne. He was already drunk. He tapped a branded pen against his glass flute. Nick held his breath. Had his father come through? What was Levi so fucking giddy about, then?

"We've been bought," Levi said. He grinned.

The room erupted in cheers.

"This is an *incredible* step for us."

After his speech, Levi locked eyes with Nick and approached, receiving back slaps along the way. "You fucker," Levi said. He poured Nick a glass of champagne, into one of the few real flutes. "Whatever you said to Matthew—" Levi paused here. "Well, whatever it was, it worked."

"Maier's buying the company?" Nick said, to clarify. "Not Pax?"

"He's buying it. Prepare to be very, very rich."

Nick's chest tightened. Could he trust his father to do what he'd asked? He'd believed Matthew was being honest: He wanted to make amends, wanted forgiveness. Had that been the truth? Levi's excessive joy suggested differently.

The phone in Levi's pocket rang. He looked at the screen, pleased. Nick saw that it said "Maier."

"Speak of the devil," Levi said. "Gimme a second." He turned away from Nick. "Hey, man. We're just celebrating the news."

The smile was frozen on his face while he listened.

"I don't understand," Nick heard him say. "Let's . . . Can we talk about this in person? We're on the verge of—okay. No, no, I'm not arguing with you. Right, right."

Levi hung up, stared into his phone.

"Well, fuck me."

"What happened?"

"He's dissolving it. The entire company. It makes no fucking sense." Levi ran an aggressive hand through his hair. Then he kicked a chair so it fell to its side. Everyone jumped back. The beginnings of a tantrum.

So Matthew had done what he asked, after all. Nick was aware it wasn't a real solution. The future was bigger than he was—bigger than the Maiers, even. Science would always move forward and not back—and that was good, of course. It meant less needless suffering. He couldn't personally allow some progress and not others. If it wasn't their company, it would be another. People would seek to control fate, for themselves and others. It was almost certain. He could only put up this small protest.

Nick didn't stay. He gathered his few things from the office, put them in his backpack, and headed back to Chinatown—to his grandmother.

I am in my own bed, thin quilts heaped over me. The apartment is warm from the heater that Nick has turned high. A humidifier puffs beside me, and I remember Ping, our afternoons on the roof of the biology building, discerning shapes in the clouds—"My spirit so high that it was all over the heavens," wrote the poet Li Bai. The kettle sounds its shrill whistle. I hear the metal scrape of it being lifted from the stove.

"Hey," Nick says, noticing I'm awake. He kneels beside my bed, worry on his face. "How are you feeling?"

Somehow, my body is both hot and cold. My chest is tight, as though my ribs have shrunk in the wash. I can't take more than a shallow breath. I manage a smile for him: The emotion is genuine. It's a comfort that he is here.

"Listen," Nick says. "Before I left . . ."

He reaches a hand into his backpack and rummages. He produces a thin vial, the size of a cigarette, clear like water. He doesn't have to tell me what it is; I already know. It's the unapproved drug he's told me Levi takes daily, to extend his life. "I know you won't want it, and we don't have the data for non-European populations, but I don't think it would hurt if you just—"

"Get rid of that."

"She could change her mind. Just give her some time."

Time. I wanted it for all my life, and now I've had enough.

"I don't want that," I say. "The elixir of immortality." I laugh a little. "Do you take me for the moon goddess?"

Nick protests. To attempt to prolong my life: What would be the harm?

"No."

I can't say it isn't tempting. There is so much I want to tell my daughter that Nick can't understand or relay completely. That I'm sorry, of course, but the word is hardly precise enough. There's so much more I want to say.

Nick's hands take mine. It strikes me as remarkable, that we are bound together—that, for a time, we were strangers, and now we mean something to each other. When I'm gone, he will miss me.

The clock ticks loudly from the kitchen. Time passes, indifferent to me. So much of my life I have let slip by, because I have not attended to it. All this while, instead of seeking more time, I could have been paying attention. I notice it now, my present: my grandson's kind face, his warm hand in mine, and the smell and sensation—here the words, in any language, fail—of being alive. Chinese is a language that exists in the present tense. In this way, it is unlike English, a language in which it is easy to say: I *had* a past, I *will have* a future. When I adopted English as my own I lived so much in the hope of what was to come. Now my future shrinks with each passing second.

I will have the boy write her a letter. I will tell her what I never could, never possessed sufficient language to say. I will tell her it was my greatest luck, to have been her mother—to have had the fortune to love her. Though I still don't have the language, between the Chinese she knows now and English, I can try.

This is what I am thinking when the door opens, and my daughter walks through.

ACKNOWLEDGMENTS

This is a book about fortune, and appropriately, I could not feel more fortunate. Thank you, Marya Spence, the best agent by light-years (it's not even a contest) and a compassionate friend, on top of that. I hope to do many more years of life and books together. Thanks, also, to Mackenzie Williams, Mairi Friesen-Escandell, and the entire team at Janklow & Nesbit.

Thank you, John Freeman, for meeting me in Istanbul, for comprehending this book and its DNA so fully from the start, for helping it become itself. Thank you for your enthusiasm, intuition, and passion; thank you for noting and for looking. Thanks to Jordan Pavlin, Reagan Arthur, Sarah Perrin, Isabel Ribeiro, Erinn Hartmann, Laura Keefe, Kelsey Manning, Kelly Shi, Noah Hoff, Maria Carella, Ruth Liebmann, Zachary Lutz, Melissa Yoon, Aja Pollock, Chris Jerome, Nancy Tan, T. C. Gardstein, Linda Huang, and everyone at Knopf. Thanks to Charlotte Cray at Hutchinson Heinemann, Mona Lang at Kiepenheuer & Witsch, Eugenia Dubini at NN Editore, and all those bringing this American story to other places. Thank you, Michael Taeckens, for getting this book to readers.

Thank you, Cameron Awkward-Rich, for granting this book its epigraph and for "Meditations in an Emergency," which was a beacon.

A wise person once said, "I want to be less afraid of friends' judgment and more enthralled by their perspectives." That wise person is Aku Ammah-Tagoe, who is among the brilliant friends whose perspectives on this book I sought and was enthralled by. Thank you, Aku. Thank you, Christie George, Lauren Ro, Sarah Bowlin, Andrea Nguyen, Nina Bai. How lucky I am, that some of my favorite writers are also my friends: Meng Jin, Susanna Kwan, Shruti Swamy.

Acknowledgments

Thanks to my peerless writing group, for insight and communion: Margaret Wilkerson Sexton, R.O. Kwon, Andi Mudd, Colin Winnette, Anisse Gross, Caille Millner, Esmé Weijun Wang, Ingrid Rojas Contreras.

The Ruby in San Francisco has, like this book, nourished and changed me. Thank you, Claire Calderón, for your stewardship and friendship. Thank you, Peggy Lee, for carrying on the baton and your continued labors. Thank you to everyone at the Ruby, including current and former members, and those who have passed through, for community and kindness. I have learned so much from you.

Thank you to the people and organizations who generously provided time and space for me to write: Fritz Haeg and Salmon Creek Farm. Jeff McMahon and Cyndy Hayward at Willapa Bay. Holly McAdams Olson and the Kimmel Harding Nelson Center. Lynn Reeves, Mary Jane Clay, and Neltje at Jentel. Wally and Celia Gilbert for the residency at Cold Spring Harbor Laboratory.

For their scientific insight and expertise (though all errors are 100 percent my own): I owe a debt of gratitude the size of a lungfish genome to Derek Jantz, who answered a cold email I sent because I read on a website bio that he liked science fiction. Thanks for helping me figure out May's work (and being the cofounder of Genet-ex, our one-parent-DNA company for divorcées). Thanks to Christina Agapakis for early conversations that informed my thinking. Thanks to the generous scientists at Cold Spring Harbor who spoke with me.

For fielding miscellaneous inquiries: Lisa Nourse, Mia Arias Tsang, Nozlee Samadzadeh.

For eleventh-hour adjustments and assurances: Weike Wang, John Inglis, and Mia Arias Tsang (again).

For friendship and support, sharing everything from chamber pots to face masks to fireside gin and tonics: Natalie So, Mimi Lok, Cassandra Landry, Kara Levy, Christina Nichol, Jessica Wang, Katherine Meckel, and Fueled by Mummies (even though only some of you believe in acknowledgments).

For sustaining me financially over the years this book took to write: Thanks to Jason Richman and Maialie Fitzpatrick at UTA for selling my intellectual property. Thanks to Recipe Club: Chris Ying,

Dave Chang, Priya Krishna, Bryan Ford, John DeBary, and our listeners. Thanks to the San Francisco Arts Commission.

I am grateful for the University of Pittsburgh's CR/10 Project, a collection of interviews with survivors of the Cultural Revolution. And for the following books and their authors: *Red-Color News Soldier* by Li Zhensheng; *The Cowshed* by Ji Xianlin; *The Cultural Revolution* by Frank Dikötter; *The Good Women of China* by Xinran; *Waiting* by Ha Jin; *Wild Swans* by Jung Chang; *The Gene* by Siddhartha Mukherjee; *A Crack in Creation* by Jennifer A. Doudna and Samuel H. Sternberg; *Winners Take All* by Anand Giridharadas; *Caste* by Isabel Wilkerson; and *America for Americans* by Erika Lee.

A note for observant commuters: The Metro-North discontinued its bar cars in 2014. In this fictional account, I have revived them.

This book is for my family: Amity Horowitz. Jesse Horowitz and Krysthel Lokan Rojas. Danny Horowitz, from whom I borrowed "We do look alike, but he's better looking." Clement Khong. Ben, Fiona, Milo, and Piper Khong. Edward and Lynn Khong (who are also Khong Choon Min and Tan Moi Ling). Bunny the cat.

Finally, thank you to Eli Horowitz, who makes me laugh every day we're together. Without your love and loving attention, this effort would have been doomed. (I would have given up in 2017.) Writing a book is an exercise in devotion, and loving you teaches me, daily, about it. How lucky I am, that you chose me.

A Note About the Author

Rachel Khong is the author of *Goodbye, Vitamin,* winner of the California Book Award for First Fiction and named a best book of the year by NPR; *O, The Oprah Magazine; Vogue;* and *Esquire.* Her work has appeared in *The New York Times Book Review, The Guardian, The Paris Review,* and *Tin House.* In 2018, she founded the Ruby, a work and event space for women and nonbinary writers and artists in San Francisco's Mission District. She was born in Malaysia and lives in California.

A Note on the Type

The text of this book was set in Electra, a typeface designed by W. A. Dwiggins (1880–1956). This face cannot be classified as either modern or old style. It is not based on any historical model, nor does it echo any particular period or style. It avoids the extreme contrasts between thick and thin elements that mark most modern faces, and it attempts to give a feeling of fluidity, power, and speed.

Typeset by Scribe, Philadelphia, Pennsylvania
Printed and bound by Berryville Graphics, Berryville, Virginia
Designed by Maria Carella